THE TARANTULA STONE

Philip Caveney was born in North Wales in 1951. The son of an RAF officer, he spent much of his childhood travelling the length and breadth of Britain and later lived for several years in Malaysia and Singapore.

His first novel, *The Sins of Rachel Ellis*, was published in 1977. Since then, he has published many novels for adults and since 2007, a series of children's books that have sold all over the world. In 2012, his children's novel *Night on Terror Island* won the Brilliant Books Award.

Find out more on his website:
www.philip-caveney.co.uk

T0312526

By Philip Caveney

The Sins of Rachel Ellis
Tiger, Tiger
The Tarantula Stone
Speak No Evil
Black Wolf
Strip Jack Naked
Skin Flicks
Slayground
Burn Down Easy
Bad to the Bone
1999
Love Bites

THE TARANTULA STONE

Philip Caveney

HARPER

This novel is entirely a work of fiction.
The names, characters and incidents portrayed in it are
the work of the author's imagination. Any resemblance to
actual persons, living or dead, events or localities is
entirely coincidental.

Harper
An imprint of HarperCollins*Publishers*
1 London Bridge Street
London SE1 9GF

www.harpercollins.co.uk

This paperback edition 2015
1

First published in 1985 by Granada Publishing
Copyright © Philip Caveney 1985

Philip Caveney asserts the moral right to be identified
as the author of this work
A catalogue record for this book is
available from the British Library

ISBN: 9780008138462

For Rachel . . .
who doesn't like adventure stories

Author's Note

I am aware that the cruzeiro did not actually become the currency of Brazil until 5 October 1942; but in the interests of the story, I deemed it advisable to disregard this fact. A change of currency seemed an unnecessary complication in an otherwise straightforward tale, which is, after all, intended as a celebration of a time when the world was not yet inextricably bound up with lengths of red tape. I trust that the purists among you will forgive this minor presumption.

PART ONE

The Last Flight

Prologue

The backstreet bar was very nearly empty. Mark Austin settled himself onto a vacant stool at the counter and ordered *cachaça*. The bar-man, a dark-skinned young *caboclo*, brought him the drink and then left him to consume it in peace. Beyond the open doorway of the bar, the streets of Rio shimmered in the afternoon heat-haze.

Austin sighed. The *cachaça* was unpleasantly warm and within moments a fine film of sweat had moistened his face, neck and armpits. He was still not sure what he was doing here; looking for a little reality perhaps. The fancy main-street bars and cafés had none of the qualities he was seeking. That was for the tourists, a category to which he liked to think he did not belong. Here, there was only grime and squalor, but at least that was more honest; and it was in places like this that he tended to pick up his stock in trade. He gazed slowly around at the interior of the bar, noting the rusted tin tables, the mottled fly-blown mirrors; and then that the other occupant of the bar was looking at him curiously.

A grizzled old-timer in a slouch hat and a grubby khaki shirt, he was gazing at Austin with the quizzical expression of a man bored with his own company. He was also nursing an empty glass.

'Drink?' offered Austin, waving his own glass to make his meaning clear.

'Hell, don't mind if I do!'

Austin was pleasantly shocked. He had expected a string of unintelligible Portuguese for a reply, but this was clearly a fellow American. In an instant, the old man was perched on the stool opposite and the two were shaking hands with the kind of warmth only employed by compatriots in a distant land.

'Mark Austin, Washington DC.'

'Martin Taggart, somewhere in Wyoming. I forget where.' The old man's eyes twinkled but there was, Austin thought, an unmistakable trace of sadness in them. His voice was slow, gruff, laconic. Somehow it seemed to speak of wide experience.

'Well then, Mr Taggart . . .'

'Martin. All my friends call me Martin.'

'Martin then! What'll it be?'

'Oh, I'll have just whatever you're drinking.'

Austin ordered a bottle of *cachaça* – the local raw white rum – and another glass. He took out a packet of cigarettes and offered one to the old man. Taggart shook his head.

'No thanks. I gave those things up a long time ago. Never went back to them. No sir . . .'

Austin shrugged, put the cigarettes away. The *cachaça* arrived and the two men drank together in silence for a while.

'So, what brings a feller like you to Rio?' asked Taggart at last. 'More importantly, what brings him to a piss-hole bar like this one?'

Austin considered the question for a moment. He'd had a couple of drinks so he thought: what the hell, come right out with it.

'Adventure,' he said.

Taggart raised his eyebrows. 'Come again?'

'Adventure. I'm looking for adventure. You see, I'm a writer and adventure is my thing. I write the stories as fiction, but I like to base them on real-life happenings. I've done my last four novels that way and it seems to work for me, so . . .'

'A writer, huh?' Taggart sipped his drink. 'That pay

10

well?'

Austin grinned. 'I don't do so bad,' he replied. 'Say, maybe you read my last one, *Children of the Kalahari*? I think it was published here.'

Taggart shook his head. 'No, I don't believe I did.' He shrugged. 'But then I don't read much, these days. Adventure, huh? Well, I'm afraid you won't find much of that in Rio de Janeiro, my friend. Not any more, anyway.'

Austin topped up Taggart's glass. 'Been here a long time?' he inquired.

'Oh yeah, hell of a long time. Since before the war. Seen some changes around here, I can tell you.'

Austin nodded. 'Well, I'm going up-jungle tomorrow. The Rio das Mortes. Maybe I'll find something there.'

Something suspiciously like recognition dawned in the old man's eyes. 'The das Mortes? Yeah ... well, even that's changed, you know. The Indians been killed off or pushed out of their territory. Hell, there's even a damned ferry on the das Mortes these days, any two-bit tourist can go and have himself a look. None of that kind of business when I was there.'

'You were there? When?'

'Oh. Long ways back. Bad story. You wouldn't be interested.' Taggart shook his head. There was something evasive in his manner, something that fired Austin's curiosity. It had been a casual incident very much like this one that had given him the basis for his bestselling book, *Hour of the Wolf*. These old-timers had their stories and the world tended to forget about them. Still, Austin was an old hand at wheedling out what people didn't like to discuss. He fed the old man a ready stream of *cachaça* and gradually Taggart's reluctant tongue was loosened.

He produced a yellowed scrap of paper from his shirt pocket. It was folded but Austin could see that it was inscribed with various pencilled lines and figures.

'Looks like a map,' he observed.

'It is,' replied Taggart, his voice slightly slurred with drink. 'Sort of a map, anyway. Place on the river. That's where the tarantula stone . . .'

'The what?'

Taggart sighed, shook his head. 'Hell, it's a long story. You don't want to be burdened with it.' He made as if to put the scrap of paper back into his pocket but Austin stayed his hand.

'Listen,' he said. 'The day's free, I've got nothing special to do and we've a bottle of *cachaça* to drink. I'd like to hear the story. Speak away, I'm listening.'

Taggart sighed again but then he shrugged. 'Well, let me see now. It all started back in 'forty-six . . . well, earlier than that, I suppose. But to get it straight, I'll begin at that point and backtrack a little. Yes, 'forty-six. The war just over with. That was one hell of a year . . .'

Chapter 1

Even in the relative cool of the airport lounge, Martin
Taggart could not stop sweating. Directly above his head,
a large electric fan clicked rhythmically round, beating the
humid air into some kind of restless motion; but the
perspiration still trickled from his armpits, making dark
stains against the fabric of his khaki shirt. It oozed in a
viscous stream down the gully of his spine, glued his
collar to the back of his neck and made the soft leather
pouch that hung round it stick like an island against the
tanned flesh of his chest.

For perhaps the hundredth time that morning,
Martin's right hand came up to touch the pouch, his
fingers probing the round hard shape that nestled in there.
The diamond seemed bigger every time he touched it. It
was the size of a chicken's egg and Martin could only
begin to guess at its true value. It would make him rich,
that was for sure . . . provided he could get away with
it.

He glanced nervously around the lounge, momentarily
afraid that somebody might be reading his thoughts,
but the motley assortment of passengers were, just like
him, waiting impatiently for their flight to Belém. Out on
the brilliantly sunlit concrete of the runway, the plane
already stood like a great silver queen bee, attended by
the restless assembly of gasoline trucks and maintenance
men; but glancing at his watch, Martin could see that
there were still twenty-five minutes to wait. It would be
the longest twenty-five minutes of his lifetime. He
fumbled in his shirt pocket for his cigarettes. Extracting
one from the damp packet, he struck a match with visibly
unsteady hands and inhaled deeply. Then he leaned back

13

in his seat, let the smoke out in a thin stream and watched as it rose for a short distance in a straight column and then went berserk as it was caught in the rush of air from the fan.

He had not wanted to think too much about Caine, because he was nervous enough as it was. But sitting there in the crowded lounge he couldn't help letting his thoughts drift back to the very beginning, the chain of events that had brought him to where he was now.

He had never had what might be called a steady job, because he had never much liked working. It was a fact that he acknowledged but not something that bothered him overmuch. As a youth, he'd travelled a great deal, taking work when he needed it and wherever he could get it. He had been born in Wyoming and, as far as he knew, his family still lived there; but he'd left home at the age of seventeen and never gone back to visit. More by accident than design, he had gravitated southwards and had spent most of his years in the territory of New Mexico, driving trucks for local contractors and doing the odd spot of manual work whenever his finances got dangerously low. He lived in cheap hotels and rented rooms, slept rough when he needed to and had no ambitions beyond staying alive. He was in his late twenties when two things happened to change all that.

Firstly, it became apparent that America would soon be entering the Second World War; and around the same time, Martin came across an article in the local newspaper that described the recent boom in diamond prospecting in Brazil. There were vast fortunes to be made there. All a man had to do was make his way over and dig it out with his bare hands. For Martin, it was an easy decision. He had always detested the mindless stupidity of patriotism and he wasn't about to get his ass blown away for any damned cause. South America seemed as good a place as any to hide himself from the draft board and, besides, he was feeling lucky around that time. So he buckled down for a month or so, worked

14

himself like a dog and managed to raise just enough cash to buy himself a one-way ticket to Rio de Janeiro. Leaving was easy. There were no ties for him in New Mexico, no family, no special girl who might have a hold on him. Of course, he had no idea about how to go about becoming a *garimpeiro* – diamond prospector – but he would cross that bridge when he came to it.

And so it was that he had arrived in Rio with nothing but a few dollars and the clothes he stood up in. He had wasted little time in making inquiries in the local bars and eating places. Of course, there had been problems. The native language hereabouts was Portuguese and few people could speak more than the odd word of English. His 'inquiries' usually consisted of his saying the one word, *garimpeiro* (he had picked it up from the newspaper article and did not have the least idea how to pronounce it), whilst striking himself repeatedly on the chest. He was rewarded with blank stares, sad shakes of the head and, occasionally, a string of Portuguese jabberings with accompanying gestures that meant absolutely nothing to him. At last, on his third day out, sunburned and riddled with mosquito bites after sleeping rough in the open, he had some kind of success. He met an old man in a dingy cantina who could speak passable English and seemed to know exactly what to do.

'If you wish to be a *garimpeiro, senhor*, you will need a patron, *patrão*. Senhor Caine is the top *patrão* around here. For fifty cruzeiros, I will take you to him.'

Martin shook his head. 'I don't have any cruzeiros, old man.'

The man's grizzled face had split into a wide, gummy grin. 'Not yet,' he admitted. 'But Senhor Caine will give you money. For now, a promise is good enough.'

Martin frowned. It sounded too good to be true. 'Well, I tell you what. This guy gives me any dough, the fifty Cs are yours.'

He had followed the old man through the sprawling

ghettos of Rio, observing, as he passed, the awful poverty that existed away from the clean, well-ordered main streets where the richest people in the world came to squander their money in the elegant stores, casinos and night clubs. Back here, reality was the sight of a skinny Indian woman begging in the streets while three emaciated children clung to her skirts. The old man led Martin to a large crumbling office building. At a paint-blistered door, he rang a bell and, shortly after, a thick-set swarthy man in an ill-fitting black suit appeared. He stared disdainfully for a moment and then leaned forward so that his ear might be whispered into. He gazed thoughtfully at Martin for a moment, as though appraising him.

'Wait here,' he barked suddenly in toneless, heavily accented English. He slammed the door and the old man turned back to Martin with a reassuring grin.

'What did I tell you, *senhor*. Senhor Caine is an important man. He'll fix you up. The . . . the money . . . you would not break a promise to an old man, *senhor*?'

'Relax.' Martin slipped off his battered slouch hat for a moment and mopped at his brow with a bandana. The heat was intense. After a few moments, the door opened again and the thick-set man reappeared. He ushered Martin inside.

Beyond the doorway, Martin followed the man in the black suit along a gloomy roach-ridden hallway. There was a vile smell in the air that suggested bad sanitation. They moved on, up a rickety flight of wooden stairs and through another doorway at the top. A small metal plaque bore the legend *Charles Caine Incorporated*. Martin's companion opened the door and stood aside to let the American enter. He found himself standing in a small airless office; at the desk a fat man in an expensive but badly crumpled suit appeared to be busy with a jumble of papers. He had a pale, almost baby-like face

16

and what little hair was left on his head had been teased into an oily series of black curls that drooped down onto his forehead. His eyes were small and piggish, but they glittered with a low animal cunning. Behind him stood an impassive stooge in a suit that must have been run up by the same tailor who had garbed the man who answered the door and who now moved round the desk to join his opposite number. The two stood flanking the fat man like attendant flunkies waiting on an emperor. Martin could see quite clearly the bulges under their left armpits where gun holsters nestled. He frowned and turned his attention back to Charles Caine.

His first reaction was one of instant distrust. An old garage mechanic Martin had known back in New Mexico had once told him, 'Never trust a guy who looks like he eats better than you do.' Caine was the first overweight man Martin had encountered since his arrival in Rio. Most people here had the sallow, hunted look of those who did not know where their next meal was coming from. Not so Mr Caine. He looked content as only a wealthy man can, and there was something about the shrewd little eyes gazing abstractedly at the rows of figures before him which suggested that this man should be trusted only as far as he could be thrown. Martin's nostrils twitched as a smell reached them, the sickly sweet odour of lavender water.

Caine glanced up as if noticing Martin for the first time, but of course this had all been a calculated ploy intended to belittle the newcomer. At any rate, it didn't cut much ice. When Caine spoke, his voice had a strange, piping, high-pitched tone, but his accent was shot through with the unmistakable tones of a cultured Englishman.

'So . . . er . . . Mister . . .? I'm sorry, I believe we have not yet . . .?'

'Taggart. Martin Taggart.'

'Mr Taggart. An American. Moreover, an American

17

who wants to become a *garimpeiro*. An interesting break from tradition, but then we get all kinds in here.' He grinned, displaying a set of even white teeth that looked too immaculate to be real. 'I would have thought, Mr Taggart, that like all true-blooded Americans you would be busy preparing yourself for the er . . . *glorious* struggle with Japan and Germany; but then, perhaps you find the whole business of war as trivial and tiresome as I do.' He studied Martin for a moment as if expecting a reply to this, then continued in a different tone. 'Ah well, a man's reasons are his own, I suppose. At least it will prevent your running back to your country for a while. The call-up brigade have never been well known for their understanding of those who evade them.'

Martin had to try hard not to register a reaction. The fat boy was obviously a good deal sharper than he looked. It hadn't taken him more than a few moments to figure out the lie of the land. 'A *garimpeiro*,' Caine continued, pretending that he was unconcerned whether his arrow had hit home or not. 'Yes, well, you might do at that. You look hungry enough . . . you look as though you can handle yourself in a tight spot. Show me your hands, please.'

Martin stepped obediently closer to the desk, extended his hands, palms uppermost. Caine reached out suddenly and took them in his own.

'Ah, now look at these hands, Agnello,' he purred, half-turning to address the man in the black suit. 'Here is a fellow who has done some hard work in his time. Not like your lily-white hands, Agnello, hands that have done nothing more than pull a trigger or wield a knife; and not like mine either, hands that have only signed papers and . . . counted money.' He gave a little giggle, a rather unpleasant sound; and he gazed for a moment at his own pudgy, stubby hands, the fingers of which glittered with a series of ostentatious diamond rings. Martin took the opportunity to pull his own hands away from Caine's grasp. The fat man smiled at him a moment, a trace of mockery in his expression. Then he nodded.

'Yes, well, Mr Taggart, I am after all a patron; I have many *garimpeiros* in my employ, hundreds. What's more, I am always ready to take on more, regardless of their nationality. Good fortune owes allegiance to no flag, my friend.'

'I'd say you're proof of that, Mr Caine. How does an Englishman come to be a patron in Rio de Janeiro?'

Caine shook his head. 'Oh, a long story, that one; and a strange and muddy path from the playing fields of Eton to this weird backwater. Let us just say that I am by nature an opportunist, Mr Taggart. It's not just diamond prospecting that I have interests in. I have my fat fingers in a whole series of delectable pies dotted about this great continent; and as you can see from the shape of me, I never tire of trying out new flavours.' He laughed drily. 'But I digress. Let's get back to the business in hand. I take it you have no money?'

Martin shrugged. 'About five cruzeiros,' he replied.

'Five cruzeiros!' Caine leaned back in his chair and cackled gleefully. 'Well, you aren't quite destitute, but you're not far away! Let me see now, you will need to buy yourself the necessary equipment, you will need your fare up to the *garimpo* – the diamond field – and you will need a gun. I think ten thousand cruzeiros will suffice.' He opened a drawer in his desk and took out a thick wad of money. With the slow relish of a man who loved the feel of paper, he counted out the agreed sum. Then he indicated to Martin that he should take it.

'What's the catch first?' Martin inquired tonelessly.

'The catch.' Caine feigned wide-eyed innocence for a moment. 'The catch, Mr Taggart? Did you hear that, Agnello? Paco, did you hear? Such a suspicious nature this young fellow has. Why, if I didn't know better, I'd

19

swear he didn't trust us!' He fixed Martin with a calculating look. 'The "catch", Mr Taggart, is a simple enough idea and one that, I can assure you, you will find the same wherever you inquire around Rio. Of anything and everything that you find at the *garimpo*, I take fifty per cent.'

Martin returned the gaze calmly. 'Fifty per cent, huh? That's a little steep, isn't it?'

Caine shrugged. 'Perhaps it is, by some standards. But you see, by lending you the necessary money I'm running the risk of your never finding a thing.'

'Some risk,' muttered Martin.

'I'm afraid that's the way things work here. Without money for equipment, I don't see how you can become a *garimpeiro* at all. Perhaps you may find a friendly backer who will loan you the money you require with no strings attached; but, somehow, I seriously doubt that. If you'd rather forget the whole thing . . .' He made as if to put the money back in the drawer, but Martin stepped quickly forward and put his hand down on top of Caine's wrist. It was an unwise move. The two *pistoleiros* on either side of the fat man went for their guns. In an instant, Martin found himself looking down two barrels aimed straight into his face. He backed quickly away, his hands in the air.

'Hey, hold it, hold it! I was only going to say that I accept the terms . . .'

There was a long and terrible silence. Martin's body crawled as he imagined the terrible impact of those unseen bullets. But then Caine spoke, his voice like warm oil. 'You must forgive my boys, Mr Taggart. They tend to be a little overprotective sometimes. You see, I pay them a great deal of money to keep my interests uppermost in their minds. They can be very excitable. You wouldn't believe the trouble it can cause.' He waved the guns away with a delicate motion of his fat hands and the pistols were grudgingly returned to their holsters. Then he indicated that Martin should pick up the thin wad of money from the desk. 'Spend it wisely,' he advised as Martin slipped the cash into his pocket. 'Here is a list of the equipment you will need. Go to the address at the top of the page and you will receive a special discount. Also, here are a set of instructions about how to get to the *garimpo*. The rest, Mr Taggart, is up to you. I wish you luck.'

Caine returned to his papers, seeming to have dismissed Martin completely.

'Is that it?' demanded Martin incredulously.

Caine glanced up in surprise. 'Was there anything else?' he inquired.

'Well, uh . . . that's for you to say. I figured there'd be some papers to sign . . . some kind of a contract.'

Caine chuckled, seemingly amused by the notion. 'Oh, we have no need of any *contract*, Mr Taggart. That's not the way things are done in Rio.'

'Yeah, but . . . supposing I do strike it rich out there. I mean, what's to stop me from just taking off with whatever I find?'

Now it was the turn of the two *pistoleiros* to laugh. They leaned back their heads and guffawed unpleasantly, revealing teeth that were riddled with dark metal fillings.

Caine gave a slow, expressive shrug. 'Nothing at all, Mr Taggart. Nothing at all. In fact, many others have tried the same thing in the past. There's a big graveyard out on the edge of the city. You'll find every one of them there. In fact, why don't you pay the place a visit before you leave for the *garimpo*. I'm sure you'd find it most interesting.'

Martin glanced from Caine to the two laughing *pistoleiros*. He studied their ill-fitting suits for a moment, with particular reference to the strange bulges beneath their left arms. He nodded slowly.

'Just remember one thing,' added Caine, beaming up at him. 'I know everything that happens at the *garimpo*. You may think it's a long way from there to this office desk but, believe me, my friend, distance does not matter when a fellow has as long a reach as I have. Once again, I wish you luck.'

Martin said nothing more. He turned and made his way out of the room, closely escorted by Agnello. They retraced their steps down the evil-smelling staircase.

Stepping out from the gloom of the hallway, he was momentarily dazzled by the harsh sunlight in the street. The old man was waiting, his little black eyes glittering greedily. 'The fifty cruzeiros, *senhor* . . .'

'Sure, sure, here . . .' Martin peeled off fifty from the wad and pressed it into the old man's skinny hand. He stood gazing at it for a moment, as though he could scarcely believe his luck. Then he glanced quickly round to ensure that nobody else had witnessed his good fortune. He grinned and scuttled abruptly away, diving headlong into the nearest alleyway. Martin was left alone in sun-baked silence. He tipped his hat back on his head a little and reached for his cigarettes.

He had come to Rio to become a *garimpeiro* and now he had the money to enable him to do it; but he didn't like the set-up one bit. Caine had been too confident of himself to be making idle threats. There was little doubt that those who had tried to cheat the patron really were out in the graveyard he had mentioned. Martin was going to have to keep his nose clean from now on.

That afternoon, he purchased the equipment he required – a pick and shovel, several round pans with wire mesh bases for sifting rubble, a good pistol and some spare ammunition, a knife and as many packs of cigarettes as he could conveniently carry. All these things could be purchased up at the *garimpo*, the storeholders told him, but would cost very much more. The following

22

morning, before dawn, he took a train through the jungle to Garimpo Máculo. It was a three-hour ride through dank, humid forest and the interior of the train was like a Turkish bath. It was packed with hopeful prospectors of every nationality, each, like Martin, sent out by a patron. For the most part they were a tough, hard-bitten bunch of men, most of them running away from something – the police, the war, or just their own poverty. There was no friendliness between any of them. They began the journey as they meant to continue, as rivals.

One thick-set bearded Englishman asked loudly if anybody could tell him what *maculo* meant. A Portuguese on the other side of the compartment shouted back in slow, heavily accented tones that *maculo* was the Portuguese word for the diarrhoea caused by dysentery and that the camp was named after it because the disease was rife there. But this was the only conversation of the journey. Martin was relieved when the train finally came to a stop and the passengers spilled out onto a muddy deserted halt in the middle of the jungle. From here, it was only a short trek across open scrubland to the *garimpo*.

Martin's expectations of the place had never been very high and yet he was unprepared for what he saw; a great ugly gash in the surface of a wide stretch of red rock which not so long before had been covered with dense jungle; and, within the gash, countless numbers of man-made pits, each with a single occupant grubbing his way frantically deeper with pick and shovel. There were hundreds of men working here, tough, scowling, sunburnt men dressed in rags who greeted the arrival of the newcomers with nothing more than a sidelong sneer. Round the edges of the *garimpo* were the living quarters, a description that was little more than a bad joke when applied to the tumble-down, ramshackle collection of squalid huts, lean-tos and canvas shelters that the

23

garimpeiros called home. As Martin and his companions disembarked from the train, a little weasel-faced man in a filthy suit and a shapeless panama hat moved amongst them, announcing that he was the *fazendeiro* on whose land the *garimpo* was situated. If anybody wanted to dig here, they would have to pay him, Senhor Mirales, ten per cent of anything they found. The man was an irritating little insect and would normally have been swatted aside like a troublesome mosquito; but, predictably, he was backed up by three venomous-looking *pistoleiros* and the newcomers were too dazed and numbed from their journey to make much trouble. They milled about in confusion while specially appointed men moved amongst them, offering accommodation for hire. The prices demanded were exorbitant but nobody was in any position to refuse. Martin was billeted in a filthy little wooden shack with no windows, no door, no toilet, not even any running water. There was simply a rough bed made out of boards with a single filthy blanket lying on it. Water could be obtained from a hand-pump on the other side of the clearing or, failing that, from the stretch of muddy river that ran alongside the perimeter of the *garimpo*. Food could be purchased from the nearby *barraca* at about four times the going rate elsewhere and would have to be cooked on open fires outside the shelter. Also from the *barraca* would come any equipment that needed replacing and the *cachaça* with which a weary miner might drink away the misery of a long fruitless day's work. For those with a little more money to spend, there was a brothel situated next to the store, haunted by a collection of dead-eyed, gaunt and miserable-looking Indian girls. They were plain and, for the most part, rife with venereal disease but, after a few months of unrelenting toil, it was surprising how attractive they could look.

Martin threw himself into the work with silent

dedication, rising every morning at first light to go and hack away the ground in the place which had been allocated to him. The first few weeks were terrible. His skin blistered in the sun, he was bitten half to death by a multitude of insects, he suffered a dose of malaria that turned his skin grey and racked him with uncontrollable bouts of shivering. His hands blistered and scarred against the hard wooden shaft of the pick and at night he staggered back to the stinking little shack to sleep only to find it crawling with rats and cockroaches. And, worst of all, in all this time he found nothing, not the smallest trace of a stone. Others found diamonds. Every few hours a wild shout would go up from some corner of the *garimpo* and there would be a sudden rush of men, anxious to see what had been discovered. A few moments later, the same men would trudge grimly back to their own claim and continue to hack at the hard, indifferent, unyielding soil. Men went down with the *maculo*, the debilitating diarrhoea that left them little more than weak skeletons. Others contracted typhoid. The sick who had any money left took the train back to Rio, the others simply died and were buried in shallow graves out in the scrub jungle by men who were well schooled in the art of digging and had no time for prayers.

When a man did grub a diamond from the earth, the word spread like wildfire through the camp; and a short time later, a buyer – a *comprador* – would appear, a professional man usually employed by the patron or the *fazendeiro*. He would examine the stone with his eye-piece while the finder looked hopefully on; and then he would make his offer with calm, well-practised disdain. 'It is not much of a stone; a good size, I grant you, but badly flawed. I could not offer you anything more than ten thousand cruzeiros for it.' The price offered was always a fraction of the stone's true value, but the presence of the ever-watchful *pistoleiros* in the background prevented any possibility of argument. The 'lucky' finder would take his share of the money and promptly go on a binge, getting blind drunk, spending a couple of nights fulfilling his tawdry fantasies in the brothel, brawling with his fellow *garimpeiros*; and a few days later he would be back at his accustomed place, hacking savagely into the soil, fuelled by the conviction that what had happened once could happen again. Sometimes really large diamonds were discovered, so big that even the *comprador*'s lousy offer would amount to a sizeable sum. Then all kinds of madness would break loose. Martin came to hate the *garimpeiros* and their stupid macho philosophy which dictated that it was a great loss of face not to squander any money that they had earned in the shortest possible time. One man who had found a good diamond went to the lengths of having a Cadillac shipped in from the United States, piece by piece, so that it could be brought in to the *garimpo* by train. Once everything had arrived, he had it put together and delighted for a few days in driving the expensive vehicle round and round the perimeter at breakneck speed, its interior packed with yelling drunken men who normally would not have bothered to talk to him. This went on until the car ran out of petrol and the owner was running short of money. Soon he was back at work and the rusting, dilapidated hulk of the car still stood at the edge of the jungle, an incongruous intruder in this remote corner of the world. Other diamond finders had more unfortunate ends. Sometimes a man was knifed in the back at the height of some drunken brawl and the remainder of his money appropriated by the killer. Others simply drank too much *cachaça*, went berserk and plunged yelling and shrieking into the jungle. Either the Indians got them or wild animals; they were never seen again.

Eventually, Martin found a diamond; not a particularly big one, but a diamond nonetheless; and though he had sneered in the past at the brutish excesses of his workmates, he found himself acting in just the same way. Long months of loneliness and frustration spilled out of him and there was nothing he could do to stop himself. He drank himself insensible at the *barraca*, he beat up some man who was too slow to get out of his way and, that night, in one of the grubby beds of the brothel, he rutted with an Indian girl who barely acknowledged his presence. The next morning, sick at heart, ashamed of his stupidity and suffering from the worst headache in all of creation, he was back at work, ignoring the jeers of men working alongside him.

Time passed with slow, relentless monotony. The long rains of his second year came, when there was nothing to do but lie in the shelter and stare out at the sorrowful yellow waters, swirling ankle deep around the *garimpo* and across the floor of the shack, bringing with it all manner of creatures – snakes, rats, scorpions. Vast swarms of mosquitoes and plague flies hovered in the air and fed on the abundance of human flesh. At a time like this, a man had to obtain credit to get those things that would keep him alive. There was always an interest rate and the next year was begun with the miner heavily in debt.

Martin had worked on, stubborn, indefatigable. The third and fourth years, he did better, found six diamonds in all, a couple of them of reasonable size. This time he forced himself to follow some kind of a plan. From each sale he put a little money aside, hiding it in the heel of his boot, and then went ahead and squandered the rest, in the usual flamboyant style, managing to convince his workmates that he had spent everything. He dared not let anybody know he was keeping some back, because inevitably a greedy man would come in the night and take it from him with the blade of a knife. He feigned poverty, asking for credit at the store, even though he no longer needed it. His plan was simple. To amass enough money to escape from the *garimpo* to something better. It might take him years but there was always the chance that he really would make it good, that he might find a diamond that was big enough to risk running with.

The news that the war had come to an end deepened his resolve. Now he should be able to get back to . . . or at least pass through, his homeland. The long rains came again. He bided his time. Sometimes, as he lay in the hammock he had constructed as a safer alternative to sleeping close to the water level, an image would come to his mind, an image of Charles Caine, fat and scented with lavender water, growing steadily rich on the proceeds he obtained by selling his diamonds on the international market; and a calm powerful hatred would come to Martin, a hatred and a hunger for revenge. But then he would remind himself that he had only himself to blame for this misery. He himself had wanted to become a *garimpeiro*; Caine had only provided the one-way ticket. There were men working at the *garimpo* who had been here for years and, what's more, it was plain they would remain here till they died.

'But not me,' vowed Martin silently. 'No, not me. I'm going to get out of this.'

And so the sixth year had begun. Martin's money stash had now become too big to keep in his shoe. Instead he had made himself a crude money belt out of a discarded piece of canvas, working at the dead of night by the light of a candle. He found another two diamonds that year and treated the money as he had done before, creaming off a little for his nest egg and frittering away the rest. He took to hiding the money belt in a small gap behind one of the roof beams of his shack, afraid that somebody might search him when he was drunk. He carried his gun with him at all times and would have been prepared to use it without a moment's hesitation, should the necessity arise.

And then the miracle occurred, the moment of destiny to which his whole life had been geared. It was late July and he was digging in the merciless glare of the midday heat. He was about four feet down into the latest of a seemingly endless series of excavations. Having broken up a large amount of rubble, he scooped it up in his pan, clambered out of the hole and strolled down to the river to sift through the contents. The yellow stagnant water washed round his ankles and he dropped the sieve unceremoniously beneath the surface, gave the rubble a quick swirl and then heaved the contents back onto the firm mud of the shore. He left them for a moment to soak through, strolling back to the hole to continue digging for a while. This was his usual procedure. After about twenty minutes, he clambered back out of the hole and wandered down to examine what he had. He did not hurry himself, since this was only one of hundreds of similar loads that he examined every day. He picked up a piece of stick from the bank and began to sort through the collection of mud and rock, poking systematically.

For an instant, something seemed to glitter, catching the rays of the sun; but then more mud slid downwards and the light was gone. Martin frowned. He probed with the stick again and found a hardness that seemed far too big to be anything but rock. He pushed his fingers experimentally into the rubble and pulled something free that was the size of a duck egg. He grunted disgustedly and was about to fling the object aside, when another flash of light caught his attention. He gave the object an exploratory wipe with the flat of his left hand, revealing a crystalline, transparent surface below. It was a diamond, the biggest he had ever seen; and he had very nearly thrown it away.

For an instant, he was struck numb, frozen to the spot. Then he opened his mouth to scream, but snatched the sound away before it left his throat, realizing that other men were working only a few yards away. He closed his hand round the diamond, stood up and kicked out with his boot at the discarded pile of rubbish, scattering it in all directions.

'Nothing but shit!' he announced bitterly. Then he moved down to the river again, crouched down in the shallows and feigned the act of splashing water on his face, while with his spare hand he doused the diamond in the water, rubbing the remains of the mud from it. He was shaking with emotion and he felt his eyes fill with tears. He dashed them away with muddy water and allowed himself the luxury of a sly glance down at his prize. He had not dared to believe that it could *all* be diamond, expecting that its size had been increased by lumps of rock adhering to it. He almost cried out a second time. It filled the palm of his hand and was unquestionably the biggest diamond found at Garimpo Maculo, perhaps the biggest ever discovered in the continent of South America. Even sold locally it would make him a rich man. On the international market, it would sell for millions of dollars.

Realizing that to linger there much longer might make his fellow workers suspicious he slipped the gem into the pocket of his trousers, testing the lining first with his fingers to ensure that there was no hole through which the precious object might slip. Then, composing himself with an effort, he mopped his face on his bandana and forced himself to return to his digging place, keeping his face stony and impassive. He hefted his pick and went on with his work, digging methodically and taking the rubble down to the water's edge every so often. At the back of his mind was the belief that, where one diamond had been, other lesser stones might occur. But all through that long afternoon, perhaps the longest of his life, he found no sign of anything else. As he worked, he considered the possibilities open to him. There was no way he would announce this find to the *compradors*. It was the discovery of a lifetime and he would either escape with the diamond or die trying. Once, he thought he saw the man working at the next dig staring at him suspiciously; but he assured himself that this was just the product of his overworked imagination.

When the brief tropical dusk came, he gathered up his equipment and trudged back to his shack. Impatiently, he waited for full darkness to fall and then, lying in his hammock, by the light of a single candle, allowed himself the luxury of a first proper look at the diamond. There was a curious shock in store for him. The stone was every bit as big as his first impressions had suggested; but what he could never have guessed was the fine, weird beauty of the rough gem. It was quite translucent and when he held it close to the candlelight, he gave a little gasp of surprise. For within the cool depths of the diamond a strange flaw had created a perfectly symmetrical and highly familiar shape. It was exactly like a spider, a tarantula, etched in a slightly grey series of veins within the heart of the stone.

He knew that shape only too well, for in the rainy season the creatures tended to seek sanctuary in the dusty corners of the hut. Though Martin knew that the bite of a tarantula was rarely very harmful, still he had a horror of their thick, hairy bodies and wriggling legs.

He replaced the diamond in his pocket and began to draw up his plans. Any man here at the *garimpo* would readily kill to possess such a stone, so he did not intend to linger. In three days' time, the regular train back to Rio would depart in the early hours of the morning, but to leave suddenly would inevitably cause suspicion. At Garimpo Maculo, there were only two reasons for leaving, death or sickness. So Martin decided that he would become sick that night. It would not be hard to fake. He suffered from recurring bouts of malaria and it would simply be a question of exaggerating the symptoms. That night he sat up sewing an old scrap of leather he had been saving to make a tobacco pouch into a bag in which he could keep the tarantula stone. He fixed a strong loop of rawhide to the bag, double testing it by wrenching the finished article with all his strength. Satisfied at last that it would not break, he hung the pouch round his neck, tucking it beneath the loose khaki fabric of his shirt. With the hard, rough shape of the diamond pressing reassuringly against his chest, he finally snatched a few hours' sleep, but he was troubled by an awful dream.

He was climbing a remote mountainside, clutching precarious holds on some sheer granite rocks. Far below, the jungle spread out in every direction, the huge trees dwarfed by distance. He had no idea what he was doing in this place, nor what he had come to find. He only knew he had to go on.

Reaching a particularly tricky section, he was obliged to put up both hands in order to pull himself onto a ledge. He began to do this, reluctantly lifting his feet up from their holds and letting his legs dangle above a terrifying chasm, and started to haul himself up; and then, with a sense of shock, he felt a movement under the fabric of his shirt, against his naked chest. Glancing down in terror, he saw that beneath the fabric something was moving, wriggling, pushing against the folds. Martin opened his mouth to yell but the sound died in his throat as he saw something dark and horribly furry begin to edge out from beneath the shirt. His fingers were aching on the ledge, a thick sweat bathed every inch of his body, but he could not move so much as a muscle; he could only hang helplessly as first one leg, then another, came creeping out into full view. Then there was a squat, heavy body and a whole series of quivering tiny jaws. He knew suddenly, with a terrible conviction, that the tarantula was going to

32

crawl up onto his face.

Martin woke, his body caked in acrid sweat. The first light of day was spilling through the open doorway of his shack. Remembering his plan, he stayed in his hammock much later than was his usual custom and then, after several hours of this, collected his tools and stumbled down to his digging place. He wore two layers of clothing to give the impression that he felt cold and of course this made him sweat profusely. The only difficulty was faking the shivering attacks, but even though nobody was taking a great deal of notice of him, he kept the act up all through the day, getting very little work done.

In the early afternoon, he was startled by the sound of a heavily accented voice just behind him. He turned and had to suppress a look of shock. Standing by his dig was the man who had been working opposite him the day before. He was Portuguese, a thick-set, bearded fellow with an enormous belly that jutted out over the belt of his jeans. He had moved to a new site that morning and Martin had not expected to see him again; but he stood now, his hands thrust into the back pockets of his jeans, regarding Martin with a calm, slightly mocking expression.

'You are ill, *senhor*?'

Martin shrugged, mopped the sweat from his brow with the sleeve of his shirt. 'Yeah ... just a touch of malaria, that's all. I get it from time to time ...' He turned away to recommence digging.

'Funny ... you don't look so ill to me,' the *garimpeiro* muttered. This was said in such a sly way that Martin was shocked; but he forced himself to continue digging grimly and when he turned round again, the man was gone. Back in the shack, Martin pondered the matter. Could the man have seen anything yesterday morning? Was his remark just coincidental? Was Martin himself becoming paranoid, seeing enemies at every turn? He did not sleep that night and the following morning his feeble attempts at digging were less of an act than they had been the day before. After a couple of hours of ineffectual fumbling, he gathered up his tools and stumbled off in the direction of the *barraca*. Behind the roughly made counter, he found Hernandez, the man who ran the store. Martin trudged slowly over to him and set the tools down in front of him, shivering violently as he did so.

'You are ill, *senhor*?' inquired Hernandez patronizingly.

'Yeah . . . Hernandez, what'll you give me for these tools?'

'Tools?' Hernandez glanced down at the well-worn equipment. 'You are quitting, Senhor Taggart?'

'I guess so. I've got to get back to Rio and sort out this damned malaria. I can't take another rainy season feeling this way.'

Hernandez chuckled. 'You should count yourself lucky, Senhor Taggart. At least you have not yet the *maculo*. That one, she is a real killer . . . malaria, a man gets to live with. You will see, in a day or so, the badness will pass . . .'

'I ain't planning on waiting a day or so. Come on, Hernandez, how much for these?'

Hernandez gazed at the tools disdainfully, prodding them with his fingers. 'These . . . there is little life in them, eh, *senhor*? I give you fifty cruzeiros.'

'Fifty! They damned near cost me five thousand!'

Hernandez shrugged expressively. 'That is what they are worth to me, Senhor Taggart. Maybe you should keep them. You may decide to come back, eh? They say a garimpeiro never quits until he has made his fortune . . . or died trying for it.' He chuckled unpleasantly.

'I can buy more in Rio, if I ever decide to come back to this rat-hole. Come on, give me a hundred for them, at least.' He shuddered violently and swore beneath his breath.

34

'Sorry, *senhor*. Fifty. That's my offer.'

'All right, dammit, give me that! At least I'm not in debt to you for anything and I guess I can just about afford the train fare back to Rio.' He accepted the notes that Hernandez counted out from a cigar box under the counter. Martin knew that Hernandez kept a double-barrelled shot-gun beside the box.

'The *senhor* should try a bottle of my *aguardente*; it's very good for the fevers.'

'No thanks, Hernandez, I couldn't afford your prices.' Martin leaned forward across the counter. 'Unless, of course, you were offering me a bottle free, out of the goodness of your heart . . .'

Hernandez shook his head. 'Alas, *senhor*, nothing in this life is free.'

Martin sneered and turned away from the counter; he froze for an instant when he recognized the figure standing in the doorway: the bearded Portuguese who had questioned him the day before. He was gazing at Martin with interest, leaning against the edge of the doorframe.

Goddammit, thought Martin desperately. *The bastard knows something*! But he kept his face impassive as he pushed by the man and trudged slowly outside. The man turned and came quickly after him.

'*Senhor*, wait a moment! You leave tomorrow, yes?'

'Maybe.' Martin did not pause or look back.

'Sure, I hear you tell Hernandez! Hold up a moment . . .'

Martin turned round, his expression threatening. 'So all right, I'm leaving. What the hell's it got to do with you?'

The man nodded and an arrogant smile played on his lips. 'Yes, I figured so . . . you found something, no?'

'What? What are you talking about?'

'A diamond, *senhor*. You found a diamond, two days ago when I was working near. I wasn't sure then, but I had an idea . . . just . . . something in your face; so I say to myself, Orlando, you wait to see what he does next. He will show you yes or no. And now suddenly you are ill and you have to leave . . . it is for sure you found a diamond, a big diamond or you would not risk to run with it.'

'You're crazy,' snapped Martin.

'I don't think so, *senhor*. Can I . . . have a look at it, huh? Listen, I'm not a greedy man, you know. We could be partners you and me . . . What do you say?'

'I say you're crazy. There is no diamond. I'm leaving because I'm sick.'

'Oh yes, of course! The malaria. Well, *senhor*, you're a good actor. But I have seen malaria many times. In cases as bad as this, the skin of the face turns grey . . . but yours now, *senhor*, looks perfectly good to me. So you tell me where is the diamond? Can I see it? You keep it on you somewhere, no?' The man stepped forward and began to finger the fabric of Martin's shirt; then he lurched backward with an oath as Martin's right fist clipped him hard against the jaw. He stood there, smiling ruefully and massaging his chin. 'A strong arm for a man with malaria,' he observed.

Martin said nothing. He glanced quickly about. Nobody seemed to have observed the fight but there were people around who would come running if the thing escalated. He fixed the man with a contemptuous glare and said, 'Just keep away from me. You're crazy. I don't know what you're talking about.' And he turned and walked away, remembering to keep his gait slow and awkward, just in case anybody else was observing him. He was terrified.

Back at his shack, he threw his meagre belongings into an old carpet bag and made his plans. The Portuguese was wise to him, but what did he plan to do about it? It seemed likely that he'd try to get to Martin before the

36

morning train arrived. Well, let him come; if he was foolish enough to try anything ... But would he tell anybody else? Martin guessed not. The man was as greedy as any other *garimpeiro* and would not wish to share the diamond with any 'partners'. Besides, he could have no idea how big this particular gem was. Martin could only hope that this reasoning was sound. If several men came after him in the night he wouldn't stand a chance of holding them off. One man he figured he could handle.

When dusk fell, he bundled the carpet bag and whatever bits of rubbish that were lying about the place into the hammock and covered them with a blanket. He lit a candle and placed it a short distance away, so that it just about illuminated the shape. Then, taking his razor-sharp, big-bladed knife from its sheath, he dropped down into the shadows in the corner of the shack. As a last resort, he placed his pistol where he could grab it in an emergency but he was hoping there would be no need of it. A shot would alert everybody in the *garimpo* to the fact that he had something worth defending.

He resigned himself to a long, monotonous wait. The hours began their slow, laborious journey towards the dawn. He sat crosslegged in darkness, sweating in the stifling heat. Mosquitoes worried relentlessly at his forehead and bare neck but he remained stock-still, staring out at the slightly lighter rectangle of blue that was the doorway of the shack. The candle gradually burned its way downwards through the wax and from time to time a large moth fluttered jerkily round the halo of light before moving away to rest in darkness. Time seemed suspended and Martin began to wonder if he really had any reason to be afraid. He had slept little over the last couple of nights and now his eyelids grew heavy, his head inclined downwards by degrees until his chin rested against his chest. He slept, a deep, dreamless slumber of exhaustion.

And then he was awake, suddenly, with the intense conviction that something was about to happen. His legs were badly cramped and his mind woolly; but, glancing towards the doorway, he was aware of a shape moving there, crouched down by the floor to the left. For a moment he thought it was some animal that had wandered in from the jungle after food; but then the shape inclined upwards and Martin recognized the fat silhouette of the bearded *garimpeiro*. The man remained in the doorway for what seemed like an eternity, his gaze fixed to the huddled form in the hammock. The candle had burned very low now and the faint glimmer of light only just caressed the soft curve. Now the man moved slowly forward into the shack, placing his feet on the wooden boards without making a sound. He was obviously barefoot and Martin silently cursed the fact that he had not considered this. His own heavy boots would be sure to make creaking sounds on the warped planking, but there was no time to remove them now. The man was approaching the hammock and between his outstretched fists something glimmered faintly. It was a length of cheese wire. Martin shuddered at the thought of the wire slicing into the vulnerable flesh of his neck. Setting down his own feet with as much care as possible, he got up, using the wall of the shack for support. He did not have long. As soon as the man realized that the hammock was a decoy, he would be on his guard; and even now the assassin was leaning forward over the blanket.

Martin took two quick steps forward, threw his left hand up to cover the man's mouth and with his right hand slammed the long blade of the knife into the small of the *garimpeiro*'s back. The man's fat body shuddered with the force of the blow and Martin began to lever the blade upwards, searching for the heart; but then the

38

bearded man's right hand let go of the cheese wire and he brought his elbow savagely upwards into Martin's face, knocking him back across the room. The man spun round like an overweight dancer doing a macabre pirouette, his hand clawing ineffectually at the handle of the knife that protruded from his back. He was making a strange guttural noise deep in his throat and the length of cheese wire still dangled uselessly from his left hand. Knocked half senseless, Martin leapt in again, terrified that the man's noises might alert the rest of the *garimpo*. He grabbed the wooden peg at the end of the cheese wire, whipped the man's left arm upwards round his own neck and, when the wire grew taut, gave it a quick turn round the *garimpeiro*'s throat, pulling it tight until the sounds he was making ceased with an abrupt gurgle. The man stood in the centre of the room, thrashing hideously for a moment with his free arm. Then he gave a last jolting spasm, his head tilted sideways and he fell into Martin's arms. Snatching the rubbish free of the hammock with one hand, Martin man-handled the body into its place, pausing only to wrench the knife free of its fleshy sheath. He wiped the blade thoughtfully on the dead man's shirt, rolled him over onto his back and threw the blanket across him so that there would be no need to look into those glazed, staring eyes again that night.

Martin sighed. He undid the bandana round his neck and mopped his face dry of sweat. It was too bad that it had to happen this way. Now it would be obvious why he had left and of course people would be looking for him. He would have to move quickly as soon as he got to Rio. At least the body in the hammock would buy him some time. People would simply think he was lying in, suffering with his malaria. Only Hernandez at the *barraca* knew of his intention to leave next morning and he never came down to the diggings. It should be hours before anybody bothered to glance in at his shack, and by then, with any

39

luck, he would be on his way to Europe. He had already decided that Rotterdam would be the best place to sell the diamond; and, with careful planning, he figured he had just enough money put by to pay his fare to there. That was surely one place where even Caine couldn't reach him.

Glancing at his watch, he saw it was just a few hours to dawn. He remained seated in the corner of the hut, chain-smoking, and gradually the light began to brighten. Now Martin could make out the hunched shape in the hammock and the dark red stain that was spreading across the underside of the fabric. A swarm of plague flies buzzed curiously round the stain, settling and resettling upon it. He felt no sense of guilt at the killing. The man had come to steal a diamond and had paid for his greed in the most fitting way.

Glancing at his watch again, Martin saw it was time to make his move. He stubbed out his cigarette, reached up to the gap behind the roof beam where he kept the canvas money belt and tied the device in place beneath the loose fabric of his khaki shirt. Then, collecting his carpet bag, he ducked out of the doorway of the hut, glancing cautiously around in the half light. There were few people about yet, but he made his way slowly to the railway halt, walking as though with great difficulty. He left the great ugly scar of the *garimpo* behind him and moved on through the brief stretch of scrub jungle that bordered the trail to the railway halt. The vegetation was sodden with morning dew and the legs of his trousers were soon soaked through. Once he reached the rough earth banking that passed for a platform, he settled down to wait. His pistol was tucked in the waistband of his trousers, in case anybody should challenge him; but the only other people to arrive were a couple of feeble *garimpeiros* who were genuinely sick. Martin wisely kept his distance from them. Off to the east, lost somewhere in jungle, a few unidentified birds greeted the rising of the sun with a distant squawking. Then, at last, he heard the wheezing of the rusty old train as it came lumbering up out of the jungle. It clanged to a halt in a spasm of steam and ancient metal, disgorging a motley collection of would-be fortune-hunters, a pack of arrogant, snarling tough guys who had yet to be broken by the jungle. Martin watched them pass by, remembering his own arrival here six years earlier. More human fuel for the furnaces of men like Caine. The newcomers strode noisily away towards the *garimpo*, where the *fazendeiros* and their henchmen were waiting to greet them.

Martin hauled himself aboard the train and took his place on one of the hard wooden seats. The carriage stank of a mixture of sweat, *cachaça* and urine, but to Martin it was the vehicle that would carry him away from the living hell that was Garimpo Maculo. An impassive Indian guard came along collecting fares; and a few moments later the train lurched into motion, heading back into the dark, mysterious jungle. Martin sat quietly through the journey, staring out of the dust-streaked window.

Arriving at Rio three hours later was something of a shock. It was six years since he had seen anything of the trappings of civilization and clambering off the train to be swallowed whole by a sea of humanity in the process of hurrying to work was a weird experience. It seemed inconceivable that Rio de Janeiro, with its great glittering skyscrapers of glass and concrete, its traffic-jammed streets and its bewildering mixture of races, could actually have been here all the time, perched on the edge of the jungle like a bizarre oasis on the perimeter of a vast green wilderness. But now was the time to move fast. Martin's first step was to seek out a cheap clothing store where he purchased a new khaki shirt and trousers to replace his rotting rags. Then he went to a public wash-house, where he was able to bath and shave himself. He was, all the time, horribly aware that the hours were passing and that each minute he wasted would bring him nearer to discovery; but he also realized the stupidity of turning up at the airport looking like a tramp. Once he was satisfied that he looked fairly presentable, he dumped his old clothes in a trash can and hailed a passing cab, directing the driver to take him straight to the airport.

A short while later, he was pushing his way through the crowds of people inside the main building. The presence of so many strangers made him nervous; every couple of moments, he glimpsed a man who could well be one of Caine's *pistoleiros*. He made his way to the check-in desk and impatiently tagged himself onto the end of a long queue. When he finally reached the desk, he was met with an engaging smile from the pretty, dark-haired receptionist.

'You er . . . speak English?' he inquired.

'Yes, *senhor*.'

'Fine. Well now, I need to get to Zürich just as soon as possible. I er . . . had a telegram this morning, a friend of mine is seriously ill.'

The girl looked taken aback. She shook her head. 'I am sorry, *senhor*, but . . . do you not have a reservation?'

'No. See, I only found out this morning. When could you find me a seat?'

Again she shook her head. She gestured vaguely at the papers in front of her.

'Now is a very busy time for us. There is certainly nothing until early next week, for sure. Of course, there may be cancellations . . . Have you perhaps a phone number where I could contact you?'

'No, you don't understand. I have to leave right away, today. You see, my friend . . . is dying, he . . .'

'I'm very sorry, *senhor*, but –'

'Is there no other way I could go today? I don't have to go directly to Zürich, you see. Perhaps I could go to some

42

other place first ... Britain, Paris ... I could pick up another flight from there.'

'Well ...' The girl scanned her lists thoughtfully. 'There's a place tomorrow night on –'

'Tomorrow night is too late!' Martin snapped.

'Well then, *senhor*, I'm afraid that ...'

Martin did not hear the rest of her words. He nodded at her, but her voice did not reach him. This was something he hadn't figured on. He'd just assumed he'd be able to clamber aboard a plane and take off. If he was obliged to hang around Rio till tomorrow night, he might as well go straight to Caine's office and turn himself in. He moved away from the desk, his mind turning over furiously. Whatever happened, he had to put as much distance between Rio and himself in the shortest possible time. An internal flight perhaps? Yes, that might be the answer. Brazil was a big country; a simple hop up the coast involved a trip of several thousand miles. Lighting a cigarette, Martin manoeuvred his way across to the local flight desks. Various details were chalked up on blackboards. He found details of a domestic flight to Belém on the north-east coast, at the mouth of the Amazon. There was an overnight stop first at Recife, an eight-hour haul up the coast from Rio; and the second leg across to Belém would involve a journey that was barely shorter. While it was nothing like the distance that Martin wanted to put between himself and Caine it should at least buy him time to wait around for a flight to Europe. Best of all, this flight was due to depart in just under an hour's time. He inquired at the desk and was relieved to find that there were still a few seats available. He purchased a ticket and strolled gratefully through to the small lounge at the far end of the building. It was quieter here, with only fifteen or so other passengers to worry about. At last he began to feel that his plan could succeed.

The fan above his head came back into focus. He had

43

drifted for a moment into a half-sleep and his mind was a hazy jumble of confused thoughts. Instinctively, he lifted a hand to stroke the hard shape beneath his shirt. The touch was reassuring, but he was suddenly uneasy. Something had woken him and, sleep-dazed as he was, he could not direct his thoughts to identify whatever it had been. He yawned cavernously, shook his head to clear away the last shreds of sleep. Then the something happened again, making the blood in his veins turn to ice.

It was the firm, powerful grip of someone's hand on his shoulder.

Chapter 2

Mike Stone pushed his foot firmly down on the accelerator, urging the old jeep up to its top speed. The engine growled a noisy mechanical protest, the wheels leaped and bucked over the uneven surface of the road. However, such measures were entirely necessary. Mike was late; he was usually late for something; and there was still a considerable distance to the airport. He sat hunched behind the wheel, his grey eyes fixed on the way ahead. Despite the heat, he wore the scuffed leather flying jacket that was the uniform of his profession. Occasionally, he turned to glance slyly at the woman in the passenger seat, but she was still ignoring him. She leaned back, her eyes hidden behind a pair of sunglasses, her long naturally curly red hair trailing in the wind. In the white cotton blouse and tight navy blue skirt her slim but curvacious body looked particularly inviting. Mike wondered wryly if he'd be able to last out the long trip to Belém without going crazy for her. Her name was Helen Brody; she was Mike's stewardess and had been for nearly a year now. The two shared several things: a similar sense of humour, a tough, tenacious ability to survive; and on the regular overnight stops in Recife and Belém, a single hotel room and a double bed. It would have been a perfect arrangement but for one major problem: the wife and two children that Mike supported in his home on the outskirts of Rio de Janeiro. That was the main reason why Helen had not spoken a word since he had picked her up an hour earlier. Mike appreciated her troubles but didn't feel inclined to do anything about them.

Like most airmen, Mike had found himself at the end of the war with few prospects. His role in the affair had not been a martial one though he had seen plenty of action in the South Pacific. He had flown 'Gooney Birds', the rugged, ubiquitous and ever dependable DC3 airliners, hauling troops and equipment to wherever there was a suitable runway hacked out of the jungle. The surrender of the Japanese in 'forty-five had left him somewhat out on a limb. What was there for a man whose only ability was to fly a battered old crate around the airways of the world? The answer should have been obvious, but oddly enough, he had never even considered the idea until Willy Borden had suggested it. Willy was a ground crewman, a little fellow with big ideas and a tidy sum of money put away for safe-keeping. What Willy had in mind was a charter airline; oh, nothing fancy, mind you, just a single plane to begin with, perhaps a couple more in time if things went well. It would be a way of utilizing the particular talents that the war had given them and, as Willy was so quick to point out, one thing that there was bound to be a lot of at a time like this was surplus equipment. So, they had pooled their resources, purchased a Gooney and sought out a stretch of the earth's surface where there were guaranteed transport problems. Mike's wife, Mae, was loyal enough to go wherever work might be found and willing to take two young toddlers with her. Things had gone surprisingly smoothly and the only item missing was a capable stewardess.

Helen had answered the advertisement.

From the moment he saw her, Mike had wanted her and she had felt pretty much the same way about him. Helen was the daughter of some stuff-shirted diplomat at the American embassy in Rio. She had grown tired of attending boring functions and opted for making her own way in the world. As she'd told Mike at the interview, she'd never done this kind of work before, but she figured she could turn her hand to just about anything. Helen had got the job and, shortly afterwards, had got Mike. The affair was by now a fixture and, typically, everybody knew about it but Mae.

A horsedrawn wagon appeared in the road ahead of the jeep, a rickety vehicle loaded with cans of latex. A lone driver dozed at the reins while his skinny horse plodded placidly to some unknown destination. Mike did not slow the jeep for an instant but accelerated around the rear of the wagon, cutting perilously close to the side of it. Startled, the horse reared up with an indignant snort and a couple of cans of raw rubber went hurtling back into the road. A stream of livid Portuguese curses were flung in the jeep's wake but Mike just grinned, rejoicing in the petty annoyance he had stirred up.

Helen glanced at him contemptuously. 'Big shot,' she sneered.

Mike glanced at her in mock surprise. 'Say, you *do* speak!' he exclaimed. 'I was beginning to think it would be like this all the way to Belém.'

She scowled at him. 'Grow up,' she advised.

'All right, all right, I get the message. I'm not the world's most popular man today, am I? You want to talk about it?'

She shrugged. 'What's the use? It never gets us anywhere. I mean, I talk to you and talk to you, but

46

sometimes I wonder if you ever hear a damned word. It's obvious you didn't tell Mae.'

'Hell no I didn't! It isn't that damned easy, believe me! I ... *wanted* to tell her but ...'

'The trouble with you is you want everything, Mike. You want me on a string so you can have your fun when it pleases you. And you want Mae and the kids to be there waiting for you when you fly home, to make you feel like a big man back from the war. But what about what *I* want, Mike? I've been patient for a long time now ... surely you could have brought yourself to –'

'Aww, it's easy for you to say!' retorted Mike. 'You're unattached, you don't know how difficult it is. You can't just slap somebody in the face like that, not after all the years we've had. Mae's been a good wife to me.'

'I could be a better one,' replied Helen calmly. 'You said yourself that you no longer make out with her.'

'Sure, but there's more to a marriage than that. You don't know the half of it, that's your trouble. How old are you, twenty-three, twenty-four? Mae's given up a lot for me. Heck, she's trailed halfway round the world hanging on to my shirt-tails; she's had my kids; she ...' His voice trailed away into a long sigh. He glanced at Helen reassuringly. 'I *will* tell her, honey, but I need time, that's all.'

'There *is* no time,' she told him. 'This is the last flight, Mike.'

He chuckled, shook his head. 'You said that last time,' he observed.

'This time I mean it, believe me, Mike. I've waited for you nearly a year now and that's as long as I'm prepared to wait for anyone. Besides, I ... I've had another offer of work. A *better offer* as it happens.'

He glared at her. 'From who?' he demanded.

'Felix Walsh over at WBA.'

'Walsh?' Mike sneered. 'Yeah, I might have known.

47

Jumped-up little creep, throwing his old man's money around. Give me three months and Stone's airlines will be pushing Walsh's off the airlanes. That jerk probably just wants to get you into the sack.'

Helen smiled wryly. 'Sure he does. But then that's his privilege. *He* isn't married.'

'Goddammit, Helen!' Mike smacked his fist down heavily on the dashboard of the jeep. 'What money is Walsh offering you? I'll match anything that he can put up.'

'You jughead. It's nothing to do with money, surely you can see that?'

'Well listen, honey, you've got to give me a little more time, that's all . . .'

Mike slowed the jeep as he approached the entrance to the airport. The guards recognized him, pushed back the high wire-mesh gate and waved him through. He glanced at his watch in silent irritation and then accelerated through the gate and out onto the airfield. 'We'll talk about this in Belém,' he said quietly.

'There's no point in discussing it further.'

'We'll talk about it,' he repeated forcefully; and then they both lapsed into moody silence. Mike headed over to the corrugated iron hanger at the edge of the airfield decorated with the SA logo. The word Stone was hardly one to engender confidence in the air. The Gooney was already out in position, its silvered metal surface glittering in the harsh sunlight. The fuel trucks were pulling away but Willy was still fussing around in his sweat-stained overalls, making a few last-minute checks. Mike clambered out of the jeep and stalked across to the plane leaving Helen to stroll along behind.

Willy glanced up as Mike approached. The mechanic was a grizzled monkey-like man who looked much older than his forty-five years. He was wearing an oily Boston Red Sox baseball cap the wrong way round on his slightly

48

balding head, so that the peak would shield his neck from the sun; and the habitual stump of a foul-smelling cigar was clenched tightly in his teeth. He gave a scowl which in Willy's world passed for a friendly grin.

'Punctual as ever,' he observed. A complete stranger meeting Willy for the first time would deduce that the man had an enormous chip on his shoulder, from the way he snapped out sarcastic comments but actually this was just his way of doing things. The fact of the matter was that he thought of Mike almost as the son he had never had. Willy was the archetypal crusty old bachelor, yet beneath his rough surface there really was a heart of pure gold. He was the most generous of men and ever sensitive to the moods of those around him.

'Ricardo here yet?' Mike asked.

'Sure. He's been here a half hour. Some people believe in being on time.' Willy jerked his thumb in the direction of the cockpit where Ricardo Ramirez, the co-pilot, was already going through the flight check. Willy glanced at Helen. 'Morning, Trojan,' he said. This was Willy's perpetual term of endearment for the girl and had something to do with Helen of Troy.

'Morning, Willy. How's Matilda this morning?'

Willy reached out an oil-blackened hand to touch the silver flank of the plane with the fondness of a country squire stroking his favourite horse.

'Well, she's in one piece and that's something, I suppose. Which reminds me, Mike, I've got a list here of those parts we need. We'll have to order them just as soon as this trip is finished. The old girl isn't going to hold up for ever you know.'

'What're you grouching about, Willy? She got through all the safety checks, didn't she?'

'Yeah, sure, this time. But things are changing, Mike, the war's over now. People don't fly by the seat of their pants any more. You've been pushing Matilda too hard

49

on that first leg up to Recife. You've barely got a reserve of fuel as it is; it would only take some small problem and any one of these parts could give out. Sure the plane is sound, but it's a helluva responsibility we've taken on here. It's simply a question of keeping in a proper reserve . . .'

'OK, OK, I get the general idea. You order whatever you need and I'll sign the papers. Did you get that problem with the undercarriage straightened out?'

Helen clambered up the couple of steps to the door and went inside to check that everything was tidy. She worked her way along the cramped interior and then went through the doorway into the cockpit. Ricardo glanced back at her with a good-natured grin on his tanned, handsome face. At twenty-six, with his thick jet-black hair, his dark hazel eyes and his perfectly spaced, even white teeth, he was probably regarded as the most eligible bachelor currently working the airlines. Happily though, he was a shy, unassuming boy who didn't seem to have much time for fooling around. But he was genuinely fond of Helen, she was sure of that. Sometimes Helen wished that she could become interested in a younger man like Ricardo, but she always found herself gravitating back to the more mature male and, nine times out of ten, there was a wife tucked away somewhere, like a nagging conscience. Mature! That was a joke. Mike was the most immature man she had ever encountered but she was stuck on him anyway. Helen returned Ricardo's smile. If nothing else, she enjoyed flirting with the boy.

'Hello handsome,' she said.

'Hello, Trojan! How's tricks?'

'Not so bad. You know me, Ricardo, always a good girl.'

He chuckled. 'Yeah, that's what I heard.'

She tousled his hair affectionately. 'Hey you, keep your mind on your work.'

'I'll try. Where's our great captain?'

'Outside, arguing with our great mechanic. Think there's a chance we'll get this crate up in the air on time, for once?'

'Hey, now that would be something, wouldn't it?'

Mike appeared in the doorway. 'What would be something, Ricky?'

'Oh, we were just saying. Maybe for once we can take off on time.'

Mike shrugged. 'What's the hurry?' he muttered. 'We don't charge enough to make that worthwhile.' He turned to say something to Helen, but she was already pushing past him, back into the passenger section. Mike frowned. He watched her for a moment as she prowled slowly along the length of the plane. Then he turned back to find Ricardo staring at him thoughtfully.

'For God's sake then,' muttered Mike irritably. 'Let's get this show on the road.' He closed the door behind him and then clambered into his seat. As he lowered himself into place, his hand brushed automatically against the butt of the sawn-off shot-gun that rested alongside his leg space.

'One of these days that things gonna go off and blow your foot away,' observed Ricardo.

Mike stared at him impassively. 'Flight check,' he announced tonelessly.

'Oh, it's all right. Everything's fine, I've been through it.'

Mike's expression didn't alter. 'Flight check,' he said again.

Ricardo sighed. When Mike was in this kind of mood, there was no sense fighting it. He started the procedure again, right from the very beginning.

Martin gazed up into the face of a stranger; but the expression on the face was a warm smile and, after a

51

moment's hesitation, he began to relax. The man was a stocky Portuguese dressed in crumpled khakis. His swarthy face was quite handsome, dominated by a pair of dark, intelligent eyes, and he wore an immaculately clipped Zapata-style moustache. In one hand he was holding an unlit cigarette. He gave Martin an apologetic grin.

'Forgive me, *senhor*. But I was afraid you would sleep through and miss your call for the plane . . . and also, I am out of matches.'

Martin nodded, reached in his pocket and handed the matches to the man.

'Thank you, *senhor*. You are English, yes?'

'No, American.'

'Ah.' The Portuguese lit his cigarette, exhaled smoke and nodded enthusiastically. 'I wish myself one day to visit your country. Allow me please to introduce myself. Claudio . . . Claudio Ormeto.' He indicated the seat opposite Martin. 'May I?'

Martin shrugged. 'It's a free country.'

Claudio sat down. He was obviously not going to let his enthusiasm be dampened by Martin's aloofness. 'You are going to Belém, yes?'

'That's right.'

'Is it . . . how do they say it in American movies . . . er, business or pleasure?'

Martin smiled. 'Well now, I don't think I've quite figured that out yet. How about yourself?'

'Oh business, business . . . To be honest, *senhor*, there's not a great deal of pleasure to be found in Belém. But my work sends me there. I work for the Brazilian Government in the capacity of an Indian observer. At this time, there are many reports of bad treatment filtering in to our agency. *Garimpeiros* and *seringuiros* – rubber tappers – are travelling down the headwaters of the Amazon and laying claim to land in the interior . . . Indian land. It seems that these men are simply killing off any Indians who oppose them.'

Martin nodded. 'Yeah, that sounds likely enough. From what I hear, the Indians have always had a rough time of it, ever since the Conquistadores first came over and started kicking them around.'

Claudio nodded. 'If you had seen the reports that arrived this month . . . women raped, men strung up and cut open with axes. It's hard to believe that men can be capable of such things. Now, of course, the big *fazendeiros* are becoming aware that there are vast areas of jungle land that they can buy up for a few cruzeiros an acre. Certain government departments turn a blind eye to the deal and that only makes our job more difficult. I heard last week of a *mateiro* – a forester – who has been travelling amongst many of the tribes, distributing clothing to them.'

'Well, what's wrong with that?' inquired Martin.

'The clothing had come from a smallpox hospital in Belém. A clever man that *mateiro*. He knows only too well that the Indians have no immunity to such diseases. They die like flies, whole villages at a time . . . and then the *fazendeiros* move in to pick up the pieces. So neat, so efficient. There can be no murder charges when the assassin is a microbe or a virus. I've seen a common dose of influenza decimate a village in a few hours. And what frightens me, *senhor*, is that this is just the tip of the iceberg. In time, the problem will get worse . . . much worse.' Claudio shook his head, looked abstracted for a moment. 'Ah, but you must forgive me,' he continued. 'Always I talk too much about troubles that others may not wish to share. You are staying in this country for long, *senhor*?'

Martin shook his head. 'Just passing through,' he replied. 'Fact is, I took this flight as something of a last resort. I don't aim to be staying in Belém for long.'

'Well, amen to that my friend.' Claudio leaned forward

slightly as if to impart a secret. 'It is a pity we cannot choose our fellow travellers, eh?'

Martin frowned. 'What do you mean?' he inquired.

Claudio nodded in the direction of two people sitting at a table on the far side of the lounge. Martin glanced at them from out of the corner of his eye. One was a middle-aged man dressed in an expensive-looking black suit. He was a short, rather tubby fellow and would have looked insignificant if it were not for a rather distinguished grey beard that seemed to lend him an air of dignity. He was smoking a huge Havana cigar and had one arm draped protectively around a young girl who sat beside him. She was a pretty, frail-looking girl, with straight blond hair and a pair of large blue eyes that seemed to hold a perpetually startled expression. She was surely no more than eighteen years old, dressed in a rather revealing white cotton dress. She was nursing a drink in one hand whilst glancing nervously around at her fellow travellers.

'Look at that pig,' muttered Claudio with undisguised hatred.

'Who is he?' inquired Martin.

'His name is Carlos Machado. He's a *fazendeiro*, one of the richest in Brazil; owns a fancy villa up in the city. He's currently in the market for buying land and it's well known that he isn't too particular how he comes by it. I don't doubt for one moment that he's heading up to Belém to pull off some shady deal.'

Martin raised his eyebrows. 'Nothing you can do about him?' he inquired.

Claudio grimaced. 'In Brazil, my friend, a man is considered beyond the reach of the law when he has enough money to buy himself out of trouble; and Machado has money enough for a thousand men. Money can buy most everything a man requires.'

Martin nodded. He glanced at Machado again. The man was now stroking the girl's hair with slow sensuous movements of his left hand, and occasionally she giggled as he whispered some remark into her ear.

'How else would a middle-aged guy like him get hold of a pretty little kid like that one,' agreed Martin.

Claudio chuckled. 'Oh, that's one thing he has not had to buy, *senhor*. You see, that is his daughter.'

Martin turned back to face Claudio, a look of mild disbelief on his face. 'His daughter? Say, you don't think . . .?'

'What would I know, *senhor*? Maybe they are just very close. But a slug like Machado, I would think that he is capable of much that would make a decent man sick to his stomach.' Claudio sighed, then smiled apologetically. 'You must forgive me. I do not mean to sound this bitter but somehow . . . ah, the hell with it!' He made a conscious effort to change the subject. 'What time do you have by your watch, please?'

'Oh, it's er . . . a little after twenty past twelve. They'll be calling us in a few minutes. I think I'll go and freshen up a little.'

'Oh, *senhor*, I hope my foolish talk has not upset you. Believe me, I am not usually a vindictive man. It is just that –'

'Forget it!' Martin got up from his seat. 'We'll talk some more on the plane.' He turned and made his way in the direction of the washroom. Now that he had assured himself that Claudio meant no harm, Martin was glad to have somebody to talk to. It took his mind off the doubts and worries that were assailing him. He followed the signs for the men's toilets, pushing through a swing door set in the end wall of the lounge, and found himself in a short, poorly lit corridor with another swing door at the top end of it some twenty feet ahead. After the comparative bustle of the lounge, it seemed strange to be alone again. He strolled forward, whistling tunelessly to himself, and then pushed through the second door. The washroom was completely empty. Martin moved towards a handbasin. He set down his carpet bag and let the basin fill with cold water. Meanwhile, he examined his face in the mirror above the taps: he had aged terribly in the six years at the *garimpo*. There were crow's feet etched into the sunburned skin around his eyes. He raised one hand to finger them thoughtfully for a moment. Little matter, he was still young enough to enjoy the benefits that the diamond would bring. With a sigh, he leaned forward, lowering his face until it was completely immersed in the water. The coldness was a delicious, tingling shock to his sleep-dulled senses. Now he put his hands into the basin, splashing more water around his neck and shoulders, smoothing handfuls of it back through his hair. When he heard the slight creak of the door opening behind him, he willed himself to act normally. Of course, he reasoned, other people would come here, it was a public facility. No reason to stiffen or jerk around in alarm. He went on splashing the water into his eyes for a few moments and then straightened up, giving his head a flick to remove the last traces of liquid from his hair. He felt revived now, fully awake.

And then he became aware of the second reflection in the mirror in front of him. A man's face was peering intently over his shoulder and there was a terrible silence in the room. The face was a familiar one, though Martin had not seen it for over six years. It was the *pistoleiro* who called himself Agnello, the same man, in the ill-fitting black suit, who on the occasion of that last meeting had been working for a certain Mr Caine.

Agnello's face broadened into an ugly grin. 'Ah, Senhor Taggart,' he said, in slow, toneless English. 'I have been looking for you everywhere.'

The boy pushed his way impatiently through the crowds of people that surrounded the reception desks, his dark eyes glancing nervously this way and that. He was perhaps sixteen or seventeen years old, a thin rangy *caboclo* – half-breed Indian – who looked very out of place in his grubby, too-large cotton shirt and baggy trousers. He wore cheap rope-soled sandals that flapped as he walked and the airline ticket that he clutched in his right hand was damp with perspiration.

He moved out from the press of noisy tourists waiting for international flights and hurried over to the quieter desks that handled domestic routes, finding the right place and joining a short queue of latecomers. His eyes strayed again and again to the face of the large clock that overhung the reception area; he had not meant to cut things so fine and he was aware that in the departure lounge anxious eyes would be looking for him in vain. The trouble was he had been too confident, wanting to give his companions the impression that he had everything under control; and then it had all gone wrong, a stupid mistake that he had not even envisaged. The car he'd stolen to get him to the airport had simply broken down on him. In a blind panic, he had been forced to hitch a lift from a passing stranger, a farmer in an old pickup truck that had got him to his destination with only minutes to spare. *Diabo*, what a fool he'd look if he were to miss that plane!

The queue moved forward a step and the man in front of him, a tubby drawling American tourist, began to flirt with the girl at the desk as though there was all the time in the world. The boy sweated uncomfortably. The barrel of the gun was rubbing his flesh raw where it was tucked into the waistband of his trousers, the heavy butt obscured by the loose folds of his shirt. He noticed with a sense of unease that a uniformed security man was lounging against the wall, just behind the receptionist. His job, no doubt, was to run a critical eye over everyone and question any whose face did not seem to fit. For the first

57

time since he had set out, the boy felt acutely aware of the shabbiness of his clothes. He had been advised more than once to purchase new ones, but had argued against it, maintaining that he would look even more out of place in a business suit. He had the face of a poor man and no amount of fancy clothing could disguise the fact. Better, he had concluded, to present himself as he really was. After all, poor men did sometimes travel by plane ... didn't they? Now he was almost at the moment of truth, the argument seemed somehow less convincing.

'Take it easy,' he warned himself; but his stomach gave an abrupt lurch and he had to close his eyes a moment and will his frayed nerves back into some kind of order.

'*Sim, senhor?*'

He took a deep breath. Everything would be all right so long as he kept his nerve. He'd gone over every detail again and again, allowing for anything that might conceivably go wrong. All that remained was to get himself onto the plane and the rest ... the rest would ...

'*Senhor?*'

He opened his eyes abruptly, realizing that the girl was talking to him. The American had disappeared and now the receptionist regarded him irritably. Behind her, the security man was smiling mockingly, his eyes inscrutable behind the dark lenses of a pair of sunglasses. Flustered, the boy shuffled forward and handed his ticket to the girl. She took it gingerly, holding it between thumb and forefinger as though it were daubed with excrement. She laid it on the counter, gave it a cursory check and rubber-stamped it with a sigh. Then she glanced up at him as though reflecting on the strangeness of a scruffy young *caboclo*'s possessing such a ticket.

'Baggage?' she inquired.

'*Nao.*' He shook his head and somehow could not meet her gaze. 'I travel light,' he mumbled; and instantly wished he had said nothing. The security man had stepped forward, still smiling dangerously. The boy wished he would take off those damned glasses. You needed to see a fellow's eyes to know what he was thinking. He glanced at the black butt of a heavy pistol that jutted from a holster around the man's waist as he leaned forward over the girl's shoulder to look at the ticket.

'Kind of young to be travelling alone,' he observed.

The boy shrugged. 'Old enough, I guess,' he replied.

'What takes you to Belém?'

'I've got a job waiting for me there. A cousin of mine is a big man with a mining company. He's promised to give me a good start . . .' With an effort, he wrenched his gaze up to stare right back at the man. 'I can't seem to find anything that suits me in Rio.'

There was a long uncomfortable pause, broken only by the distant echoing drone of a flight announcement. The security man seemed to be thinking and it was impossible to tell whether his eyes were on the boy's face or searching the folds of his cotton shirt for a tell-tale bulge; but then, inexplicably, his mouth lapsed into a friendly smile.

'You'd better hurry on through,' he said. 'The flight will be leaving any minute now.'

The boy smiled, nodded, had to suppress a long sigh of relief. He turned and began to walk in the direction of the departure lounge.

'*Um momento, senhor!*'

He froze in his tracks. The man's voice was suddenly terse and rigid with authority. The friendliness had been simply a ploy to put him off guard. The boy's blood seemed to run cold. He turned slowly, fully expecting to see the guard's pistol pointing at his chest . . . but the man was grinning at him and holding out his ticket.

'You won't get very far without this.'

'*Nao . . . nao*, of course not . . .' The boy grabbed the

59

ticket and hurried down the short corridor that led to the departure lounge. He went in just in time to hear the first call for flight SA119 to Belém and followed the stream of passengers that were already moving towards the open doorway at the end of the room. Before he stepped out into sunlight, he raised his right hand in an exaggerated fashion and wiped the back of his neck, a sign to those who were watching that nothing had gone wrong.

Out on the tarmac, the plane waited and the boy strolled towards it, whistling to himself. He knew all about this kind of plane, had devoted a year of his life to learning everything he could about it. He knew its range, its weight, the intimate workings of its navigation systems, anything and everything that could be gleaned from books on the subject. He had never actually been inside one before but was fairly confident that, should it become necessary, he could even fly it to its destination. But that would only be if something went wrong. He did not intend to make any more mistakes.

Chapter 3

Martin winced as the point of a switchblade knife dug painfully into the freshly shaved flesh at the side of his throat.

'Put your hands onto the basin,' advised Agnello calmly. 'If you try anything fancy, I'll slit your throat.'

Martin stayed absolutely rigid, gazing sullenly down at the carpet bag by his feet. His pistol was inside. He cursed his carelessness as Agnello's large left hand searched methodically up and down the length of his body and, predictably, discovered the leather sheath strapped to his right shin. The knife was quickly removed and tossed contemptuously to the other side of the room.

'Now you can turn around,' announced Agnello; and the pressure of the knife blade slackened momentarily. Martin turned slowly, his stomach lurching with fear. Agnello regarded him with silent disgust. 'An amateur,' he said tonelessly. 'Where the hell did you think you were going?'

Martin forced his voice to respond, as he desperately tried to play for time. 'You were quick,' he murmured.

'We got a telegraph about the guy you killed. It was certain you had found something. This was the first place we figured you'd come.' Agnello's tone was one of mild irritation. He was like a schoolteacher who had been given the irksome task of punishing a disobedient pupil.

'So what happens now?' croaked Martin. 'Do we go and see Caine?'

'What for? You ain't going anywhere, my friend.' Agnello grinned unpleasantly and then glanced in the direction of the door. 'But we don't wanna be disturbed, do we?' He motioned to a toilet cubicle, the door of which was open. 'In there,' he ordered. 'Get moving!'

Martin's guts seemed to turn to ice. He began to back away from the advancing blade; the moment he was inside the cubicle Agnello would kill him. He could scarcely control his breathing. 'Listen,' he gasped. 'Listen, Agnello, we can make a deal on this. The diamond I found, it's big, really big. It would bring millions on the open market. We could make a deal, fifty-fifty.'

Agnello sneered, shook his head. 'Only a stupid man would try to cheat Senhor Caine. No diamond is worth such trouble.'

'This one is!' Martin began to fumble with the pouch around his neck. There were only a few more steps to the cubicle and he had fixed on the notion that the diamond might be his one hope of escape. Everything seemed to be happening in a terrible slow-motion. His eyes took in each vivid detail: Agnello's cold merciless eyes, as cold as

61

the glittering steel blade that hovered several inches in front of Martin's face; the great sinewed fist that clenched the handle of the knife, the knuckles whitening slightly from the pressure of holding it; Agnello's badly made suit, worn at the elbows and cuffs and with a few unidentified foodstains spattered down its front. And now the pouch was in Martin's hands; he was shaking the diamond out onto the palm of his hand, at the same instant that he was passing into the gloomy confines of the cubicle. He glanced up hopefully but Agnello had not even noticed the jewel, his gaze was fixed on Martin's chest, seeking out the right place to bury the blade of the knife.

'For Christ's sake, look!' snapped Martin.

For a fraction of a second Agnello's gaze dropped to examine the diamond; then his eyes widened perceptibly, his jaw fell a few degrees and the blade of the knife wavered. He was standing framed in the doorway of the cubicle, his arm outstretched. He was frozen into immobility because he was looking at the biggest diamond in God's creation. And now his eyes had caught the strange perfect form of the tarantula shimmering in the diamond's heart. For a split second only, mesmerized, Agnello had forgotten the instincts that years of violence had taught him; Martin was just beginning to learn them. He let the diamond fall to the floor.

Agnello could not help himself. He made an instinctive lunge to catch the jewel with his free hand and in that instant Martin grabbed the edge of the door and slammed it with all his strength on the arm that held the knife. Then he threw the entire weight of his body against the metal door, snapping the bone beneath the flesh like a dry twig. From behind the door there came a hollow, formless scream of agony and the switchblade clattered to the floor. Now Martin wrenched the door open again, grabbed a fistful of Agnello's hair and pulled the *pistoleiro* into the cubicle, hoping to make a quick end of him; but he had reckoned without the man's brutish strength. Agnello came blundering in, lashing out with his left arm, catching Martin a stinging blow across the eyes. For a moment Martin reeled back against the cistern while Agnello tried ineffectually to grope for his shoulder holster with his useless right hand. Martin unleashed a savage punch that slammed Agnello back against the door, banging it shut again. His hands clamped around the *pistoleiro*'s thick throat and he began to squeeze with all his strength. Agnello aimed a knee up between Martin's legs, but Martin twisted away from the full force of the blow. He swung Agnello around and pushed him back against the toilet seat, banging the man's head with sickening force against the white enamel of the cistern. Then he continued with his squeezing, gouging his thumbs deep into the hollows at the sides of Agnello's jaw. His eyes bulged grotesquely as the realization struck him that he was about to die. He struggled helplessly, his already swelling right hand clawing ineffectually at Martin's face.

And then, to his horror, Martin heard the door to the washroom swing open. He glanced nervously back. The cubicle door was shut. He released one hand and clamped it roughly over Agnello's mouth before a moan for help could issue from it. He applied all his strength into the pressure of the other hand, but somehow, Agnello clung on to life. His feet began to move weakly, the heels making dull scraping noises against the tiled floor. It was horribly quiet for a moment; then a familiar voice spoke.

'*Senhor*, is that you?' It was Claudio, the man that Martin had chatted to in the airport lounge.

'Yeah, it's me.' Martin sweated helplessly as he strove to finish Agnello off. He hoped the tone of his voice did not sound too strange.

'I thought perhaps you had not heard the call for our flight in here.'

63

'Oh yeah, I heard it all right. You go ahead and save me a seat, huh? I'll be right with you.'

Agnello's face was now a curious shade of purple. His tongue had emerged from his mouth but he still made one last spasmodic attempt to free himself. Then his body gave a series of convulsions and he began to relinquish his hold on life. Outside, the door opened again. There was a short silence and then it swung shut with a final thud. From beyond, there came the muffled second call for the plane's departure.

'Die, God damn you,' hissed Martin savagely. But there was barely any movement in Agnello's limbs now and his eyes had begun to cloud over. Frantically Martin began to look about for the diamond. It was nowhere in the cubicle and the possibility that it might have been kicked out through the space beneath the toilet door occurred to him for the first time with an abrupt conviction that Claudio might have found it lying on the floor. He wrenched Agnello's lifeless body up onto the toilet seat. The *pistoleiro* sat there, hunched and grotesque, his expression amply displaying the horrible manner in which he had died. Now, Martin realized grimly, he *would* have to run, as fast and far as he could.

Quickly, Martin picked up Agnello's gun. Then, fixing the bolt on the toilet door, he slid out through the wide gap beneath. He collected his carpet bag, dropped the pistol inside. Casting around the washroom, he found his knife lying against one wall and returned this to the sheath on his right shin. In the next cubicle, he found Agnello's switchblade and dropped that in his bag. But where was the diamond? He searched frantically through every corner of the washroom and had just come to the conclusion that Claudio had indeed found it when he spotted a glimmer near the skirting-board beside the door. With a sigh of relief, he snatched the jewel up and slid it back into its leather pouch, dropped the rawhide loop

64

around his neck and settled the pouch back into its accustomed position beneath his shirt. Then he glanced into a mirror to check that he looked all right. Apart from a slight discoloration below his left eye where a fist had struck him, there was no outward sign that he had been in any trouble.

From the airport lounge, there came the muffled tones of the third and final call for the flight to Belém. Martin could only hope that Agnello had come to the airport alone. He opened the door slightly and peered along the hallway. That area at least seemed deserted.

'Well, here goes nothing,' he murmured softly as he hurried out of the washroom, slamming the door behind him.

Helen glanced irritably out through the open doorway of the plane, the checklist tucked underneath one arm. Everybody accounted for but one. There always had to be some joker who kept everybody waiting. The intercom beside her head crackled into life and she snatched up the receiver.

'What's the hold-up?' Mike's voice, edgy and irritable.

'We're one passenger short, Mike.'

'Well, we'll have to leave him behind. We're a couple of minutes late as it is.'

'Your wish is my command, great white captain,' she replied mockingly. She turned to motion to the mechanics by the door that they could remove the steps; but then she saw the lone figure, running hell for leather across the tarmac. 'Oh, hold it a minute, Mike. I think Little Bo Peep has just turned up.' She watched impatiently as the man drew near, running as though his very life depended upon catching this plane. He was a slim, dark-haired man of no great height, obviously an American, though it was plain that he had been in Brazil for quite some time. His skin was tanned a very dark shade of brown and his

65

clothes were not the usual ill-suited selection of a tourist. He clambered up the few steps to the door, panting softly from his run, and then stood regarding Helen intently with deep-set, grey eyes. There was a frankness in the gaze, a challenging, assured quality that threw her for a moment.

'You er ... must be Mr ... Taggart,' she ventured quietly.

He nodded and she ticked the final name.

'It appears that I cut things a little fine there,' he observed.

'You could say that.' She motioned him into the plane's interior and signalled to the attendants to remove the steps, then pulled the door shut, moving the heavy bar down and across to seal it. When she pressed a buzzer beside the door, a signal that everything was ready, the plane began to taxi away.

Martin moved down the centre aisle. The seats were nearly all taken, but about halfway along he found Claudio sitting by himself.

'Ah, *senhor*! I was beginning to think you were having trouble back there!'

Martin forced a smile. 'I was.' He settled into the vacant seat and patted his stomach. 'Something I ate back at the hotel, I think. Sea-food.'

Claudio raised a hand in sympathy. 'You do not have to tell me, Mr ... forgive me, I still do not know your name.'

Martin smiled. Now he was on his way, he saw little reason to be cagy about his name and it seemed unwise to offer one that differed from what was on his passport.

'It's Taggart. Martin Taggart.'

'Ah, Senhor Taggart, you do not have to tell me about sea-food. When it is good for you, it is like swallowing little pieces of heaven; and when it is bad for you, it is like throwing up several acres of hell.' He chuckled. 'Are you

66

nervous of flying, *senhor*?'

'Me? No, not at all.'

'Me neither. I only wish the view was better.'

Martin glanced across the aisle and saw the heavy, grey-bearded figure of Carlos Machado sitting in the opposite seat. He had evidently placed his daughter by the window so that she could observe the wild scenery over which they would fly.

'In the old days, cattle always travelled in freight cars,' Claudio observed, making no attempt to lower his voice. 'These days they go by aeroplane. It makes no sense to me!' For a moment, Machado glanced at Claudio with a kind of smug, distant aloofness that seemed to suggest that the man's wealth made him somehow above the retribution of ordinary people. Then he turned away and whispered something to his daughter that elicited a high-pitched giggle.

The plane had come to a halt at the top of the runway. Helen moved along the aisle, asking everybody who had not yet done so to fasten their seat belts. She paused beside Martin. 'Your belt, Mr Taggart,' she reminded him.

He glanced up at her, grinned wickedly. 'Well now, I tell you what the problem is. I can never seem to get the damn thing fixed together. Perhaps you could show me?'

She gazed at him coolly. 'I'm sure you'll be able to work it out.'

Martin laughed and winked at Claudio. 'Can't blame a guy for trying.'

'Oh, no, to be sure. And I guess you've been starved of pretty girls for a long time now.'

A sharp twinge of suspicion cut into Martin's voice. 'What do you mean?'

'Oh . . . only that a *garimpeiro* does not have much opportunity to see pretty girls, that is all.'

'I never said anything to you about being a *garimpeiro*.

67

I didn't say anything about my work at all.'

Claudio nodded easily. 'You didn't have to, *senhor*. It is all written in your hands.'

'My hands?' Martin glanced at his outstretched palms and then he understood. Those scarred, calloused, iron-hard hands could belong to only one profession.

'Tell me,' he muttered wryly. 'Is everybody in Brazil a natural detective?'

Claudio laughed. 'No,' he retorted. 'It's just that we practise all the time.'

Martin's reply was drowned as the two one-thousand-horsepower engines roared abruptly into life. The plane accelerated along the runway, its momentum pushing the passengers back in their seats. Within a surprisingly short distance, the glittering silver fuselage began to lift upwards into the empty air, leaving nothing but a fleeting black shadow on the hot surface of the runway to mark its passing.

Martin leaned over to peer out of the window, watching in fascination as the buildings, vehicles and people below dwindled to the size of children's play-things. A few moments later, the plane was banking around towards the north-east and there, far below, perched on the edge of the glittering South Atlantic Ocean, was the famous sugar-loaf mountain, a strange humped shape dwarfed by the vast stretch of blue water. From this height, it looked somehow inconsequential, like a half-melted cake that had collapsed at the edges. He settled into his seat with a sigh of content. Now at last he felt he was really on his way to freedom. He glanced up as the stewardess came walking down the aisle.

'Say, Miss, can I get a drink now?'

She shook her head. 'Not just yet, Mr Taggart. I'll announce when the bar is open.'

'I'll look forward to that.' He grinned at her but she turned away, her face expressionless, and continued to the front of the plane. Martin studied the rhythmic sway of her buttocks beneath the tight blue fabric of her skirt.

'I think you're right, Claudio,' he murmured. 'It *is* too long since I've seen a pretty girl. Now why do you suppose that one is so unfriendly?'

Claudio grinned. 'Maybe because you made her late,' he suggested. 'Or maybe just because she figures you are a little too fresh with her.'

'Fresh? Well, I oughta be fresh. I've been keeping it on ice for the best part of six years. The dame sure is a looker though. What's the betting she's the captain's personal piece of ass?'

'She could just as easily be a respectable married lady,' reasoned Claudio.

Martin shook his head. 'Maybe you're not such a great detective after all,' he retorted. 'For one thing, the lady ain't wearing a wedding ring; and besides, women who look the way she does are never married. You know why? Because men are afraid to trust them, that's why. If I was married to a broad like that I wouldn't be able to sleep nights, worrying about some other guy sniffing around when my back was turned. That's why most men are married to ugly women and get their fun chasing around.'

Claudio shrugged. 'I am afraid I am no expert on the subject,' he said. 'I have no wife.'

'Hell, neither have I!' Martin watched as the stewardess opened the door that led to the pilot's cabin and went inside, closing it behind her. 'Don't plan to have one either. Got a lot of fun to catch up on.' He glanced at his companion. 'Oh, just for the record, Claudio. I was a *garimpeiro* for six years and I never killed a single damned Indian in that time. Didn't mistreat one, so far as I can recall, though I'll admit I've seen it happen from time to time. It was never my style.'

Claudio nodded, waved his hand in dismissal. 'There are good and bad in all walks of life, *senhor*. I had no suspicions, I can assure you; and look, don't go thinking I'm some kind of plaster saint. It's just my job and I do it the best I can.'

'What happens when you get up to Belém?'

'Oh . . . I charter a boat, head down the Amazon. I am already friends with some of the chiefs around the headwaters. Wherever civilization is advancing, I try to be just a little ahead of it. I talk to the people, organize immunization, try to prepare them for the shock that is coming. You might say my function is that of a cushion. I try to push myself between the axe and the tree. Sometimes we get there too late. A man cannot be everywhere at once. Sometimes we find the remains of a massacre.' He turned to stare out of the window beside him. The plane was already flying over thick, impenetrable jungle, scarred here and there by the meandering muddy coils of a river. It was one of the most striking features of Brazil: only a few minutes out of its biggest, grandest city and already there was nothing below but a wilderness of dank, green rain forest. 'Ironic, is it not, senhor,' murmured Claudio. 'Here we sit in this newfangled, metal flying machine; while down there, it is still the Stone Age. Time has not reached those jungles yet. Sometimes I think that man was never meant to inhabit Brazil at all; no, not even the Indians, and they are the only people who could ever survive for long in that inhospitable world.'

Martin sighed. He eased his hat down over his eyes and slumped back in his seat. 'Wake me up when the bar's open,' he murmured.

Claudio continued to speak, but his voice soon became a formless drone that mingled with the low steady hum of the aircraft. Martin settled down for his first spell of real rest since finding the diamond. In a matter of moments, he was fast asleep.

70

'Everything OK back there?' asked Mike as Helen entered the cabin. He was obliged to shout over the roar of the engines but still somehow contrived to sound indifferent. She wondered why she was so helplessly and miserably attached to Mike Stone and wanted, suddenly, to hurt him.

'I think I've picked up an admirer,' she said.

'Oh yeah? You always find one token jerk, every flight.' Mike's voice was devoid of any emotion, but she knew how jealous he was about such things.

Helen shifted her attention to the co-pilot. 'Hey, how's it going, Ricardo?'

'Just fine, Trojan, just fine. The weather people have been on, it's gonna be a nice smooth flight all the way. I arranged it specially.' He flashed a grin at her. 'Now listen, any of those guys back there give you a hard time, you just come and tell me, OK? Then I'll give you a hard time!'

'Cut the cackle, Ricardo,' Mike snapped.

Ricardo looked mortified. 'I'm sorry, chief! What is it, you get out of the wrong side of bed this morning?'

'Yeah, somethin' like that.'

'Well, I tell you what I'm gonna do. When we get to Belém, I know a nice little nightclub there. I'm gonna treat the both of you to the best cocktails in all Brazil, now wha'dya say, huh?'

'Ricardo, when Helen and me hit Belém, we're just going to hole up in a quiet hotel room with a bottle of *aguardente*.'

'Who says so, big shot!' Helen's mood had abruptly boiled over into outright anger. She was furious that, despite everything she had said that morning, Mike had simply assumed that the set-up would continue in the usual way. He turned a little now to stare at her, a smug, half-smile on his face. She hated that look, the way his eyes seemed to say 'in the end, you'll do it my way'. But

71

worse was the knowledge that this was most probably true. She had always given in to him, allowed herself to be humiliated. But not this time, she had promised herself that much. She turned back to Ricardo. 'I'd love to come to a nightclub with you,' she said brightly. 'If Mike is feeling too tired, I expect we can manage just as well without him.'

Mike's expression turned to a dangerous glare. 'Helen, you're not making a lot of sense,' he growled. For a moment, the two exchanged vitriolic glances.

Ricardo began to grow uncomfortable. 'Hey, well look,' he murmured. 'I don't want to cause any . . .'

'. . . trouble, Ricardo?' finished Helen mockingly. 'But why should there be any trouble? After all, I'm a free agent. It's not as though I'm married to anyone. I'm not even engaged, so what could be the harm in —?'

'Helen, I think it's time you chased through some coffee to us,' snapped Mike forcefully. In the ensuing silence, the thunder of the engines sounded deafening.

'Yes . . . *captain*,' replied Helen at last, her voice loaded with ridicule. 'That's something you *can* make me do . . . after all, it's part of my job.' She threw him a last defiant sneer and then stalked out of the cabin, slamming the door. She stood for a moment, regaining her composure and ordering her face into the professional smile, aware that eyes were watching her from the rows of seats, then began to move slowly forward along the aisle, inquiring if everybody was comfortable, was there anything that they required? She hoped that her true feelings did not show in her eyes. In the last few minutes, she had made her mind up for sure. When she reached Belém, she would hand her notice in to Mike Stone. She would not let herself be influenced by his glib tongue or helpless expression, as she had so many times in the past; and furthermore, she would not go to work for the other airline either. She would simply get as far away from this business as she could, pursue some other line of work. She was adaptable; she would surely survive.

She reached the seat where the arrogant American had been sitting and found him asleep, his hat tilted over his eyes. In repose, his undeniably handsome face looked serene, almost childlike. The man's Portuguese companion smiled across at Helen.

'I was just about to tell him that he could have his drink now,' she said quietly.

'He told me to wake him,' confided Claudio. 'But I think it's better that he sleeps. There will be plenty of time to drink later.'

Helen nodded. 'Can I get you anything?'

'No thank you. I believe I might take a nap myself.'

Helen moved on, noting as she did so that the bearded gentleman sitting to her left seemed to be enjoying a perturbingly familiar embrace with the girl who was entered on the flight records as his daughter. He had his arm around her shoulders in a gesture that spoke of something worlds apart from normal paternal protectiveness. The man glanced up and beamed an oily smile at Helen as though aware of her thoughts.

'Just a moment, miss!' He beckoned to her authoritatively and she turned back to stand beside his seat. 'I believe I'd like a drink,' he said in stilted, though fairly accomplished English. 'A Scotch, I think. I don't suppose you have any ice on board?'

Helen shook her head. 'I'm afraid ice is a rare commodity in Brazil,' she replied. 'But Scotch, we do have. And something for your . . . daughter?'

The man inclined his head to the side. 'Miranda, my dear, is there anything you would like?'

She gazed up at him a moment as though she did not comprehend, her large blue eyes wide, her head tilted slightly to one side. For a moment, a sense of shock ran through Helen, for she could see quite clearly that there was madness in those young eyes, a stark, tormented insanity that seemed to stand out as plain as day. Then the girl leaned forward to whisper something into her father's ear and the man nodded. He glanced up at Helen.

'My daughter says that she thinks you are very pretty,' he said.

'Well . . . thank you.' Helen leaned forward a little to catch the girl's attention; but the blue eyes just seemed to gaze through her. 'I said, thank you, you're very pretty too.' Nothing. The child's gaze seemed to burn through Helen as if to view some distant mystery.

'You must forgive my daughter,' said the bearded man abruptly. 'She rarely speaks to anyone but me. Some . . . mental problem. I have taken her to see all the best doctors but alas there is nothing anyone can do. Thank the lord I am here to protect her, otherwise who knows what might become of her?' He leaned forward suddenly and placed his lips against his daughter's ear. Helen saw quite clearly that his tongue came out, to lap suggestively inside it. The girl gave an abrupt meaningless giggle, her eyes still staring sightlessly ahead.

Helen felt a wave of revulsion. 'I'll get your drink,' she announced coldly and moved quickly away.

She went back along the aisle, taking orders for drinks from various people. Huddled in a seat in the back, she found a young man sitting alone. He was a *caboclo*, a thin boy with a shock of thick black hair and handsome brown eyes. He was dressed rather poorly and Helen had thought when he boarded the plane that he did not look the sort who could normally afford a plane ticket. He looked rather ill at the moment, his gaunt face covered with drops of perspiration, and Helen wondered if he was feeling airsick. It was quite possible that this was his first experience of air travel.

'Is everything all right?' inquired Helen, in Portuguese.

The boy glanced up at her as though startled. Then he

74

frowned and nodded curtly.

'*Sim*,' he replied.

'Is there anything I can get you? A drink perhaps . . . a wet towel for your forehead?'

'*Nao*.' He shook his head and returned his gaze to the floor as though dismissing her from his thoughts. She shrugged and moved back to the narrow corridor between the tiny galley and the lavatory. You met all sorts of people aboard aeroplanes, she observed to herself as she prepared the drinks, and not always the kind you wanted to meet. That bearded man . . . she glanced at the flight list . . . Machado, his name was; there was definitely something very unpleasant about him. Still, she would be getting out of this life soon and she did not think that she would miss it overmuch. She would miss Mike, of course, for a time. But in the end, if she stayed firm, it would be no more distressing than the removal of a bad tooth. It would ache for a short while but then she would not even be aware that it was gone. She was remarkably adept at the art of healing her own wounds, simply because she'd had a lot of practise over the years. Before Mike, there had been Adam, an aide to her father at the embassy, a man several years older than her and, of course, married. Before that, there had been Tom, a plantation owner, and before him, a whole string of male disasters, not one of whom could have afforded Helen any future. Married men had been her singular passion and her greatest pitfall and, try as she might, there seemed to be no way she could shake off the obsession. The fact was that younger men had always bored her. Older men had more grace, more sensitivity, they were better lovers. Perhaps it was simply that her first stumbling attempts at high-school affairs with boys her own age had been so disastrous. A psychologist friend had once spent an entire evening trying to convince her that she subconsciously wanted to make it with her father, but the idea had seemed too

75

ludicrous to contemplate. Her father was a pompous, overbearing, money-orientated bigot who treated his daughter as just another possession; more likely, she was trying to find a father figure whom she could find acceptable. Yes, she could buy that.

On her way back from serving the drinks, she noticed that the young boy in the last seat was heaving violently into a paper sick-bag. She stopped, meaning to comfort him, but he waved her away, presumably humiliated by his illness. Helen frowned. How like a man, she thought sadly. Caught up in senseless arrogant pride from the day they were old enough to spit. She sighed, wearied by the thought of the long, uneventful journey ahead. It was good that she was getting out of this business. She ought to have done it a long time ago.

As she came out of the galley, she saw the young man coming towards her along the aisle, his face rather pale beneath the tanned surface of his skin. Assuming he was heading for the toilet, Helen stepped back through the doorway of the galley to allow him to pass by. She was taken totally by surprise when the boy moved suddenly towards her, pushing her back out of sight with a quick shove of his hand. Helen was about to cry out in alarm, but the sound died in her throat as the black barrel of a gun was pointed unceremoniously at her face. For a moment, she was too stunned to register what was happening.

'Is this some kind of joke?' she asked brightly; but then she looked at the boy's face, the grim, desperate expression on it and the wide, staring eyes that were shot through with fear, and she knew, with a terrible tightening of her stomach, that this was not meant to be funny. This was not funny at all. She seemed to lose the ability to control her breathing as she tried to stammer a question out.

'What . . . uh . . . do you . . . uh . . . what . . . *please*?'

'Shut up,' he hissed fiercely; and he pushed the cold steel of the gun barrel against her throat to silence her. It felt like the touch of death and she recoiled from it instinctively, her elbow catching a metal coffee jug that stood on the counter behind her. It rolled over with a clatter and the boy threw out a hand to still it. Then he stood, the gun pushed up against Helen's throat, while he listened intently for the sound of advancing footsteps. But nobody had heard. In the silence, the hum of the plane's engines seemed to rise to a terrible crescendo.

Helen spoke again, more slowly this time, in a soft measured whisper. 'Please . . . what is it you want? You must . . .'

'I told you to shut up!' snapped the boy. 'I talk, you listen. I tell you what's gonna happen, lady, you do like I tell you and you don't get killed, understand?' The boy was staring at her, his eyes bulging grotesquely in their sockets. There were thick beads of sweat on his forehead.

'How old are you?' asked Helen abruptly.

The boy ignored the question. 'Here's what's gonna happen,' he said. 'You and me, see, we're gonna take a walk up to where the captain sits. You're gonna go first and I'm gonna be behind with my gun in my shirt pocket like this, see? It's gonna be pointed straight at you, all the time and you say or do anythin' makes me nervous and I'll put a bullet in your back, can't miss. And there's five other shots here for anyone tries to get to me. You believe this I tell you?'

Helen gazed at the boy for a moment. There was not a trace of compassion in his face. She nodded. 'I believe you,' she said.

'OK. Here's the story, like in the movies, understand? You're sorry for me, sick n' all . . . gonna take me up to sit with the captain now, make me feel a whole lot better. Anybody asks you where you're going, that's what you tell 'em. Believe me lady, you try one thing that don't seem right to me, I'm gonna waste you. Now, get walkin' up there! Hurry!'

'But why . . . why do you want to . . .?'

He jabbed the gun into her ribs. 'I don't have time to waste, lady. Move out, now.'

Helen moved rather unsteadily to the door. She had recovered a little from her original shock but her legs still felt like columns of rubber. She stood in the doorway for a moment, taking a deep breath and trying to steady her nerves. But another prod against her back started her on her way. She glanced back once and saw that the boy was indeed just behind her, his right hand pushed into the pocket of his baggy shirt. The boy glared at her and she turned back again, began to move slowly along between the rows of seats. The thought of a loaded gun pointed at her back filled her with unspeakable dread and she could only hope that her emotions did not show on her face. At the moment though, everybody seemed to be either asleep or engaged in conversation. Nobody so much as glanced up as she went by. The short distance to the pilot's cabin seemed to take an eternity. At last she had the handle firmly in her grasp and was opening the door. She stepped through and the boy pushed in behind her, closing the door. The two pilots were intent on their instrument panels. They did not bother to look up.

'I thought you were grinding that coffee grain by grain,' yelled Mike over his shoulder. Helen stood there helplessly, willing them to look up; but it seemed a very long time before Ricardo glanced up and grinned good-naturedly.

'Hey, who's this you've brought with you?' he inquired. Then his grin faded as he saw the gun in the boy's hand. Mike glanced back now. His eyes widened and then narrowed to slits.

'What the hell is this?' he demanded angrily.

'He pulled a gun on me, Mike,' began Helen. 'There

78

was nothing I could . . .'

'Shut up, lady!' The boy motioned with the gun. 'Move ahead of me, where I can see you.' He licked his lips nervously and surveyed the two pilots for a moment. 'OK, now here's what we're gonna do . . .'

'Who the hell are you?' interrupted Mike. 'What's the idea of coming in here like this?'

'I'm about to explain that to you,' retorted the boy. 'Just take it easy. You do like I tell you and nobody . . . nobody on this plane's gonna come to any harm. You got my word on that.' The boy raised his left arm to mop at his clammy forehead with his sleeve. 'Now what I want is for you to make a little change of course, OK?'

Mike frowned. 'Oh, so that's it. I suppose I should have realized. What are you, some kind of rebel or something? Planning to overthrow the Government?'

The boy waved a hand to silence Mike. 'You shut up. It don't matter what I am. All that matters is I have this gun and I will use it if I have to.' He fished in the breast pocket of his shirt and brought out a crumpled scrap of paper. 'These here are the map references.'

'Map references?' Mike stared at the boy for a moment, then turned to his co-pilot. 'Say, you hear that, Ricardo? This guy doesn't belong to some chicken-shit organization; he's got some damned map references!'

Ricardo smiled feebly. 'A professional,' he yelled back.

'Damned right. This kid knows exactly what he wants.' Mike glanced down between his feet, where the stock of the sawn-off shotgun lay inviting his touch. It seemed a strange irony. Mike had always kept the thing there, all through the war and on every flight since, believing that one day something like this might happen. Now it had, he was afraid to use it with Helen in the cabin. He would have to get her out of harm's way first. He turned back to look at the boy. 'And supposing, sonny, I was to say to you that on no account am I going to alter this plane's course. Then what would you say?'

The boy shrugged. He moved forward until he was standing directly behind the co-pilot's seat. He pushed the barrel of the gun up against Ricardo's neck and cocked the trigger. Ricardo gasped and glanced helplessly across at Mike.

'First, I will kill this man. Then your stewardess here. And if I have to, then I will kill you.'

'The plane won't fly without somebody at the controls, boy,' observed Mike. 'What use would it be to you then?'

'No use at all. But, see, I don't think you will let me go that far. I don't think you want to see your friends die. And believe me, I *will* kill them . . . if you are stupid enough to put me to the test.'

There was a long silence.

Then Ricardo spoke, his voice clumsy and guttural with fear. 'Mike, I think the kid means it,' he gasped.

'I'm sure he does, Ricardo,' Mike nodded. 'All right, take the gun out of my co-pilot's neck and hand him those Goddamned references. Calm down, Ricardo, nobody's going to get hurt if I can help it. Have a look at the kid's instructions and let's see where he wants to take us.' Mike glanced up at Helen. 'You all right, honey?'

She nodded dumbly. Mike turned back to face the boy. 'Kinda young to be pulling a hijack, aren't you?'

The boy shrugged. 'Old enough, *senhor* . . . and don't go gettin' no fancy ideas about me, because I've killed a lot've men who figured I was too young to handle this gun.'

Mike nodded. 'Oh yes, I'll bet you have. You speak good English for a *caboclo* . . . a college kid, I shouldn't wonder.'

'*Que Diabo!*' exclaimed Ricardo suddenly. He glanced up from his charts. 'These figures would take us way north-west of here . . . ain't nothing out that way but a few savages and a hell of a lot of jungle.' He glanced at

80

Mike. 'It's Mato Grosso territory ... I'm not even sure offhand if we'd have enough fuel to make it that far.'

'You got enough fuel,' snapped the boy. 'You started out with eight hundred and four gallons. You keep in cruise and conserve it properly, you'll make it with just a little in reserve.'

'The kid's done his homework,' observed Mike dryly. 'But like Ricardo says, if there's nothing out there –'

'There *is* something out there! You think I'm *louco*, huh? There's an airstrip, cut out of the jungle. It's rough but it will do to land this old crate on. I know it's there, because I helped to build it ... but if we're going to make it there, we have to change course right now. Understand, *Capitão*?'

'Yes, I understand.'

The boy stepped forward again and jabbed the gun barrel against Ricardo's neck. 'Now you give an order,' he snapped at Mike. 'And make it the right order or you'll be scraping this guy's head off the windscreen.'

'All right, take it easy. Ricardo, you do like he says.'

'And don't try anythin' stupid like headin' off in another direction,' added the boy. 'I can read a compass pretty good.'

'You're a talented kid,' said Mike sarcastically. 'With everything you've got goin' for you, I'm surprised you don't just fly the Goddamned plane yourself.'

'Shaddup!' The boy watched the compass needle closely as Ricardo brought the plane around onto its new course. 'That was a shaky turn,' he observed when the manoeuvre was completed.

'I don't fly so good with a gun against my head,' Ricardo sneered.

The boy reached up an arm to mop his forehead again. Then he glanced over at Helen. 'Hey you! C'mere ... yeah, c'mon, I ain't gonna hurt ya.' He grabbed her wrist as she stumbled uncertainly forward. 'Now listen, lady, those people back there, they're gonna start wanting drinks and things; so here's what we're gonna do, OK? You're gonna go back out there like nothin' in the world has happened, you're gonna act like it's just a normal flight. Anybody gets suspicious, you throw them off, see, 'cos if anybody tries to come through that door before I want them to, I'm gonna kill one of these guys.'

Helen nodded. She glanced down at Mike and he gave her a reassuring smile. 'Do just like he says, honey. Don't worry about a thing; it's going to be all right.' He reached out and squeezed her hand gently.

'All right, all right, that's enough.' The boy jerked his thumb back at the exit door. 'Get out there and remember what I told you.' He backed slowly away from Ricardo, swinging his gun back and forth to keep both pilots covered. When his back was against the wall, he reached out his left hand and opened the door so that he was hidden behind it. Then, with an abrupt flick of his head, he signalled Helen to go out.

'Pretty girl,' the boy observed casually as he slipped the door's heavy bolt into place. 'You guys use your heads and she'll stay that way. We don't want to have to kill anybody, we just need the plane.'

'I take it you've got fuel at this strip of yours,' said Mike. 'This thing won't be much use to you without it.'

'Sure, we got fuel.'

'What do you want the plane for?'

'That's our business.'

'Uh huh.' Mike turned around to the boy. 'And what about us ... the passengers and the crew? You really trying to tell me that you plan to let us go after we land?'

'Sure, why not?'

'It just doesn't seem very likely, that's all. We'll know where your base is; we'll be able to recognize members of whatever tinpot political group you belong to. Seems to me that out there in all that jungle ... well, I figure it'll

82

just be a case of a few more unmarked graves.'

The boy laughed harshly. 'Well, I guess I really don't know what the plans are about that. But I think you'd better start hoping that the people I work with are in a good mood when we arrive. Right now, all I want you to do, is fly.' He moved across and prodded Mike roughly with the gun barrel. 'You think you can do that?'

Mike leaned forward slightly to peer down at the stock of the shotgun tucked away between his feet. He licked his lips. 'Oh yes,' he murmured softly. 'I think I can do that.'

Chapter 4

Martin was running down a long fleshy tunnel, its walls misty and ill-defined; but at the far end of it, the tarantula stone glittered enticingly, spinning around on the empty air like some mysterious alien planet. It seemed to have grown in size, as large now as a football, and within its glittering heart the spider pulsed, its body seeming to rise and fall as though it were actually breathing. He concentrated all his energy on reaching the end of the tunnel, but his actions were sluggish, his legs heavy, as though he were rooted in the thick clinging mud of a jungle stream. The harder he strove to cover the distance, the farther the end of the tunnel seemed to be.

He woke with a start and sat blinking in momentary confusion. Then he remembered and he instantly slid a hand to the inside of his shirt; with a shock of pure terror, he realized that the pouch was no longer there. He turned to speak to Claudio, but it was not the friendly Portuguese who sat beside him now; it was Agnello, his purple face wreathed in a friendly smile. He opened his mouth to speak and something came tumbling out, something fat and furry and obscene. A *tarantula*. It fell into his lap with a dull plopping sound and it was followed by another and another and another . . .

'Jesus Christ!' Martin opened his eyes and the back of the seat in front of him came abruptly into focus. He reached out a hand to stroke the fabric of it, anxious to reassure himself that this time he really was awake. His trembling fingers found the leather pouch against his clammy chest; and when he turned, fearfully, it was to find Claudio Ormeto sleeping peacefully beside him. 'Jesus Christ,' he whispered again and gave a long sigh of relief. He fumbled for his cigarettes and placed one in his mouth, which felt as dry as a desert. He leaned over and glanced back along the aisle, searching for the hostess. She came forward with an undisguised scowl on her face.

What is this charm I have? thought Martin dryly. She looks like she hates my guts.

Helen came and stood beside Martin's seat. 'Yes?' she inquired mechanically; and Martin noticed that she was not even looking at him but that her eyes were fixed intently on the door to the pilot's cabin.

'I was wondering if I could have that drink now?'

'Drink . . .?' She seemed hardly to have registered what he had said. 'I uh . . . what kind of . . .?'

'Excuse me, but is there something wrong?'

She turned now to stare at him. 'Wrong? What do you mean? Why should there be anything wrong?'

Martin shrugged. 'Well, I don't know. You just seem a little disturbed, somehow.'

Helen shook her head. 'I'm tired, that's all. I'm sorry, Mr . . .'

'Martin. My name's Martin.'

'I'm sorry Mr Martin. Now what drink was it you wanted?'

He ordered a Scotch and soda and watched as the girl

84

threw another intense look at the pilot's door and then moved away. Probably had an argument with her old man. He glanced back at his sleeping companion, then at his watch. He had slept for just over an hour. He found his matches and lit the cigarette that still drooped from the corner of his mouth. When he got to Belém, he'd search out the best hotel and just climb into bed and stay there until it was time to pick up his flight to Europe. Right now, the luxury of sleeping between clean sheets in a soft double bed seemed the most incredible experience a man could wish for. Later he would think of much more imaginative pleasures.

A glass was pushed unceremoniously into his hand.

'Er, thanks a lot.' He gazed at the whisky. The contents were nearly slopping over the brim of the glass. There must have been nearly four shots in there. 'Say lady, if you're planning to send me back to sleep, you're going the right way about it.' He glanced up at her but she was staring apprehensively at that damned door. 'Look, honey, what's the matter? Is somebody in there giving you a hard time?'

She glared at him. 'No,' she snapped ungraciously. 'Of course not!' She turned and stalked away. Martin sighed.

'If I carry on at this rate,' he murmured to himself, 'she'll be wanting to marry me by the time we land.' He chuckled and took a large swallow of his drink. It tasted warm and unpleasant, making him long for a handful of crushed ice.

He leaned across Claudio and stared out of the window. Below there was nothing but a wilderness of jungle, stretching in every direction as far as the eye could see.

What a Godforsaken place, he thought. Brazil must be the ass-hole of the world. Nothin' down there but trees, snakes and savages ... He felt suddenly very vulnerable, comparing the tiny, insect-like plane to the vast all-encompassing jungle far below.

Mike was getting desperate. The plane was fast approaching the point of no return and still the kid with the gun had not let his guard down enough for the pilots to risk jumping him. He stood just at the back of their seats, tense and watchful, swinging his gun from right to left at the merest sound from either of them, and he would question every little move they made towards the control panel. It was clear that at some time the boy had received extensive training on the subject of aircraft and it would clearly be unwise to try and hoodwink him in any way. There was only one point in Mike's favour. The boy did not know about the shotgun tucked away by the pilot's feet. But to have the gun there was one thing; to use it quite another. It would take several seconds to snatch the gun up, swing it around and fire – no need to aim of course, in the cramped confines of the cabin, but without some kind of diversion, it was folly to even attempt it. The boy's gun was already aimed and he was jumpy enough to fire at the slighest movement. Besides, there was Ricardo to consider. So Mike just kept asking questions, hoping to needle the boy into making a mistake.

'Look kid, why don't you tell me about this organization you're workin' for, huh?'

'I don' work for no organization,' the boy sneered.

'Well, whatever you call it. If I'm gonna fly all this way on account of something, I figure I ought to know what it's all about.'

'You don' need to know nothin'! Just keep doin' what you're doin'.'

Mike turned to grin at Ricardo. 'Helpful kind of guy.'

'Sure is.' Ricardo fixed Mike with a curious stare, trying to transmit a silent message in his eyes. The co-pilot's gaze moved rapidly across and down to the area at

Mike's feet, then came back to glare encouragingly at him. Mike stiffened, because he had recognized the message and he didn't like it. It seemed to say: 'I'm going to try something. Back me up.'

Mike framed the word *no* with his lips, but Ricardo was already starting.

'Hey kid, listen, I gotta go take a leak, you know? It's been ages ...' As he spoke, he began to unbuckle his safety belt, as though taking it for granted that the boy would give him permission to leave.

The gun swung across to cover him. 'You just stay right where you are, *senhor.*'

'Hey, but look, you know ... we've been flying for over three hours. We've still got a long way to go. What am I supposed to do, piss in my pants?'

'Yeah, if you have to. I sure as hell ain't gonna let you go out back.'

'Hey, but look, I gotta go real bad ...'

Surreptitiously, Mike reached his hands into his lap and unclipped his seat belt. Ricardo was still talking, half-rising from his chair, his arms outstretched. Mike began to lean slightly forward, so he could reach down to touch the butt of the shotgun.

'Hey you, whatcha doin'?'

Mike turned his head to look back at the boy. 'Nothin', just stretching a little ...'

'You hold still!' He waved the gun at Ricardo. 'And you, I'm tellin' you to sit down. Do it now!'

Ricardo would not let the idea alone. He began to move forward, out of his seat, his hands held up above his head. 'I tell you what, I'll make a deal with you –'

That was as far as he got. The boy stepped forward and brought the barrel of his pistol down with sickening force against the side of the co-pilot's head. He reeled back and collapsed against his seat. He was out cold.

'You little bastard!' snapped Mike. 'Why did you do

that?'

'Because he was trying something, that's why.' The boy prodded Ricardo's inert form with his right foot.

'You could have killed him. You didn't have to hit him so hard.'

'Maybe not. Anyway, we don't need him.' He leaned forward and, picking up Ricardo's charts, threw them contemptuously into Mike's lap. 'It's easier to watch one man than two. Now, Captain, don't do nothin' stupid. Remember, you're responsible for all them good passengers back there . . . and the girl too. I guess you wanna get her ass back down in one piece, huh?'

'You lousy bastard,' said Mike tonelessly.

'Sure, *Chefe*,' the boy chuckled, 'that's the way. You just call me whatever you like; and make damn sure you get us to that airstrip. Look at the distance we're puttin' behind us. Soon, there won't be any other place in reach.'

Then it's gotta be soon, thought Mike calmly. Ricardo's out of the way now and if the bastard doesn't give me an opening I'll have to make one.

He unfolded Ricardo's chart and placed it on his lap, pretending to study it intently; but all the time he kept his gaze fixed on the wooden butt of the shotgun. He figured he had maybe another fifteen minutes to wait for an opening; then, ready or not, he would have to make his move.

Claudio woke with a yawn. He stretched himself luxuriously and ran a hand through his black hair. He scratched himself and turned to blink at Martin.

'Oh, how I hate these long flights! Forgive me, *senhor*, but you looked so comfortable, I decided to join you.'

'Don't mention it! Would you like a drink? They do an interesting warm triple whisky here.'

'Oh no thank you. Too early in the day for me. You have the time, please?'

'Sure. It's a little after four, so I guess we've done about half of it. First thing I do when I get to Belém is find a good hotel room with a hot shower.' The hostess moved past him to take drinks to the seat in front. He watched thoughtfully as she bent forward and handed the glasses to the old couple who sat there. 'On second thoughts, make that a cold shower.'

Claudio chuckled. 'Oh, Senhor Taggart, I fear that you are beyond saving! But at any rate, I think I can recommend a good hotel that . . .' Claudio's voice trailed away in mid sentence. He was looking out of the window at the landscape below.

'Somethin' wrong?' inquired Martin, puzzled by his silence.

'Well . . . it is only that we . . . appear to have changed direction.'

'What?'

'I have flown this route many times. The jungle below looks different somehow.'

'Hell, I wouldn't know one piece of Brazil from the next. Maybe we're just flyin' a different way.'

'I hardly think so.' Claudio was standing up now, craning his head around to peer this way and that through the window.

'Hey, take it easy, Christopher Columbus! I'm sure the crew know where they're headed.'

'Yes, but you see, there's something of a mystery here.' He sat down in his seat, looking vaguely perplexed. 'When we took off this morning, flying almost due north, the sun was, of course, to our right and slightly in front of us. Now, at . . . just after four, I think you said . . . we would surely expect it to be to our left.'

Martin nodded. 'Sounds logical.'

'But it is not! It is right in front of us.'

'Which means?'

'Which means we are flying west . . . back towards the

89

middle of Brazil, towards the headwaters of the Amazon.' He shook his head. 'But that doesn't make any kind of sense. There's nothing that way but jungle.' He stood up again and began to peer back towards the rear of the plane.

Martin frowned. He looked up at the hostess again. The old people in front were asking her interminable questions in Portuguese and she was answering them, but her gaze was, once again, fixed on the door.

'Maybe there *is* something wrong,' murmured Martin. He waited until the hostess had finished with the questions and then, as she turned to walk past him, reached out and grabbed her wrist.

She looked down at him in surprise. 'I asked you before if there was anything wrong,' he told her quietly. 'Now I'm asking you again.'

'What do you mean?' she blustered. 'Everything's fine . . . now, please let go of my arm.' But Martin kept hold and pulled her gently but firmly closer.

'My friend here seems to think we've changed course,' he said beneath his breath. 'And you seem damned interested in what's going on behind that door. If anything *is* wrong, I think you'd better tell us, now.'

She stared at him for a moment, a look of indecision in her eyes. 'It's a . . . a temporary change of course,' she stammered. 'A fuel correction, that's all.'

But Claudio shook his head. 'That doesn't make any sense. We're heading inland, aren't we?' She lowered her head, her lips pursed. 'Aren't we?' repeated Claudio, a little louder.

Helen glanced nervously around. 'Please, the other passengers . . .'

'Then tell us the truth,' persisted Martin.

'All right, I'll tell you, but please keep your voices down. I don't want a panic on my hands. There's a man in the cabin . . . a young man, seventeen, maybe eighteen. He's got a gun.' She waited a moment for this to sink in, then she continued, talking quickly and methodically. 'He marched me in there hours ago. He made them change course; as you said, inland towards the Mato Grosso. I heard him say something about an airstrip in the jungle. That's all I know, but please, I beg you not to try anything. He said if anyone tried to go in at the door he'd shoot Mike ... he'd shoot the captain and his co-pilot. Besides, the door's bolted from the inside. There's nothing anyone can do.'

Martin and Claudio exchanged glances.

'I hate to admit it,' muttered Claudio, 'but I think she's right.'

Martin nodded. He glanced back at the girl. 'And you've known this for the last few hours? Christ, no wonder you've been such a grouch.' He brightened a little. 'Say, does this mean there's still a chance for me?'

She stared at him in mild disbelief and then, despite herself, she had to smile. 'I'll tell you the answer to that if and when we get out of this mess.'

'Lady, you've got some style,' observed Martin. 'What's your name?'

'Helen. Helen Brody.'

'Well, Helen Brody, I think you're a brave girl. And now you can have your arm back.'

She shook her head. 'I don't believe this conversation,' she said simply; and she turned and made her way back to the rear of the plane, feeling better for having shared her problems.

'What happens now?' asked Claudio blankly.

Martin shrugged. 'You got me, Mister. I guess we'll just have to sit tight and sweat.' He tilted his glass and drained the remainder of its contents. 'Like the lady said, we can't risk going in there. Even if we could kick the door down, the pilots would be dead before we could help 'em. Of course, the kid with the gun could be bluffing but I wouldn't like to take that chance.' He stared

91

blankly ahead for a moment, then brought his fist down suddenly on his knee. 'Of all the Goddamn flights I have to wind up on a Jonah!'

Claudio sighed. 'I feel as bad about it as you do, but surely we aren't going to sit here and do nothing?'

'I don't see what the hell else we *can* do; not while we're still in the air. Maybe when we touch down at wherever it is we're headed for . . .' He glanced slyly at Claudio. 'You carry a gun?'

Claudio shook his head. 'There's a handgun in my luggage; a couple of rifles too.'

'Not much use to us there,' observed Martin dryly. 'Well, Claudio, you're in luck. I just happen to have a spare pistol in my carpet bag here.' He nudged the bag with his foot and Claudio raised his eyebrows slightly.

'Do you always travel so well prepared for trouble?' he inquired.

Martin declined to answer the question. 'The way I see it,' he continued, 'the kid'll have to come out this way when we land. If he comes past us, it shouldn't be too much of a job to blow him away, though we'd have to be damned sure the pilots didn't stand a chance of being hit.'

'Why just the pilots? There are other people on board.'

'Yeah, but we don't need any of them to fly our way out of there. The trouble is, I can't see the kid taking us way out into the jungle unless he's expecting a sizeable reception committee.'

'And what are we meant to do meanwhile? Just sit here and wait?'

'Well, I can't think of anything better, I must admit.' Martin chuckled bitterly. 'You know, Claudio, for a little while there I really thought that for once things were going to happen like I wanted.'

'You found a diamond, didn't you?' said Claudio unexpectedly.

Martin choked on his own breath. He turned slowly to

92

face the Portuguese. 'Claudio,' he murmured. 'You keep saying things that make me very nervous. A little while ago, I suggested you might be some kind of detective. Bearing in mind that I had to kill the last guy who found out, I'd sure like to know what made you say that.'

Claudio's dark eyes gazed back at him, frank and unafraid. 'It was a very easy deduction to make, *senhor*. You must remember, I know the *garimpeiros* well, half of my work is with meeting them. I know too that there are only a small number of ways that a man can escape from that life. He can die . . . he can become ill with the *maculo* and be carried away on a stretcher . . . and just once in a while, he may find a diamond big enough to chance running with. You clearly do not fit the first two descriptions . . . so it follows that you are making a run.' He smiled. 'I can assure you that I have no personal interest in your find. Wealth holds no great lure for me. On the contrary, I wish you luck.' And then he added, cryptically. 'You will need it.'

Martin looked at Claudio. The man's face was open, peaceful and somehow without the slightest trace of deceit. 'I must be getting old or soft in the head,' he muttered at last, 'but I think I believe you. Still, just the same, I wish you hadn't told me what you know.'

Claudio looked puzzled. 'Why is that?'

'Because if the diamond ever goes missing . . . it's you that I'll have to come looking for.'

Claudio smiled disarmingly. 'Believe me, Senhor Taggart. You are probably looking at the last honest man in all of Brazil.' He brightened a little. 'At least there is one good thing to come from all this.'

'Yeah? What's that?'

'The ones you are running from will never think of looking in the middle of the Mato Grosso.'

Martin grinned. 'I guess I never looked at it that way.'

The point of no return had long been passed, the designated last fifteen minutes had elapsed fully an hour and a half ago and still Mike's opportunity had not come. He glanced sideways at Ricardo. The young pilot remained slumped against his seat, his forehead matted with congealed blood. Apart from the steady rise and fall of his chest, there had been no sign of life since he had fallen. Meanwhile, the kid with the gun remained vigilant, standing just a few feet to Mike's rear. It was silent in the cabin, for Mike had long since given up the idea of breaking the boy's concentration by flinging questions at him. What he needed now, he mused glumly, was a miracle, an act of God; as if in answer to some silent prayer, one came along.

The plane began to lurch and buck alarmingly.

'Hey, what's this?' snapped the boy suspiciously. He jabbed the gun barrel into Mike's neck.

'Relax, it's just some air turbulence. We're passing over a range of hills.'

The boy peered out of the window to validate this statement; then he became alert again as Mike reached for his intercom.

'OK, leave it be. I don't want any messing around.'

'I said relax!' Mike turned to gaze at him stubbornly. 'I'm just going to warn everyone to fasten their seatbelts, that's all. It's normal procedure.'

The boy shook his head. 'Not this trip it ain't! I don't want you sayin' nothin' to them people.'

'Don't be stupid. If I don't say anything, they'll start to worry. Next thing you know, you'll have one of 'em trying to get in here and ask questions.'

The boy bit his lip nervously for a moment. The plane lifted in the air and then dropped alarmingly for ten feet or so.

The boy nodded. 'OK, say your piece. But make it quick.'

Mike lifted the intercom and pressed the button. 'This is your captain speaking. We have entered an area of air turbulence. There is absolutely no cause for alarm ... I repeat, no cause for alarm, but will all passengers please fasten their seat belts. That goes for you too, Helen.'

He returned the intercom to its hook and the boy glared at him.

'Helen is the stewardess,' Mike explained. 'I was just warning her to take a seat. That's normal procedure on this plane. You'd better strap yourself into Ricardo's seat. It could get rougher.'

'What, you think I'm *louco*?' the boy sneered. 'I'll stay right here, thanks!'

Mike almost whooped with joy. It had been something of a gamble, but he'd figured the boy would automatically ignore any advice he might be given. Now the odds were in Mike's favour. Everybody behind was securely tied down and, though the move he had in mind might cause some injury to Ricardo, it was a chance he had to take. He waited for the next wave of hot air to buffet the plane. For a few moments, he thought that they might have passed out of the area, but then a strong shudder rivered through the fuselage and, at that instant, Mike turned to stare out of the window to his right.

'Jesus Christ!' he yelled; and the boy turned his head to look – for just a moment. And in that moment Mike stamped his foot hard on the rudder pedal, throwing the plane over to the right in a reckless sliding movement until the wing was pointing straight at the ground. With a yell of sheer terror, the boy was flung sideways against the racks of metal shelving that lined the side of the cockpit. He fell heavily, the impact driving the breath from his body, but he still retained his hold on the gun, which he tried frantically to bring to bear on his tormentor; but immediately Mike flung the plane in the other direction, throwing the luckless boy the full width of the cabin again. This time he came down head first but his hold on the gun was tenacious. Mike kept see-sawing the plane left and right, not allowing the boy a chance to take aim, until finally the *caboclo*'s head connected with a metal shelf support and his body went limp. As the plane levelled the boy slumped in an untidy heap on the floor. Mike unbuckled his seat belt and reached down to pick up the shotgun. He straightened up, rising as he turned; and that was when the boy shot him, blasting a bullet deep into his chest.

Mike slammed back against the windscreen with an exclamation of pain and surprise, the shotgun still grasped in his hands. The boy was getting slowly, painfully to his feet, bleeding from a dozen wounds; yet the gun was still clenched in his bruised fist. For an instant, time seemed suspended. Mike's eyes were fixed on the slow thread of smoke that curled from the barrel of the boy's gun; and a little further back he could see the boy's knuckle whitening as he began to squeeze the trigger again. Everything seemed frozen in the hot dazed interior of the cabin. The gun, the smoke, the dark eyes sour with hatred. Mike's ears pounded with a strange ragged thudding, the laboured sound of his own heart, and he was dimly aware of his own finger, so very far away from the vacuum that was his body, his own finger, curled around the cold steel of the shotgun trigger. He willed the finger to move, to tighten, to spew death back at the boy in return; and then his hands seemed to explode with flame.

It was as though the boy had been struck by a great invisible fist. His whole body shook with the force of the blow and then his chest collapsed beneath the impact and came spilling out in a red explosion behind him; at the same instant, he was jerked abruptly backwards, so that his body struck the door behind him with a dull thud of finality. He stood framed there for an instant, his arms outstretched as though in mockery of the crucifixion, his mouth hanging open dribbling blood and saliva. His dark eyes glazed abruptly as though he had passed beneath the shadow of a cloud, and then he slid slowly down to the floor, his limbs bereft of any power to hold him up.

The shotgun dropped from Mike's hands and tipped uselessly away onto the floor. A terrible pain shuddered through his chest, making him snatch at his breath. He put his fingers to the wound and they came away caked in blood. He sniffed at the fingers and then groaned and gazed at the bolted door which he knew he did not have the strength to reach now. He could dimly hear the sounds of fists thudding against the exterior of it as he twisted around with a gasp and sank back into his seat. He clung grimly to consciousness, but the world was reduced to a violent red buzzing behind his eyes and a terrible numbness was spreading through his body. He fumbled for the intercom, but it slipped from his clumsy hand and clattered to the floor. Peering dimly out from the windscreen, he could barely register that the plane was now on a downward course. They had lost a lot of height already and far below the jungle was lunging greedily up to swallow the plane. Desperately he took hold of the steering column with both hands and attempted to bring the nose up; but the extra effort sapped what was left of him. A huge black pool seemed to open up in front of him and he fell headlong into it, leaving not so much as a ripple on the surface to mark his passing.

'What the hell is happening in there?' whispered Martin. He glanced quickly around, aware of a sense of rising panic within him. The events of the last few minutes had been heart-stoppingly dramatic and it was only now, in the aftermath, that there was time for fear. To begin with there had been the warning of air turbulence and everybody had dutifully strapped themselves in, but there had been something cryptic in that last casual instruction to Helen that suggested to Martin something unusual might follow. He had glanced back at Helen and noticed the puzzled expression on her face; but she went obediently to a vacant seat as the tremors buffeted the plane. For a moment, all seemed normal enough. The other passengers, unaware of the drama being enacted up front, laughed and chattered nervously as the plane dipped and bobbed in the sky; and then suddenly nobody was laughing any more.

The plane gave a great stomach-lurching shift to one side. Glasses and magazines went flying in all directions and people screamed in undisguised terror. Then the plane was see-sawing crazily from side to side like a Coney Island pleasure ride. Thankfully, the awful manoeuvres had been mercifully brief and the plane had seemed to level out again, but then there had been the two shots, loud enough for everyone to hear. First, the sharp staccato crack of a pistol; then the dull, sonorous boom of a shotgun and, an instant later, the heavy impact of something thudding against the door. The effect on the passengers was quite magical. Where a moment ago, the plane had been filled with a hub-bub of cursing, weeping and shouting, now there was an abrupt and terrible silence as every pair of eyes stared helplessly towards the door. Martin was the first out of his seat, grabbing for his pistol as he went; but he was halted by the tubby figure of Carlos Machado.

'What is going on?' he demanded hysterically. His plump hands clung to Martin's lapel and his face was grey. 'What's happening in there?'

'How the hell should I know?' Martin pushed him back into his seat and moved to the door. He listened for a moment but the only sound was the low thunder of the engines. 'Hey! Open up in there! What's happening?' He rapped loudly on the door with the butt of his gun but there was no reply.

And then Claudio had shouted from his seat by the window. '*Que Diabo*, I think we're going down!'

The fear came back, as everybody turned to stare out of the nearest windows. A long moment of realization. Then a murmur that rose quickly to a tumult of shouts and sobs.

'Shut up, all of you!' snapped Martin. 'We've got to stay calm!' But his own voice was ragged with fear. Helen came running along the aisle, stopping at intervals to try and give reassurance, but nobody was listening to her. She came slowly up to Martin, a frightened expression on her face.

'What's happened in there?' she whispered hoarsely but Martin could only shake his head. He turned and threw his shoulder against the door; it did not budge.

'Goddammit!' he growled, rubbing his shoulder. His inability to do anything communicated more fear to the other passengers. Suddenly, everybody was yelling at once. The old Portuguese couple to Martin's left began to babble and gesticulate and Helen turned to them, did her best to quieten them a little. Just across the aisle, a lone, fat priest slid frantically from his seat onto his knees and started to pray out aloud, his voice a rhythmic whining irritation.

'Say one for me,' snapped Martin sourly; and he launched himself at the door again, nearly dislocating his shoulder. 'This is no Goddamned use!' he screamed at Helen. 'Look, there must be some tools around here . . . an axe, a crowbar, *something* . . .!'

Helen shook her head. 'All the tools are kept in a locker in the captain's cabin,' she said miserably.

'Oh great, that's just great.'

'We're still going down,' yelled Claudio from his seat by the window. 'We seemed to lift a little a moment ago, but now . . .' His voice sounded surprisingly calm in the circumstances. 'Try shooting the lock off.'

'It wouldn't do any damned good. The door's solid metal and it's bolted. The bullet would most probably bounce off and hit somebody back here.'

'Try it anyway! We don't have a lot to lose.'

'All right.' He turned to Helen. 'Move everybody back as far as possible.' She went to move the old couple out of their seats while he prodded the priest unceremoniously with his foot. 'Get your ass out of here,' he told the man. The priest stared at him uncomprehendingly and he waved the gun in the man's fat face. 'Shift,' he snapped threateningly, and this time the order was promptly obeyed.

'You'd better hurry up,' advised Claudio calmly. 'We're getting low.'

'Tell me the good news.' Martin glanced around to check that everybody was seated and then sized up the door, estimating where the bolt would most likely be. He stretched out his arm now, at something like a forty-five-degree angle, keeping his body as far away from the door as possible; then he took a deep breath and squeezed the trigger.

The report of the gun and the heat of the bullet as it fanned his cheek seemed almost simultaneous. The spent slug smacked harmlessly into the roof of the plane. Martin fingered the burn on his face and gazed ruefully at the round dent that the bullet had made in the door.

'I won't try that again in a hurry,' he observed. He glanced over at Claudio. 'Any more bright ideas?'

Claudio shrugged. 'Belt yourself into a seat and pray,' he suggested. 'That's what I'm going to do.'

A sense of dry, abject fatalism took Martin now. The conviction that all his striving this far had been in vain. There was nothing for it but to take a seat and wait; if he wasn't meant to survive this, then nothing he might do

100

now would help him. He turned away from the door and saw rows of white faces staring as though begging him to effect some miracle. It occurred to him suddenly that he had nearly been killed by his own bullet just then, and all to no avail: there was nobody here who knew how to fly a plane.

Helen came running back, a look of anguish on her face. 'You're not giving up?' she demanded. 'You've got to try again!'

'There's no use,' he told her. 'We'd need a cannon to blast through that.'

'Give me the gun. Let me try.'

'I said no, dammit! Now come and take a seat back here . . .'

'But Mike . . . I have to get to Mike!' Her voice dissolved into a flurry of hysterical weeping and she began to beat at the doors with her fists.

'There's no use in this,' Martin told her. 'There were two shots in there. The first a pistol, the second a shotgun. If there was anyone left alive, they'd come and open this Goddamned door. Now come on!' He reached out and took hold of her shoulders, pulling her bodily backwards along the aisle.

'No! Let go of me, let go, damn you!' She began to hit out at him, slapping at his face and chest in a hysterical fury. He twisted her around to face him, pushed her back one step and then brought his clenched fist across her jaw in a powerful right cross. He caught her around the waist as she fell, lifted her neatly up across his shoulder and hurried back along the aisle in search of two empty seats. He dropped her into place, fastened the seatbelt around her, horribly aware out of the corner of his eye that the ranks of green vegetation beyond the window were rather too close for comfort. Helen was lying with her head tilted back against the seat; she looked extraordinarily composed and quite beautiful. Against the whiteness of

101

her jaw there was just the faintest blue tinge where a bruise would soon develop. He leaned forward and kissed her softly on the lips. It had occurred to him that this might be his last opportunity to kiss a woman.

Then he moved back a little, settled himself into his own seat and clipped the safety belt tight around him. It was horribly quiet in the plane now. Somewhere ahead a young girl was crying; and just behind he could hear the monotonous drone of the fat priest as he worked rhythmically through a prayer.

How long before we hit? thought Martin calmly. Ten minutes? Five? And how do you fill the time in between? Smoke a cigarette? Tell a dirty story? Hell, I could think about all the great times I've had, but that would only take up thirty seconds.

'Senhor Taggart? Good luck, my friend; I hope you make it!' Claudio's voice called unexpectedly from up ahead.

'I hope you do too, Claudio. Otherwise I'll never find my way out of this mess.'

Silence then as the aeroplane swung relentlessly downwards through the empty sky, the drone of its engines a long protesting scream of mechanical death. Martin took a deep breath and unconsciously slipped his hand beneath the fabric of his shirt, so that he could hold once again the round reassuring hardness of the diamond.

Life came fleetingly back to Mike Stone, like a terrible nightmare in the midst of peaceful sleep. Life was pain, a tortured, gasping spasm of misery, but nevertheless he emerged back into life to find himself piloting an engine of destruction. The topmost fronds of the jungle canopy were snatching at the undercarriage and it was not heroism but simple, unyielding instinct that urged him to try and level the plane out again. The effort caused a hideous ripping sensation deep in his chest and his breath exploded from his mouth in a warm crimson spray; but he managed to edge the nose up a little while his failing eyes searched in vain for some kind of clearing in the dense hostile world that lay below him. And then, suddenly, ahead of him he saw the river ... a wide shallow stretch of muddy yellow water, knifing through the greenness like a twisted vein. He was running parallel with it and, though he knew the chance was a slim one, it seemed infinitely better than no chance at all. The question was, could he hang on to consciousness long enough to put the old girl down? He edged gently over until the plane straddled the yellow line and was aware of foliage thundering against the fuselage as he began to ease her down; and that was the last thing he was aware of. He died abruptly, his heart giving out in one last wrenching spasm. He slumped over the controls and never knew whether or not his aim was good.

The plane came down in a chaos of splintering foliage and crashing metal. Its shadow haunted the muddy shallows for an instant and then there was the deafening rending of steel as the wings connected with the thick tangles of vegetation that flanked the river. Then they were torn away, with mocking contempt, like the puny wings of a child's toy. Weighted with its own terrible impetus, the fuselage slid onwards like a vast beached whale, bellying into the shallows with a roar that shook the ground. The nose of the plane ploughed a great furrow into the river bed, throwing out a huge ponderous baptism of mud and filthy water. The front section buckled under the impact, smashed itself open and tore sideways in a chaos of splintered glass and metal; but the fuselage lumbered onwards, the metallic booming of its hollow shell drowning the screeching of thousands of birds that launched themselves skywards for miles in every direction. An abrupt curve in the river brought it to a premature halt. It breasted the muddy bank and tore a deep ugly scar in the vegetation that topped it; and there at last, with a long, gonging din of capitulation, it stopped and gravity eased it down into a great humid pillow of undergrowth. It lay dead, a shattered vestige of civilization flung headlong into a primeval swamp.

With the abrupt cessation of noise, the screeching of the birds became more audible as they wheeled and soared like restless wounds against the cloudy fabric of the sky.

Over the next hour, they gradually quietened and, one by one, settled back into the leafy sanctuary of the *selva*. Before long they had lost all recollection of the noise that had startled them. But in the dank shadowy jungle of the river's edge, the wreckage lay stark and ugly in the terrible silence of death.

In the long afternoon, the jungle waited.

Chapter 5

It was pain that brought Martin back to the realization that he was alive. Not the sheer magic of his own phenomenal luck or the overwhelming celebration of survival against all the odds; just an ordinary, mundane throbbing over his right eye and a dull, constant ache in his ribs. He gave a low groan of misery and sat where he was for a moment, blinking the thick stream of blood from his eyes. It was very gloomy in the interior of the plane and it took several moments for his vision to focus. When it finally did, there was nothing more spectacular to see than the back of the chair in front of him; it had tipped backwards at a crazy angle until it was mere inches away from Martin's nose. Strangely, he did not remember anything of the actual crash; his last mental image was of green palm fronds flashing by the window. He had steeled himself for the inevitable impact but oddly had not

104

experienced anything of it. His next memory was only a few moments old; waking in the wreckage, battered but as far as he could tell in perfect working order.

He wondered vaguely how long he had been unconscious and peered at his watch in the half-light only to find that the dial was smashed and the hands missing. He cursed and turned his head to look at Helen. She was slumped beside him, her eyes closed and her face unnaturally pale. For a terrible moment, Martin thought she was dead, but then he discerned the rise and fall of her breasts beneath her tight blouse. The window beside her had smashed, showering her with glass fragments; but apart from a few small cuts on her face and neck, she looked uninjured.

Abruptly Martin became aware of a restless, murmuring sound that seemed to be issuing from beneath the floor of the fuselage. His first instinct was that the wreckage might be on fire. He fumbled at his safety belt, unlatched it and clambered his way drunkenly from his seat. He stood for a moment in the rubbish-strewn aisle, glancing nervously this way and that. There was no evidence of fire and he quickly identified the sound as the restless lapping of water. He took an exploratory step forward and nearly fell over. Puzzled, he stared out of the nearest window and then realized that the wreckage was lying at a steep angle to the ground. To his left he could see the wide sweep of a sluggish yellow river. Ahead where the cabin had once been, there was now a gaping ugly rent with thick undergrowth crowding into the fuselage. The frontmost seats were a heaped jumble of débris, but amongst them one or two people were stirring and moaning. Martin shook his head to clear away the last woolly traces of unconsciousness. He leaned down to Helen, grabbed her shoulder and shook her roughly. She moaned in response like a late sleeper, unwilling to rise; but when Martin slapped her face lightly a couple of times, she opened her eyes. She lay uncomprehending for a few moments. Then she remembered and her eyes grew moist.

'Mike,' she whispered softly. 'Where's Mike?'

Martin shook his head. 'Get up,' he told her gruffly. 'People need help.' He left her now and moved to the seat in front, where the priest had been sitting. The man was still kneeling in the attitude of prayer, his hands clasped, his head bowed.

'All right, Father, you can knock it off now,' suggested Martin. 'We're down.' The fat man made no reply and Martin reached out and shook his shoulder. But the body was absolutely rigid. Martin noticed how close the seat in front was. It had torn loose from its mooring and slid backwards, crushing the priest's body as though caught in a vice. The man's thick beard was sodden with blood. Despite his prayers, luck had deserted him.

Martin grimaced and turned away to inspect the old Portuguese couple, who had been moved back earlier on to sit opposite the priest. As he leaned over them a familiar figure came stumbling out of the chaos at the front of the plane. It was Claudio, his face streaked with oil, his jacket hanging in shreds and stained here and there with patches of blood. He grinned fiercely. 'Well, by God, it looks like we both made it! You are injured?'

'Not badly . . . you?'

Claudio shrugged. 'I'm all right, I guess.' He thumbed his hand back towards the front of the plane. 'Fellow sitting behind me seems all right too. Big guy, Portuguese. Says his name is José. A lot of the seats near the front got smashed up pretty bad. I've already found six dead up there . . .'

He broke off as he heard the sharp intake of breath from Martin, who had turned to lean over the old couple. The woman was dead. A heavy tree limb had smashed through the wall beside her, crushing her head like an

106

eggshell and narrowly missing her husband. He, though still alive, had problems of his own. The seat in front of him had collapsed onto his legs, snapping them like twigs. He was barely hanging onto consciousness and he was muttering something under his breath in Portuguese.

'Claudio, what's he saying?'

Claudio leaned closer. 'He's asking about his wife.'

'Tell him she's all right.' Martin glanced around and found a discarded raincoat on the floor beside him. He reached out and draped the coat over the woman's head in case the old man should turn. Claudio leaned over the man and whispered some reassurance into his ear. The old man nodded, smiled through gritted teeth and then closed his eyes. 'Let's get this damned seat off him,' suggested Martin. The two set to work in the gloomy dust of the wreckage, lifting back the twisted metal framework. The man who called himself José came over to help. He was a big shambling bear of a man with huge shoulders and a dark gentle face but prodigiously strong; the other two quickly learned that it was wise to let him handle anything that required any great effort.

'You're doing a good job,' observed Martin, slapping him on the back, but José just smiled blankly.

'I don't think he speaks any English,' said Claudio.

Helen clambered out of her seat, cradling her forehead in her hands.

'About time,' muttered Martin, unsympathetically. 'Look, you carry any medical supplies on the plane? This old guy's going to need morphine . . .'

Helen frowned. 'There *is* a first aid kit back in the galley. There'll be bandages and plasters . . . maybe a couple of splints. But drugs are hard to get out here. I doubt if we have anything stronger than aspirin.'

'Aspirin!' exploded Martin bitterly. 'My God, what kind of two-bit operation is this? You shouldn't be flying over territory like this without the right equipment.'

Helen gazed back at him defiantly. 'I'll pass on your remarks to the captain,' she replied, her voice loaded with sarcasm.

There was a brief silence while they glared at each other. Then Martin took a deep breath and wiped his forehead on the sleeve of his shirt.

'Well, you'd better search it out anyway,' he told her. 'But first, check over the seats up front for any signs of life. It's too damned quiet for my liking.' He turned away to help with the old man. Claudio and José were just lifting away the seat and Martin could see the broken legs clearly now. They were twisted and bent at impossible angles, and at one point, below the left knee, a piece of splintered bone was actually protruding through the blood-soaked fabric of the old man's trousers.

'Oh Jesus!' Martin grimaced and ran his fingers through his sweat-damp hair. He turned to Claudio. 'Can you and José get the poor old devil outside?' he asked. 'There's no room in here to splint him up. I'll check the seats at the back.'

Claudio nodded. 'He'll need something for the pain,' he said. 'When you go looking for that first aid kit, see if you can come up with a bottle of spirits that hasn't been smashed. It won't be as good as morphine, but it might help a little.' Claudio turned and muttered some instructions to José. The big man nodded, then squatted down and scooped the old man up in his arms, cradling him as gently as a baby. Then he stood up and began to follow Claudio towards the front of the plane, where he had already opened up the square escape hatch in the middle of the fuselage which offered a relatively easy climb down to the river bank beyond.

As Claudio came alongside Helen, he paused. She was standing helplessly, staring down into the jumble of smashed seats that littered that part of the aisle. Claudio moved nearer and recognized the broken bodies of Carlos

108

Machado and his daughter. Even in death they seemed intimate. Their arms were tight around each other as though still trying to offer protection from the impact. They lay in a deep puddle of their own blood.

Helen seemed riveted to the spot, hypnotized by the horror of the scene. Claudio put an arm around her shoulder and edged her away towards the escape hatch. 'There's nothing to be done there,' he told her gently. He helped her out onto the river bank, then helped José manipulate the old man's body out through the opening. He turned and glanced back towards the rear of the plane, where Martin was poking about in the gloom.

'Anything back there, *senhor*?' he called out.

'The whole of the Goddamned galley's come down,' replied Martin. 'It's a hell of a mess back here. I think they're all dead.'

'I'll be back in a moment,' Claudio called as he clambered down onto the slippery, vegetated slope of the river bank and was immediately assailed by the terrible damp heat of the rain forest. It was like a great clammy hand caressing his body, wrenching sweat from every pore. He ran the back of his hand across his forehead as he gazed slowly around in a full circle. To his left, the sweep of the shallow river, veined here and there with the dank black smudges of mud-flats. Ahead the river veered sharply away to the right, behind green impenetrable depths of jungle. Overhead, the sky was just visible along the line of the river, a jagged, brilliant scar through the restless canopy of vegetation; a few steps into Mato and the sunlight would be gone, replaced by the gloomy claustrophobia of the rain forest. Claudio licked his lips nervously and tried to think optimistically about his future. It wasn't easy.

A polite cough from José brought him back to the present. The big man was waiting patiently, the old man's frail form draped like a rag doll in his arms. 'Where shall

I put him?' he asked softly in Portuguese, his gentle voice strangely at odds with his massive frame.

Claudio frowned. He scanned the bank for a suitable place and after a few moments located a flat, wide ledge a short distance away from the plane. 'Put him there,' he suggested. 'We'll try and find him a blanket. There'll be room for a fire tonight.'

José laid the old man carefully on the ground, staring in horrified fascination at the smashed legs.

'He looks bad,' he murmured. 'It's a mercy he's asleep.'

'We'll need to splint those legs later; but somehow, I don't think he'll live out the night.'

José looked up in shock. 'Is there nothing we can do for him?'

'We need drugs . . . proper equipment.'

'Well . . . then we must get him to a doctor as soon as possible.'

Claudio almost laughed as he stared down at the old man's mangled legs.

'It must be hundreds of miles to the nearest white settlement,' he murmured.

José studied Claudio's face for a moment. 'But we'll . . . we'll get home OK . . . won't we?'

Somewhere, away in the green depths of the jungle, a jaguar roared, a long sonorous boom of hunger; and an instant later the call was answered by the anxious wailing shriek of a howler monkey.

'Sure,' replied Claudio tonelessly. 'We'll get home.' He turned at the sound of a footfall behind him. Martin had just dropped down from the escape hatch. He stayed where he was for a moment, resting on his haunches. His face was grey.

'I was just coming back to help you,' said Claudio.

Martin shook his head. 'Don't bother,' he retorted. 'There's nobody back there that we can help.'

'No one? Are you sure?'

110

'Check for yourself if you like.' He shrugged expansively. 'I guess we just had the best seats in the house, that's all.' He fumbled in his shirt pocket and cursed bitterly. 'Claudio, you got any cigarettes?'

'Huh? Oh, yes, of course . . .' Claudio found his own pack, extracted two and handed one to Martin. He held the pack out to José but the big man shook his head. It was rough local tobacco but a cigarette had rarely tasted better. Martin inhaled deeply and blew out a slow cloud of smoke. The sick feeling in the pit of his stomach began to subside.

'Jesus,' he murmured at last. 'Here's a fine mess.'

Silence descended on the small group as they began to face up to what had happened to them. Martin looked for Helen and saw her standing a short distance away, staring silently downriver. She had recognized an ominous dark shape that lay in the shallows several hundred yards away: the twisted wreckage of the cockpit which had wrenched itself sideways in the first impact as the plane struck the ground. As he watched, Helen's shoulders began to move and her hands came up to cover her face. Martin took an exploratory step towards her but abruptly she broke away from the shore and went running frantically through the shallows towards the wreckage.

Martin made as if to follow her but Claudio put a hand on his shoulder and stilled him. 'Best to let her go,' he murmured softly.

'What's the point? There isn't going to be anybody alive in that mess.'

'I know that. But if there had been somebody you loved in there, wouldn't you want to see for yourself?'

'Hell, I suppose so . . .' Martin took another deep drag on the cigarette and then he gave a groan of despair. He looked slowly around at the endless vista of jungle that surrounded him. He looked at the old man lying broken and unconscious on the river bank and at José standing

111

grim-faced and hulking beside him. Then he turned and glared at the useless, battered wreckage of the aeroplane, where it lay like a beached whale against the river bank.

'I should've known,' he murmured bitterly. 'I should have realized right from the start that nothing could go right for me. The one chance of my life to do something right and look at me . . . LOOK AT ME!' His voice had exploded into a bellow of impotent rage and he vented his scorn on a clump of scrub, lashing out at it with his right foot, snapping the dry wood in two.

'When you've finished with that, perhaps you'd like to give me a hand back in the plane,' suggested Claudio.

'What's the fuckin' point?' snapped Martin. 'I told you, they're all dead.'

'And so will we be soon, if we don't prepare ourselves. There's a lot of equipment in there that needs salvaging. Amongst the luggage, provided it's not been damaged . . . and I pray to God it hasn't . . . there's my case containing a handgun and two good rifles, some ammunition and a compass. If we can reach them, we'll all stand a better chance. We also need to find the first aid kit, and before the sun goes down, we'd better lay in a good supply of firewood for tonight.'

Martin stared at him. 'You've got it all figured out, haven't you?' he sneered. 'But Christ, Claudio, what's the *point*? Look at this place! You really trying to tell me that we've got a chance of making it out of here.'

'Sure there's a chance,' retorted Claudio. 'Getting down alive was the hardest part and we've already done that. If we keep our heads and stick together, there's every chance of coming out of it, but we don't have a moment to waste. In three, maybe four weeks' time, the rains begin. I'm sure I don't have to explain to you why we must not be still in the jungle then.'

Martin nodded bleakly. The rains. The constant, torrential downpour that would transform this already

112

inhospitable place into a stinking quagmire in which no white man could hope to survive for long. First there would be the awful bouts of malaria that would leave them grey and shaking in the heat of the day; then the terrible debilitating dysentery that would swell their stomachs and rack their bowels until, too weak to forage for food, they would die slowly as the cold rain hammered their bodies. It would be hard to envisage a more miserable death.

'So what's your plan?' demanded Martin.

'I'll tell you that when I see what we manage to salvage out of this.' He jerked his thumb at the dark opening of the escape hatch. 'Me and José will make a start in here. If you would, Senhor Taggart, I'd like you to go over and bring back Miss Brody now. It's best if we all stay together as much as possible. For one thing, we don't know how close we are to this airstrip we were headed for; and also there could be hostile Indians about.'

'Oh, that's great. That's just great.' Martin threw down the butt of his cigarette and ground it beneath his heel. 'Got another smoke?' he demanded instantly.

Claudio shrugged, smiled. 'You shouldn't smoke so much, it's bad for your health.' He found the pack which contained his last three cigarettes and handed them to Martin, together with a box of matches. 'Here, you have them. I was thinking of giving up anyway. Maybe we'll find more in the plane.'

'I sure do hope so,' replied Martin earnestly. 'A plane crash in the jungle is one thing, but no cigarettes . . . that's something else.' He turned and strolled away down the river bank, trudging resignedly into the shallow water. Claudio issued a few brief instructions to José in Portuguese and the two men clambered back into the plane.

Martin moved out into the jagged scar of sunlight that ran down the centre of the river. The late afternoon heat

113

was still fierce and reflected up from the rippled surface of the water, making him squint. The slight effort of movement brought new sweat oozing from every pore of his body and after a short distance he was drenched in perspiration again. To compound his misery, a halo of buzzing sweat bees quickly formed around his head, frantically alighting and resettling on his face to lick the salt from the damp trails on his forehead and neck. After a few ineffectual attempts to swat them away, Martin resigned himself to the misery of their presence. He splashed his way glumly upriver until he found Helen.

She was kneeling down on a muddy flat, gazing silently at the shattered wreckage of the cockpit, ripped apart by the impact of the collision and flung like so much litter against the far bank. There was little that was recognizable; just a haphazard assemblage of steel plates, twisted spars and broken glass; and here and there amongst the mechanical carnage was strewn rubbish of animal origin; lengths of red glistening meat, around which clouds of flies greedily buzzed . . . stained, tattered rags of clothing occasionally identifiable as something a pilot might wear, but impossible to say with any conviction whether the cloth concealed an arm, a leg, a torso . . . only one thing was for sure. Nobody could have had the slightest chance of surviving such an impact. Nobody.

Martin felt a bitter wave of nausea well up in his throat and he forced his horrified gaze to move away from the puzzle of steel and flesh. Helen was kneeling in the mud, her head bowed in misery and totally unaware of the flies that were an ominous tormenting cloud around her head. She did not move a muscle as Martin's hand closed upon her shoulder.

'Come away,' he said simply. 'There's nothing you can do here.' He hated the clumsy gruffness of his own voice.

Helen raised her head to stare blankly up at him. Tears

114

had worn white channels through the dirt that smeared her face.

'We were going to be married, you know,' she said tonelessly, her voice a hoarse, exhausted whisper. 'After this trip he was . . .' She shook her head, swallowed hard, annoyed by her own inability to speak easily. 'He never . . . really loved his wife . . . you see. Not like he loved me . . . and you know, I said some bad things to him before we left on this trip, but I never really *meant* . . . he *knew*, I didn't really mean it; when I said those things. But you see, I had to let him know that I was tired of waiting. You know how it is, when you've waited for a thing for so long . . . and then it begins to feel like you'll never . . . never in this world . . . never.' Her voice faded to a whisper and she clearly didn't have the strength to say any more.

Martin squeezed her shoulder again. 'Come away,' he repeated, softly but firmly. 'The others back at the plane . . . they need your help.' He took hold of her arms and pulled her to her feet. 'It doesn't do any good to sit out here alone.'

She nodded, stumbled upright, leaning heavily on his arm for a moment. Her skirt was torn and filthy with mud while her stockings were no more than occasional shreds of silk, clinging tenaciously to her legs. Her hair was matted and tangled and hung in wild confusion on either side of her dirt-streaked face and yet, for all that, Martin thought that she possessed more dignity than any woman he had ever encountered. She moved a step away from him, intent on standing on her own two feet. Then she cleared her throat, flicked her hair back out of her eyes and pointed to Martin's cigarette.

'Could I have some of that, please?'

'Sure.' He handed the cigarette to her and she took a long steady drag, letting the smoke out in a sigh. 'Funny,' she murmured. 'I don't even smoke.'

115

'Good time to start.' Martin took her arm and led her away from the wreckage. She glanced back briefly and then looked away again.

'I don't suppose we can even bury them,' she said helplessly.

'Be difficult without any tools.'

She nodded. 'And tell me, Mr Taggart . . . all things considered, how do *you* rate our chances?'

Martin frowned. 'Er . . . well, Claudio seems to think . . .'

'Don't bullshit me!' She glared at him defiantly. 'I asked what *you* thought.'

'Well . . . to be honest, I don't think there's much hope; leastways, not for *all* of us. One or two might make it, barring accidents, but even then they'll be pushing their luck. Between us and any kind of civilization there's two or three hundred miles of the worst kind of jungle on this planet. There's malaria, wild animals, poisonous snakes and hostile Indians. In fact, if I was asked to choose the place in the world I'd least like to be stranded, I guess this would be it.'

Helen nodded, took another drag on the cigarette and then handed it back. 'Well, that's more or less what I figured,' she said. 'But thanks for being honest with me. I learned a long time ago to set my expectations as low as possible. That way, if things turn out for the best, there's a nice surprise in store.' She threw one final glance back along the river at the already distant wreckage by the water's edge. 'It's funny,' she murmured. 'I'd already told Mike that this would be the last flight . . . I didn't know how right I was.'

'Come on,' suggested Martin. 'Let's get back to the plane.'

116

Chapter 6

In the great dank blackness of the night, the flickering light of the fire was comforting. The survivors sat hunched around it in a ragged circle as though trying to soak up the heat of it, even though it was far from cold. It was simply the light that drew them, with the same basic reassurance that has drawn mankind to the flames since the beginning of human life. The fire was a beacon, a sanctuary, a protection from every unspeakable danger that prowled the periphery of the campsite, out beyond the restless cloak of darkness.

Even in lighting the fire there had been problems. The various boxes of matches they possessed had quickly become too damp to be of any use; but luckily, José owned a petrol lighter, a strange turn of events since he didn't seem to smoke. It had been a present, he explained, from his late father. It was quickly acknowledged a most precious possession and Claudio insisted that it be given over to his safe-keeping and used for nothing but the sacred ceremony of fire-lighting. He knew only too well that, once the lighter ran out, he would have to resort to the more traditional methods of raising sparks by wood friction, a slow and laborious task with dry wood, let alone the rain-soaked twigs and branches of the *selva*.

Around the survivors was piled the jumble of luggage, implements and odds and ends that had been salvaged from the plane, a formidable collection that would be sorted through the next day. A few items of food, biscuits, sweets and a little fruit had been found and shared out. It had amounted to very little but had at least taken the edges off their appetites. At Claudio's suggestion, Helen Brody had exchanged the torn remains of her dress for more practical but rather oversized men's clothing rummaged from amongst the suitcases. In a land that teemed with poisonous snakes and blood-sucking insects,

117

large areas of bare flesh were clearly a disadvantage. Shirt and trousers could simply be turned up at the wrist and ankle if they were too big, and Helen had even found herself a hat amongst the rubble, but shoes provided a real problem. Her own lightweight ones were clearly of little use in the jungle; the solution seemed to be to pad out her feet with rags until she could wear any men's boots that she could salvage. She had as yet not found any, and she could scarcely bring herself to contemplate the possibility that she might have to rob one of the corpses.

Claudio, meanwhile, had located his luggage and was relieved to find that both the rifles and the compass were still intact. He sat nearest to the fire, cleaning down one of the guns with an oily rag and talking enthusiastically.

'Now we'll be able to shoot some breakfast in the morning. José tells me he's a good shot, so the two of us will go out at first light . . .'

He was interrupted by a long groan from the old man who lay hunched and still beneath a blanket. His head was resting on a mound of clothing and his thin face was grey and etched with pain. The plane's medical kit had still not come to light and the assumption was that it must lie somewhere beneath the tangled wreckage of the galley. Helen had wanted to try and splint the legs but a few fumbling attempts had quickly shown her that it was hopeless to even try. She could do nothing but pour a little *aguardente* down his throat on the few occasions when he returned to consciousness. Three bottles of the rough brandy had miraculously survived the impact of the crash. Nobody had argued when Claudio demanded that it all be kept for medicinal purposes. A large metal coffee jug from the galley had been filled with muddy river water and boiled over the fire to provide a safe but absolutely revolting drink. The loss of sweat was so great that large amounts of the vile stuff had to be forced down and the

118

jug was for ever being refilled.

The old man groaned again and Helen got up and went over to look at him. His forehead felt dangerously hot to the touch and his lips were moving as he muttered something over and over again. She leaned closer to listen but his voice was the merest ghost of a whisper; she could not make it out.

'How is he?' asked Claudio.

She shook her head. 'Not good. I wish to God there was something we could do for him. Those legs . . .' She grimaced, lacking the words to fully articulate the horror she felt about the shattered lengths of bone and flesh. She sighed and moved back to sit beside Martin, who was leaning back on one elbow, smoking a cigarette. It was his last one and he was trying to extract the maximum amount of pleasure from it, inhaling deeply and holding the smoke in his lungs for a long time. He turned his head a little to glance at Helen. She sat stiff and hunched beside him, looking faintly ridiculous in her shapeless felt hat, a large check shirt and a pair of baggy grey trousers tied round with string and turned up several times.

'You know, I think I prefer you dressed like that,' he murmured. 'You look a little like my kid brother.'

She shot him a look of intense irritation. 'I hate to point this out,' she snapped, 'but we're in serious trouble. There's an old man over there in a bad way; we're stranded in the middle of nowhere and frankly, I don't think your attitude is helping very much.'

Martin considered the statement for a few moments and then replied. 'Well, princess, I hate to point *this* out, but I know we're in serious trouble, I know we're stranded in the middle of nowhere and, what's worse, I'm smoking what may possibly be my last cigarette ever. As for the old man, he'll be dead by morning, so out of the whole bunch of us, I'd say he's got the least to worry about.'

119

Helen gave a brief exclamation of disgust. 'How can you talk like that?'

Martin shrugged. 'I just move my lips and the words come out.'

A silence fell and then, out in the night, there came a long eerie howl.

'What the hell was that?' inquired Helen nervously.

'A jaguarundi, Miss Brody. A little cat. Don't worry, it's not going to hurt us.'

'It just sounds so *lonely* out there,' murmured Helen apprehensively. 'Golly, I'm feeling hungry.'

'We'll all have to try and hold on till morning,' Claudio told her. He gazed at Helen in undisguised admiration. The kid was pretty tough. For a while Claudio had thought that it was just adrenalin that was carrying her along and that any moment, when the full shock of Mike's death hit her, she would collapse. But the time for that had long since passed and it really looked as though she was tough enough to come to terms with what had happened.

'We'd better keep a watch through the night,' Claudio broke the silence that followed. 'Two-hour intervals. I don't like the idea of being caught out here in the open and, like I said before, we don't know how close we might be to the friends of that hijacker. Anybody got a watch that still works?'

'I have,' replied Helen.

'Good, that's something to be grateful for. If I may, Miss Brody, I'll take it from you and place it on this treestump so that we can all use it. I'll take first watch; José here has already agreed to do the second. Senhor Taggart, I trust you will be prepared to handle the third?'

Martin sighed. He threw the spent butt of his last cigarette into the fire. 'What's the point?' he muttered flatly.

'The point? Well, there's every point. I'd feel a lot safer

120

if . . .'

Martin cut him short. 'Yeah, yeah, sure, if that's what you figure, put me down for third base. You want to play boy scouts, that's all right with me. But look, Chiefy, you'd better shape up a little. You've already made one big mistake today.'

'I did?' Claudio looked puzzled. 'What was that?'

'You told me there'd be more cigarettes in the plane. There weren't. I know, I spent hours looking.'

'Well, I'm sorry about that. Maybe we'll find some when we look through the cases.'

'I hope so. I get real irritable when I don't have cigarettes. Jesus, even in Garimpo Maculo, I could get cigarettes, though the price was eight times too much.'

'*Garimpo*?' Helen turned to stare at him with a look of accusation. 'So that's it! You're a diamond-jacker.'

'Yeah. What of it?'

'Oh nothing, it's just that I should have guessed, that's all. I've met a few of 'em in my time and they're basically all the same. Full of those dumb get-rich-quick schemes that never amount to anything; and for some reason, I don't know why, they're the world's biggest complainers. The least little problem and they let you know about it.'

'I see,' said Martin quietly. 'Anything else?'

'Well, only that they're really all little boys who've refused to grow up and take on the responsibility of a steady job.' She thought for a moment. 'You hit me back there, didn't you?' she said abruptly. 'On the plane, just before we were going to crash. I'd forgotten about it for a while, but you *did* definitely hit me.' Her fingertips traced the bluish bruise on her jaw for a moment as though reassuring herself that the incident had actually occurred. 'Well, I hope it made you feel manly hitting a woman.'

He glared at her angrily. 'How would you like to make it the best of three rounds?'

'Oh yes, well that's typical, isn't it! I suppose violence is

121

your only answer to criticism.'

'Listen, I hit you on the plane, sure, but you were hysterical. If I hadn't clipped you one, you'd still have been up by the cockpit when we came down. You saw what happened to those first rows of seats.'

But clearly Helen was not in the mood to listen to any more of this. She lay down, pulling the blanket over her, and turned her back on Martin. 'Goodnight, Mr Ormeto,' she said. 'I trust someone will wake me when it's time to take my watch.'

'Oh, that's all right, Miss Brody. I don't think we'll need you tonight.'

'Nonsense! I insist on doing my full share, the same as everybody else.'

'Well, you're certainly giving out more than your full share of bullshit,' Martin growled. There was an uncomfortable silence.

Claudio was beginning to wonder what the chances were of keeping this little group together. Only the first night and already there was friction. It was difficult to keep up his outward show of confidence, but in situations like this, people needed a leader. For better or worse, he had taken on that role. He reached out, grabbed a large branch from the pile and dropped it onto the fire, A flurry of sparks kicked themselves skywards and then died in a pall of grey smoke. He glanced around at his companions again. Both José and Helen were settling themselves down for the night. Martin Taggart was leaning back against a fallen tree trunk, his arms crossed against his chest, a scowl on his face as he stared sullenly into the fire.

Just get through tonight, thought Claudio, that's the thing. We've got the fire, tomorrow we'll get something to eat. Then I can outline my plans to them ... He settled back a little, tilted his hat back on his head and sighed. He could have used a cigarette himself right now. The warmth of the fire was comforting, though. If it hadn't

122

been for the thought of what lay ahead of them, he would have felt surprisingly content. With a frown, he went back to the mechanical task of cleaning his rifle.

Chapter 7

Claudio came abruptly awake from a shallow, restless sleep. He lay for a moment gazing up at the jagged scar of sky that overhung the river. It was a gunmetal grey at the moment but rapidly paling in the first glow of dawn. For an instant, he was confused by his surroundings; but then it all came flooding back: the plane, the crash, the aftermath. He groaned softly and remembered an incident from his childhood. He had suffered a terrible and very vivid nightmare in which he was being hunted by an unseen killer. He had awoken sobbing, convinced that the dream was true in every detail. But then his mother had come into the room and had sat beside him on the bed, stroking his hair and murmuring softly to him in the early morning light, assuring him that the dream was safely locked away from him in darkness, that it could not reach him now. The relief he had felt! The blissful, all-pervading relief . . . But glancing around at his sleeping companions, Claudio knew that this was no dream. The reality would be here waiting for him, every time he woke.

He sat up and rubbed at his eyes. Who was supposed to be on guard right now? Martin, wasn't it? But the man was fast asleep, sitting up with his back against a rock, his chin sunk forward to rest on his chest. Beside him, Helen was asleep too, her tousled head resting on her arms, a serene half-smile on her face. Some guards! Claudio sat up, pushing his blanket aside, and rivulets of dew ran across the grey wool. He wished vainly for a cup of hot coffee, to drive away the last vestiges of sleep; instead, he had to make do with a mouthful of boiled water. It was warm and brackish and made his gorge rise.

Now Claudio turned and moved quietly over to the old man with the broken legs. He was hunched and still beneath the blanket and for an instant Claudio felt a terrible weight lift from his shoulders. He was dead, surely . . . but when he moved closer, he could see that the old fellow was still breathing, his face grey and contorted with pain, each hard-fought breath wheezing like a bellows in his chest. He might last another day like this. Another day of constant, unremitting agony. Claudio bent over the old man. He turned for a moment to gaze around at the others. They were all asleep.

Turning back, Claudio reached out his hand and gripped the old man by his throat. He began to exert a slow, steady pressure on the windpipe, gouging his fingers deep into the hollows at either side of the scrawny neck. For an instant, the old man's eyes flicked open, an expression of shock in them. Then the expression softened to one of acceptance, relief and finally gratitude. When the eyes had become glazed, Claudio closed them with a brief touch of his hand. Then he knelt where he was for a moment, his head bowed. He felt no sense of guilt, only a vague tiredness. He would not have allowed an animal to suffer on in such a terrible way. What distinction was there between a dog and a man in such circumstances? But he had ensured that the others were asleep, because he knew that their civilized sensibilities would be aroused.

He stood up again and gazed towards the east. The sky was rapidly minted with gold. Soon the sun would filter a little light in through the thick canopy of the *selva* and then the time would be right for the hunt. He went over to where the rifles were leaning against a rock, their barrels pointing skywards. He checked them both and then filled his pockets with ammunition.

This done, he walked across to José and kicked lightly

124

against the sole of one of his boots. The big man blinked his eyes open and yawned cavernously. He gazed up at Claudio and nodded. He pushed his blanket aside and got to his feet. Then he moved a few steps away into the bushes, unzipped himself and urinated into the undergrowth.

'Did you sleep all right?' Claudio asked his back.

'Surprisingly so, Senhor Ormeto.' José strolled back and, taking the rifle that Claudio handed him, hefted it to his shoulder and sighted upon an imaginary target.

'Think you'll be able to use that?'

'It is a fine gun,' observed José. 'Better than I am used to . . . How is the old man this morning?'

Claudio shook his head. 'He died in the night.'

'Oh . . .' José moved slowly across to the body and stared at it for several moments. 'Funny,' he murmured. 'I never saw a dead man before this crash. Suddenly, it seems I shall never *stop* seeing them.' He knelt down and lifted the edge of the blanket until it covered the dead man's face. 'Somebody should say a prayer for him,' he observed; and he bowed his head.

'We should get going,' announced Claudio irritably.

José glanced up. 'I will be but a moment.' He resumed his prayer.

You'd better say one for me, thought Claudio sadly. He turned away and gazed into the neighbouring depths of the jungle. He wished in vain that he knew exactly where the plane had crashed. That much at least would be a help.

José came and stood beside him. 'I am ready now, *senhor*.'

'We'll work our way along the river bank. The cover's pretty dense there, but we might be able to scare something out.' Claudio glanced at his compass and took a quick check on the direction then nodded and they began to move away. 'We're looking for anything that's

125

edible,' he said. 'The people back there are hungry; if we don't come up with something to fill their bellies, the chances are they'll just give up. So anything you see, José, be sure and point it out to me before you fire. That way, if you miss, we'll get a second chance.'

José nodded. They moved out of the reach of the sunlight, into the dank green cover of the *selva*. Claudio was no stranger to the rain forests of the Amazon but there was a quality to this place that worried him. It was too remote somehow and he seriously doubted that any white man had passed this way before. Alongside the river, the land was a luxuriant tangle of palms, rubber trees, ferns and lianas, above which the close-packed, straight-limbed trees soared to a height of a hundred and fifty feet, choking out the sunlight with the denseness of their leaves. But within a hundred feet of the water, the vegetation took on a sparser, more stunted appearance. It was plain that it would be harder to find game that way. Claudio knew only too well the importance of rivers in these regions. He had himself travelled extensively up the Tocantins and a considerable distance along the Araguaia, but that had been comparatively easy. For one thing there were Indian villages dotted all down those stretches of river and both of the major tribes, the Cayapos and the Carajas, were friendly and eager to trade. Here there was no such reassurance. The river they had found was a miserable dried-up backwater. Any Indians in the vicinity would more than likely be hostile. The Carajas always spoke fearfully of the tribes of the interior and it took a lot to frighten those tough little devils. Deliberately Claudio turned his attention to the big man moving alongside. Despite his size, José was moving quietly and gracefully through the thick shrubs and gnarled roots that littered his path, the rifle held ahead of him while his dark eyes scanned the trees and vegetation.

How strange it was that a man like José should have

126

been aboard the plane. It was not just his inability to speak English that made him the odd man out. Here was a man who was clearly more at home with a spade in his hands than travelling across country by aeroplane. His clothes, though probably his Sunday best, were threadbare and cheap, and his voice had the slow, halting tones of an uneducated peasant. He was also no newcomer to the art of hunting, moving across the difficult terrain as easily and quietly as an Indian.

At last, Claudio's inquisitive nature got the better of him. He had to ask. 'Tell me, José, how did you come to be aboard that mother of a plane?'

José glanced up in surprise. Then he gave a slow, bemused smile. 'I was going home, Senhor Ormeto.'

'Home?' Claudio paused and mopped at his forehead with the sleeve of his shirt. 'And where exactly is that?'

'Oh, nowhere of any importance, *senhor* ... my mother's farm, just outside Belém. It's not much of a place. We have a few cattle, some goats, chickens.' He looked suddenly wistful. 'The milk cow was due to be having her calf any day now. It would have been nice to be back to see that.'

The two men stood gazing absently into the trees ahead of them.

There's more to it than that, thought Claudio. And if I stand here quietly for a few moments ... he will tell me.

The *selva* was strangely silent. Even the warning calls of the few solitary birds had died, to be replaced by a curious emptiness. An occasional ray of sunlight knifed low through chinks in the green armour of the undergrowth and a low mist stirred upwards from the damp soil.

'The animals,' murmured José. 'They are on their guard. They know we are after them.'

Claudio shrugged. 'Maybe.'

José sighed. 'Ah God. I wish I had never gone to visit

127

Uncle Antonio. I could have been home now. I could have been feeding that calf.' He scuffed irritably at the ground with the toe of his boot.

Now we're getting to it, thought Claudio. 'Uncle Antonio?' he echoed.

'He is a big-time *fazendeiro* out in Rio. It was he who paid my passage there and back.' José grimaced. 'Always my mother's favourite brother. And Mother, you know, she always used to say, "Ah José, why are you wasting your time on our little farm? Why do you not go to Uncle Antonio's *fazenda*; he is a big man, a big *patrão*. He would see to it that you lacked for nothing." I tried to tell her that I was happy as I was. Life is quiet on the farm. I can do as I please. When the animals are fed, I can take out my old .22 rifle and shoot some birds for supper. In Rio, I told her, people are for ever having to work, work, work!' He spread his big hands in a gesture of exasperation. 'Who needs such problems? Not I!'

'But you went in the end.'

'Had to. They gave me no choice. The plane tickets arrived in the post, my mother and Uncle Antonio had cooked the whole scheme up between them. To waste such money would have been a crime.'

'And . . .?'

José shrugged expressively. 'And, *senhor*, it was as I said. Much work. And everything so big, so hard to take in. There were cows there Senhor Ormeto, but not cows such as there are on my mother's farm, each with her own name, each her own ways. Here, there were hundreds upon hundreds of these beasts, moving across the ground and stirring up the dust with their hooves, each one nothing more than a moving hunk of beef destined to end up in a can.' He spat emphatically onto the ground in front of him. 'Then there were the men of my Uncle Antonio . . . who whispered in sneers of how I was the country boy who was up to learn a thing or two, the idiot

128

whom rich Uncle Antonio had tucked under his wing. They said these things about me Senhor Ormeto and, stupidly, they said them loud enough for me to hear. So, I had to crack a few skulls and break a few jaws and it saddened me to do that because I am a man of peace.'

José looked truly offended by the memory of it all and Claudio had to grin. 'Little wonder that you didn't get on there,' he observed.

'Oh, *senhor*, that was not the worst of it! There was also Cousin Lupe.' He pronounced the name with the same kind of quiet dread in his voice that a man might reserve for a particularly venemous species of poisonous snake. Claudio nodded. He thought he could guess the rest but he allowed José to continue.

'My uncle's only daughter, *senhor*, and as fat and ugly as a prize sow. But persistent! No sooner had I arrived there than she attached herself to me, giggling and fluttering her pink hands. At every turn she was there.' He shuddered visibly at the recollection. 'My Uncle Antonio began to make suggestions. He would set me up in business as *fazendeiro* of a new ranch. Everything would be provided. Buildings, stock, workmen . . . and naturally, a wife. It will give you some idea of her ugliness, *senhor*, when I tell you that Uncle Antonio had made the same offer to many men before me . . . some of them no more than simple ranch-hands, and all of them, every one, turned it down. You can imagine that to some men with little in the world, such an offer of land and wealth would drive aside all objections; but this one, she is a sow, no man would be so reckless with his life.' José shook his head, sighed. 'I have to hand it to my uncle though. He kept on trying, never missed a chance to hint. The things he would say! "Oh, what a fine dinner, Lupe! I think it is *so* important for a wife to be able to cook, is it not, José?" or "José, you have a tear in your jacket! Give that to Lupe to mend for you, she's *so* eager to have a man to

129

sew for!" ' José grimaced. 'I was due to stay on for another month, but I could no longer stand for it. I kept thinking of that calf and how much I should like to see it. Then the foreman of the cattle drovers, who did not like me much and wanted me out of the way, told me that I could get my plane ticket exchanged for an earlier flight. Naturally, I did not have to be told twice. Which is why I am here now in this stinking jungle, with an empty belly. My only consolation, *senhor*, is that *anywhere* is better than being in the company of my Cousin Lupe.'

'Amen to that!' Claudio slapped José lightly on the back.

The big man gazed at him inquiringly for a moment. 'Senhor Ormeto?'

'Yes?'

'Do you think I will ever get back to see that calf?'

For a moment, Claudio's spirit sagged. Always the same question. It was not the first time somebody had asked for an assessment of the chances of survival and it would certainly not be the last. Sound confident, he told himself. He'll need that. But it took some effort to concoct a cheery reply. 'Sure, José. The damned thing'll be a few months old when you see it, but you'll get there, never doubt it.'

José nodded, seemed reassured. Claudio hefted his rifle and the two men went on again, deeper into the jungle. The light was improving rapidly now and ahead of them they could perceive a ragged trail where the regular passage of some animal had worn a winding track. They moved silently along it, peering intently ahead and, after a few yards, spotted some old dried-up patches of dung on the ground.

'Pig,' thought Claudio hopefully. 'God, wouldn't that be a gift.' He was suddenly aware of just how hungry he was. His belly lurched at the thought of frying bacon, but he would not allow himself to depend on the idea. He knew the folly of that from past experience. He glanced at José, pointed at the dung and winked slyly. 'Maybe Cousin Lupe is more persistent than you thought,' he whispered; and the big man had to stifle a laugh.

They crept silently onwards. Claudio licked his dry lips while his eyes stared hopefully into the half-light, anticipating the abrupt, frantic rush of a heavy body on the trail ahead; but when a movement did come, it was up in the limbs of a tree, high above their heads. Instinctively, Claudio's gun barrel jerked upwards to point at the sky.

'See it?' he hissed fiercely.

'*Sim, senhor!*' José's gun was already pointing in the same direction.

'All right then . . .' Claudio snatched a breath, sighted quickly on the leaping, scuttling, chattering target. His finger tightened on the trigger.

The two guns roared in unison.

Helen could not identify the sound that woke her. The last booming echoes of it faded into distance, distorted by the dense cover of trees that lay on every side of its source. It might have been the terrible crashing of metal through vegetation, the restless roar of a hungry predator, but whatever it was, she was grateful, for it had rescued her from a dream so vivid, so frightful that even in the coolness of the morning it had drenched her sleeping body in a thick, acrid sweat.

She lay still beneath the blanket, staring helplessly up at the sky, a thin avenue of escape on either side of which the dark ranks of jungle seemed to offer nothing but silent suffocation. Her dream had begun in actuality. She had been here asleep in this remote place, the fire burned down to a few dull embers in the darkness. But a sound had woken her, the slow unhurried tread of an approaching figure, coming out of the trees to her left. She had

131

turned to shout to her companions and had seen, in a sudden spasm of jolting fear, that they were no longer with her. She was alone and the realization of it had paralysed her. She lay waiting as the figure approached, a tall dark silhouette, black against grey. For a moment there had been a sensation of relief. It was Martin Taggart. He had come back for her.

But then a voice had come to her out of the darkness, a slow, croaking voice, that somehow suggested that the speaker was in terrible pain. 'Helen. Helen, let me in! I'm cold.'

And in an instant, the fear had come back, because the voice belonged to Mike Stone; and that could not be, because with her own eyes, she had seen . . .

An image flashed before her eyes, an image of blood and mangled flesh that coaxed a wave of nausea into her dry throat. But the voice continued.

'Helen. It's cold here, so cold. Please . . .'

And a hand had reached out of the darkness and brushed lightly against her cheek, a strong hand that yet had a touch of gentleness in it. The soft familiarity of it had reassured her.

'Mike,' she whispered. 'I'm sorry.'

'Sorry? For what?'

'For thinking you were someone else.' Her own reply confused her. Perhaps at the back of her mind was the conviction that she had *wanted* the approaching figure to be Martin Taggart. Mike's body moved against her and she could feel that it was shivering. 'I would never have made you divorce Mae,' she murmured. And she lifted aside the blanket, so that he could get in beside her.

And then a shaft of moonlight had caught his face.

She would have screamed aloud, but in the dream she was somehow not able to make a sound. She would have struggled, pushed, hit out at the face that was not a face, but a torn, ragged obscenity that moved closer, saying her

132

name over and over. She would have, but her limbs seemed locked, rigid, incapable of movement. She could only lie, inert, helpless, waiting for the hideous touch of those bloody lips on her own. And then the sound had reached her, deep in nightmare, and had snatched her out to the cool sanctuary of morning.

Lying there, she allowed herself the luxury of tears, hiding her face beneath the blanket as she sobbed her terror silently away.

Stubborn pride, she thought to herself. She had always hated what she regarded as a weakness in her sex, this tendency to cry when the going got tough. Indulging in it was bad enough, but to be seen doing it was a humiliation she had never been able to endure. Of course, there were some women who could use that ability as a weapon to manipulate. She was not of that school. Even now, she quickly gained control. She wiped her eyes on her sleeve, sniffed a couple of times and then sat up to gaze around at the others.

For the first time, she realized that she really *was* quite alone.

Claudio and José had obviously gone out after food, and a little distance away from her the blanket that had recently held the sleeping form of Martin Taggart lay rumpled and empty. The sight brought back the dream to her and a curious sense of guilt. She *was* drawn to him somehow, she could not deny it. From the very first moment, as he came running across the tarmac, there had been something. She had felt no guilt then, but of course, Mike was still alive.

She could argue with herself that she was merely gravitating towards a strong, capable personality in a desperate situation; but if that was really the case, Claudio would be the obvious choice, not cynical, wisecracking Martin Taggart who thought the chances of survival very remote and took every opportunity to say as

133

much. His flippancy over the survivors' predicament was irritating, but not half as irritating as the knowledge that, with Mike dead less than twenty-four hours, Helen was beginning to be more interested in Martin Taggart than she cared to admit, even to herself.

She shook her head. If ever a potential relationship could be labelled 'No Future' this had to be the one. She sighed, slipped a hand under the collar of her shirt and rubbed vigorously at a flurry of insect bites that had raised angry red blotches against her soft, white skin. This did nothing to alleviate the fierce itch; it simply made her aware of other, similar depradations, dotted here and there beneath her loose clothing. Overnight, it seemed, she had become a banquet for mosquitoes.

Her gaze fell on the still blanket-draped figure of the old man and her blood seemed to turn several degrees colder in her veins. So, it was just as Martin Taggart had predicted. The old man had not made it through the night. Helen stared at the strange wool-draped profile of his face and suddenly the possibility of her own death seemed horribly near.

'It's a blessing,' she told herself mechanically; but she only remembered the brief look of gratitude in his grey eyes when she had wiped his forehead with a damp cloth the previous night. He must have known how small his chances were and yet he had never complained, not once. Now, for him at least, the fear and the doubt were over.

The abrupt crack of a distant rifle shot jerked Helen's gaze up to the tree-tops. An instant later, a second shot rang out and the twin echoes died away in a long, rumbling reverberation.

That's what woke me before, she thought. She wondered vaguely what the hunters were shooting at and the thought of possible food made her realize just how hungry she was. She turned at the sound of footsteps behind her and saw Martin Taggart emerging from the

134

jungle. He was carrying an armful of wood. Ignoring Helen for the moment, he approached the ashes of the fire and, poking them with a stick, revealed a hot red core beneath the surface. He began to place small twigs on the source of the heat and after a few moments a thin plume of white smoke drifted upwards. The smoke became a spark, the spark a dancing flicker of fire. Martin fed the blaze with larger pieces of wood and, in a matter of minutes, had a respectable fire going.

Helen brought her hands together in a short burst of applause.

Martin glanced up and smiled. 'I was a boy scout,' he said by way of explanation. His eyes held a mocking expression that she somehow distrusted.

'I thought you were the one who didn't see the point of doing anything,' she challenged.

He considered the statement. 'That's as may be,' he agreed. 'But right now, I'm damned hungry and it sounds like Claudio and José might have got lucky. The way I figure it, if the fire's ready when they arrive, we all get to eat a lot sooner. I've nothing against eating. It's one of my favourite pastimes.'

She nodded in agreement. 'Well, amen to that. You know, all things considered, I slept surprisingly well last night.'

'I wish to God *I* could,' muttered Martin bitterly. 'I just keep thinking about my lousy luck ending up in this mess.' He shook his head and reached up a hand to finger absent-mindedly at the small leather pouch that hung around his neck. Then he glanced back at Helen. 'That business last night . . . about me hitting you . . .'

'Oh forget it. I was sore about everything myself.'

'We're *all* like that sometimes.' He picked up a heavy branch and dropped it onto the fire. They both watched in silence as the greedy flames ate into the wood. There was a long hiss as the sap turned into steam. Then away in the distance, two more gunshots rang out.

'Goodness,' observed Helen hopefully. 'They certainly do seem to be shooting a lot out there.'

'Maybe they're just missing all the time.'

'That's the idea, Mr Taggart. Stay cynical. It suits you.' She had said this not with venom but mild sarcasm in her voice, and they both chuckled softly.

'You know, it's kind've nice to see you smile like that.'

'Oh, you'd be surprised. Under different circumstances, I can be the life and soul of every party.'

'Well, stick around. The party's just beginning.' He stood up as though he had remembered something. 'Things to do,' he told her simply and, turning on his heel, strolled away in the direction of the plane. Helen watched him thoughtfully, noting the arrogant swagger in his step. This was clearly a man who was used to having his own way and, though the plane crash had been an unexpected set-back, it had only temporarily upset his equilibrium. Here was a survivor if ever she had met one.

She turned her attention back to the fire and fed it a few more sticks from the pile, making it crack and sputter greedily. It was now rather quiet in the camp and the presence of a dead man a few feet to her right made her feel distinctly uneasy. She scanned the ranks of deep jungle around her but there was still no sign of Claudio and José. Supposing they simply never came back? It was not an agreeable thought. She had heard so many wild stories of explorers who'd set off into the Amazon and never been heard of again. Sitting in the midst of this desolation, the stories didn't seem quite so improbable.

She turned her head and gazed back in the direction of the plane, just in time to see Martin clambering up through the open hatch in the side of it. He paused for a moment, peering into the gloom and then he went on inside.

What's he up to? she wondered vaguely. Then, her

curiosity roused, she got to her feet and wandered after him.

It was hard to associate the wreckage with the familiar plane in which she had flown countless trips up and down the continent of South America. Now it was just so much worthless scrap, broken and anonymous in the midst of green desolation. Heaped with foliage and caked with mud, it already seemed to belong here. Helen moved forward to the open hatch, craned herself upwards and peered in, but she could discern nothing. Reaching up, she hauled herself inside. Within, there was a bad smell, a sickly sweet stench of decaying flesh that made her empty stomach heave. She clasped a hand over her mouth and nose and stared along the dark aisle. Now she could see Martin. His back was to her and he was bending forward over a corpse in one of the seats. Puzzled, Helen moved a few steps nearer. Martin was systematically going through the dead man's pockets. As she watched, he pulled out a wallet, opened it and examined the contents with interest. Then he extracted a thin wad of paper money, stuffed it into his back pocket and flung the wallet carelessly aside. He moved along to the next seat where the body of an elderly woman was slumped. He rooted around by her feet for a moment and emerged holding her handbag, which he opened and peered into. But there was nothing inside that interested him and with a snort of irritation he flung the bag away.

Suddenly, he seemed to become aware that he was no longer alone. He turned around and gazed impassively at Helen for several moments. His expression bore no trace of guilt. He simply acknowledged her presence, grunted something unintelligible and calmly moved on.

'My God,' exclaimed Helen, her voice a horrified whisper. 'What are you doing?'

He glanced back at her, mild irritation on his face. 'What does it look like?'

137

'You're . . . you're robbing the dead!'

'That's one way of putting it,' he admitted. 'I was looking for cigarettes.'

'Cigarettes be damned! You took some money from that man. I saw you.' She pointed a finger at him in grim accusation.

'Sure,' he agreed. 'He didn't have any cigarettes. Anyhow, I figure that nothing they've got in here is going to be much use to 'em any more; on the other hand, it could be some use to me.'

'What do you mean?'

'I mean that even considering the slim possibility that we can haul our asses out of here alive, some of us might still have problems back in so-called civilization. Extra money could buy off trouble, if and when I manage to crawl back to the land of milk and honey. Now a few sheets of paper doesn't weigh very much, so I figure I'll take it along with me. None of these people seem to have the least objection.'

'That is the sickest thing I've ever heard. I quite understand your reasoning, Mr Taggart, but that doesn't excuse the morals of what you're doing.'

'Morals?' He gave a short derisive laugh. 'Where the hell do you think you are, Miss Brody, Park Avenue? Take a look out there!' He indicated the backdrop of dense jungle that lay beyond the opening in the fuselage. 'You see that? That's the Stone Age out there, the friggin' Stone Age. It's the quick death of all those nice little customs they observe back in the big city. Past that jungle you're looking at, there's more jungle and more, a thousand goddamned miles of it, and you and me, we're just the poor sorry bastards who've had the bad luck to fall slap bang into the middle. There *are* no morals here, Miss Brody, just the day-to-day reality of staying alive any way you can. The sooner you accept that fact, the better you'll get along.'

138

Helen shook her head. 'I don't care what you say,' she retorted. 'I would personally never sink so low as to steal from a dead man.'

Martin laughed again. He moved closer and fingered the fabric of the shirt Helen was wearing. 'And where did this come from? Those trousers too. And the boots you're going to need before very much longer. Where will they come from, Miss Brody?'

'That's different!' she argued. 'The clothes came from somebody's luggage. I don't even know who they belonged to.'

'Oh, so that's what you object to, is it? It's all right to steal if you remain in safe ignorance afterwards. What you object to is the contact, isn't it? Sure, that's it.' He grabbed hold of her arm and spun her around to face the man whose wallet he had just lifted. 'Let me see now,' he murmured. 'That shirt looks around his size, wouldn't you say?'

'Let go of me!' protested Helen. 'Goddamnit, let me go!'

But he tightened his grip and pushed her forward, jamming the arm up behind her back when she struggled. 'Take a look at him,' he growled. 'Take a good long look. It's not a pretty sight, is it?' With his other hand, he craned her forward, pushing her face to within a few inches of the dead man's white, bloated features, filling her nostrils with the all-pervading stench of death. She cried out and her eyes filled with tears. With a wrench, she pulled away from his grasp and blundered back along the aisle.

'You bastard,' she shrieked vehemently. 'You rotten-hearted bastard. There was no need for that, no need at all!'

But he had dismissed her already. His back turned, he had resumed his grisly salvage operation. 'Just wait till you've been stuck out here a few days,' he muttered over

139

his shoulder. 'Then come back and tell me if you still have morals.'

'Screw you,' she snapped in reply; and added as an afterthought. 'I hope you die.'

'Well, that's a distinct possibility for all of us,' he admitted as Helen made her way to the front of the plane. She stood by the hatch for a few moments, drying her eyes on her sleeve. The stink of decaying flesh made her stomach heave. Behind her she heard Martin's muffled voice.

'Christ, didn't *any* of you bastards smoke?'

'Sonofabitch,' she murmured. She jumped down onto the river bank and began to walk slowly back to the fire, looking up at a shout from the jungle to see Claudio and José emerge triumphantly. They were carrying two dark furry bundles over their shoulders as they hurried towards the fire. Helen quickened her pace, arriving just as the men lowered their bundles unceremoniously to the floor.

'Monkeys,' she observed with undisguised revulsion; and she stopped dead in her tracks, gazing in horror at the creatures sprawled on the ground. There were two large, thickly set monkeys with black shaggy fur and small exquisitely detailed faces, both of which were obscured by masks of blood. The mouths were open, revealing rows of tiny pointed teeth and lolling pink tongues. Helen could feel her appetite rapidly disappearing.

'We're going to eat monkeys?' she said weakly, sitting herself beside the fire.

'No ordinary monkeys,' Claudio assured her. '*Howler* monkeys. They may not look appetizing but, believe me, they make good eating. To the Amazon Indians, they are a mainstay of the diet.'

Helen nodded numbly. 'It doesn't matter what you say, they still *look* like monkeys.'

'Only for a little while, Miss Brody!' Claudio settled

himself on the ground and took out his sheath-knife. He turned to José and issued some curt instructions in Portuguese. 'José, take the spare knife and cut me a long stick, to make a spit. And two forks to rest the ends in.'

'Yes, *senhor*.' José grinned and hurried away. Claudio picked up the first of the monkeys, pushed the point of his knife into the animal's groin and made a quick, straight slash upwards along its belly, spilling a mess of vividly coloured entrails onto the ground. He picked these up and flung them away along the river bank.

'That will keep the insects busy,' he observed brightly; but he noticed that Helen had turned her face away.

Claudio chuckled. He raised the knife and brought it down on the monkey's thin neck, snapping through the bone and shearing the head clean off the body. Then he set about the tricky task of removing the fur to reveal the pink flesh beneath.

He glanced up and saw that Martin was approaching from the direction of the plane. He was carrying something tucked under one arm. As he drew nearer, Claudio could see that it was a pair of men's boots. He came to a halt beside Helen and dropped them on the ground in front of her. She glanced up with an unfriendly scowl then looked down again at the boots; but she made no attempt to pick them up.

'I found a guy with small feet,' observed Martin tonelessly. 'A couple of pairs of socks and they'll fit like they were made for you.' He did not wait for a reply but walked over to examine what Claudio was doing. He squatted down, stared thoughtfully at the bloody half-skinned carcass in Claudio's hands.

'That's a howler monkey isn't it?' he said quietly. 'I've been told that they make really good eating.'

Claudio grinned. 'For that, Senhor Taggart,' he exclaimed, 'I'm going to save you the best helping. Miss Brody here . . . she does not seem to think she will enjoy

141

eating a monkey.'

Martin nodded. He turned and his gaze settled on Helen. She was still staring fixedly at the boots, something she needed but which her pride would not allow her to take.

'She'll come round to it in the end,' said Martin thoughtfully. 'It takes a little time, that's all.'

Squashed together on the roasting spit and devoid of their usual covering of dark fur, the monkeys resembled large pink rabbits, oozing a yellow glutinous fat; but the smell of cooking meat was appetizing enough and Helen knew that she would do her best to cram the flesh down her throat, even if her stomach kept heaving it right back again. There were too many other discomforts to bear to allow hunger to be one of them. She had found herself a couple of pairs of thick socks in one of the suitcases and the boots seemed to fit her tolerably well; but she avoided meeting Martin's gaze, knowing full well the smug expression his face would wear.

Claudio presided over the feast like some bizarre master of ceremonies, turning the spit and testing the meat with his knife every so often. He was aware that the others were impatient but refused to allow the meat to be taken from the spit until it was properly cooked. From time to time, he made proud observations about the kill.

'They're a good size, these brutes! And we certainly had tremendous luck, first time out. One half monkey for each of us. I hope you won't always expect to dine this well!'

While he had got the lunch under way, José and Martin had moved the body of the old man into the plane with the others. Then the long restless wait for the meal had begun, everybody crowding around to stare longingly at the meat as it slowly turned from pink to dark brown. At last Claudio announced that it was ready. He lifted the long spit from the fire and eased the carcasses onto a large

142

flat stone from the river bed. He cut each carcass carefully in half and jabbed a couple of sharpened sticks into each piece. In a short time, everybody fell to eating, hunched over the hot meat and tearing at it wolfishly in the fierce frantic haste of real hunger. Helen found the meat surprisingly palatable, provided she kept her gaze away from a bloody pile of fur some distance away.

In the brief period of contentment that followed Claudio wiped his mouth on his sleeve and looked at his three companions. He began to speak, quietly and logically, of the plans he had formulated. 'First of all, I have to tell you that I only have a very rough idea about where we are. As you know, we failed to find the plane's charts and maps but we do know that we had travelled north-west towards the Mato Grosso. Helen tells me that the plane's top range is around one thousand two hundred miles. Now of course, we can't be sure just exactly how far we got, but looking at the terrain and making an educated guess, I'd say we're somewhere to the west of the Rio das Mortes or possibly even the Xingú.'

Martin gave a short derisive snort. 'That's a hell of a big somewhere.'

Claudio nodded. 'I know that, but like I said, I can't be more exact. Still, we've got one ace in the hole and that's my compass. Now, I'll tell you a fact. If we head due east, eventually we'll come to a river. It might take a few weeks, it might only take a few days but we'll come to one, and then . . .'

'Pardon me, Mr Ormeto,' interrupted Helen. 'You mention moving on as a matter of course. Is there any reason why we shouldn't stay here?'

'Plenty,' replied Claudio without hestitation. 'Oh, I know at the moment this place seems to represent some kind of security; there's some hunting up the river and all the supplies in the aircraft. But no search party is likely to find us here and even if an aeroplane did spot the wreckage, where could it land?' He gestured around him expansively. 'An angel would have difficulty setting down in this wilderness. Any rescue attempt that might come would have to be by river. This one is all but dried up. Now, if we can find ourselves a real river, we could maybe construct a raft and just let the current carry us back to a village or a rescue party, whichever came first.'

'You make it sound very easy,' she observed.

'Forgive me, I didn't mean to. But what we must be aware of, is time. We've got a month before the rains begin. If we're still in the jungle by then, we may as well take one of my guns and blow out all our brains. Here's what I suggest. Tomorrow morning, we get together whatever equipment we can carry and then we – DIABO!'

Claudio had stood up and was staring open-mouthed over the heads of the others. They turned to see that the plane was on fire. Suddenly, inexplicably, fire and smoke were belching out of the open escape hatch and coiling greedily upwards to lick across the metal fuselage, leaving dark sooty streaks on its silver flanks.

'How the hell did that start?' Claudio took a step forward and, in that instant, something within the plane's guts erupted with a dull thud, blasted a great waft of hot air out at the group, forcing them to back away, their hands shielding their faces. The windows shattered one by one, allowing fresh tongues of flame to claw frantically outwards.

'We'd better get the hell away from here,' yelled Martin over the terrible roar of the conflagration. 'The petrol tanks . . .'

The rest of the words were lost in a dull sonorous boom as a vast explosion rocked the bowels of the wreckage, which burst outwards in a terrible welter of flame and steel. The four onlookers were literally knocked to the ground by the impact and had to scramble desperately away on their hands and knees as chunks of debris rained down.

At a safe distance, they turned and looked back. The aircraft was now an inferno, flinging a great oily column of fire up into the sky, a surreal orange stairway that reflected strangely in the shallow water of the river.

'Look at that sonofabitch,' murmured Martin. 'I'll bet you can see that for miles.'

Claudio nodded grimly. 'That's what worries me.' He rubbed his chin thoughtfully. 'How the hell could a fire have started so long after the crash?'

Martin shrugged. 'It beats the hell out of me.'

Claudio grabbed him by the arm. 'You were in there before, weren't you? You were in there for a long time when we were hunting ...'

'So? We've all been in there at one time or another. I was just looking for cigarettes, that's all.'

'Yes? And maybe you found some! Maybe you smoked them in there and left a butt burning on a seat somewhere.'

'You're crazy!' Martin shook his hand free. 'If I'd found some cigarettes, you think I'd enjoy smoking them crouched in a plane full of stiffs? Hell, anything could have caused that fire, the sun shining through the glass of the window maybe.'

'But the plane's in the shade now.'

'Don't mean a thing. It could have been smouldering away for hours. Anyhow, what difference does it make how it started? The plane's burned now. At least it'll save us the job of burying all those bodies.'

He spat at the ground and strolled a little nearer to the blaze to watch the plane's final agonies. Claudio stared after him thoughtfully. Had there been something a little too flippant in his attitude, or was he simply telling the truth? It was unlikely that the plane could catch fire hours after the crash but not impossible. Besides, as far as he

145

knew, the only dependable source of fire in the camp was José's cigarette lighter and that was safely tucked away.

Instinctively, Claudio reached into the breast pocket of his shirt. He swore softly as he realized that the lighter was no longer there.

Chapter 8

Claudio pounded the flat piece of metal with the heavy stone, working in a slow, relentless rhythm. It was noon of the following day and the heat was at its most unendurable. Fat drops of sweat ran trickling down his face until they soaked into the already damp khaki fabric of his shirt collar. Slanting down through the broad gap in the treetops, the sun now bathed the river bank in a ferocious glare that made the least effort a major undertaking.

Claudio and Martin had moved back to sit in the comparative shade beside the burnt-out fuselage. Martin, with characteristic fatality, had quickly given up the idea of exerting himself in any way and was stretched out on his back, his hat pulled down over his eyes while he attempted to nap; but meanwhile Claudio worked on with the fierce determination that was typical of him. The hunk of metal had fallen from the plane upon impact. It was impossible to say what it once was, but now Claudio was shaping it into a long, flat strip. He had bound some strips of cloth tightly around one end to form some kind of handle; and every so often he paused to heft it experimentally before returning to his thankless task. José kneeled beside him, watching every move with great interest.

Helen too was busy. She had managed to clamber up onto the blackened roof of the plane with a great mound

146

of white clothing from the discarded suitcases and, with the aid of a series of rocks which she had also laboriously manipulated up there, was laying out the articles of clothing, weighing them down with stones. She had spent some time explaining her idea to Martin: to create a message that might be spotted by a passing plane. Martin had congratulated her on her ingenuity but at the same time made it painfully clear that he himself had no interest in helping her. So Helen toiled on in the open sunlight, while Martin did his best to blot out the terrible noise that Claudio was making.

It seemed to Martin that Claudio had been acting strangely ever since the plane had caught fire. Quiet and intense, he seemed to have retreated into himself and the only time he had exchanged words with Martin that day was to ask if he knew anything about José's lighter. Martin had replied that he disliked the atmosphere of distrust that existed and nothing more had been said.

The afternoon wore on, accompanied only by the dull clanging of stone on metal. Occasionally, when Claudio flagged, José would take over, applying his prodigious strength to the task, making more noise than ever. Then he and Claudio would examine the thing, muttering together in Portuguese.

Eventually, even Martin's curiosity was aroused. He sighed, tilted back his hat and peered accusingly at his companions. 'OK, you two, I give in. What the hell *are* you making, apart from a goddamned noise?'

Claudio paused and glanced up. For a reply, he hefted the ungainly hunk of metal again and swung it down against a large piece of fallen wood. The result was spectacular. The sharpened edge ploughed deep into the rotten timber, hacking out a great V-shaped wedge. Claudio gave a grim nod of satisfaction and wrenched the blade free.

'A machete,' said Martin, answering his own question.

'It doesn't look much, but it seems to work all right.'

Claudio turned his head to stare across the river into the green depths that awaited them on the other side. 'We wouldn't get very far through that without one,' he observed flatly. 'But forgive us if we're interrupting your siesta.'

Martin ignored the taunt. 'Say, listen Claudio, since you're so damned clever at making things, perhaps you could come up with a suitable alternative to tobacco . . . maybe some leaf that grows out here.'

Claudio smiled. 'I'll put my mind to it,' he promised. 'But right now, I'm more concerned with necessities. Maybe if you stopped thinking about cigarettes all the time, you could apply *your* mind to some of the things we need.'

'Yeah? Such as?'

Claudio got to his feet. 'Well, such as —'

The sudden, heart-stopping crack of a rifle and the dull thud as a bullet slammed into metal shortly to the right of Claudio's head were almost simultaneous. For an instant, everybody seemed hypnotized, rooted to the spot by the sheer suddenness of it. Then with an oath Claudio was flinging himself face down onto the ground, colliding with Martin who was flipping himself over onto his belly. José scuttled in the direction of the spare rifle, which he had left farther down the river bank. A second slug punched a hole in the aircraft just where Claudio had been standing an instant before.

'Helen, get down from there!' yelled Claudio, peering up at the roof of the plane. She was kneeling upright, a rock in her hands, her mouth open in surprise, presenting a perfect target to the unseen gunman. 'Down, for Christ's sake! Do you want to get killed?'

She responded awkwardly, edging herself gingerly across the curve of the plane's roof, keeping her body as low as possible. Then a bullet ricocheted off the metal a few inches to her left and she threw caution to the wind, came hurtling down from above with a yell of pure terror. She hit the ground in a sprawl, rolled awkwardly and scrambled back, hugging the side of the plane. She wedged herself in beside Martin, who was lying with his face pushed into the comforting softness of the ground.

There was a long, terrible silence, broken only by the distant shrieking of a macaw and the last booming echoes of the gunfire fading into distance. Then silence again as they lay sweating in the hot sun.

It was Martin who spoke first, his voice oddly muffled because he was reluctant to lift his face from the ground. 'For an uninhabited patch of jungle, this place is beginning to seem a little too lively.' He angled his head slowly sideways to look at Claudio. 'Who the hell do you suppose it is?'

'Most likely the friends of our hijacker,' he murmured. Then he raised his voice slightly to call back to the others. 'Anybody hurt?'

'No, we're both fine,' replied Helen quietly.

'Whoever is firing at us is up high,' observed Claudio. He lifted his head a little and scanned the screen of tall trees that flanked the forest at the top of the river bank. It presented a vista of thick impenetrable foliage behind which a hundred gunmen could easily conceal themselves. 'Up there somewhere,' he mused. Now he glanced a short distance away to where his rifle stood, propped upright against a fallen treetrunk. He judged the distance he would have to run. Ten, maybe fifteen yards. A daunting prospect under a pointing gun.

Martin followed his gaze and guessed Claudio's intentions. 'Don't do it,' he whispered. 'It's too fuckin' risky . . .'

'Yes, Senhor Ormeto. Like the man says . . . don't do it.'

Despite the unseen presence of a sniper, the new voice

149

made everybody turn their heads; because it was José who had spoken. They all turned, open-mouthed in astonishment. Good dependable José, who couldn't speak a word of English. He was crouched near the fuselage of the plane, the spare rifle grasped in his huge hands. The barrel was trained unwaveringly on Claudio's chest.

There was a long, stunned silence while the terrible truth sank home. A man could have had no better cover than that which José had enjoyed. Nothing was hidden from a man who 'didn't speak the lingo'. He could sit there for hours on end with a vacant smile on his big dumb face and all the time observing, drawing up his plans. Everyone had fallen for it.

'You son of a bitch,' growled Martin at last.

José's face creased into a mocking grin. 'You must forgive me, *senhor*. It was a bad thing I did ... but it's amazing how playing the idiot can put a man above suspicion.'

Claudio was shaking his head now as he remembered the elaborate tale the big man had spun. The little farm in Belém ... his cousin Lupe and Uncle Antonio ... right down to the newborn calf he wanted to get back and see. How much of that melodrama was based on any kind of reality, he wondered glumly; yet he had swallowed every word of it. José must have noted the expression on Claudio's face, because he gave a little bow of apology and grinned again. He was clearly enjoying his little deception. Now, he raised his voice and shouted out in Portuguese.

'Hey, out there! This is José speaking. You can come out now and stop the shooting, I've got everything under control. You hear me? Bring your sniper down or he'll be putting a bullet in my ass! Raoul didn't make it out of the crash, but I'm fine! Come on out, it's all clear!' He waited a minute and then an answering call came back from the bushes.

'José? Is that really you?'

'Of course, you asshole! Is that Jorge? Come out, you idiot, everything's all right. I've got these pigs covered.'

He leaned back a little and smiled at his captives. 'So ... now we wait,' he suggested. 'My friends won't be long.'

'Who the hell are you people?' demanded Claudio. 'It's obvious you were working with our hijacker.'

'That's right. I was supposed to be his back-up man, there if anything went wrong. But how was I supposed to know he was going to lock himself in the cabin that way? So when the time came, there was nothing I could do. I decided to sit tight and take my chances with the rest of you.'

'And this ... organization ... you belong to ...'

'We're rebels.'

Martin laughed derisively. 'Somehow, I had a feeling that word was going to be used.'

'We support Getulio Vargas.'

'Vargas? Hell, the country's had fifteen years of his kind of dictatorship. It was the best thing that ever happened when they kicked his ass out of the President's chair ...'

José swivelled the gun in Martin's direction. 'I should be careful what you say, *senhor*,' he advised.

'Why did you need the plane?' inquired Claudio.

'For mobility, naturally. There are many other factions of Vargas's supporters hiding out in the jungle. The plan was to use the plane to transport the other followers to this camp and to ferry weapons and ammunition from place to place. We had already amassed a sizeable fuel dump, ferrying the gasoline drums downriver by raft. All we needed was the plane but Raoul messed it up. It seemed we were right back where we started ... but luckily, Senhor Taggart, I met you. And what you are carrying will buy us several planes and a lot more besides.

151

Martin glared at him. 'I don't know what you're talking about.'

'Sure you do. I mean the diamond; the one you carry in that pouch around your neck. I can't say exactly how much it's worth but it must be a good one or you would never have risked leaving the *garimpo* or the employ of your patron. I've been watching you, Senhor Taggart. I've noticed how your hands are always reaching out to touch it, to reassure yourself that it's still there. To what use would you put such a stone? Stupid frivolous pleasures no doubt! But I . . . I will ensure that it is put to the support of a worthy cause. So . . . I will trouble you to hand it over my friend.'

'Over my dead body,' snapped Martin sourly.

José nodded, smiled. 'Just as you prefer.'

Helen glanced nervously back at the trees that concealed the gunmen. She was aware of figures emerging slowly from cover.

'They're coming,' she whispered hoarsely, her voice trembling with the certainty that she was soon to die.

'Let them come.' Claudio's voice was so calm and assured that Helen could not help but stare at him in surprise. He was smiling back at José, gazing straight into the big man's eyes. 'One thing, José. How did you rig the plane to go up that way? It was no accident but a signal for your friends back there . . .'

'It was easy. A simple time-fuse made from a length of string and a small container of petrol.' He fumbled in his pocket and took out his cigarette lighter, which he displayed with a proud flourish. 'Amongst my many talents I am also a good pick-pocket. And after all, I was only taking back my own property.'

'Jesus,' snapped Martin in disgust. 'And you suspected me, Claudio. I hope you feel good about that!'

Claudio shook his head. 'On the contrary, Senhor Taggart, I feel ashamed and relieved at the same time.

You see, it was my distrust of *you* which prompted me to take all of the bullets out of the spare rifle. A happy accident you might say.'

José's eyes bulged for an instant; but then he sneered in disbelief. 'I'd have to be pretty stupid to fall for a line like that.'

'Indeed you would,' agreed Claudio; and then he made his move, snatching his hand down to the leather sheath at his belt and then up again in a single lithe action. His hand came up glittering with heavy steel and he flung the knife at José with all his strength. The blade buried itself deep in the big man's shoulder, the wooden handle juddering, the impact rocking him backwards but not completely over. He came up again, his teeth gritted in pain, his eyes blazing hatred. He squeezed the trigger of the rifle.

The loud click of the empty chamber sounded somehow louder than the shot that Martin and Helen had anticipated. There was a momentary stillness which to Helen's racked imagination seemed to last an eternity; the scene was frozen like a grisly waxworks exhibit. José was staring vacantly down at the empty gun, his mouth hanging open in dismay. Around the wooden handle of the knife which jutted incongruously from his shoulder, a large red stain was spreading, soaking the grubby fabric of his shirt. And then abruptly all was chaos as Martin and Claudio launched themselves headlong at the big man, wrestling and punching him to the ground. But they had underestimated his enormous strength. He came up again roaring like an angry bear, lashing out with the rifle as though it were a club. Claudio grabbed the stock in his hands and wrested the rifle away, but then received a blow in the face that sent him sprawling. Martin aimed a wild punch at José's back that did nothing more than annoy him. He spun around and dashed his huge right fist into Martin's stomach, doubling him over with a grunt of

153

pain. He rolled desperately sideways, narrowly avoiding the kick that was intended as a follow up.

Now José reached up and gripped the handle of the knife with his right hand and wrenched the blade free, causing the blood to pump copiously down the front of his shirt. Hefting the knife, he advanced on Martin, his arm held ready to strike. At that instant, Claudio stepped back into the fray, using the butt of the rifle to aim a savage blow at José's head. The impact would have floored an ordinary man, but José merely stumbled, shook his head and turned around, directing his fury at Claudio instead. He came lumbering forward, swinging his knife hand from side to side in a series of deadly arcs and Claudio could do nothing but retreat, feebly trying to parry the blows with the rifle butt. Martin, meanwhile, had got back to his feet and, realizing that there was no time to locate a suitable weapon, went racing back into the fight with a flurry of wild punches at José's kidneys. This slowed his adversary enough for Claudio to bring the rifle down hard on José's right hand, knocking the knife from his grasp. For a few moments, the three men swayed in a tight, cursing bunch as each of them tried to go after the knife. Then a wild swing from José connected with the side of Claudio's head with a loud crack. He sank down with a groan and José, twisting about, pushed Martin's hands contemptuously aside and grabbed him in a vicious bear hug. He began to exert a slow, steady pressure on his victim's ribcage and Martin gave an involuntary scream as he felt the awesome power in the big man's arms. It was as though somebody was slowly tightening a band of steel. He lifted his fists and dashed a couple of blows into José's face, but to no avail. With a cruel laugh, José exerted more pressure, lifting Martin's feet clear of the ground and driving the last reserves of breath from his body. Martin gave a low groan of agony, opening his mouth wide in a vain attempt to draw air into his burning

154

lungs. He squirmed and struggled, clawed feebly at the face that seemed now to hover in front of him like a great white moon, but the strength in his arms was waning fast and it seemed that nothing would ever make José relinquish that terrible hold. A foggy blackness seemed to fill his head; it seemed that his ribs were about to collapse like dry firewood. He barely heard the sound of the gun.

The first bullet buried itself in José's spine, smashing through vertebrae and muscle and jolting his whole body with the force of the impact. The second ploughed an ugly furrow across the top of his head, spattering warm blood over Martin's upturned face. The gun kept on firing, pumping shot after shot into José until his lifeless body swayed, tottered and finally crashed headlong to the ground, half crushing Martin beneath its weight, obliging him to lie there for several moments, spreadeagled and gasping for air. Then, realizing with a grunt of revulsion what lay on top of him, he levered José's body away and scrambled clear. The last booming echoes of gunfire receded and, glancing up, Martin realized for the first time what had happened. He had expected to see Claudio standing there with a confident grin on his face. Instead, there was Helen, kneeling a short distance away, her eyes still staring wildly at José's body. The rifle was cradled awkwardly in her arms, its barrel emitting a thin plume of grey smoke.

In the heat of the moment, she had acted from sheer instinct, scrambling for Claudio's gun, oblivious to the advancing rebels who had been no more than thirty yards from her when she started shooting but who had scattered into cover at the first sound of gunfire. It was only now as she regarded the shattered body that the full realization of what she had done struck her. It was certainly not the first time she had used a rifle. She'd often gone out hunting with Tom, the plantation owner with whom she'd been involved some years back, and had at one time been considered a fair shot. But this had been the first shot she'd ever fired in anger, and now she was taken by an abrupt numbness.

Claudio was the first to recover. Shaking his head to dispel the woolliness that lingered there, he scrambled over to her, relieved her of the gun and began frantically to reload it with cartridges from his belt.

'You needn't have wasted so many shots,' he chided her, his voice brusque and businesslike. And then he added, 'But you were fantastic.'

Helen opened her mouth to speak, but the words wouldn't come. She gestured vaguely at the body and her eyes filled. Sensing she was close to breaking-point, Martin moved nearer to her, put an arm protectively around her shoulders.

'I'm . . . all right,' she assured him haltingly. 'Really . . . I . . .'

'Those other bastards sure as hell went to ground,' interjected Claudio grimly. 'It must have sounded like World War Three had broken out. It's going to take 'em a little while to get organized again.' He surveyed the surrounding ranks of jungle intently, the rifle held ready to fire. For the moment, there was no sign of life. He glanced at Martin. 'You'd better locate your pistols, Senhor Taggart. We may need them.'

'Sure.'

Martin gave Helen's arm a reassuring squeeze and then, keeping his head low, moved back along the fuselage of the plane to the place where his carpet bag was lying. Reaching inside, he found the cool reassuring grip of his pistol. He hefted the unfamiliar weight of the gun he had never fired and then made his way back to Helen's side. He noticed how she kept glancing back at the body, as though half expecting it to come back to life.

'You did what you had to,' he assured her. 'He sure as hell wouldn't have had any qualms about doing the same

156

to any of us. Anyhow, you saved my bacon there and I want to thank you.'

She nodded, forced a thin smile but her eyes were heavy with grief. Martin turned his attention to Claudio, who seemed to have spotted something out in the bushes. He was squinting along the sights of the rifle and murmuring savagely beneath his breath.

'Come on, you son of a bitch. I see you! Just one more step out from cover, that's all I ask. One more . . . oh yes, that's it. Come on, come on.' His voice had the tone of an excited adolescent and Martin was momentarily shocked. Now the flesh of Claudio's index finger whitened against the trigger and the sudden crack of the rifle made Martin's skin crawl. Thirty yards away there was a brief commotion in the bushes and a high-pitched unearthly scream that died as abruptly as it had begun.

Claudio lowered the rifle with a slow sigh of satisfaction. 'That's one less,' he observed calmly. 'But they'll be a good deal more careful from now on.'

Another silence descended, this time long and tense, while the three lay sweating in the afternoon heat. Martin found himself wondering how many unseen men there were out there in the trees, each of them plotting death for these three luckless intruders into their territory. It was an unsettling thought. He glanced sideways to look at José's blood-spattered body, which had already acquired a grubby halo of flies. How well the big clumsy 'farmer' had played his role; and just like Agnello before him, he'd died in pursuit of the diamond. Martin fingered the pouch around his neck. He was filled with a powerful, irrational desire to fling the gem away, but it was a desire that was very short-lived. In seconds it was replaced by the conviction that he would hang on to it till the bitter end. He noticed Helen gazing at him thoughtfully.

'I always wondered what you carried in there,' she murmured. 'I figured maybe it was something of sentimental value.' He thought he detected a trace of sarcasm in her voice. 'Is it really worth as much as José seemed to think?'

He nodded and felt a tinge of sadness. She had just saved his life, yet now she knew of the diamond, he doubted whether he would ever be able to trust her. He started slightly at the sound of a shout from the bushes away to his left.

'José? Hey . . . what's going on?'

'José's not able to talk right now!' yelled back Claudio. 'He's done for and the same will go for any of you who stick their noses over here.' He grinned at Martin. 'Let's see what they make of that.'

Another long silence. Then the same voice went on, stumbling awkwardly over the English phrases. 'Hey! You is *norte americanos*! Lissen, you come out here, OK? Throw out all weapons and come out. We don't shoot you. *Americanos* is friends.'

Claudio laughed mockingly. 'If we're friends, then why shoot at us?'

'Is just a mistake.'

'It'll be a bigger one if you try and come over here. We're all armed and there's plenty of bullets.'

Another pause.

'Lissen, you come on out here. Is last chance. We is many persons. Don' want to kill you but we will if we have to. I wait five more minutes. Then we come for you . . . understand?'

'Yes, we understand! We'll be waiting.'

'Jesus,' said Martin apprehensively. 'Do you think they mean it?'

Claudio shrugged. 'Maybe, maybe not. But they're not entirely stupid. If they use their heads, they'll just surround us and wait us out. You've got to remember, they probably daren't take the chance of letting us talk to anyone about their little hideaway. Sure, the plane's no use to them now, but if we were lucky enough to get back to civilization, questions would be asked about how we got out here. They're the ones with everything to lose. I wish I knew how many there are.'

'I counted at least six before,' said Helen glumly. 'And maybe that was just a small party, sent on ahead.'

Claudio frowned. 'Well, whichever way you look at it, I think it would be a mistake to stay here very much longer. We were planning to leave anyway and this seems like the right time to go. We haven't collected as much equipment as I would have wished but ... well, it's a question of now or never.' He reached out and took Helen's hand. 'Here's what we'll do. We'll make them think that we've run out. I want you to collect up as much gear as you can carry, then head across the river here, making enough noise for the three of us. Martin and myself will hang back awhile and see if we can't leave them something to remember us by. You can manage for a moment?'

Helen nodded curtly. 'I guess so.'

'All right, move on out. Remember, plenty of noise, but keep your head down. I'll keep you covered from here.' He slapped her lightly on the shoulder and she moved quickly away on her hands and knees, keeping close to the side of the plane until she reached the spot where the equipment was stored. Martin watched as she swung a haversack over each shoulder and hefted the precious water container, which had been filled and sealed with an improvised cover. Thus burdened, she moved down to the water's edge and began to wade across, splashing the water with her spare hand as she went. Claudio had sighted his rifle on the surrounding bushes to give covering fire. He realized that the rebels might be thinking ahead of him, might already be waiting across the river; in which case, he would have sent Helen into a trap.

After what seemed ages, she was across the river and had clambered up the far bank, out of sight.

159

'Well, that went all right,' observed Martin. 'Now what?'

'Now we find ourselves a place to hide. How are you bearing up?'

'I'm OK, but I don't know if I'm going to be much use to you.' Martin waved his pistol clumsily. 'I'm a lousy shot.'

Claudio raised his eyebrows in disbelief. 'A man who carries so many pistols in his bag? That's hard to swallow.'

'I'm afraid it's true. I just seem to collect these things, that's all.'

Claudio seemed unperturbed. 'Well, we'll just have to wait until they're so close that you can't miss them.'

Martin grimaced. The idea was not comforting.

'Come on,' murmured Claudio. He indicated a small declivity, farther down the slope. 'We'll wait for them down there.' He began to edge his way towards the spot, pausing only to collect the machete where it lay beside José's body. He also reached into José's pocket and took back the lighter. Martin collected his carpet bag and followed, keeping low. They reached the gully and slid gratefully down, pressing their backs up against the hard earth wall. Once again, a deadly silence had settled. Across the river, there was no sign of Helen.

'She's keeping herself well hidden,' observed Claudio, more for his own reassurance than Martin's. He indicated the pistol that Martin was holding. 'You'd better check that it's loaded,' he said.

'Of course it's loaded. It's *always* loaded.' But he checked anyway, hoping that Claudio would not comment on his shaking hands.

'They won't all come out,' predicted Claudio. 'They'll send a few men to check first. We'll have to be sure of them. That means waiting until they're right on top of us. I'll hit your shoulder when the time comes. Just take out the man nearest to you.' He looked intently into Martin's eyes for a moment. 'And don't forget, it's my skin as well as yours; so don't foul up, OK?'

Martin nodded dumbly. He gazed down at the gun in his hands. It looked like a clumsy toy and for a moment he seriously doubted that it would fire. In all the years he'd owned it, he'd never used it, nor even cleaned it more than once or twice. Claudio was always oiling and polishing his guns. He wondered vaguely if he should ask for the spare rifle but somehow couldn't bring himself to speak.

The two men waited while an eternity passed. Nothing happened to break the terrible silence. Once, a large, beautifully coloured butterfly skimmed past their heads and went weaving away across the shallow water, a rare, gorgeous jewel of blue and yellow. In different circumstances, it would have been a pleasure to watch.

Martin opened his mouth to speak but froze as Claudio nudged him. He turned and saw that his companion was holding a finger to his lips. Then he jerked a thumb quickly over his shoulder to indicate that somebody was coming. Martin's stomach gave an abrupt lurch and he waited, his spirit wilting at the confrontation to come.

Now he could hear the footsteps, several sets of them, pounding dully on the earth as the men approached. They were running, pausing, moving on again. Already, they sounded terribly close. Martin wished that he could see them, assess their fire-power. He dreaded the moment when he and Claudio bobbed up from cover, to find, what? Twenty men and all of them armed? He turned his head slightly to stare at Claudio, who was sitting with his head tilted back, listening intently, a strange half-grin on his face as though he was enjoying this. The light of recognition dawned in his dark eyes and he glanced at Martin, held out three fingers in front of his face.

Now the ground seemed to shudder beneath the impact

of running feet. Martin could hear their voices whispering in Portuguese, fierce frantic instructions that he could not comprehend. The voices were strained, nervous. They too were obviously scared and that made Martin feel a little better about the ambush.

The element of surprise, he thought vaguely. That hollow clichéd phrase. How often had he heard it bandied about by self-styled soldiers of fortune? But crouched there in the dirt, with his mouth dry and his belly lurching, it seemed to stand for something. He wished to God Claudio would give him the signal and they could get on with it. The men were close now, so close that Martin could almost smell them. A piece of dry mud dislodged itself from the top of the gully and clattered down past Martin's ear. He had to stop himself from yelling out in fear. He looked again at Claudio, his eyes imploring action; but still Claudio's face wore that serene, almost casual expression. It was as though he was relishing this moment, wishing to prolong it.

A few more long silent seconds passed. Martin dared not even breathe now. Abruptly a change came over Claudio's face. His eyes widened, seeming almost to bulge from their sockets; and a look came over his face, an expression of crafty, animal cunning. Then his hand slapped Martin's shoulder with surprising force. The two men bobbed up from cover, their guns ready to fire.

What happened next took only fractions of a second, but to Martin seemed like a slow, clumsy melodrama, frozen in time, encapsulated in ice. His terrified eyes took in every tiny detail. Claudio had been right in his estimate. Three men stood at the edge of a gully, three men looking big in the sunlight, but their faces were small with terror. Each of them held a rifle, but none was aiming his weapon. '*Take out the man nearest to you*,' Claudio had said; and it was with an abrupt sense of sickness that Martin regarded the nearest man; who was

162

not a man at all, but a boy. A boy, maybe sixteen, seventeen years old. A thin, black-haired boy, his rangy body hidden in a man's shirt. His face wore an expression of unspeakable dread as he looked into the dirt-stained face only a few feet in front of him; for he was looking into the face of his killer and he knew it. The boy made a clumsy, futile move to bring his gun around but then the pistol in Martin's hand seemed to go off of its own accord. It bucked wildly and seemed a hundred miles away, along the long, lonely highway of his arm. He had not even aimed it properly. The bullet struck the boy in his thigh, shaking his body with the force of the blow. The boy swayed, stared down dully at the large ragged hole in the fabric of his trousers. He opened his mouth to scream, but then the gun, which Martin could not control, spewed lead a second time. This time, the bullet ploughed deep into the boy's throat, jerking his head back convulsively and smashing a bloody exit through the back of his head. His limbs become those of a marionette whose strings have suddenly been cut. He fell backwards to crash heavily against the dirt, where he lay shuddering violently while a dark slow pool spread outwards from beneath his shattered skull. From the corner of his eye, Martin was dimly aware of another body falling to his right; and when he glanced up he saw that the third man was running away, back towards the jungle. He had dropped his gun and was running wildly, desperately, flinging his arms backwards and forwards like a champion sprinter.

Claudio lifted his rifle and took slow, deliberate aim.

'Let him go,' croaked Martin dully. He felt sick, aware of the strange stench of blood in his nostrils. But Claudio simply shook his head and squeezed the trigger.

The blow struck the running man square in the middle of his back, but he continued to run for some considerable distance as though unaware of the wound.

Then, rapidly, he began to lose control of his limbs. He staggered drunkenly, wove from side to side, his arms flailing like a man on a tightrope losing a battle with the forces of gravity. His legs could now hardly hold him upright but he struggled defiantly onwards. Blood was pulsing from his mouth and Martin could hear quite distinctly that he was sobbing aloud, calling out a name that was incomprehensible. For Martin, this was the worst thing of all.

At last, the man's legs gave out. He pitched unceremoniously forward, his face scraping a bloody furrow in the river bank. But he was not finished yet. He began to crawl laboriously onwards, his gaze fixed resolutely on the trees ahead.

'For Christ's sake finish him off.'

'He's finished anyway,' announced Claudio. He clambered up the bank and snatched up one of the fallen rifles, then glanced quickly around. 'Let's get the hell away from here.'

Martin needed no second bidding. He turned and splashed his way into the shallows, still holding the pistol out in front of him as though it had been somehow infected with death. Claudio followed more cautiously, scanning the bank behind him for any signs of threat.

They found Helen crouching, grim-faced, on the other side of the river. She breathed a sigh of relief when she saw the two of them running towards her.

'The shots . . .' she murmured. 'I was so worried.'

'Everything's fine, princess,' Martin told her, but he couldn't mask the expression of dread in his eyes and his face was oddly pale beneath his suntan.

Helen recognized the look only too well. 'Welcome to the club.'

'We can't waste any time,' Claudio urged. He took one of the haversacks from Helen and swung it onto his own shoulders. He handed the rebel's rifle to Martin and

164

wielded his improvised machete. 'I'll lead,' he announced. 'Martin, you bring up the back and keep an eye open for anyone following. You see the least thing that makes you suspicious, sing out. This is going to be a hard slog, but I want to put as much distance between us and them as we can.' He stood for a moment gazing apprehensively at the green depths that lay ahead, a dark shadowy labyrinth of dank vegetation that seemed to wait greedily to swallow the three of them. There came to him the powerful conviction that none of them had a hope of surviving this journey; but he shrugged the notion off with quiet determination. 'Let's go,' he said simply.

Slowly, stumblingly, they began their long desperate trek.

The leader of the rebels moved cautiously down the river bank, sweating uncomfortably beneath his khaki clothes. He was a small, monkey-like man with a grizzled, sun-blackened face and ragged black beard that was flecked with grey. He had ventured out himself because he dared not risk any more of his men. What should have been a routine skirmish had backfired horribly; he had just passed the bodies of three of his best fighters. He crouched low, his pistol held out in front of him, while his brown eyes examined every inch of the ground. He could see the big hunched shape of José's body a short distance ahead.

The man cursed softly beneath his breath. Everything had gone wrong. First the plane and then José calling out like that, saying that he had everything under control . . . well, it was obvious that José had paid for that misconception. Five men dead at a time when they could ill afford to lose one.

He scrabbled forward a few more paces until he could survey both banks of the river. There were footsteps in the soft mud where somebody had recently crossed over.

They could be holed up anywhere on the far side now and there was every reason to believe that they were as well armed as they had implied. Of course, he could take his men some distance down river and work his way back to them, but . . .

The man frowned, mopped his brow on his shirtsleeve. This stinking place! He hated it with a venom he could never feel for the enemy. A low buzzing drone reached his ears and he saw that a thick mantle of insects was buzzing furiously around José's body. He grimaced, turned back to stare at the far bank of the river, weighing up the natural desire for vengeance against practicalities. He already had a lot of explaining to do to his captain and news that he had killed three survivors of the plane crash wouldn't do much to improve his chances. Five dead already and how many more trying to get across?

Besides, he assured himself, the fugitives were not going to tell their stories to anyone now. The jungle would see to that. They were making for some of the most inhospitable country in the whole of the Mato Grosso. At best they might hope to survive a week or so. It was unlikely that they knew in which direction they were heading. No doubt they would wander around in circles until they succumbed to hunger, fever or wild animals; and if they were really unlucky, the Xavantes would get to them first.

The rebel leader spat. Then, turning, made his way back into the jungle.

PART TWO

Before the Rains

Chapter 9

The light aeroplane came buzzing effortlessly in from the east, an incongruous red speck against the vastness of the afternoon sky. Its single engine made a pugnacious, mosquito-like hum.

At the controls, Paolo Estevez stifled a yawn as he gazed blankly down at mile upon mile of undulating green vegetation. He wondered vaguely what his chances were of finding what he was looking for. When he had set up his little charter business some months earlier he had anticipated an exciting and unpredictable career, but the reality had proved somewhat different: routine hops across the jungle carrying sweating businessmen to various destinations; occasional mail deliveries transporting sacks of boring letters to boring little people in Recife or Belém. Worse still, for the last few weeks there had been *no* work worth speaking of and Paolo's credit at the local bars had been stretched just about as far as it would go. So it had been with mixed feelings that he'd accepted this latest assignment. He doubted very much that he'd be able to find any trace of the missing plane but his client seemed prepared to put him in the air every day for the foreseeable future and that at least would settle some debts.

Paolo sighed. For him life was all too predictable. A slim, good-looking twenty-three-year-old, Paolo had never quite got over his dejection at being too young and of the wrong nationality for the last war. As a youth, raised on a steady diet of Clark Gable-Spencer Tracy movies, he had never had any doubts about his chosen vocation; and the fact that his old man worked as a baggage handler at Rio airport had provided the

169

connections that got him his pilot's licence at an unusually early age. He was by nature a loner and indeed there were few men who cared to be his friend; many maintained that Paolo had let his dark matinee-idol looks go to his head. He habitually wore his black hair quiffed and brillianteened in emulation of the cinema heroes he idolized and he had acquired a reputation with the young ladies that hung around the local bars as something of a Romeo. In truth, he did not care half as much for the ladies as he did for himself. It was only by inhabiting his own narcissistic dreamworld that he could make reality more agreeable. Reality had a habit of bringing him down to earth. Take this job, for instance. For once, he had thought, here was a task that was distinctly different from the usual routine; and hadn't there been an element of mystery in the way his new employer had approached him? He was to look for the missing DC3 but not along the established route, where a major search had already been made with no success. Paolo was to work around a map reference far inland, deep in the heart of the Mato Grosso, systematically checking off a series of squares on his charts . . . and that, of course, was where numbing reality crept back in.

Flying over a patchwork quilt of green and brown intersected here and there only by the sluggish yellow trail of a river was clearly nobody's idea of an exciting time. After only a few days of it Paolo was bored rigid and had already decided that he would stick with this imposition only until his debts were squared.

Reaching out, Paolo fiddled about with his radio receiver until he homed in on a rhumba station and the sounds of a big Latin-American band. He grinned, displaying a set of even white teeth and, glancing at the fuel gauge, consoled himself with the thought that in ten minutes or so he would have to turn back. No doubt his employer would be waiting to pester him with the usual questions. A decidedly persistent fellow, that one. Paolo didn't like him at all; but he had a healthy respect for the contents of the man's wallet.

Paolo eased the plane lower, gliding steadily downwards until its sleek belly was skimming dangerously over the treetops. The sound of the rhumba band filled his head with a frantic pulsing of maracas, the shrill jangle of guitars, the throaty bellow of horns. Below, the jungle sped away and back, a green blur of desolation. He couldn't say with any certainty that there were no survivors from that damned plane somewhere below, but gazing down into the primeval wilderness of swamp and forest, he couldn't hold out much hope of finding any of them alive.

They had been walking for three days. Claudio acknowledged the fact with a dull weary resignation as he moved slowly forward through the dank sunless reaches of the *selva*, his blistered hands stinging with every swing of the heavy machete. He had expected it to be an ordeal but that did not make the resulting misery any easier to bear. The ground over which they trudged was a treacherous tangle of ferns and roots which made them stumble again and again, and there was the constant misery of clouds of attendant insects that battened themselves onto every square inch of unprotected flesh. But most destructive of all was the heat, a damp, wearisome exhalation that seemed to exude from everything. It coaxed sweat from every pore of their bodies, saturating their clothes and making them weak and sluggish. The small amount of water they carried with them had to be severely rationed to a couple of mouthfuls each per day and there was now no more than an inch or so, sloshing tantalizingly in the bottom of the metal jug.

Each evening the three would stumble into a make-

171

shift camp and would have to undergo the tiresome ritual of collecting firewood for the night. Claudio was thankful that in the hurried flight from the campsite he had remembered to snatch up the lighter; otherwise the task of starting the fire would be unbearably complicated.

Hungry, exhausted, they would collapse beneath their woollen blankets and sleep like the dead; and each morning at first light, Claudio would creep grey-faced and shaking from his blanket and set off to hunt for breakfast. It was a rude reminder that they had strayed far from the relative bounty of the river banks. Here, in the sparser environs of the deep jungle, game was scarce. The first morning out, he came trudging back to camp with a solitary spider monkey, a skinny creature that made a miserable repast for three ravenous people. The second morning, he found nothing at all and the three were obliged to set off with their bellies groaning for food. Some hours later, they had chanced upon a large slow-moving tortoise. Its head was unceremoniously smashed by the butt of Claudio's rifle. When they made camp that evening, the tortoise was shelled and eaten, though it tasted every bit as revolting as it looked. The third morning their luck had seemed to change a little. Stalking bleary-eyed through the undergrowth, Claudio chanced upon two sleeping mucucaure birds and slaughtered them before they knew what was happening. Their delicate white flesh had made a welcome change from the tough greasy meat of monkeys. But water was still the main problem. Their dry cracking lips and swollen tongues craved it and every morning, they were driven to seizing handfuls of dew-soaked vegetation and pulling it frantically between their lips.

As time passed and still there was no river, a dull sense of resentment arose between Martin and Claudio. At first

172

nothing was said but the American became slower and more reluctant to carry out any tasks Claudio required of him. It was almost as though he were blaming Claudio for the situation he was now in, though he knew as well as anyone that it would have been folly to have remained with the plane. Claudio was also aware that some kind of bond was rapidly developing between Martin and Helen. She would not have readily admitted it, but she was attracted to the American, had been from the start. She still acted sullen and indifferent to him but every glance betrayed her true feelings. This worried Claudio, because he realized how easily he might become the 'outsider' of the group. For the time being, he was still the leader, but the orders he was compelled to give were guaranteed to make him unpopular. How long, he wondered, before Martin began to dispute his authority openly? If that happened, all sense of discipline would be lost; and then they were all as good as dead.

The rebels had not bothered to follow and somehow this was the most disconcerting thing of all. It was plain that they felt there was no danger of the fugitives making it out of this wilderness alive.

Claudio paused to examine his compass. They were constantly veering left or right of their intended course, so bearings had to be taken with irritating frequency. Martin and Helen lurched to a halt and stood swaying wearily. In the silence, Claudio sensed Martin's goading question.

'You sure that thing's working all right?' His voice was a hoarse stab of accusation, spat from between blistered lips.

'It's working,' replied Claudio quietly. He knew quite well that his own temper might easily rise to boiling point and was determined to avoid that at all cost.

'And how long before we reach this famous river of yours?'

'It's not *my* river; and you know perfectly well that I

cannot say how long it will take.' Claudio replaced the compass carefully in his breast pocket and buttoned the flap awkwardly with his swollen, bleeding fingers. He felt a great weariness pulling at his body but, gritting his teeth, he hefted the machete again and eased off in the new direction. A screen of lianas hung like a curtain across his vision and he hacked at them viciously, releasing some of his pent-up anger. The lianas fell aside and he moved on, his gaze fixed intently on the shadowy trails that lay ahead and oblivious to the fact that, for the moment at least, the others were not following him.

Martin licked his crusted lips and stared at the dark V of sweat that extended down the back of Claudio's shirt. 'That son of a bitch thinks we'll follow him till we drop,' he muttered blankly. 'I ought to . . .'

Helen reached out a hand and squeezed his shoulder. 'He's doing the best he can. It's not Claudio's fault that we're in this mess. We just have to go on. And hope.'

He glanced at her. She looked haggard and was burdened like a pack-horse, a huge haversack across her shoulders and the water jug clutched in her arms like the precious possession it really was.

'Sure,' he admitted. 'I know all that, but somehow, knowing it doesn't make it any easier. I just wonder how much longer we can keep this up.'

'Maybe the river is only half a mile away.'

'Yeah,' he murmured wearily. 'And maybe it's a hundred miles away. Maybe there *is* no river, did you ever think about that?'

Helen forced a hollow laugh. 'That's what I like about you, Mr Taggart. You're such an optimist.' She moved on again, stumbling in the direction Claudio had taken. 'Come on, we'd better shake a leg . . . the great white leader will be halfway to Belém by now.'

Martin nodded, but for the moment he remained where he was. He gazed upwards, wanting to see sky, but there

174

was only the dark, oppressive canopy of foliage. Here and there a solitary beam of light broke through but could do nothing more than fleck the greenery with the occasional swaying patch of dappled light. Martin felt crushed, suffocated by his surroundings, and in his bones he felt the first unmistakable shivers of fever; yet he knew Helen was right. There was nothing to do but go on. The only alternative was to lie down in the mud and die. No alternative at all. Meanwhile, he had the tarantula stone and he could still make plans for the money it would bring him. If anything could carry him through this mess, it was those plans. He would hold them constantly in his mind, go over them, reconsider, refine them; and thus he would continue the mechanical action of walking, placing one blistered foot in front of the other.

With a sigh, he readjusted the haversack on his raw back, slung the heavy rifle across his right shoulder and set off after his companions. Somewhere, away in the distance, a macaw shrieked and there was a brief flapping of wings overhead. Then, as before, the *selva* was as quiet as death.

The plane's wheels touched concrete with a slight thud and as the tail eased down onto the runway, Paolo Estevez throttled back hard, slowing the four-seater Beech. He coasted to the left, off the main runway, and taxied slowly past the series of buildings that lined this back stretch of the airport. To his right, he passed the low concrete building carrying the SA logo. In there, he knew, a receptionist and clerk still hung on in the hope of some good news. Paolo could see their white staring faces watching his arrival from the grubby windows. Mike Stone's charter operation wasn't a big deal by any stretch of the imagination, but to Paolo it had always represented the next rung of the ladder; now, it was beginning to look as though the founder of the unfortunately named Stone

Airlines would never be coming back. Paolo noticed the familiar figure of Willy Bordern, Mike's mechanic and partner, hurrying from the direction of the aircraft hangar. He was waving his arms so Paolo let the engine idle down and flipped open the window as he eased the plane to a halt.

Willy's already grizzled face seemed to have aged several years over the last few days. He gazed up at Paolo entreatingly.

'Anything, kid?'

'No, Senhor Bordern, I'm sorry.'

'Goddamn.' Willy shook his head, stood there uncertainly a moment, his hands deep in the pockets of his overalls. 'I er ... see your *friends* are in to visit.' He jerked a thumb in the direction of the ramshackle hut that served as Paolo's headquarters. A huge black Cadillac was parked outside.

Paolo nodded. 'I saw the car from the air.'

'Paolo, what's the angle with those guys? Think they know something the regular authorities don't?'

Paolo shrugged. 'I couldn't say, Senhor Bordern. All I know is they pay my time and they tell me where they want me to look. The way things are, I'm glad of any work, even if it's only what you call a ... wild-duck chase.'

'Goose.'

'Huh?'

'A wild-goose chase.'

'Yeah, well, whatever, I figure there's no law against it. Anyhow, I'd better coast on over and give them my report.'

'Listen, kid, you find out anything, you be sure and let me know, huh?'

'I will, Senhor Bordern. Don't lose hope.'

Paolo watched as Willy turned and slouched slowly back in the direction of the hangar. It was a tough break for him, Paolo decided, but what could he do about it? People wanted miracles, that was the trouble.

He gunned the engine and rolled on again until he reached his own 'offices', a beaten-up hangar and the dilapidated wooden shack which stood alongside. His own mechanic, Miguel, came slowly out from the gloom of the hangar with an indignant expression on his fat face that told Paolo the noise of the plane had just woken him up. Miguel's habitual resting place was a hammock strung across one of the corners of the hangar and he slept there whenever he could avoid doing something else. He was lazy, rude and generally incompetent and if Paolo hadn't owed the man six months' back wages he would probably have fired him. Miguel stood there now, scratching his backside sullenly as the pilot flipped open the door and jumped to the ground.

'*Hola*, Miguel! I'm back.'

Miguel looked unimpressed. So? his eyes seemed to say.

Paolo frowned. In every American movie he'd seen about fliers, the pilot and his mechanic were supposed to have a great relationship, all wise-cracking one-liners, while the mechanic worked valiantly against the clock to keep the pilot's plane airworthy; but Miguel had obviously never seen any of those films. He just stood there, a great resentful lump, yawning and scratching his ass.

Paolo sighed. 'The starboard flap's a little stiff. Check it over for me, will you?'

'My *pleasure*, Senhor Estevez.' Miguel gave a mocking little bow and sneered in the knowing way that only a man who is owed a lot of money can. 'By the way your *friends* are –'

'Yes, yes, I know!' Paolo waved Miguel to silence and strode haughtily past him in the direction of the hut. He felt abruptly rather irritated. Both Willy and Miguel had used the same sly, insinuating tone when they said that

177

word; *friends*. What they were both trying to imply was that Paolo's employers were somewhat short of being model citizens. Well, perhaps they were but what was that to do with Paolo? He was doing his job and he was being paid for it. It was as simple as that. These people were no friends of his.

He moved past the long predatory shape of the black Cadillac. One of the men sat inside, behind the wheel. His hat was tipped forward over his eyes and he appeared to be asleep but as Paolo drew level with the open window, he said, '*Boa tarde, senhor.*'

Paolo nodded but did not check his pace. He reached out and, opening the door of the hut, stepped inside. As he had expected, the other two men had made themselves as comfortable as possible within. The tall blond European who called himself Schiller was lounging against the wall at the far end. He wore an immaculate dark grey suit and a silk fedora hat. As was his usual custom, he was picking at his fingernails with the blade of a pearl-handled stiletto knife. He glanced up as Paolo entered and the pilot felt an involuntary chill run through him as he looked briefly into Schiller's piercing grey eyes. They were cold, mirthless, devoid of any expression. Somehow, they were the eyes of an old, old man set in a lean, sallow face that could have been no more than thirty or thirty-five years of age. The eyes scrutinized him for a few moments and then flicked away, returned to the careful study of his fingernails.

Schiller's patron had commandeered the one chair in the room, a rickety wooden affair that looked as though it might not be able to cope with the man's considerable bulk. His outstretched legs rested on Paolo's desk. Dressed in a crumpled panama suit, he sat regarding Paolo, his chubby hands resting across his prodigious belly. There was the powerful but by now familiar smell of lavender water, and a look of inquiry in Charles

178

Caine's deepset, piggy eyes.

Paolo shook his head. 'Again, nothing, Senhor Caine. Only jungle and more jungle.'

Caine shrugged, grinned and displayed rows of perfect teeth. 'Ah well. It is early days yet. We must not expect too much, too soon. Show me on the chart the area you have covered today.' He swung his heels down from the desk and the chair creaked protestingly.

Obligingly, Paolo moved around the desk to stand beside him. He searched in the pocket of his leather flying jacket, found the well-worn stub of a pencil and, leaning forward, sketched a small square in place beside the three already there. He indicated the vast expanse of untouched map that lay on either side.

'I'm afraid it may be hopeless,' he confessed. 'The sheer scale of the country is against us. We could go on like this week after week and still there would be no guarantee of finding a thing. The official search party with all their equipment have not come up with anything.'

Caine gave a low grunt of contempt. 'That does not surprise me in the least! The "official" search as you call it has shown a singular lack of imagination. All they have done is go over and over the flight path to Recife, expecting no doubt to find some wreckage, but if the plane really had crashed along that route, somebody would be sure to have seen and reported the incident. No, our information suggests that the plane is somewhere in this area.' He tapped the squares with a fat index finger around which an ostentatious diamond was wrapped. Then he glanced up at Schiller. 'I trust my information is good.'

Paolo frowned. 'Well, you may be right. But you must try and appreciate my position in this matter. I mean . . . I've been flying for you for three days now and I'm still in the dark about what's going on. First you come to me and tell me I'm to look for the missing plane. So naturally enough, I tell you that it will be like looking for a needle in a haystack. It doesn't matter, you say, look anyway; and besides, it's not just a *plane* I'm looking for and I'll know what it is when I see it.' He spread his hands in a gesture of hopelessness. 'Now tell me, Senhor Caine, what am I to think? I could go on flying blind like this for months.'

Caine shrugged. 'Is it so necessary to *know* everything, Paolo? Is it not enough that I pay you what you ask and that I'm prepared to keep you employed as long as it takes?'

Paolo shook his head. He opened the drawer of his desk, took out a half-empty bottle of *cachaça* and a grubby glass. He poured himself a drink and gulped at it eagerly. 'We don't *have* very long,' he pointed out. 'We have at best three weeks before the rains start. After that I can't do any more flying; the plane will be laid up in the hangar till January. And if there *are* any survivors out there now, they'll be finished, as good as dead the moment it begins. So you see, it's in your interests to tell me as much as you can, anything that might help me to know what the hell I'm supposed to be doing.' He waved the *cachaça*. 'I've got another glass if anybody wants a drink.' Both men declined with a curt shake of the head. 'Suit yourselves,' he muttered and topped up his own glass. Drink had always been his weakness and he made no secret of it.

Now Caine turned and glanced at Schiller, who was still absorbed in the finicky task of cleaning his fingernails. 'What about it, Otto?' he demanded. 'You're absolutely sure that this is the right area? You haven't made some mistake?'

Schiller looked up, his eyes still expressionless. Carefully he folded the blade of his knife and slipped it into the breast pocket of his jacket. He strode over to the table and glanced perfunctorily at the map.

180

'You know I cannot be precise,' he said in a strange, clipped tone. 'But it is somewhere in this vicinity, you can depend on that. Perhaps tomorrow, if he tries a little more to the west ...'

'But I still don't understand how you can *know* where the wreckage is ... Unless ... unless maybe you're expecting to find it in one piece!' The slight narrowing of Caine's eyes told him that he was on to something. 'Is that it?' he persisted. 'You think the plane's been hijacked or something? But how could that be possible? There's nowhere for it to land!'

Caine and Schiller exchanged glances then, abruptly, Caine gave an unpleasant snicker and a brief nod of mock capitulation.

'Very well, Paolo, I can see that it's high time we filled you in. It's not that we intended to keep anything from you, you understand; we simply deemed it wiser to tell as few people about this as possible. You see, it's quite likely that we may be way off beam with our suspicions and it would be unfortunate to build up everybody's hopes.'

'Yes ... yes, I can see that.'

'And I trust we can count on your complete discretion?'

'Of course. Go ahead.'

'Otto, perhaps you'd like to tell Paolo here what we know.'

Schiller shot Caine a look of sheer doubt, as though he suspected the wisdom of doing such a thing.

'Go ahead,' Caine reassured him. 'Paolo here is a smart boy and a *wise* one. I know he wouldn't do anything to betray any confidence.'

Schiller gave a small, barely perceptible nod. Then he began, talking slowly in that same curious clipped tone, his voice as flat and unemotional as his expression. As he talked, he slipped one hand into the pocket of his jacket to play absent-mindedly with something he kept there; something that rattled.

181

'I have not been in Mr Caine's employ for very long; only a matter of days, in fact, though for a few months before I was working for a friend of his, another patron. Mr Caine made me a better offer.'

Charles Caine chuckled gleefully. 'Poor Enrico,' he said with exaggerated concern in his voice. 'So sure of his employees' *trust*. I always told him that money was the only real consideration that any *pistoleiro* has!'

Schiller did not acknowledge this statement. He continued with his story. 'The man who previously held my position was called Agnello. He was murdered by an American called Taggart, Martin Taggart, who, as fate would have it, tried to escape by boarding the missing DC3. Mr Caine is most anxious to see the man brought to justice.'

Paolo nodded. 'I see . . . but isn't all this effort going to be a waste of time if the plane blew up somewhere over the jungle?'

'I don't think it did. But to explain why I think that, it is necessary to go back over three months, before I began working for the patron from whom Mr Caine . . . persuaded me. At that time I was very much a free agent. I had acquired a certain reputation around Rio for being a useful sort of fellow in a tight spot. I was good with the gun and with the knife and there are always people ready to employ such men.'

'Mercenaries,' said Paolo quietly.

For the first time, the ghost of a smile played across Schiller's lips. 'If you care to call it that. I have personally never had much time for the word; such a sanctimonious expression. Anyway, as I was saying, about this time I was approached by a man who was looking to recruit a number of these, er . . . mercenaries, as you call them. It wasn't really my style but I was interested enough to look into the matter. It turned out that this fellow was a rebel, a supporter of Getulio Vargas. Vargas had just been

182

deposed and this fellow was looking for men with strong political convictions. I told him flatly that he should talk money or forget the whole thing, and it became clear that he was quite desperate for help. In his panic he disclosed things he would have been wiser keeping to himself. He told me that his people were holed up east of the Serra da Roncodor, the so-called Snoring Mountains, and that they were at work on an airstrip in the middle of the jungle. Their plan, it seems, was to hijack a passenger plane and they wanted me to be one of the two men to carry out this task. But ... they had no money up front, just a lot of promises. "*When* we are in power," they said, "*when* the plane is delivered". "I am a businessman," I told them. "You can take all those political convictions and stick them up your asses." So, I told this fellow that I was not interested and he went away. Later, he must have got cold feet about telling me too much. A couple of nights later, he sneaked into my hotel room with the intention of shutting me up for good. I had expected something like this and I was ready for him. Instead, I shut him up.'

Schiller made a quick sawing motion across his throat with one finger. He was not bragging of his exploits but simply mentioning the matter in an offhand sort of way, as other men might discuss the weather. For the first time, Paolo began to realize just what kind of a man this was. The knowledge should have made him feel distinctly uneasy. On the contrary, it thrilled him, made him feel as though he was a party to momentous events.

'The arm of coincidence has a long reach,' observed Schiller. 'When Mr Caine here told me about Taggart, I naturally put two and two together. Allowing the rebels three months or so to complete the airstrip and ferry in the necessary fuel, it would be about this time that they would make their move.'

'So you figure that the plane's still in one piece, on that airstrip?'

'It seems a likely bet.'

'Hmm.' Paolo stroked his chin for a moment. 'All right then, supposing you're right . . . supposing in a day or so I do find the airstrip and the plane sitting there? Then what? I can't just land and wish them *boa tarde*, now can I?'

Caine giggled. 'I think that would be very unwise, Paolo . . . unless of course, you would like your skinny little ass blown out from under you. No, you just concern yourself with finding the airstrip and the plane, if it's there. Then report back to us. We'll make any necessary arrangements.'

Paolo took a long swallow of *cachaça*, feeling the warmth of it blossom in his stomach like sweet fire. It gave him a false sense of bravado and this in turn kindled into a determination that he was not going to be saddled with the role of messenger boy. He had seen this situation played out in so many American movies that he knew every role by heart. Why should he not adopt one to his own ends? Almost without thinking, he slipped into character, speaking in the terse gruff tones of the stars he idolized.

'Senhor Schiller here said something about this guy Taggart having killed one of your boys, Senhor Caine. Surely you're not going to tell me that you're going to all this trouble on account of revenge.'

Caine's eyes narrowed to suspicious slits. 'Why not, Paolo? It's a powerful emotion, you know, and Agnello was a dear friend of mine . . .'

'Excuse me, but I don't go for that! It's very likely that this guy you want is already dead, killed by the hijackers. It seems to me that for somebody to spend so much time and money there has to be something more. I think maybe it's time you levelled with me all down the line.'

By the uncomfortable silence that followed, Paolo knew he'd pushed his finger onto an exposed nerve. For an instant, Caine's sweaty face registered an expression of outrage and his little eyes glinted dangerously. Nervously, Paolo fumbled in his breast pocket for a packet of cigarettes. He extracted one, placed it between his lips and, taking out a box of matches, managed to ignite the thing on his fifth attempt. All the time, he was aware of the two men watching him silently, but when he blew out a cloud of smoke and glanced up he saw that Caine was smiling at him.

'Very astute, Paolo. Very astute!' Caine glanced back at Schiller and winked. 'You have to hand it to this boy, eh Otto? He's a sharp one! A fellow would have to get up very early in the morning to put one over on such a sharp lad.' He took a silk handkerchief from his breast pocket and mopped at his face, which was perspiring heavily in the unventilated confines of the hut. 'Yes Paolo, you are, of course, quite correct. There *is* something in it for me. But I don't think you need concern yourself with that.'

He gazed intently at Paolo, a half smile on his face, as though daring the young man to continue with his ploy. The pilot shrugged and slowly refilled his glass. He kept his own face expressionless but his mind was doing some rapid thinking. So far so good; but dare he push his luck? He licked his lips, swallowed another mouthful, waiting once again for the resulting glow to fire him up. 'Well now, Senhor Caine,' he chose his words carefully, 'a moment ago you said you were going to fill me in on the details. Why stop there?'

'Paolo . . .' Caine frowned and a look of mild irritation came into his eyes. 'I hired you to do a job and I'm paying you well for it. That seems a perfectly fair arrangement to me.'

'Yes, but I've been thinking . . .' Paolo paused for effect now, vaguely aware that he was steering into dangerous waters. His argument, on the other hand, was a sound one; he was fairly sure of that. Engrossed as he was in his own thoughts, he was unaware of a brief interplay between the other two. Schiller's hand had slipped into the breast pocket of his jacket to fondle the pearl handle of his knife and he was looking inquiringly at Caine; but the big man gave just the slightest shake of his head before leaning towards Paolo.

'Go on my boy. What have you been thinking?'

'Just this. You depend on me to do the airwork right now. I've been over it in my mind and it occurs to me that I'm the only one who can. I'm the only operation small enough and independent enough to undertake that kind of work ... at least, the only one here in Rio. Oh, you might find another in Recife or Sao Paulo but that would take time ... and you don't have a lot of time, do you, Senhor Caine?'

Caine shrugged, then nodded. 'I'll admit you have a point there. So ...?'

'So I was thinking. I'm a pretty important link in this whole operation. I'm doing the donkey work and I'm being paid peanuts for it. Now, if I do locate the plane, whether it's crashed or in one piece, you're still going to need my help to get to it, isn't that right?'

'Yes, I suppose so.'

'And if I did find it, there would be nothing to stop me flying straight to the authorities and telling them of its whereabouts before contacting you.'

'Once again, you have a point.'

Paolo nodded, grinned. He was now convinced that his plan would work. 'So what I had in mind is a partnership. Not a big deal. I'm not a greedy man. Let's say, a straight twenty per cent cut of whatever it is that you're so anxious to get your hands on. Whatever it is, it has to be something that this man Taggart is carrying with him ... money, diamonds, cocaine. All I want is twenty per cent of it. How does that sound to you?'

There was another long, seemingly interminable silence.

Caine leaned back in his creaking chair. He had put the tips of his fingers together and was tapping them rhythmically against his pursed lips. He actually seemed to be giving the matter serious consideration. Paolo inhaled on his cigarette, blew out a cloud of smoke which hung in thick tendrils on the windless air. He turned and glanced across at Schiller, then looked away again, not enjoying the way the European was studying him, much as a butcher must examine a carcass before he begins to slice it up.

'And if we don't find anything?' murmured Caine at last.

'Then we call it quits. I go on being poor and you go back to whatever it is you do for a living. End of story.'

Caine smiled sweetly. 'Well, Paolo, it seems as though you have thought everything out; and, of course, you are quite correct in your assumptions. I *do* need your help. So after proper consideration, what else can I say but . . . we have a deal?' He held out his ring-encrusted hand and Paolo let out an audible sigh of relief as he shook it.

'We . . . are . . . partners then?' he ventured, hardly daring to believe that his terms had been accepted.

'Partners,' echoed Caine warmly. 'It's as you said, Paolo. You *are* doing all the donkey work. I'm a fair man. I believe a fellow should get what he deserves; isn't that right, Otto?'

Schiller smiled coldly. 'That's right, Mr Caine,' he said.

'One thing occurs to me, Paolo . . . you . . . wouldn't have found the airstrip already by any chance? You wouldn't be holding out on me until you could mention this little deal of yours?'

'Oh no, Senhor Caine, not for a moment! I've been strictly on the level with you, believe me. And the moment I find anything, anything at all, you can bet I'll come straight to you. I'll work a lot better now that I've got a stake in this myself.'

187

Caine nodded. 'Be sure that you do. Like I said, I'm a fair man but I *hate* anybody holding out on me. Remember that.' For an instant, his smile disappeared to be replaced by an expression of warning. Then it was gone, the eyes were jolly again, the lips curved into that familiar oily smile. He glanced at his wristwatch casually as though he had dismissed the incident from his mind. 'Well, we'd better be on our way. I have some business to attend to in the city. You'll go up tomorrow of course?'

'Just try and stop me, Senhor Caine! I promise you, you won't be sorry about this.'

'I know I won't.' Caine reached suddenly into his jacket pocket and Paolo stiffened involuntarily; but when Caine brought his hand out again it was holding nothing more threatening than a brown paper envelope. 'Your fee for today's work,' he announced quietly and slapped the envelope down onto the desk. Then he eased his bulk up out of the chair, straightened his jacket and headed for the door. Schiller followed, but not before throwing a glance in Paolo's direction, a look of cold, meticulous scrutiny that made the younger man feel decidedly edgy. The two men went out into the long shadows of the descending tropical twilight and Paolo watched as they climbed into the back seat of the Cadillac and the sleek black convertible rolled away, as smooth and powerful as a metal panther. One day, thought Paolo, maybe I will own such a car. He had been rash and headstrong to pull such a stunt on Caine and yet it looked as though he had got away with it. Suddenly, life was spicy and exciting. He was on his way. Sure, he would have to play things very carefully. At this stage of the game, Caine and Schiller had need of his talents and they knew it. Later, when he was no longer indispensable, he would have to watch out for himself.

He leaned over the desk and opened the single drawer. The pistol was there where it had always been, huge, ancient, riddled with rust. Paolo had bought it from a pawnshop one night when he'd had a little too much *cachaça*. He took it out now, hefted it, sighted along it at an imaginary target. He cocked the action, squeezed the trigger and enjoyed the heavy click as the hammer snapped down. Yes, he'd need to hang onto this now he was a big operator. He slipped the gun into the pocket of his flying jacket and patted the bulge with an air of satisfaction. He'd have to remember to buy some bullets next time he was in town.

He reached for his bottle and poured the last few drops of *cachaça* into the glass, then folded the brown envelope and pushed it into the breast pocket of his shirt. Tonight, he might just drive into the city and do a little celebrating. He'd got the taste for drinking now and it had been a long time since he'd called at Orlando's Bar. But he would not drink so much that his tongue began to wag. That would not be professional; and besides, he had his partners to think of.

He tilted the glass against his lips and savoured the warm taste on his tongue. The last mouthful was always the best. Beyond the window night was falling fast.

Martin held the single drop of warm brackish water in his mouth for as long as he could, knowing full well that it was probably the last he would get for a long, long time. He rolled it over his swollen tongue and in an instant it was no more than a memory, as if it had simply evaporated in the desperate heat of his parched throat. He gulped, swore miserably and, passing the jug across to Helen, watched enviously as she took her own meagre share of the contents.

She looked across at Claudio, who was hunched intently over a pile of dry sticks, coaxing a tiny flame at its base to spread upwards and outwards. 'There's a mouthful left for you,' she croaked.

He nodded but did not look up. 'I'll have it in a minute,' he replied. 'I just want to get this fire going.'

'Now *that's* will-power,' Martin observed mockingly. 'The brave leader denies himself sustenance so that the mission may go on.'

Claudio glanced up at Martin for an instant but said nothing. He leaned closer to the flames and blew gently, fanning the fire until it burned more fiercely. He kept this up for several minutes until the flames had taken a good hold. Then he leaned back, wiped his forehead on the sleeve of his shirt and reached out to take the water jug.

'Enjoy it,' growled Martin bitterly. 'It's all we've got.'

Claudio slammed down the empty jug and glowered back at him. 'I took no more than my share!'

'Didn't say otherwise.'

'No, but you *implied* it. I'm tired of your implications, Taggart.' Claudio snatched up a stick and poked angrily at the fire, sending a flurry of sparks dancing skywards. 'Anyhow,' he muttered, 'before much longer we may be getting all the water we can handle.'

'You . . . you think we're near the river?' inquired Helen hopefully.

'No, unfortunately that's not what I meant. But I've got a feeling it might rain.'

'Rain?' Martin stared at him disbelievingly. 'Are you trying to be funny? Or maybe you know something we don't. Sure, that's it! Claudio's been listening to the weather forecasts on his secret radio.'

'It's just a feeling I have,' persisted Claudio, stolidly attempting to ignore Martin's jibes. 'There's something in the air; it's hard to explain in words. An electricity. Of course, I could be wrong . . .'

'Damned right you could!' Martin's voice was loud now, on the point of boiling over into outright anger. 'You had a *feeling* about the river, Goddammit and it's been four fucking days of promises so far! You've got a feeling! Christ, I trust your judgment like I'd trust a snake to share my bed-roll!'

'Martin, for God's sake stop needling him!' Helen, sensing a potential fight, stepped quickly in to referee. 'You've got to get it in your head, it's not Claudio's fault. Can't you see that he's doing his best? If we start to fight amongst ourselves, what chance do we have?'

Martin stared at her wildly, shock on his face as though he had somehow been betrayed by her words; but then a softer expression came into his eyes as he realized how unreasonable he was being. He shook his head, buried his face in his hands.

'Yeah . . .' he groaned. 'Sure . . .' He took his hands away and glanced sheepishly at Claudio. 'Hell, I'm sorry,' he admitted gruffly. 'I don't know what's gotten into me, I just get so angry all the time. I guess I feel useless depending on you for every damned thing; and meanwhile here we all are, hungry, half-dead from thirst and just about too weak to stand up. I don't see how we're supposed to keep going.'

'We've *got* to,' snapped Claudio fiercely. He leaned forward across the fire and the others could see the strange fanatical gleam in his eyes. He was staring back at them but it was as though his gaze was blazing right through them. 'We've come this far; we can do the rest. We *can* do the rest. We can. But we have to keep together, that's all. Together we're strong, and just think . . . think of the distance we've put behind us already. Just remind yourselves that every step . . . every single step . . . takes us nearer and nearer to the river. And while you walk, pray that it will rain tomorrow.'

God help us, thought Helen horrified. *He's cracking up.*

'Rain . . . yes, that's all we want. Rain. Too early for the real thing and besides, that wouldn't be good for us. All we need is a shower, just enough to fill that water jug there.' He giggled, tilted back his head to stare up at the

191

vast slab of blackness that hung over them. 'There's something happening up there. I feel it. Electricity. Don't you feel it too?'

They could only stare back blankly at him, too exhausted to feel anything but fear and the need of sleep.

'Trust me,' he concluded quietly; and then, seeming to forget them, he hunched his body a little nearer to the fire and sat staring thoughtfully into the yellow flames as the long night began.

The black Cadillac purred effortlessly along a tree-lined street, its headlights knifing the darkness ahead. Leaning back against the luxurious leather upholstery in the back, Charles Caine allowed himself a little chuckle.

'The little lush,' he giggled gleefully. 'Did you hear him, Otto? Wasn't it a performance?' He mimicked Paolo Estevez's distinctive accent. 'What I had in mind, Senhor Caine, was a partnership. Not a big deal, I'm not a *greedy* man ...' He tilted back his head and laughed unpleasantly. 'I could scarcely believe it. There he sat, a snot-nosed little drunkard and he's feeding me lines that he must have memorized from some cheap detective novel!'

Schiller nodded but his gaunt face remained expressionless. 'I don't know why you didn't let me take care of him back there,' he muttered. 'The kid is getting too big for his boots and, what's more, he's an amateur. I hate amateurs.'

'I couldn't agree with you more! But in a way, he *does* have a point. He's the one with the plane and right now we need a plane. So ...' He shrugged. 'For now, we go along with the game. When we have no further use for him, I shall very much enjoy watching you kill him.' He took his handkerchief from his breast pocket and mopped his clammy forehead and neck. 'Gods, this heat!' He glanced ruefully at Schiller who seemed quite unperturbed by the humidity. 'Don't you ever sweat?'

'I'm cold-blooded,' replied Schiller, with the faintest trace of a smile. 'You know, the kid did make an interesting observation.'

'Oh. What was that?'

'He said something about revenge not being reason enough for all this effort; he thought the money must mean more to you. But I wonder. You're a very wealthy man already, Mr Caine. So maybe *it* is the vengeance that drives you.'

Caine shrugged. 'Well, Otto, as you know, Agnello was very dear to me. We had a very ... *special* kind of relationship.' In saying this, Caine allowed his plump right hand to settle on Schiller's knee. His companion's expression did not falter for a second but his lean body stiffened, became rigid with distrust. After a few moments Caine allowed the hand to slide back into his own lap. 'Yes, a very special relationship. He was almost like a son to me. I brought him up from nowhere, just another poor *caboclo* trying to make his way in the world. I made him everything that he was and in the end he would have done anything for me ...' Caine shook his head, and his voice, for once, was tinged with something that sounded remarkably like sincerity. 'I misjudged the American. I felt sure Agnello could handle him alone. But I was wrong and it was Agnello who paid the price for my carelessness. So yes, vengeance *is* important to me. As for the money, well, like you said; I am a wealthy man. But no matter how much money a man has, he will always crave more. It's like a sickness somehow, the more you have, the more you want.' He turned his head a little and stared thoughtfully at the low ramshackle dwellings of adobe and corrugated iron that lined this part of the road. On each porch there was the dull glow of a hurricane lamp and around each pool of light families of poor ragged farmers and plantation workers were seeking relief from the oppressive heat indoors. They watched the rich man's

193

car glide past with envious eyes. Around the lamps, dark clusters of moths flapped in frantic agitation.

'There is a third reason,' announced Caine unexpectedly. 'One that to me is most important of all.'

'Oh?' Schiller was intrigued by this statement. 'And what is that?'

'The American I'm seeking. He thought he could get the better of me. He thought that by putting distance between us he could escape retribution. But nobody ever gets the better of me, Otto. Nobody. You'd do well to remember that.' Caine's eyes were now burning with a strange fanatical gleam and his voice was hoarse with menace. 'I've met this man Taggart. He's not a hero, not the sort to take a risk if it can be avoided; and yet he's killed two men to defend the diamond he has found. It must be worth a very great deal for him to do that. But you see, Otto, that diamond is half mine! Taggart has stolen it from me and that I cannot . . . I will not allow.'

Schiller nodded slowly, as though he understood. 'Well, I hope, after all your efforts, that the American is still alive.'

'Oh, he's alive! Never doubt that! I feel it in my guts. The thought of it sticks in my throat every time I take a breath. He's out there somewhere, with *my* diamond, and I'll find that bastard if I have to spend every penny I own. Oh yes, Otto, I'm going to find him . . . shall I tell you why?' Abruptly he was gazing slyly at his companion, a mocking expression in his little eyes. 'Shall I tell you why it is only a matter of time before I turn the tables on this . . . maggot?'

Schiller was rapidly losing interest. 'If you must.'

'Because, Otto, I am a clever man. A very clever man. I take a great deal of trouble and I use my brains. Nobody ever out-thinks Charles Caine. Another thing, people who come to work for me . . . it's funny, but somehow, they never want to leave. Isn't that right, Paco?' Caine leaned

194

forward and clapped the driver heartily on the shoulder.

'That's right, Senhor Caine.' The reply was too quick, too mechanical to be entirely convincing.

'Yes, Paco knows! He joined up with me, what, three years ago? He only meant to stay a month or so and yet, here he is, driving my car just the same as always.' He giggled, turned back to Schiller. 'Let me make a little prediction, Otto. In three years time, *you* will still be working for me.'

Schiller laughed, shook his head. 'Oh no, Mr Caine, that is hardly possible. We made no contract at any time. I only said that I would come into your employ for as long as it suited *me*. I thought you understood that I like to be free to move around from time to time. I had a similar arrangement with your friend Enrico. Being in one job all the time, it stifles me.'

Caine grinned, nodded. He seemed to be enjoying some private joke. 'Indeed, Otto, I remember the arrangement we made. But that, my friend, is about to be superseded. I want you as a *permanent* replacement for Agnello.'

'I'm sorry but that will simply not be possible.'

'Oh, but it will, it will! You see, Otto, I do my homework. I've been doing some on you for quite some time, long before I engaged your highly specialized services. The very first time Enrico introduced you to me, I made an observation about you. I noted to myself that you were almost certainly an ex-military man. There's some strange quality about a fellow who wears a uniform for much of his life. Afterwards, he never looks quite comfortable in civilian clothes.'

'Uniform? What are you talking about?'

'I think you know, Otto . . . or perhaps I should call you by your real name. Your *German* name.'

'Have you gone mad? I'm a Swiss citizen and, what's more, I have a passport to prove it.'

Caine gave a short derisive laugh. 'Your passport? My

195

dear fellow, you'll have to do better than that. Why, for the right price, I could get myself a perfectly convincing *Chinese* passport made up in Rio, but it wouldn't make me Chinese. Otto, you are as Swiss as I am.' Caine reached into one of the pockets of his jacket and brought out a small black and white photograph which he tossed contemptuously into Schiller's lap. 'Have a look at that,' he suggested. 'I think you will find it amusing.'

Schiller sat very still, gazing down at it. 'What is it?' he asked suspiciously.

'Pick it up,' demanded Caine, a new hardness in his voice. 'Go ahead, take a good look. It's very interesting.'

Slowly Schiller picked up the photograph. In the dark interior of the car, he had to peer at it very closely in order to make out the image. It was a picture of several German officers dressed in the distinctive black uniform of the *Schutzstaffel*. They were young men, all of them, poised arrogantly on the steps of some huge building. Behind them, between two great marble columns, a vast banner hung emblazoned with a swastika. Schiller felt a sense of dread.

'Where . . . did you get this?'

'It doesn't matter *where*,' retorted Caine. 'The simple fact is that I *have* got it and that one of those young lions, Otto . . .' He tapped the photograph with his finger. 'This handsome young fellow here . . . is you. Oh, I have to admit somebody has done a good job on your face; plastic surgery or whatever they call it these days. But there are things about a man that surgery cannot alter. His eyes, his frame, the way that he stands. You are not Otto Schiller at all. You are Manfred Guessler, a prominent member of the SS and one of Heinrich Himmler's favourite angels of death. You were personally responsible for a great many political executions, the torture and extermination of vast numbers of Jews, you masterminded some interesting medical experiments at

Auschwitz during the year and a half you spent there, and where you also acquired the rather dubious title of *Doctor* Guessler; a bizarre honour for a man whose experiments were chiefly centred upon finding out how much pain a human being could endure. Your colleagues at Auschwitz had their own affectionate nickname for you. They called you "MacHeath" because of your curious habit of passing over the scalpel in favour of a stiletto blade. It's also presumably the place where you acquired a liking for those strange little trophies that you carry with you everywhere you go.' Caine reached into the breast pocket of his jacket, took out a slim cigarette case and flipped it open. He extracted a cigarette and lit it with an ostentatious gold lighter. He inhaled, blew out a slow cloud of smoke. 'There's more,' he announced at last. 'I was very thorough. I shall continue if you like . . .?'

Schiller shook his head briefly. 'I think you've made your point. Am I to take it that you intend to blackmail me?'

Caine laughed briefly. 'Nothing so crude, Otto. Of course, there are many people who would be interested to know all about you, but you can rest assured, your secret is entirely safe with me . . . as long as I remain in a good frame of mind. The only thing guaranteed to put me out of sorts is the thought of one of my most trusted employees letting me down.' He glanced at Schiller, raised his eyebrows slightly. 'So you see, Otto, it probably would be in your interests to stay in my employ.'

Schiller turned to look Caine full in the face. For an instant, the German's usually expressionless eyes blazed with open hatred. Caine must have read the message in them all too clearly, because he continued more forcefully than before. 'In case you get any ideas about shutting me up, Otto, I'd better tell you about the letters.'

'Letters?' Schiller's voice was now barely more than a whisper.

'Yes; the sealed letters I have left with the managers of three banks. All of them contain full details about your past ... er, achievements; and I have left instructions that the letters are to be opened in the event of my death.' He patted Schiller softly on the shoulder as though consoling him. 'All things considered, Otto, it would be wise if you were to do your very best to ensure that nothing ... *untoward* should happen to me. From now on, you're going to be my guardian angel!'

Caine seemed to find this last statement most amusing. He tilted back his head and began to laugh, his big shoulders bobbing rhythmically, his eyes squeezed shut. The effort coaxed fresh drops of sweat from his flabby face and, in the stuffy confines of the car, the sour smell of perspiration mingled with the all-pervading odour of lavender water.

Schiller sat hunched and silent, staring silently at the black and white photograph in his lap as the Cadillac accelerated into the gathering darkness.

Chapter 10

The mouse-opossum had barely moved an inch in the last twenty minutes. A tiny golden-brown rodent with a long shrew-like face and great clownish black orbs for eyes, he had systematically eased his five-inch frame along the edge of the fallen treetrunk in a series of nervous stops and starts until he was mere inches away from his intended victim, a huge black and orange grasshopper. The insect rested on a moss-covered outcrop at the very edge of the log, his great spring-like hind legs ready to propel him headlong away from danger; but his quivering antennae had not yet detected the opossum, who crouched in a torment of anticipation only a short leap away. The opossum was hungry and, after a morning's fruitless hunting, was determined not to let this juicy banquet elude him; and so he remained still, every muscle rigid, while he awaited the correct moment to make his play. Only his tiny whiskered nose was in constant motion, twitching in a frenzy as he prepared to pounce.

The opossum, too, was being observed. A foot or so behind him, farther down the fallen trunk, a smooth brown head watched with cold, malignant eyes. Behind the head, draped in a sensuous spiral around the trunk, stretched the creature's body, a shiny highway of glittering coils that, pulled out into a straight line, would extend twelve feet from nose to tail. It was a boa-constrictor, a non-poisonous snake that killed by crushing its luckless victims within those powerful brown and tan patterned coils. The rodent would offer no more than a quick morsel to a snake of this size, but the boa-constrictor was also hungry and had come upon an opportunity that was too good to miss; so the snake eased its body in a slow gliding run along the length of the treetrunk, moving over the rough bark as silent as a shadow.

The opossum, intent upon its own prey, had not the slightest inkling that death waited only inches behind his tiny heels, that the sands of his own life were fast running out. The constrictor's great jaws hinged silently open, ready to swallow the opossum whole.

And then there was an abrupt swish as a heavy object cleaved downwards through the air. Something thudded forcefully into the treetrunk, making it shudder. Alarmed, the grasshopper flipped away into the undergrowth, an abrupt blur. The opossum gave a shriek of alarm and went bouncing off in another direction, his hunger momentarily forgotten. The snake's heavy body writhed and coiled spasmodically away from the blade of the machete, trailing a warm fountain of crimson from the neck where the head had been savagely hacked away.

Claudio reached down and, with an effort, yanked the clumsy weapon out of the rotten wood. He put the heel of his boot down onto the squirming coils, judging just how much of it he could manage to carry. Then, arriving at a decision, he brought the machete down a second time, cleaving the reptile's succulent body in two and leaving a thick fleshy section some five feet long. Fixing the machete in his belt, he stooped and hefted the body up across his shoulders. In his present weakened condition this took some considerable effort and he was glad that he did not have a long journey back to camp.

He hesitated for a moment, sniffing the air, aware of the dull, electric heaviness that was in it. As if to confirm his suspicions, somewhere off in the distance there was a low growl of thunder. His instincts of the previous night had clearly not betrayed him. There would be rain and it would give them the water they craved; but after that? He shrugged his heavy burden into place and began to walk. He did not want to think about that.

He moved through rustling shadow, his eyes intent on the way ahead. After only a short distance, his shoulders were aching and he was painfully aware how weak he had become. He licked nervously at his cracked and swollen lips, imagining the expressions of his two companions when he brought home this latest offering. It was not what anybody in their right mind would choose to eat but Claudio had been searching in vain for most of that morning and he could no longer afford to be particular. Besides, it wouldn't be the first time he had eaten snake. Once, in a Cayapo village, he had been served a very agreeable stew and had not found out until some time afterwards that the large meaty chunks he had made such

200

short work of were actually prime cut of anaconda. He smiled briefly at the memory of his own revulsion at the time.

As he walked, his gaze flicked left and right, locating the knife scars slashed at regular intervals to mark his entry route. It was all too easy for an unwary traveller to lose his way. Not for the first time, he wondered resentfully what Helen and Martin would have done without him; and perhaps more important, how they would ever cope if something happened to him.

He found the two of them exactly where he had left them crouched sullenly beside the small fire and dropped to his knees, dumping his bloody burden in the dust and ignoring his companions' horrified stares.

'What the hell is that?' Martin muttered in disbelief.

Since the answer was obvious, Claudio made no attempt to reply. He took out his knife and tore a straight scarlet incision along the snake's belly, channelling out some half-digested monstrosities with the flat of the blade. Helen murmured something beneath her breath and turned her gaze away. She was too weak and hungry to offer any kind of protest.

'First monkeys, then a tortoise and now a snake,' observed Martin wearily. 'Next thing you know, we'll be chewing on rats.'

'If we have to,' agreed Claudio briskly. He turned his attention to a half-constructed spit Martin had abandoned and willed his fingers to work properly. He felt feverish and light-headed, but he didn't know how much of that was just hunger.

Another peal of thunder shouted from the unseen sky. Martin glanced upwards at the forest roof. 'Looks like you were right, Claudio,' he observed. 'Damned if I know how you could tell.' He swallowed with an effort. 'We can sure use that water though.'

Claudio nodded but again said nothing. He took the

sharpened length of wood that Martin had cut and began to impale thick sections of snake on it, forcing the point through the dense rubbery flesh. When the pole was laden he hung it over the flames.

'Hope it tastes better than it looks,' mused Martin, but Claudio was in no mood for casual conversation. He worked methodically at the fire, coaxing the flames higher until they licked greedily at the hunks of greyish brown meat on the spit. A strange sickly sweet aroma began to reach them that would have been unpleasant had they not been so ravenous.

The bursts of thunder grew louder and more frequent and the tiny patches of sky visible beyond the forest canopy were occasionally lit by the fierce, abrupt flares of lightning. The temperature seemed to rise until it was almost suffocatingly hot and they could almost sense the first drops of rain hanging frozen in the air high above their heads; but still it did not fall.

The chunks of snake looked only minimally less disgusting when Claudio lifted the spit from the flames and passed the food around. Helen took her share gingerly and sat gazing at it in apprehension for a few moments, trying to banish from her mind the thought of what this actually was. She raised the flesh slowly to her lips and took an exploratory bite. The meat was tough and dense; she had to wrench at it with her teeth. Then she was left with a warm, rubbery lump and, for an instant, felt her empty belly rebel at the thought of accepting such a thankless gift; but tenaciously she swallowed and took another quick bite before her stomach had a chance to reject the first. It was hard work but she was soon able to settle into the kind of routine that people invariably adopted for taking medicine; and at least she could feel that the food was doing her some good, channelling strength to her badly weakened body. She glanced at Martin and could tell by the expression on his face that he was undergoing similar hardships. Only Claudio appeared to be taking it all in his stride, chewing energetically at this nightmarish repast as though tucking into the very best steak.

A wind stirred the undergrowth around them and Helen noticed that suddenly the jungle was silent. The constant background of bird-song and insect-noise had shut off abruptly as though some unseen hand had simply flicked a switch. They sensed rather than saw the blackness in the sky above them and began to eat more frantically, realizing that the rain was almost upon them.

A peal of thunder startled them with its power, seeming to shake the ground upon which they sat, and then what little light there was fell away, as though night had inexplicably arrived in the middle of morning.

The first drops of rain came knifing down through the trees, big, fat globules that exploded as they smashed into the dry vegetation. For an instant it sounded oddly like a roomful of people applauding. Then the heavens tore themselves open and the deluge came roaring down, cannoning crazily off every surface. In seconds, the campfire was extinguished and the three people sitting around the ashes of it were soaked to the skin. The scraps of meat in their hands were momentarily forgotten as they tilted back their heads and opened their parched mouths to receive the fresh water.

After a while, Helen remembered to uncover the water jug and set it upright on the ground. She watched in awe as it began to fill, the rain drops hammering a lively tatoo on its metal shell.

'When that's filled up, we'll get moving,' announced Claudio, shouting over the tumult of the falling water.

'Wouldn't we be better off sheltering somewhere?' suggested Helen.

Claudio laughed dismissively. 'Where?' he demanded. He gestured around. Everywhere the eye could see the undergrowth was being battered by a relentless fusilade, a force that the densest foliage could do nothing to diminish. The only question that troubled Claudio now was how long would the rain last?

A couple of days of this could finish us, he thought gloomily. At some point we'd have to sleep and then . . . He left his own thoughts unfinished and returned his attention to the jug, watching as its level rose steadily upwards. It was already half-full. He crammed the last remnants of snakeflesh into his mouth and chewed thoughtfully. Rain drummed hollowly against the brim of his hat and overflowed from it, trailing a thick curtain of water across his eyes. He glanced at Helen and Martin, knowing that he would have to push them hard again and knowing, too, that their resentment would come flooding back. He'd been right about the rain and that of course would restore a little of their confidence but the ordeal that was coming would soon wear that away. If only they could find the river today! Once again, he tilted back his head and opened his mouth, letting the sweet cool liquid gush into his throat. For the moment at least, the rain could be enjoyed. That would soon change.

Now the water was spattering around the jug's brim. For an instant, he experienced a sense of all-pervading lethargy. Supposing he sat right where he was, just waited to see what happened? He was tired and it would be so easy to succumb to the embrace of some much-needed sleep, to lie down in the mud and let the rains absolve him, wash away all his weariness and pain . . .

He shook the thought away. Move. They had to move. He willed his legs to lift his body upright and, reaching out his dripping arms, scooped up his rifle and haversack, swinging them heavily onto his shoulders.

'All right,' he shouted. 'Let's get moving.'

He watched the other two as they fumbled their equipment slowly together, clumsy and sloth-like now, as though the rain was simply washing the last shreds of vitality from their bodies. At last they stood hunched and silent, waiting for the order to move out. Helen clutched the corked water jug against her body, preparing to carry its contents through the deluge. Another irony.

With a brief nod, Claudio took the machete in his right hand and, turning, trudged away. The others followed, moving painfully and shivering in their wet clothing. The rain kept falling all the rest of that day.

'Goddamn!'

Paolo Estevez peered out of the grimy window of his office and cursed his bad luck. Bouncing up from the concrete surface of the runway, the rain resembled a thick layer of mist hanging over the backlot of the airport like a gloomy shroud. There had not been a hope in hell of taking the plane up that morning. It remained in the great gloomy shell of the hangar, where Miguel tinkered half-heartedly with its iron guts. There was nothing to do now but wait for the rain to stop, and how long that might be was anybody's guess. The sky was a great slab of bruise-black fury that looked content to spit down its wrath for the next ten years. The suspicion that the unthinkable had happened, that the long rains really had come early this year, nagged repeatedly at Paolo's mind. A fine mess that would be! For once, he'd managed to brazen his way into something big and now his newly acquired knowledge was of no use to him. He shook his head. This couldn't be the rains, it was a prelude, nothing more. He had to believe that. Meanwhile, he would have to occupy himself with the more routine necessities of outstanding paper-work.

He moved back to his littered desk and slumped down in the chair, only to see that a rapid stream of droplets was falling from the ramshackle ceiling of the hut right onto the page of his laboriously scrawled accounts. The freshly inscribed figures had blurred to a series of indecipherable smudges and stains. He swore viciously, balled the accounts in his fist and flung them into the wastepaper basket. Hours of work wasted. Wasn't that always the way? The drops continued to spatter rhythmically against the desk and, after a few moments, he slid an empty *cachaça* bottle under the stream. The dripping sound became a little more treble in tone but was no less irritating. Opening a drawer of the desk, Paolo took out a fresh bottle, uncorked it with his teeth and poured a little fire into his stomach.

His attention was caught by the sound of feet thudding against wet concrete and moving back to the window he saw Willy Bordern running from the direction of Mike Stone's hangar, a canvas sheet held protectively across his head and shoulders. A few moments later, the door of the hut burst open and Willy stepped in. He shook the canvas by the doorway, folded it and set it down against the wall.

'Just came over to say goodbye,' he announced gruffly.

'Goodbye? You giving up already?'

Willy shrugged, nodded towards the window. 'If there *was* any hope, I figure this must have settled it. I don't see any point in hanging on over there . . .' He shook his head and shrugged. 'Mike isn't coming back.'

Paolo waved the bottle of *cachaça* and moved to the desk to get a glass. 'Have a drink with me.'

'Sure. Why not?' Willy put his hands into the pockets of his overalls and wandered across to the window. He stared thoughtfully out at the rain. 'God, I hate this place.'

'Think the rains have started early?' asked Paolo, as he poured *cachaça* into a glass.

'Who knows? I've known 'em start early before now. I don't see that it makes a hell of a difference.'

'It might to somebody out in the jungle.'

Willy shook his head and fished the stub of a cigar out of his breast pocket. 'There's nobody out there, Paolo; nobody who's worth saving anyway.' He lit his cigar and walked back to the desk, accepted the glass that Paolo held out. He blew out a cloud of smoke and then took a long swallow of his drink. There was a brief silence before he asked, 'What about these friends of yours? You figure out their angle yet?'

Paolo smiled. 'Well, I guess the only "angle" is that, you know, they want to help.'

Willy gave a snort of indignation. 'Oh sure, Paolo! You've seen those guys, they look like Goody Two Shoes to you?' He puffed at his cigar. 'I've seen guys like that before. I know the type. Guys who dress that way, drive those fancy cars, they've got a lot of names but they all mean the same thing: *trouble*. No, there's got to be more to it than meets the eye . . .'

Paolo raised his eyebrows. 'Like what, Willy?'

'Hell, I don't know! You just take my advice, kid, don't get involved with people like that.'

'I figure I can look after myself.'

'You do, huh?' Willy shrugged. 'Well, I guess it's your business. But you know, Paolo, with Mike gone, you could do a lot of good for yourself.'

'Oh, how's that?'

'Well . . . it figures that there'll be more work coming your way now. You're the only operator around here in a similar league. Maybe if you could get a little money put by, you could move up to a bigger plane, start running that Recife-Belém hop that Mike established.'

'Yeah, maybe.' Paolo grimaced. 'Tell you the truth, Willy, I haven't decided whether or not I want to stay in this line of work. I don't know, I might start looking for something more . . . interesting, you know?' He leaned forward and refilled Willy's glass. 'I'm getting a little tired of busting my ass out here and getting peanuts for it.'

Willy gazed at him for a few moments. 'At least it's honest work,' he observed sourly. 'Paolo, don't fall in with those slickers. I'd hate to see you get mixed up in something you couldn't handle.'

Paolo glanced away, took a swig from his bottle. 'So er . . . what are your plans now?' he enquired.

'Oh, I'll be OK. I've already got something lined up as a matter of fact. Felix Walsh phoned me; wants me to work over at WBA overhauling some planes he's just acquired so they'll be ready for use at the end of the rainy season. I felt like a heel saying yes, but I figure I'm in no position to argue. I just plan on working long enough to earn my passage back to the States. I've had a gutful of this stinking country.'

'Walsh, eh? He didn't waste much time getting to you.'

'Well . . . his is a money operation, kid. They don't leave much room for sentiment. I guess what me and Mike were trying to do was something a little different. But those days are over now, flying is turning into just another business. We just didn't see it sneaking up on us. Which is why Walsh is running a big-deal operation and I'm going to have to bust my ass for the next three months.' He laughed and drained his glass. 'I could say more but it would sound suspiciously like sour grapes. Anyhow, thanks for the drink. I'm on my way. Listen, I left a few bits and pieces in the hangar there, anything you figure's any use to you, just help yourself.' He set down the glass, nodded briefly and moved back to the door, where he unfurled his canvas sheet. 'Be seeing you, Paolo. And think about what I said. Good luck.'

'Luck, Willy; and thanks.'

Willy opened the door and stood for a moment, staring apprehensively out at the deserted runway, the empty rain-punished buildings. Across the way, the gaunt dilapidated curve of Mike Stone's empty hangar looked somehow forlorn and spectral, a ghost from happier times. For an instant, Willy's mind filled with a cherished image: the day when Mike had hired a photographer to come out and record a picture of the newly formed SA crew, posed in front of their DC3. He could see them all standing together, laughing, their arms around one another's shoulders. Mike Stone, slightly uncomfortable in his new uniform, pretending to be eager to get the picture over with but secretly loving every minute; Ricardo Ramirez, flashing the dazzling smile that was his trademark; and saddest of all, poor Helen Brody, a lovely intelligent lady who somehow always seemed to deserve better than she got. Gone now, all of them. Gone to the terrible green purgatory of the jungle where there was no forgiveness for anyone.

Willy sighed, shook his head. The image faded and there was just the rain hammering on the roof of his grey saloon. Parked in front of the hangar, it stood, ready to take him away from this place of sad memories. He took a deep breath and launched himself through the doorway.

It was less than thirty yards to the car but by the time he reached it he was soaked to the skin.

It seemed as though it had been raining for ever.

Helen, Martin and Claudio stumbled wearily through the deluge, their clothing saturated, their aching feet sinking deep into ground that was now a tenacious quagmire. They were chilled to the bone and their bodies smarted from the impact of thousands of heavy raindrops as they came ricocheting crazily through the dense vegetation high above their heads.

Claudio still led the way, his breath clouding on the air as he swung the dripping machete back and forth to hack at the sodden undergrowth. Behind him stumbled Martin, his head bowed with weariness, his body moving with the lurching spasmodic gait of a man who was close to collapse. He was constantly having to pause and extend a

209

hand to Helen. Her ill-fitting boots padded out with rags had functioned well enough when dry, but once wet they had chafed her ankles red raw and now the simple action of placing one foot in front of the other caused her agony. She went on with it as gamely as she could, but as the hours inexorably unfolded, she fell farther and farther behind. At last, beaten, she sank to her knees in the mud and began to cry.

'I can't walk any more,' she sobbed bitterly. 'I've got to rest . . .'

Martin paused, turned back and stooped to take her arm. 'Come on, princess,' he urged her. 'You can do it.'

She shook her head, pulled her arm free of his grasp. 'No! I'm finished I tell you! Just leave me alone, leave me!' She covered her face with her hands and dissolved into a frenzy of frantic weeping. Hearing the noise, Claudio paused for a moment and looked back down the trail. Then he turned and came stalking back, his hands on his hips. He stood for a moment staring down at Helen, his eyes fierce and devoid of any compassion.

'Get up,' he snapped; and his voice was so hard that Helen stopped crying in surprise.

'I . . . I can't . . .' she began haltingly.

'Sure you can! Just get back on your feet and stop this snivelling. You're wasting your breath, there's no audience here to appreciate your performance; and neither I nor Senhor Taggart is going to waste time waiting for you to calm yourself. I'm getting a little bit tired of you playing the helpless female.'

Helen stared at him through the thick curtain of rain and for the first time she began to hate him. 'That's . . . that's not fair,' she protested.

'Isn't it?' he sneered. 'Well, forgive me, but that's how it looks to me. So all right, you're tired. We're *all* tired, Goddammit! But I'll tell you something for a fact. Sit there much longer and you *won't* get up again, you'll die there.

210

Do you want to die, Miss Brody?' He leaned forward and pushed his face up close to hers. 'Do you want to lie here in the rain till the vultures come and peck those pretty eyes out? We don't have the strength to carry you, but we're going on now, with or without you. The choice is yours.' He straightened up, turned and continued on his way as though he had dismissed her from his mind.

'That bastard,' muttered Helen. 'That lousy bastard. He's not leaving me behind . . .' The tearfulness had gone from her voice to be replaced by a newfound defiance. This time, she allowed Martin to help her back to her feet and she resumed walking, limping along as best she could. They travelled for some distance in silence. Helen kept her gaze fixed on Claudio's back as he moved forward some way ahead of her. 'That sonofabitch,' she whispered at last. 'Who the hell does he think he is? You hear what he said?'

Martin nodded. 'Yeah, I heard.'

'You agree with that stuff . . . about being a helpless female?'

'No. And neither does Claudio. He just wanted to make you angry so you'd get up and prove him wrong. It seems to have worked. And besides, he was right about one thing. We have to keep moving, at least until this rain stops.'

Helen glared at him. Her face was white and washed raw by the rain. 'It sounds strange to hear *you* defending him. I thought you were the one who didn't give anything for our chances. I thought you were the one who didn't care.'

He shrugged. 'Maybe I found a reason to change my mind.' Their eyes met for a moment and something passed between them, there in the midst of rainy chaos, something unspoken, an exchange.

'I've been a fool,' confessed Helen abruptly. 'I've been telling myself that I hate you, Martin Taggart. But I don't.

I don't hate you at all.'

He smiled through cracked lips. 'Ever get the feeling you should be hearing something in another place?' he asked her. 'A bar, a hotel room ... anywhere but in the middle of a rainstorm in the Mato Grosso. But thanks for telling me anyway. Here now, come on. We'd better try and catch up with the boy wonder.' Keeping one arm around her, Martin coaxed her along and she stepped out more confidently while she tried to close her mind to the spasms of pain that shot through her legs.

The march went on, slow, stumbling, desperate. In the late afternoon, the miracle happened. The rain gradually eased off, wound down and finally stopped.

But the trees still dripped cold misery onto them as they made camp for the night. With every scrap of wood in the forest soaked through, there was no point in even thinking about a fire; they spent the night huddled in the darkness, shivering and uncomfortable.

Martin and Helen sat side by side, their backs against a huge tree, clutching their wet blankets in a vain attempt to keep warm. Fatigued as they were, it was impossible to sleep, so they talked instead, breaking off occasionally as an icy drop of water found its way past the brim of their hats onto unprotected flesh. Helen had removed her boots and wrapped her stinging ankles with some relatively dry rags which she had found in one of the haversacks. She had not spoken to Claudio since their earlier exchange and he had chosen to shelter in a spot some distance away. They could not see him but they could both picture him listening to their disembodied voices in the darkness.

'I'd forgotten how cold it can be here,' muttered Martin. 'Somehow, when you're walking through the heat, you just get to thinking that it's always that way. Then comes the rain. I don't know which I hate most.'

Helen nodded. 'Well, at least we can console ourselves with the fact that things couldn't possibly get any worse

212

. . .' She lifted a hand from beneath the blanket and stroked the bark of the tree with her fingers. 'Touch wood,' she added warily.

Martin laughed. 'Since we've got the whole night ahead of us and not much hope of sleep . . . perhaps you'd like to explain to me how a nice girl from the right side of the tracks winds up flying a cheap-rate airbus around the ass-hole of South America?'

'Why from the *right* side? For all you know, I could be the kid from Coney Island.'

Martin shook his head. 'Nah . . . oh, I'll admit, you're *gritty* enough to be from Skid Row, but your voice doesn't fit. You're a poor little rich girl, I'd bet my pants on it.'

'All right, so you found me out! Yes, I suppose you could say I'm from a good family. Washington DC originally . . .'

'Heck, I think I know the place! Big white house on the square.'

Helen chuckled. 'No, not *that* good a family; but a similar line of work. My father's cultural attaché at the American embassy in Rio.'

Martin gave a low whistle. 'Well, I don't know exactly what that is, but whichever way you say a title like that, it comes out sounding worth a few bucks. So, by rights, you shouldn't be here at all. You should be wearing a cocktail dress, sipping champagne at some fancy reception.'

'Sure. By rights. But I did all that and it was just like this little misadventure. The novelty soon wore off.'

'Not cut out for the high life, huh? Still, at least it's good to know that your old man will be organizing a big search party on your behalf.'

'I doubt if he even knows about it yet. You see, my father and I, we parted company a long way back. He was so enraged by my little show of independence, he's declined to speak to me ever since. Not a letter, not a

213

phone call, not a birthday card. Like you said, *poor* little rich girl. When he hears what's happened to me, he'll no doubt point out that he always *said* I'd come to no good.' She sighed. 'All right, now it's your turn.'

'Huh?'

'I told you a little about myself. The least you can do is return the favour.'

He shrugged. 'Not much to tell. Born Wyoming thirty-six years ago. Left home at seventeen, bummed around, driving trucks mostly. Then it started to look as though there might be a war. Came out here, worked the garimpos for six years; and then . . .'

'And then you found your diamond?'

'Yeah, that's right.'

'And now you're making a run with it, is that right?'

'That's about the size of it . . . but how come you know so much about it?'

'Oh, I don't, not really. Only what Mike used to tell me; he had a few friends in that line of work. From what he used to say, making a run can be a pretty dangerous business.'

Martin laughed, 'So it would seem; but I hadn't counted on anything like this!' He gestured at the unseen jungle all around them. 'Well, at least there's one consolation. Caine won't think of looking for me out here.'

'Caine?'

'My patron. The man who likes to think he owns half this lump of rock. An Englishman, big, fat but deceptively dangerous. I sure as hell hope I never have to cross tracks with him again. I have to admit that, right now, the chances seem pretty remote.'

'It feels as though we've been marching through this damned jungle for ever. I keep wondering if we'll ever find our way out. It's not so much that I'm afraid of *death*; but to die here, so far from home. To never be found. To have nobody speak over your grave. That's what really frightens me.'

They fell silent for a while. Out in the chilly darkness, a big cat roared, a long lonely sound. Then they heard Claudio's voice, mumbling in the halting, delirious tones of a disturbed sleeper.

'On . . . we go on . . . till the river. River. Where . . . is it? On. On. Go on . . .' His voice faded down to the irregular rhythm of his breathing.

Helen shivered. 'Beats me how he can sleep,' she said. 'There's a lot of pressure on him. Sometimes I think I can see him beginning to crack. The trouble is, he *knows* he's the only hope we've got. But he's drifting away from us. It's like there's a barrier between us and it gets higher all the time. It won't come down again, not till we find the river.'

'Or die trying.'

Again there was silence, deep, unfathomable, oppressive.

'Tell me,' said Helen abruptly. 'If you could have one luxury right now, what would it be?'

Martin thought for a moment. 'Pack of cigarettes,' he replied.

'Is that it?' she asked incredulously. 'I mean, you could choose anything at all, no matter how fantastic. You'd still choose cigarettes?'

'Sure. I'm a man of simple tastes. If I could choose *two* luxuries, I'd ask for a five-course meal with the cigarettes to follow; but since it's just one, I guess it would have to be the smokes.'

'You must really like cigarettes.'

'A guy gets used to having them around, I suppose. How about you? What would you choose?'

'A hot tub,' she said without hesitation. 'A big luxury bathtub filled to the brim with scalding water, laced with bubbles and French cologne. I could just lie there for hours and *wallow*. Then, if *I* could choose a second luxury . . .'

'Sure, why not? I'm feeling generous tonight.'

'A big double bed in a hotel. Freshly laundered cotton sheets. And a "do not disturb" sign on the door.'

Martin nodded enthusiastically. 'Sounds pretty good. And I'm impressed. So far, there's been no mention of any food. You must have an iron will.'

'Well, not really. But this is a fantasy. You can't waste it on something as mundane as a steak with all the trimmings.'

'Hmm. Say, I just had an idea!'

'What's that?'

'Well, since I couldn't possibly eat all of my five-course meal, the two of us could share it. That way, you'd get a third luxury thrown in.'

'Sounds good. What about the cigarettes?'

'What about 'em?'

'Would you share those with me as well?'

'But you don't smoke.'

'No, but I think I'd like one after my meal.'

'Well, I suppose that would be OK, only . . .'

'Only what?'

'I'm not making anything on this deal.'

'I see. Umm . . . you could have my bath water after I've finished with it.'

Martin considered this for a moment. 'Nah. That won't do. I think in all decency you'll have to offer to share the double bed with me.'

'Ah well, I think you may have the wrong idea, Mr Taggart. You see, I had it in mind to *sleep*.'

'So did I. Eventually.'

Helen smiled; and then was assailed by an image from an earlier time. A frowsy hotel room in Belém. A sign on the door, 'Do not disturb'. And Mike Stone, stretched out on the double bed, clutching a bottle of *aguardente* in his

216

hand; and on his face, that old familiar smile of arrogance. And herself, standing by the door, holding the handle, wanting to walk out on him but knowing that she lacked the strength. She had gone back to the grubby, rumpled bed, the half full bottle, to his powerful encircling arms. As he made love to her, that smile . . . that hateful, knowing smile, had never left his lips. She had always hated herself for going back to him like that, time after time.

Her eyes filled with tears and she was dimly aware that Martin was talking to her. 'Well, princess, what do you say? Have we got a deal?'

'Mr Taggart,' she replied; and her voice was husky with suppressed emotion. 'I *always* sleep on the left hand side. Would you be content to take the right?'

'I guess that would be OK.'

'Then yes, we've got a deal.'

His hand found hers beneath the blankets and she did not resist its grip. She squeezed it gently and drew reassurance from the contact. The image of Mike Stone seemed to grow distant, to fade gently from her mind. Somehow, she knew that his memory would never trouble her again. The edge of the blanket lifted and Martin moved his body up against hers, his arm coming up to rest around her shoulders. He made no attempt to do anything more, but the long warm contact of his body was comforting and she began to believe that she might make it till morning, after all.

The first heat of the day wrenched clouds of vapour from the land. It billowed upwards in a thick spectral haze, lending everything a strange ethereal quality as the three travellers got themselves up onto cramped, aching legs. Claudio stood for a moment, peering uneasily this way and that before making the inevitable, heartbreaking announcement.

217

'It's no use trying to hunt in this. We'll just have to go on and hope that something turns up when the mist has cleared.'

The others were too numb to complain. They shambled after Claudio like a pair of zombies, staring straight ahead through reddened, sleep-deprived eyes.

We've just about come to the end of the line, Claudio thought. *How much farther can we expect to go without decent food?* He himself was a great deal weaker than he cared to admit. The blisters on his hands had developed into a series of suppurating sores which made the smallest task a major undertaking, though he took the greatest pains to conceal this from the others. Grimly, he took hold of the heavy machete and began to hack a path. Then they moved off through the mist, a trio of phantom silhouettes bobbing and lurching in a short ragged procession.

Please God, thought Claudio desperately. *Let the water be near* ... But the hours passed, the mist evaporated in the growing heat and still they found nothing to lift their flagging spirits. They settled into the awful, relentless treadmill of another day's march through the jungle. Helen's feet hurt every bit as badly as they had the day before, but now she had somehow managed to inure herself to the pain, blotting it from her mind while she concentrated on the terrible aching void in her empty belly. Martin felt the same way. If he didn't eat something soon, he decided, he would simply sit down and wait for food to come to him.

A little after midday, he nearly fell over Claudio, who had dropped to his knees in the middle of the trail. Martin was about to speak but Claudio whipped around and held a finger to his lips. He pointed to a scattering of animal droppings alongside the trail they had been following.

'Wild pig!' he whispered, unable to keep the excitement

218

out of his voice. 'Looks like a regular track and it's been used recently.' He swallowed with difficulty. 'You'd better unsling your rifle and be ready to shoot. Both of you, try to move as quietly as possible. And pray. Just pray that they're still around.' He got carefully back to his feet, jammed the machete into his belt and unslung his rifle.

Suddenly, everybody was wide awake. They moved into the shady silence ahead, putting their clumsy feet down as silently as they could. Claudio found himself praying beneath his breath. He glanced quickly at Martin. The American's face was expressionless, but he passed the tip of his tongue nervously across the dry sores on his lips. Pushing gently through a screen of ferns, Claudio could dimly perceive a small clearing ahead. A few speckles of sunlight had fought their way through the canopy of the trees to dapple the forest floor with light. This gave a curious impression of movement and, nervous as he was, Claudio almost fired then and there.

Steady now, he warned himself. He narrowed his sleep-deprived eyes and edged forward a little. Again, that strange impression of movement startled him; but then he heard Martin make a sharp intake of breath and realized that there *was* movement in the light; something large and slow, walking from left to right across his vision, the light making patterns upon its bristly back. Claudio swallowed hard and his empty belly lurched in anticipation. Against all his hunter's instincts, he nearly cried out when he recognized that it was a big heavy sow, rooting aimlessly across the floor of the jungle and quite unaware that she was being observed. Claudio brought up the rifle, which felt horribly clumsy in his blistered hands. He drew a bead on the sow's fat neck and wished vainly that he could stop the sights from shaking. There would be two chances. Martin, a poor shot, would be waiting for Claudio to fire first. The target was some twenty-five yards away but he did not dare risk getting any closer.

219

The pig was carrying enough succulent flesh to gorge everybody ten times over. He must not miss.

He breathed deeply, blinked the haze from his eyes and took a more steady aim. Then, gently, he squeezed the trigger.

The roar of the two rifles, firing fractions of a second apart, shattered the silence. The sow's body jolted with the shock of impact as two bullets slammed deep into her flesh. She stood for a moment, her stubby legs splayed outwards in a vain attempt to hold up her body; then she pitched abruptly sideways, struck the ground heavily and lay there, shuddering, gouts of blood pumping from her open mouth.

With a long formless yell of exaltation, Claudio ran towards the carcass. Flinging the rifle carelessly aside, he threw himself down on his knees and embraced the dead sow, unmindful of the warm blood that smeared his face. He was sobbing with gratitude and he kept saying, 'Thank you, thank you, thank you!' over and over again. Behind him Martin and Helen danced a bizarre waltz, laughing like a pair of schoolchildren.

'We got her, Goddammit!' screamed Claudio. 'We got her!' He turned to yell triumphantly to the others. 'Did you see the way she went down, like a –'

He broke off with a gasp of surprise as something came smashing out of the dense undergrowth to his left. Something big and powerful and deadly.

The boar was massive, a great bristling monster intent on avenging the death of his mate. He came racing straight at Claudio, his head lowered and his sharp tusks gleaming dangerously in the half-light. Glancing desperately about, Claudio saw his rifle lying a good ten feet away; and in the same glance, he saw Martin break away from Helen and begin to fumble frantically with the bolt on his. It had jammed.

Claudio had time to swear and then the boar was upon

220

him, the huge head sweeping sideways in a terrible ivory-tipped arc. He flung himself desperately to one side and managed to evade the tusks by inches. He rolled awkwardly, got to his feet and began to sprint in the direction of his gun. But the boar was right on his heels and within seconds there was the sudden lunge of a snout against his running legs. Claudio tipped backwards with an oath, somersaulted over the boar's back and fell in an ungainly heap, winded but so far largely unhurt. With a squeal of rage, the boar spun around on its back legs. Claudio had a fleeting impression of a great ugly head descending onto his chest; and then abruptly, inexplicably, the boar was rearing up on its hind legs and tipping backwards, bellowing indignantly. To his horror, Claudio saw that Martin had dashed up behind the creature and grabbed it by its tail.

'Martin, NO!' screamed Claudio, but his cry was lost in the furious shrieking of the boar as it turned its rage in Martin's direction. Now it was the American's turn to run, which he did at the best speed his weary legs could conjure up. The boar lumbered after him, inches behind, its great head scything left and right and ripping out clods of earth and vegetation. At the last instant, Martin flung himself around the base of a great gnarled tree-trunk and the boar's head collided with solid wood, the tusks gouging deep furrows in the rough bark. Martin snapped around, hugging the contours of the tree and began a deadly game of catch, keeping the trunk between himself and the boar, which continued to vent its blind fury on the wood as it lunged madly after the American, bellowing with frustration whenever it glimpsed his flying heels.

Claudio, meanwhile, had got to his feet and retrieved his fallen rifle. Pumping another cartridge into the breech, he raced to within ten yards of the tree and tried to take aim, but could not safely draw a bead on the furious anticlockwise scramble without endangering Martin as well.

'Try to lead him out into the open!' he yelled; and in that instant, Martin tripped over a tree-root and sprawled headlong to the ground. With a squeal of triumph, the boar came lunging around the tree; then, abruptly, it was bellowing in pain as a large rock bounced off its head. Helen had leapt into the fray. The boar, blind to everything except this latest source of pain, promptly forgot Martin and took off after Helen instead.

'*To me*!' screamed Claudio, lifting the gun to his shoulder again. 'Draw him out where I can get him, for God's sake!' She must have heard his shout because she veered sharply round and came running back in his direction, hobbling pitifully on her chafed legs. He could see the expression of agony on her face, her teeth gritted against the spasms of pain that jolted through her at every step; and he saw, too, that the boar was rapidly closing on her, that she had undertaken a race that she could not possibly win. Martin was scrambling up, dazed, from beside the tree, too far away now to be of any use. With an oath, Claudio ran forward, snapping the rifle up to his shoulder only to see that Helen's body was directly in line with his target. He flung himself desperately sideways, saw the great bristling head sweeping in for the kill. Scant inches separated the tusks from Helen's legs.

There was no time to aim properly. Claudio dropped down onto one knee, swung the sights quickly up to his eye and squeezed the trigger. The gun bucked in his hands, the crash of the shot echoing through the selva. For a long terrible instant, nothing seemed to happen, he was convinced that he had missed; but then, in what looked like a terrible slow motion, the boar's right eye erupted in a gout of viscous crimson and its whole body arched and twisted sideways as it was struck by a prodigious impact. The impetus of the charge carried the carcass onwards, tumbling it over and over until, finally, it crashed headlong into a tangle of ferns and bushes beside the trail.

Helen gave a cry and she too collapsed, flopping face down onto the ground. Martin raced over to her while Claudio approached more cautiously, pumping another cartridge into the breach just in case the beast was not dead. Martin reached Helen and turned her, cradled her in his arms. She was panting heavily and the expression of agony on her face made him think she had been wounded; but then she grinned and lifted one hand to make a circle of her thumb and forefinger. He hugged her close again.

'You idiot,' he said gruffly. 'What the hell were you trying to do?'

She shook her head. For the moment, she was too winded to speak. She allowed Martin to help her back to her feet and stood there, her hands on her hips, her head bowed, while she tried to regain her breath.

'It's a wonder you weren't ripped wide open,' observed Martin grimly.

'You came ... pretty close ... yourself, buster,' she gasped in reply. 'Besides ... I thought I done ... pretty good.'

Martin glared at her for a moment and then, despite himself, he grinned.

'Yeah,' he admitted. 'You done pretty good.' He stroked her face fondly.

Claudio had waded into the undergrowth to examine the body of the boar. It had been a lucky shot that brought the creature down. More by accident than design, the bullet had pierced the right eye socket and slammed its way deep into the creature's brain.

'You all right?' he asked Helen. His voice had a strange, matter of fact quality as though he wanted to suggest that he had not been worried about her.

'Just bumps and bruises,' she replied. 'Thanks to you.

223

Look, I want to thank –'

But he was already turning away, waving his hand as though dismissing the matter. 'The most damn fool move I ever saw,' he muttered and strode back across the clearing to examine the other carcass. Helen and Martin exchanged smiles.

'He's a strange one,' mused Helen. 'I keep wondering what makes him tick.'

'Me too. Though I'm beginning to get a good idea.' Helen stared at him quizzically but he did not elaborate. He took her arm and led her across to where Claudio was crouched over the body of the sow. 'And now, having *earned* our dinner,' he said, 'I vote that we get down to some serious eating.'

'Amen to that,' murmured Claudio. In a rare display of humour, he affected the jaunty air of a well-to-do Englishman hosting a dinner party. 'I trust you're both peckish enough to do justice to some roast pork? I'll carve while you chaps light the oven!'

Weary as they were, they ran to fetch firewood.

The prime cuts of pork hung sizzling invitingly in the flames but Claudio, knowing the dangers of eating undercooked pork, made the others wait until the portions were roasted through and through. It was maddening to wait and watch, their hollow bellies screaming in protest, their crusted mouths salivating uselessly at the rich aroma of cooked flesh. But at last the food was ready and they fell on it wolfishly, gorging themselves on the white, fatty meat, gulping it ravenously down with mouthfuls of clear water from the metal jug until their bellies were swollen with food.

The luxury of having more than they could possibly eat had a tremendous psychological effect. For the first time since the crash, the atmosphere around the fire was optimistic, even jovial. Helen lay on her back, her boots off, drying her bandaged feet beside the fire while she gnawed on a massive shin bone. Beside her, Martin, perhaps for the first time, was not thinking wistfully about a cigarette to round off the meal; and even Claudio was unusually animated.

'We'll cook some extra portions and carry them with us,' he said. 'We can eat them cold along the trail, they'll be good for a day or so. We *must* be getting close now. I think what we should do is rest up now, until tomorrow morning. It'll give us a chance to digest all this food.' He patted his stomach ruefully and belched.

Helen laughed. 'Yes, I know what you mean. You kind of get out of the habit of eating. You know, I'd decided that if I had to eat another of those damned monkeys, I –'

'Hey, quiet a minute!'

Claudio and Helen turned to look at Martin. He had sat upright, an expression of urgency on his face. His head was tilted to one side and his eyes stared upwards to the trees.

'What is it?' demanded Claudio.

'Ssh! Listen . . . I thought I heard . . .' He stood up and walked away from the fire so as not to be distracted by its crackling. He turned slowly around a full circle as though homing in on something, then halted, facing south-east. 'Yes, listen!' His voice was suddenly fierce and rigid with conviction.

Claudio and Helen listened too, infected by Martin's excitement. After a few moments, they could hear it, a steady mechanical buzzing dwarfed by distance and coming down from high above them. As they waited, the noise grew steadily.

'A plane,' whispered Martin. And then again, his voice rising to a yell. 'A plane Goddammit!' He glanced desperately about and then lunged for Claudio's rifle. Lifting it up, he loosed off a shot at the unseen sky. The abrupt crack rang through the surrounding jungle. 'Jesus,

225

it sounds like it's right overhead . . .' He worked the bolt of the gun feverishly and raised it to shoot again; but before he could pull the trigger, Claudio stepped in and snatched the gun roughly away from him.

'You're just wasting bullets!' he snapped. 'He's not going to hear a rifle shot from up there.'

Martin stared at him. 'We've got to do something.'

Claudio considered for a moment. 'The fire!' he suggested. 'Make smoke. Throw some damp grass onto it. He may just think it's an Indian fire, but he's got a better chance of seeing that than of hearing a gun.'

Everybody ran to snatch up handfuls of grass. The sound of the plane seemed very close now, a weird alien noise in this place of solitude. Within seconds the fire was smothered beneath a layer of damp vegetation and a black pall of smoke rose steadily skywards. They watched fearfully as the column coiled to the treetops, losing itself in the thick foliage that blotted out the sky; and they listened intently, hoping for the variation in tone that would suggest the plane was circling the area. But for a minute or so the engine noise remained more or less constant and then it gradually began to fade away. It was moving on across the great green wilderness of *selva* that stretched on into the west and the deep lost heart of the Mato Grosso.

'Maybe they'll circle back,' said Helen hopefully; but though they stood quite still and listened for several minutes more, the sound slowly diminished back to silence. The plane did not return.

'Oh, God help us!' cried Martin bitterly. He raised his hands in a gesture of supplication to unseen forces. 'Right above our heads and they didn't even know we were here!'

'There was nothing they could have done anyway,' retorted Claudio flatly. 'And besides, we don't know for sure that they didn't see the smoke. Somebody might

226

report it.'

Martin flung him a contemptuous glance. 'You never give up, do you?' he growled. 'Mister Optimism, nineteen forty-six.' He spat emphatically at the ground by his feet and then slouched sullenly back to the fire, where he began to lift away the smoking heaps of grass with a length of stick. The rare feeling of wellbeing had been surprisingly short-lived.

Claudio sighed, turned away a little to stare off into the undergrowth to his right. A halo of *pium* flies worried at his already badly bitten face but he had long tired of swatting them.

Helen moved nearer to him, gazing at him inquiringly. 'How near?' she asked quietly.

'Hmm?'

'Just before we heard the plane, you were saying that you thought the river was near. Think we'll be there tomorrow?'

He gave a brief derisive laugh. 'Did I say that?' He shrugged, his expression glum. 'Perhaps Senhor Taggart is right about me. Mister Optimism. Yes, well . . . the plain fact is that I don't know any more. When we set out, I was *sure* that we'd reach the river, that it was only a matter of time. But as the days unwind, I begin to doubt that there really *is* a river.'

'You mustn't talk like that,' whispered Helen anxiously. She was horribly aware of how infectious fear could be; aware too that if Claudio were to weaken in his resolve, then they were, all three of them, lost. 'You were right about the rain.'

He nodded, but his glum expression did not lift. 'That was different,' he said quietly; and without another word, he turned and walked back to his place at the fire. He slumped down, eliciting no more than a brief indifferent glance from Martin.

Helen frowned. She thrust her hands in her pockets and

wandered down the trail a little, preferring solitude for the moment to the gloomy company of the others. She went over to the place where the great boar had finally come to rest, feeling that the glimpse of an earlier victory might lift her flagging spirits. She reached the spot and stooped to pull aside a thick screen of ferns. Behind it, everything was inexplicably *movement*. She stared for a moment, her eyes momentarily deceived, and then she gave an involuntary cry of horror; for the carcass was alive with a thick moving mantle of driver ants, millions upon millions of dark shiny bodies that seemed to pulse and flow like waves of liquid in their frantic haste to get at the boar's dead flesh. Leading away from the heaving mound, a broad trail of the ants led back into the jungle in two streams of movement to and from the recently discovered source of food. The once mighty boar was being carved up and carried away, piece by tiny piece.

Helen shuddered. It was a vision of death more terrible than mere bleached bones or congealed blood. This was the awful finality of death here in this terrible place. She let the ferns swing back to mask the hideous image from her eyes and stood uncertainly for a moment, glancing wildly about, her flesh crawling, her eyes still swimming with that hideous image. On every side the *selva* waited, shadowy, ancient, hungry. It seemed to breathe out a great dank stench of death and decay; and suddenly she no longer wanted to be on her own. That was the last thing she wanted.

She turned and made her way back to the meagre comfort of the campfire.

Chapter 11

Paolo tapped the tiny pencilled cross on his chart and gave a brief shrug. Most likely it was nothing at all, a solitary Indian campfire; but on the other hand, it was the only sign of life he'd seen over the last couple of hours and the action of making a map reference had, if nothing else, passed away a little time. He glanced back out of his side window at the pall of smoke that snaked up out of the sea of greenery hundreds of feet below. It had thickened considerably since he first saw it, the smoke denser, almost as though somebody was trying to . . .

He grinned self-consciously. It was all too unlikely. Maybe he really *had* been watching too many movies. He returned his gaze to the way ahead. After the day of inactivity initiated by the rain, it had been a relief to get the battered old plane back up into the air and now, here he was, following Otto Schiller's suggestion by coming back into the interior on a course fifty miles west of his last attempt. He would then spend the remainder of his airtime flipping to and fro across the square of land he had designated for the day. Perhaps this time his luck would change and he would locate the airfield.

He had phoned Caine's office from a public booth the previous evening and had been worried by the Englishman's off-hand attitude.

'So, you didn't go up today, Paolo. Hardly surprising considering the inclemency of the weather, but hardly an auspicious start to our er . . . partnership.' And then the cultured voice had lowered slightly, to a silky, dangerous murmur. 'To tell you the truth, Paolo, I'm beginning to have second thoughts about the whole business. I hadn't anticipated it being as *complicated* as this. I do hope you come up with something very soon.'

A device, no doubt, designed to make Paolo take his work more seriously; or was it intended to be more than that? Paolo slipped one hand into the pocket of his flying jacket to caress the handle of his ancient revolver. He'd spent the previous night usefully, driving into the city to buy a couple of boxes of .45 ammunition. If matters should come to a head, he didn't want to be caught unprepared.

The plane puttered its way steadily north-west. Paolo's eyes scanned the stretches of forest below, his gaze flicking methodically left and right, searching for any break in the uninterrupted belt of green. His mind, though, was on other things.

He was thinking about his parents and the crummy childhood he had spent with them in their dilapidated two-room shack. It was much like thousands of other houses on the outskirts of Rio, a low, flimsy construction of adobe and corrugated iron that stank of bad sanitation. Paolo had lived in this place with his brother and two sisters until he was eighteen years old. His father's job as a baggage handler at the airport brought in barely enough to keep the family alive, and the children, from the very earliest ages, had been obliged to pick up whatever casual work they could find. It was not exactly poverty. For most families in Brazil at that time, it was more or less the norm. But Paolo had always hated it, had always felt in his heart the supreme conviction that one day he would rise above it. His mother jokingly referred to him as 'The Dreamer', and it was certainly true that whenever he had earned a few coins for his own pleasures, he would invariably spend them on a seat in the local cinema. In that dark humid environment he had seen the image that changed his life. On the peeling, fly-pocked screen, the monochrome face of Clark Gable had peered down at him from behind the controls of an aeroplane; and in that instant, young Paolo had decided that, one day, he would be a pilot too.

From that day his campaign started. He began to save every cent that he could put aside. He pestered his father to introduce him to anyone at work who could, in turn, introduce Paolo to a pilot. He wrote away for aircraft periodicals and magazines and he steadfastly ignored the jeers and taunts of his sisters and brother who took a singular delight in assuring him that the only way he would ever fly would be by growing a pair of wings. At eighteen he left home and acquired a menial job at the airport, clearing up refuse around the offices of some of the big airline companies. He used his good looks as a useful introduction to many of the women who worked either as hostesses or receptionists, gambling that eventually he would find one who had a pilot for a friend. He used the money he had saved to buy himself some of the flying time he needed for his licence and made up the rest by spending his entire weekly earnings on it. Meanwhile he lived on bread and hope.

Getting the licence had been easy compared to his next planned step: his own business. For some considerable time, he had been cultivating the affections of a rich and lonely widow who, like many younger women, was easily swayed by Paolo's charm and good looks. Now, he really went to work on her, sending her flowers, escorting her to boring functions in Rio and gradually gaining her confidence by the inevitable route of her bed. One evening, the widow was rash enough to make Paolo a loan to set him up in business. Once the money was transferred to Paolo's bank account she never saw Paolo, or her money, again.

Thus, after five years of scheming and planning, Paolo Estevez had risen from the squalor of his childhood, and yet, for all that, he was not satisfied. It was a rude shock to discover that his Gable-vision was a hopelessly distorted one and that the small airline business was drab and monotonous. He had simply exchanged one form of squalor for another. It was around this time that he first began to drown his sorrows with the harsh taste of *cachaça*. The single battered aeroplane and the ramshackle office hut may have impressed his family but he

231

wanted more, much more than that. Perhaps this business into which he had stumbled had shown him the way. Now, he nurtured in his mind a new image. He would arrive at the door of his father's house in a new car; a long sleek Cadillac like Senhor Caine's but in a brighter colour. He would be wearing a new, immaculately pressed Panama suit and he would have a matching hat worn at a rakish angle. In his mouth, a good cigar, Havana naturally. And he would just saunter up to the door and knock on it, with a hand that glittered with diamond rings . . .

Paolo came abruptly out of his daydream. The sky away to his left was dotted with *urubú*, the ragged black vultures of the *selva*, and they were swooping downwards to join some others on a *praia*. an exposed sandbank of a shallow river that cut a series of erratic curves through the vegetation below. Paolo banked the plane sharply to the left and dropped lower, coming around in a slow, lazy circle. Now he could see some commotion on the *praia* at a point where the river veered sharply to the right. The *urubú* were fighting over something that lay stretched out in the mud . . .

But Paolo was not for the moment interested in identifying what lay there; for as he accelerated into the curve of the river he could see the great metal carcass that lay beached against one of the high banks, its once silver flanks burnt to a dirty black. The wings were gone, torn away no doubt in the first terrible impact of the crash. The nose too was lost, now no more than a twisted, shattered obscenity. If Mike Stone had been at the controls when it hit, there was surely no chance of his being alive now. All this Paolo saw in an instant; then his own plane was thundering past the scene of devastation, leaving the wreckage behind. In that same instant, Paolo knew the bitter taste of defeat.

So the plane had never made it to any damned airfield!

232

Whatever it was doing so far from its intended route, it had failed to reach any kind of objective and instead had plunged down the empty sky to muddy oblivion here in the heart of no-man's-land. There *were* no survivors, not from a crash like that. Paolo was a partner in an enterprise that could yield nothing worth anyone's trouble. He cursed bitterly but forced himself to be logical. Throttling back, he turned the plane and went back for a second look. Racing in again, he could see the long jagged scar in the shallow river where the hurtling plane had dredged up a great trough of mud and debris. His gaze moved on to the plane itself . . . and he realized in an abrupt stab of exaltation that his initial reasoning had been misplaced. Somebody *must* have survived the crash, the person who had painstakingly arranged a series of white articles on the plane's fire-blackened roof and joined them together to form a huge white arrow. It was unfinished, as though whoever had been making the sign had been interrupted, or had simply grown tired of the task; but there was no doubting that it *was* intended to represent an arrow, pointing back along the plane's body towards the tail. Clearly some kind of message . . . but what did it mean? Nothing lay in the direction indicated but mile upon mile of dense, largely unexplored jungle. Paolo himself had just approached from that direction . . .

Diabo! The smoke! Grabbing his charts, he quickly plotted the plane's position and marked it down in pencil. The sign indicated a direction due east and that was, more or less, where Paolo had recorded the smoke of a campfire. He gave an involuntary groan as he remembered how the smoke had thickened suddenly, as though somebody might be attempting to signal; and how he had dismissed the idea as a fantasy.

They must have heard me, he told himself. A million-to-one chance and I just kept on going.

And yet, he reasoned, what could he have done? There

would be no way of landing in that kind of forest. The best he could have done was to circle the area for a while, assure *them* that their message had been received. The question was, what were the survivors doing so far away from the plane? Where were they headed?

He studied his maps for a moment and then he began to understand. The more he considered it, the more sense it seemed to make. He buzzed the wreckage a few more times to ensure that nobody had remained behind, noticing more details on each successive pass. He saw how suitcases had been removed from the wreckage and their contents rifled, presumably by people putting together equipment for a long march. He noticed too what looked like the remains of a campfire on the *praia* beside the plane. On his last run, when he came in recklessly low, the vultures scattered at the noise of the engines and he was able to discern that the half-eaten remains lying in the mud were wearing the tattered remnants of a brightly coloured shirt. But there was nobody here who would benefit from any help. With a nod of finality, he lifted the plane's nose skywards and retraced his original course, pushing the little plane up to maximum speed so that it jolted and juddered alarmingly. Paolo was anxious to correct his earlier mistake, realizing that people who had wandered in the jungle for days on end would take heart from the sound of a plane's engines circling overhead. To this end, he kept his eyes peeled as he approached the area, but this time he found no smoke. Puzzled, he double-checked his calculations, but there had been no mistake. He circled aimlessly about for several minutes, aware that he was already fairly low on fuel. He shrugged, told himself that it was of no great importance. Perhaps the fire had gone out. Perhaps the travellers had simply pushed on again. But if Paolo was right about their intended destination, then he would almost certainly meet up with them there . . . at the River of Death.

He eased the plane around in a slow, lazy curve and then, accelerating upwards, took off in the direction of home.

Martin woke briefly from sleep and lay for a while, hunched and uncomfortable on the hard earth, blinking in the unfamiliar sunlight. Pestered even in his dreams by mosquitoes, he had been haunted by the vision of one particularly big brute that buzzed relentlessly around his head in a great circle, seeming to double in size every time it completed a circuit while he struck out ineffectually at it with his fists. He sniffed, yawned, peered around at his companions. Lulled by the heat and their full bellies, they too were sleeping and the fire had burned to a pile of cold ash beside them. It hardly mattered. It could be relit when the chill of the evening descended.

Sleep was creeping insistently back, numbing his thoughts. Curious, but he still seemed to hear the fading sounds of that damned mosquito, buzzing around in his head. Funny, because . . . it was almost like . . . He tried to martial his senses so that he could listen for a moment, but his will was sapped, a grey smoke danced at the back of his eyes. He let his eyelids close, lead-lined covers that he had neither the strength nor the inclination to lift again. In seconds, he was asleep. This time, there were no dreams to trouble him.

There was a sense of desperation about the following day's march. The substantial meal had given them a fresh shot of vitality and they had, for the first time since the crash, the luxury of carrying food along with them. But hunger and thirst were not the only considerations on a journey like this. They were, all of them, approaching the condition where their nerves could shatter as easily as a pane of fragile glass. The long days of being trapped in the claustrophobic gloom of the *selva* had got to them just as surely as the first tell-tale aches of malaria had crept into their bones.

They set off at first light, Claudio dictating an even more crippling pace than usual. He strode well ahead of his companions, his machete swinging left and right as though he had declared personal war on the undergrowth. Martin and Helen followed as best they could, for Helen's legs, though freshly bandaged, still troubled her terribly. At every other step she was obliged to lean heavily on Martin's shoulder for support. But she went gamely on, never complaining, as the hours creaked inexorably by. It was a particularly hot day. The temperature climbed remorselessly into the eighties. They were enveloped in damp, clinging, energy-sapping heat and they were plagued by vast clouds of *borrachudos* – tiny black insects that bit at every inch of exposed flesh and left a series of red bumps that itched maddeningly.

Just as he had the previous day, Claudio forged on, getting farther and farther ahead of his companions, his concentration centred on the one, all-important task of making good progress through the vegetation. He was so intent on this that he hardly seemed to be aware of the considerable distance between him and the others. Martin, fearing that he and Helen might become separated from the leader, tried calling out to Claudio several times, but he did not acknowledge the shouts in any way.

'Our leader . . . seems preoccupied,' Helen gasped.

Martin looked at her in concern. Her face was beaded with sweat and she was panting with the sheer effort of staying upright. Her shirt was sodden and her flesh, underneath the mottled fly bites, was disturbingly pale.

'How are you making out?' he asked her doubtfully.

'Oh, I'm . . . all right,' she assured him. 'Just a little pain . . . in my ankles.'

He leaned over, hitching up the loose folds of her baggy

236

trousers to examine the tightly bound rags that swathed her ankles. They were stained crimson with blood.

'Hell,' said Martin grimly. 'These have got to be changed before we go any farther.'

'We can't do that. Claudio . . .'

'Fuck Claudio!' he snapped emphatically. 'Claudio will have to wait five minutes, that's all. He's pushing us too damned hard anyway.' He detached her arm from around his shoulder and lowered her gently to the ground. 'Wait here a moment. I'll go and tell him.' He patted her reassuringly, shouldered his rifle and turned to hurry after Claudio, who was now some fifty yards ahead, hacking his way through a thick tangle of lianas.

'Hey, Claudio! Hold up a minute, will you? Helen's in a bad way back here.'

But still Claudio took no notice. He continued his assault on the undergrowth, his arm rising and falling in a blind frenzy, his gaze fixed resolutely on the way ahead.

'Claudio?' Puzzled, Martin moved nearer. As he drew close, he could see the thick sweat stains on Claudio's shirt, could hear the shallow, hoarse gasps that escaped from his lips; and he was muttering to himself, a rhythmic jumble of Portuguese sprinkled liberally with English swear words. He kept shaking his head from side to side and, even though Martin was now right beside him, did not seem to be aware of him.

'Claudio! Listen to me! What's got into you for Christ's sake? You hear me? Claudio!'

Martin reached out and grabbed the other man's shoulder, wrenched him around face to face; and the next second was ducking frantically beneath the blade of the machete, for Claudio was still hacking at the undergrowth, even though now his blade was cleaving nothing more substantial than thin air. His face wore a blank, staring expression that suggested he had momentarily lapsed into madness.

'For God's sake!' Martin backed away, holding his hands up above his head. Another vicious swing slashed the air inches in front of his face. 'It's me, Claudio. It's Martin. Just . . . take it easy, will you.'

Claudio's strokes slowed and realization dawned on his face. He stood there a moment, his mouth open, fat globules of sweat trickling down. Then he lowered the machete and stared at Martin as though noticing his presence for the first time.

'What . . . what's the matter?' he asked. His voice was hollow, toneless, as far away from this place as a fall of winter snow.

'It's Helen. She can't be expected to go any farther. She needs a rest and she needs to have her ankles rebandaged. They're bleeding real bad.'

For an instant, the old Claudio resurfaced with an expression of concern. He took a step forward and then froze as his new, more ruthless personality asserted itself. As Martin watched in disbelief, Claudio's face seemed to recompose itself into an expression of fanatical indifference.

'Leave her,' he said bluntly. 'Leave her and carry on. We have to keep on going.'

'What do you mean, *leave her*?' Martin glared at Claudio threateningly. 'I'm not going to leave her here alone. Jesus man, anything could happen to her.'

Claudio considered this statement for a moment. 'Very well. You stay too. I'll push on ahead and when I find the river, I'll come back for you both.'

Martin shook his head. 'I don't like the sound of that either. Too risky. We don't know how much farther it is, you could be gone for days.'

'No! No, it's near here, I'm sure of that. It may only be a matter of miles from here. This is our last fling, don't you see that? Either we find it today or we never find it. Now, you have the spare rifle, there's food in your

238

haversack, all you need to do is get a fire going and sit tight. But I must go on.'

'No Claudio. We *don't* split up. At this stage of the game, that would be a big mistake. Now listen, here's my suggestion. We could all do with a rest and it won't take long to fix those bandages. I figure if we just hole up for a half hour or so, we —'

'I'm not losing any more time!' Claudio's eyes bulged with anger and his voice rose to a shrill shout. 'Who the hell do you think you are, Taggart, questioning my authority? I'm leader here and I make the decisions, understand? You just continue to do what you've done so far. Nothing. Now, get out of the way, I'm going on.' He gave Martin an unceremonious push and turned to go.

Suddenly Martin too was angry. A wild, unreasonable rage came burning into his chest, throwing a hot redness behind his eyes and jerking his reflexes into instant retribution. He stepped forward, grabbed Claudio's arm and spun him round. Then he punched him on the chin with all the force he could muster, flinging him backwards into the tangle of bushes at his rear.

There was a brief instant of terrible silence. Martin stood waiting, his fists clenched, his breathing heavy and shuddering with anger. Then Claudio was stumbling back to his feet, a slow trickle of crimson pulsing from the corner of his mouth. If there had been any semblance of his old self before, now it had vanished. His eyes blazed with cold venom. With a formless exclamation of hatred, he lurched forward, the machete still clutched in his hand. He aimed a terrible blow at Martin's head but the American weaved aside, caught Claudio's wrist in his two hands and held it there. For a few moments, the two struggled ineffectually, the machete glittering dangerously between them. Then, unexpectedly, Claudio swung his forehead down against Martin's, the two skulls colliding with a loud crack. Martin reeled back with an oath, half-

239

blinded by the blow, and Claudio plunged after him with a yell, swinging the machete like a deadly pendulum from left to right. Desperately, Martin clawed the rifle from his shoulder and swung it around to intercept the blade. Metal struck metal and the shock of the impact smashed both weapons out of their hands. They reeled back from each other, their eyes glaring dull hatred; and then they began to circle cautiously around, each seeking an opening in the other's defence.

Claudio attacked first, flinging a flurry of blows into Martin's face and driving him back a few paces; but then Martin brought his knee up hard into Claudio's groin, driving the wind out of him and pushing him back into the bushes again. He tripped on a root and went sprawling onto his back. As he attempted to rise, Martin moved in on him, kicking him hard in the ribs with the toe of a heavy boot. Claudio roared with pain and rolled aside, but managed to grab Martin's leg as he did so, bringing the American crashing down on top of him. For a moment, they grappled clumsily in the undergrowth and then Claudio's hands closed on Martin's throat, constricting with a terrible force. Weakened by days of marching, Martin could barely summon the energy to push his assailant off; and Claudio, incensed as he was, seemed to possess powers that belied his small stature. Martin felt a terrible blackness plucking at his mind. With one last, desperate effort, he brought his hands up to clap the palms against Claudio's ears. The Portuguese screamed, relinquished his hold for a moment, and Martin, jerking up his knees, flung Claudio, head over heels, deeper into the bushes.

Gasping for breath, Martin struggled up onto his hands and knees. His heart was pounding like a trip hammer; he had about reached the limits of his endurance. He prayed that Claudio would stay down this time; but as he glanced up, he could see that his adversary was already

240

struggling upright, a fuzzy dark silhouette against a background of irridescent green.

With an effort, Martin raised himself into a half-crouch and launched himself headlong at Claudio, headbutting him in the chest. The two men lurched backwards, crashing through the thick screen of vegetation and tumbling beyond it, still locked resolutely together. Inexplicably, they emerged into fierce sunlight. Martin had just enough time to think how odd this was, when something hard and unyielding collided with his left shoulder. He rolled awkwardly and bumped against Claudio, who was a moving tangle of arms and legs. There was a brief sensation of falling and then the hardness struck Martin again, this time in the small of his back, driving all the breath out of his body. He tried to check his tumbling motion but was unable to do anything. A brownish blur sped past his astonished gaze and he realized that he was falling down a steep incline, rolling headlong between the trunks of trees. Ahead he caught a chilling glimpse of a place where the hard earth ended abruptly in a sheer drop. He flung out an arm in a vague attempt to halt his impetus and his hand slapped painfully against tree-bark, the fingers clawing ineffectually as gravity urged his body onwards. Suddenly, he was twisting and turning upon empty air. He opened his mouth to yell, his body shrinking at the thought of the hard earth waiting far below. And then he hit the water.

The delicious shock of the impact disorientated him. He sank deep, his mouth still open, and got a chestful of river water for his trouble. But the sudden inability to breathe galvanized him and he kicked out, clawed himself upwards again. He broke the surface, spluttering violently. Treading water, he gazed around in awe. The river was wider and deeper than he could have hoped in his wildest dreams. The slope he had just tumbled down rose precipitously on his left. On the right, a more gentle incline led up to yet more jungle, a solid brooding slab of vegetation that now looked inconsequential to him, who told himself that he would never have to march through that. The river would be his highway now. He flipped contentedly onto his back and did a couple of lazy leg kicks in the direction of the near bank, gazing out across the still, olive-green surface of the water; and then, with a shock, he remembered Claudio.

He lurched upright, doing a frantic dog-paddle as he scanned the river for signs of movement; and then, as if in answer to his thoughts, a familiar figure came bursting up from the depths, right in front of him. Spluttering, Claudio flicked his black hair out of his eyes, sending a long glittering arc whirling back over his head. His face was a picture, his eyes, too large, darted left and right in disbelief. Then his gaze came to rest on Martin. The two of them trod water in silence for a moment, briefly reminding themselves that, a moment before, they had been deadly enemies.

As if at some prearranged signal, their faces split into triumphant grins and, with a couple of wild yells, they launched themselves at each other; not to fight, but to play like a couple of excited children, splashing water, tousling each other's hair.

'We did it, by God!' yelled Claudio, his former madness cleansed by the absolving touch of the river. 'We did it!'

'We sure as fuckin' hell did!' agreed Martin. He turned an ungainly backflip and came splashing back to the surface with a whoop of joy. Then again, he launched himself at Claudio, pounding his back, ducking his head under the water. 'You crafty sonofabitch!' he yelled. 'You Goddamned three-star *genius*! You said we'd find the river and we did! Jesus, if only we'd known it was this close, we needn't have wasted so much *energy*!'

They both laughed. Claudio jerked a thumb over his shoulder and shook his head. 'Back there,' he muttered. 'I don't know what happened, I was crazy I guess.'

'Me too. Hell, I didn't hurt you too much, did I?'

'No. You?'

'Damned near broke my fuckin' jaw!'

Again they laughed.

'We'll be all right now,' announced Claudio with conviction. He pointed upriver. 'The way home,' he said.

Martin nodded. The word 'home' had a beautiful ring to it and for the moment, he did not intend to worry too much about Caine. He turned and struck out for the shore.

'I'd better get Helen,' he shouted back. 'Hell, she still doesn't know about any of this.' He reached the bank and clambered out, then stood searching for an easy way up the steep slope. He located a track and started up it, but then found his hat lying a few feet away. On an impulse, he snatched this up, doubled back and scooped up a hatful of river water. Then he hurried on his way again, anxious to get to Helen before the precious liquid seeped out. He staggered drunkenly up to the treeline, found the place where he and Claudio had crashed through the undergrowth and retraced his steps along the trail. Holding the hat carefully out in front of him, he pushed through a screen of ferns and saw Helen up ahead.

She was coming slowly towards him, limping painfully, no doubt worried by the interval of time that had passed since Martin had left her. She had to stop every few yards to get her breath back and it was clear from her agonized expression that this last effort was stretching her to the very limits of endurance. She could hardly have been prepared for the sudden whooping attack of a complete maniac who bore her gleefully to the ground and upturned a hatful of water on her head.

She collapsed in an ungainly heap with a shriek of pure terror mingled with rage. She drew back her fists to strike out at her tormentor; and then she froze, her eyes wide

243

and staring, her mouth hanging open, as she recognized the cool substance that was trickling down her face and neck; and as she took in the fact that Martin's clothes were soaking wet.

'The river?' she whispered fearfully. She hardly dared hope that the miracle for which they had all been praying could actually have occurred. But Martin was nodding, grinning. When Helen spoke again, her voice was a fierce, joyful shriek of exaltation. 'The river! You found the river!' And then her weariness was forgotten, she was on her feet, leaping up and down like an excited child, clapping her hands and yelling at the top of her voice. They fell into each other's arms, performed a strange celebratory waltz; right there in the middle of the jungle, they spun round and round until they were giddy and fell in a heap on the ground.

And then there was a sudden intense stillness as they lay staring hungrily at each other, their eyes saying the things that their tongues would have been too clumsy with. They moved closer, their mouths locked together, and they embraced tightly. Martin pushed Helen back against the ground and they lay for a long timeless moment, their lips and tongues exploring. Then Helen pushed him gently away and they gazed inquiringly at each other.

'I'll have to find a river more often,' observed Martin wryly.

Helen lowered her gaze. She felt suddenly a little self-conscious. 'I must look a sight for sore eyes.'

'You look just fine to me.'

'Well, maybe once I've had a good *wash*, I won't look quite so . . .' For the first time, she noticed the collection of new bruises that adorned Martin's face. 'What happened to you?' she inquired.

'Oh, I had a little disagreement with Claudio. It's all right now but at the time, we were pretty het up over it. Luckily we found the river; or rather, *it* found *us*. We kind of . . . fell into it.'

'I *thought* you were gone a damned long time. I got panicky, started imagining all kinds of things. Bad things.' She reached out and stroked his bearded face gently. 'Here, help me up will you? What I want most in the world right now is a bath.'

They got to their feet and Helen placed an arm around Martin's shoulders. She walked better now that she had the promise of something good waiting at the end of the trail. As she walked, her spare arm came across to hold Martin's hand very tightly in her own. Neither of them spoke, but as they approached the fringe of light that dappled the top edge of the high bank, it felt as though they were emerging from a long, dark, airless tunnel into the first welcome touch of a new day. They paused at the top of the bank for a moment, gazing down at the long serene sweep of the river as it knifed through the jungle and away. Martin glanced at Helen and saw that her eyes were brimming with tears. Still saying nothing they picked their way down the bank and stepped, without hesitation, into the water's cool embrace.

Caine leaned forward across the grubby wooden table and his eyes narrowed slightly. In the sunless gloom of the little back-street bar, his face looked pale and unreal, as though it had been built up from handfuls of glistening white putty.

'You're sure it's them?' he whispered.

Paolo sipped at his glass of *cachaça*. 'As I said before, Senhor Caine, I cannot be one hundred per cent certain. But it seems very likely that Taggart, a tough *garimpeiro*, should be one of the people to escape . . . and tomorrow, maybe the day after, I should be able to get a look at them.'

Caine nodded thoughtfully. He leaned back, his hands folded across his fat stomach. 'He is alive,' he breathed. 'I feel it in my blood.' He took a white silk handkerchief from his pocket and mopped at his sticky forehead, glancing disdainfully around as he did so. The bar was deserted and it was oppressively hot. Above the table, an electric fan clicked disconsolately and beyond the open doorway the occasional shadow of a passing pedestrian danced in the heat-haze. The proprietor, a stooped little man with a rat-like face and a drooping moustache, had quickly tired of trying to eavesdrop on the conversation of Paolo's unusually well-heeled friends and had retreated to the far end of a long wooden counter, where he washed glasses with a slow, indolent air. Caine glanced disgustedly at his own glass of gin, which had come to him without so much as an ice-cube in it. Beside him, Otto Schiller sat slumped in his chair, staring sullenly at Paolo while one hand played absent-mindedly with the things he carried in his pocket. Not for the first time, Paolo found himself wondering what they were. By the sound they were numerous, small and hard; pebbles perhaps, or beads. He was on the point of asking about them when he was distracted by Caine's abrupt grunt of dissatisfaction.

'What on earth made you choose this pigsty to meet in? There isn't even any air-conditioning.'

Paolo shrugged. 'I phoned the office yesterday, but you weren't there. Naturally, I didn't want to leave details with just *anyone*, so I suggested the first place that came to mind. This is where I usually drink. It's cheap and the glasses are clean, that's about all you can say for it. Perhaps when this business is all tied up, I'll be able to drink in a *better* class of place.'

Caine bowed his head slightly, a mocking smile curving his lips. 'Indeed, Paolo, perhaps you will.' He pushed his glass away with a grimace and, taking out his cigarette case, offered the young pilot a smoke. As Paolo accepted he was aware that Schiller was still staring at him, like a snake at an intended victim.

246

'What the hell's he looking at?' he demanded uneasily.

Caine lit his own cigarette and chuckled. 'I think, Paolo, he's rather taken with that lovely film star's smile of yours. But you needn't worry about Otto. He wouldn't dream of harming a hair on your head; not unless I *instructed* him. And we're partners, aren't we, Paolo? So he's going to treat you as thoughtfully and considerately as he would his own grandmother ... isn't that right, Otto?'

After a few moments Schiller nodded. The rattling sound from his pocket was extraordinarily irritating and Caine suddenly turned on the German, a tone of anger in his voice. 'Oh for God's sake, Otto! Why don't you make yourself useful? Get me some ice for my drink!'

Schiller glanced perfunctorily at the bar. 'They don't have any here.'

'I know that, you fool. So, go *out* for some. There must be somewhere around here that sells ice. Get along with you, I'm sick of looking at your stupid face!'

For an instant, Paolo saw something flare up in Schiller's eyes, a cold, venomous hatred that suggested Caine had overstepped the mark; but almost at once the spark died. Schiller's shoulders sagged perceptibly, the eyes became bland, innocuous. He bowed slightly, got up and walked quickly towards the exit.

Why? Paolo found himself wondering. Why does he take that kind of crap from Caine? The fat man must have some kind of hold over him. But what?

Caine had turned back and was gazing thoughtfully at Paolo. 'Now then,' he said, 'show me the map you were talking about.'

Paolo reached into the breast pocket of his jacket and took out a crumpled chart. He unfolded it and spread it on the table. He glanced slyly across at the counter to ensure that the barman was out of hearing range.

'Here's where I saw the smoke.' He indicated a small

pencilled cross. 'And this line, you see, indicates the wreckage of the plane and the direction of the sign. They are heading for the Rio das Mortes.'

'It looks like they're *close*, too.'

'Yes, very close. I figure that at the very slowest walking pace, they will have reached it before nightfall.'

'And then what will they do?'

'Well, my guess is they'll try to build a raft or a boat of some kind. Then they have only to let the current take them downriver.'

Caine frowned. 'How far before they reach some kind of outpost?'

Paolo traced the course of the river with his index finger. 'Here,' he said. 'You see this point where the das Mortes joins the Araguaia? There's a small mission station run by an order of monks, at a place called Bananal. It's the first place where they would be likely to meet up with white men. But don't forget, it will take them at least a couple of days to build their boat and something like a week to sail as far down as this.'

'Very well,' Caine nodded. 'Now, tell me how *we* can get to that point before them.'

Paolo glanced up quizzically. 'We?' he echoed. 'Surely you are not intending to go on this trip yourself?'

'What if I am?'

'Well, forgive me, Senhor Caine, but . . . this would be no pleasure trip.' He gestured at Caine's glass and smiled. 'There would certainly be no ice in the drinks there.'

'Don't be impertinent. As I told you before, Paolo, this is a personal matter. It will be worth a little discomfort just to be sure that everything is done to my satisfaction. This business is very important to me and I don't intend to entrust it to anybody else. So . . .' He tapped the chart with a stubby forefinger. 'Assuming you do locate them tomorrow. What's our plan?'

'I take you in my plane to this village, Conceiçao,

248

farther north along the Araguaia. There's a stretch of *campo* alongside it where we can land. It's a long trip so we'll need to refuel, here, at Goian. My plane will take four, along with the necessary provisions for a trip up river. In the village, there's a man I know, Hernandez. From him we can hire a *batelão*, a small boat with a good, powerful outboard motor which will get us up to the mission station in three, maybe four days. So, when your friends arrive there; we'll be waiting for them.' Paolo spread his hands in a gesture of superiority.

'Paolo, that's marvellous! You seem to have everything figured out. You've done a good job.' Caine reached out across the table and his big hand came to rest on the young pilot's shoulder, where it gripped with a surprisingly powerful hold; then the grip relaxed and the hand stroked its way down Paolo's arm with a disturbing show of intimacy. 'You're a good boy, Paolo; and there's no doubt that you are one of *my* boys now. So . . . let's have no more slumming in places like this, understand? The boys that work for me, I like them to look good and be seen in all the right places.' He reached into the pocket of his jacket and brought out an envelope which he threw onto the table. 'There's a little money on account,' he said. 'Buy yourself a good suit. Have yourself some fun in the city. When this business is over, you may be a rich man.' The hand was back on Paolo's shoulder, gripping him with a steady, menacing power. 'And from now on, *I'll* choose where you drink.'

While the men talked together on the flat *praia* they had chosen as a campsite, Helen wandered a little distance along the river bank and sought out a place where a curve in the river had created a deep little lagoon surrounded by rocks. She undressed quickly, tossing her discarded clothing into the water so that it too could be washed. Then she lowered her body gratefully into the warm

249

water, wincing at first as her raw ankles went in but then
settling down with a sigh of contentment. She washed the
clothing first, kneading each item vigorously between her
hands and then spreading them on the rocks to dry. Then
she got down to work on herself, rubbing at her insect-
bitten nakedness with the palms of her hands, wishing
vainly for a bar of perfumed soap. She dunked her head
repeatedly beneath the water and ploughed her fingertips
agonizingly through the knots and tangles in her hair.
Then she straightened up and saw Martin Taggart, sitting
on a rock a short distance away, watching her with
interest. A rifle was cradled across his knees and he was
smiling at her with a familiarity that should have
embarrassed her; but she did not even make a move to
conceal her exposed breasts. In this primitive place, it
seemed a ridiculously *civilized* way to behave. So she just
returned his gaze for a moment, smiled and went on with
her bathing.

'Where's Claudio?' she asked after a while.

'Oh, you know him. He's set off on an expedition
already ... looking for suitable wood to build this
damned raft. He left me in charge.' Martin waggled the
rifle. 'I wasn't sure what I was supposed to be watching
for, so I figured I'd come down here and guard you.'

'That's very thoughtful.'

'Don't mention it. How's the water?'

'It's good. Why don't you try it for yourself?'

'Oh, I'd sure like to; but I'm supposed to be on guard.'

She turned and looked at him for a moment. 'I won't
tell Claudio,' she said.

It took him perhaps thirty seconds to strip off his
clothes and pouch and plunge in beside her, where he set
about a furious mimicry of her own bathing ritual,
splashing water into her face and generally behaving like
a naughty child. She reciprocated, laughing gleefully.
They were, both of them, in high spirits.

'Hell, I'll tell you something!' he shouted. 'I never expected to see this Goddamned river!'

'Me neither. Not really. I hoped of course but . . .' She spread her arms dramatically. 'Anyway, here we are!'

He nodded, quietening suddenly. 'Yeah, here we are. You know, a couple of nights back . . . I don't know if you remember. The rain and all . . .'

'I remember.'

'We . . . made a deal, did we not?'

She nodded, unafraid. 'We made a deal.'

He moved a little closer to her, until he was standing mere inches away. He lifted his arms to encircle her waist.

'I'm here to collect,' he said.

'Don't worry,' she told him. 'I never welched on a deal in my life.'

'That's what I figured,' he said and kissed her.

A pair of harpy eagles drifted lazily on the air currents, hundreds of feet above the river. Martin lay on his back in the hot sand gazing up at them, shielding his eyes with the flat of one hand. Beside him, Helen dozed. She had turned onto her side and Martin could see where her firm buttocks had made two smooth impressions in the damp sand. It had surprised him, the ferocity of their love-making; had surprised and delighted him. It was with a shock now that he realized how long it had been since he had made love to a woman. Years; and then he couldn't attribute his last coupling to anything as noble as love. A skinny Indian girl at the Garimpo Maculo brothel. Her once fierce and independent tribe had been decimated by the white diamond hunters and she had been obliged to take up the only role left to her. Martin remembered the cheerless grubby room, the cheap body-stained mattress, the way the girl had counted the paltry sum of paper money so carefully before putting it into an old cigar box. But mostly he remembered her eyes – big, vacant, devoid

251

of any interest in the white man who had just possessed her. She was probably fourteen or fifteen years old. Martin had asked her, but she was not sure herself.

The eagles began to soar away, following the line of the river, and far off Martin heard one of them call, a tiny questioning shriek in the silence. Then they were gone, chasing their shadows downriver, going home to their roosts in some secret place. Martin envied them.

He started abruptly at the sound of a footfall on the sand. Claudio was going to catch him, quite literally, with his pants down. He turned, a smile of apology on his lips, and then he froze, his eyes widened in shock. It wasn't Claudio.

It was an Indian, a small wiry man, naked and ominous because of a wooden disc that distended his bottom lip to a long, bill-like obscenity. His hair was sleek black, cut to his shoulders, and the lobes of his ears were pierced with eagle feathers. In his left hand he held a string of silvery fish; in the other, a long vicious-looking spear which he had raised threateningly above his head. Some way back along the sandbank, a second warrior was approaching.

All this Martin registered in the flash of an eye; and in an abrupt sidelong glance he saw that his rifle still lay on a rock some ten yards away.

'Shit,' he murmured softly; and instantly regretted it. It seemed to antagonize the Indian. He jabbered something that sounded decidedly unfriendly and, raising the spear a few inches, took a step towards Martin, staring at him as though he was looking at something incomprehensible. Martin, as slowly as he could, raised himself to his feet, keeping his hands raised out in front of him. He was terrified and his flesh crawled as he imagined the impact of that terrible yard-long spear, the tip of which had been fashioned from the jagged, barbed tip of a sting-ray's tail. The Indian jabbered again, something that might have been a question. Martin could only spread his arms

252

imploringly, shaking his head from side to side. Then Helen woke up.

She sat abruptly upright and her eyes widened in terror. Her mouth opened to scream.

'Helen, no, don't make a sound!' Martin implored her. 'Get these two excited and we're both dead!' The Indian was confused now, glancing from one stranger to the other in amazement. His companion had halted some distance away and Martin saw, with a sense of dread, that he was unslinging a bow from his shoulder. 'Hold your hands up and smile at them,' he told Helen, speaking from between gritted teeth like a ventriloquist. 'I'm going to try and move backwards towards the gun . . .'

Helen nodded. 'I hope to God he doesn't speak English.'

Martin took an exploratory step backwards and the Indian shouted and pointed the spear straight at his heart. 'He doesn't seem to like that,' observed Martin helplessly; but he forced himself to take another step and another as the Indian advanced, studying every move the white man made. Now the second warrior was coming closer, an arrow notched in his bow. In a few seconds, he would be close enough to make any move out of the question.

'Helen, you've got to distract him,' he said desperately.

'How?' she gasped.

'Hell, I don't know. Just *do* something!'

Helen took him at his word. She began to sing 'Yankee Doodle Dandee'. That did it. The Indian turned his head a fraction to stare at Helen and Martin took what he knew would be his only chance. He sprang forward, seized the shaft of the spear in both hands and pulled with all his strength. Caught off balance, the Indian lurched forward and Martin aimed a savage kick into the man's unprotected testicles. He sank to his knees with a scream and a second kick into the throat pitched him back onto the sand just as his companion came running in to loose off a shot over the fallen man's head. There was no time to get out of the way, but luckily, the shot went a fraction wide. Martin felt the swift terrible hiss of the arrow as it whizzed by, scant inches from his face.

He did not wait for anything else to happen. Turning on his heel, he raced back towards his rifle, grabbed it, pumped a cartridge into the breach and spun around. The fallen Indian was struggling awkwardly to his feet, clutching at the handle of a knife that hung from a girdle of string around his waist. Martin fired from the hip and the crash of the gun mingled with a brief scream from Helen. The bullet smashed a large hole in the Indian's chest, the impact flinging him backwards a second time onto the sand. He lay staring sightlessly up at the sky, his distended bottom lip flapping spasmodically as his last breath escaped. The echoes of the shot faded on the air. Helen covered her face with her hands.

The second Indian had frozen in an attitude of shock, another arrow notched but not drawn back. He was staring in disbelief at his companion, noting the dark trickle of blood that pulsed from his shattered chest.

'Don't try it,' muttered Martin and he took a threatening step forward, pumping the rifle bolt as he did so. The Indian gave a curious guttural cry, dropped the bow and arrow and turned to run back along the *praia*. Martin followed the man a few paces, indifferent to his fate at first; but then he saw what the Indian was running *to*. He swore vividly and launched himself in pursuit.

The canoe lay some hundred yards away, beached on the *praia* just above the waterline. It was a long, slim craft, fashioned painstakingly from the trunk of a single tree. To the Indians, it was simply a form of locomotion; to Martin, it was a gift from the gods, and in that instant, he knew that he could not allow the Indian to reach it. He paused, raised the rifle to his shoulder and took a careful aim on the running figure. He squeezed the trigger and the gun kicked back hard. The Indian spun round with a howl of terror as his left shoulder blade erupted in a gout of blood and shattered bone. He went down, face first, onto the sand; but incredibly he was up in an instant and racing off in a new direction, towards the jungle which bordered the river on his left. Martin had time for just one more wild shot before the Indian plunged into cover and was gone. As the sound of the last shot faded, it was abruptly very quiet.

Martin shook his head, spat disgustedly onto the sand. He'd have felt a lot easier in his mind if he'd made sure of the man. He approached the canoe cautiously, scanning the ranks of jungle as he did so, but everything seemed quiet. He knelt beside the slim craft, silently praising his good fortune. The Indians had evidently come out on a long fishing expedition. Inside the canoe, along with a pair of carved wooden paddles, there were a large number of spears, a formidable collection of fish and several sacks. Opening one of these, Martin found that it was full of turtle's eggs. He turned and saw that Helen was approaching. She had partially dressed herself and was carrying some of his clothes. She gave the Indian's corpse a particularly wide berth.

'You all right?' he asked her.

'I guess so.' She handed him his clothes and he began to pull them on.

'Your rendition of "Yankee Doodle Dandee" was a little off key,' he told her.

'I'm better with a more receptive audience. Still, I'll work on it.' She turned at the sound of approaching footsteps and was relieved to see a familiar figure racing breathlessly towards them. Claudio slowed to a halt, panting for breath as he stared down for a moment at the dead Indian. Then he moved around it and came towards his companions, looking oddly at Martin who was still pulling on his trousers.

255

'What the hell's been happening here?' he demanded. 'I heard the shots —'

His gaze had fallen on the canoe. He pushed past the others, fell on his knees beside it, stroked its rough hull with the fingers of one hand. Then he turned his head, glanced back at the dead Indian.

'What happened?' he asked quietly.

Martin shrugged. He finished buttoning his trousers and reached for his shirt. 'They must have been fishing and just chanced on us.'

'*They*?'

'Yeah. There was another one. I put a bullet into him but he managed to make it to the jungle, over there.' He pointed. 'It was a bad moment. One minute we . . .' he glanced quickly at Helen '. . . were alone and the next they were standing right over us. They near frightened the shit out of me, I can tell you.' He noticed again that Claudio was staring curiously at him and he spread his arms in a gesture of explanation. 'I was bathing,' he said.

Claudio nodded; but he glanced at Helen, noticing that her clothes were wet and mostly unbuttoned. An expression came to his bearded face, a frown of reprimand such as a parent might make.

'I thought I left you on *guard*,' he admonished Martin; but happily he did not wait for an answer. He moved instead to the corpse of the Indian. He knelt beside it, examining it carefully. The cheeks of the man's face were marked with bold designs in *urucu* – red dye – and it was to these that Claudio paid most attention.

'Recognize the tribe?' Martin inquired.

Claudio nodded grimly. 'Xavante, I think. I've never seen one close to, but I've heard descriptions, mostly from other Indians who came off worst after a fight. They're supposed to be very *bravo* – fierce.' He turned his head and stared towards the trees. 'Was it absolutely necessary to kill this man?'

256

'Well, hell, yes, I think so ... he was shouting and waving a Goddamned spear in my face. I guess I didn't feel much like giving him the benefit of the doubt. Then the other one tried to make a run for the canoe. I *couldn't* let him take that away from us.'

Claudio sighed. 'No, I suppose not.'

'The other one fired an arrow at us.' Helen had moved to stand beside Martin and had slipped an arm protectively around his waist. In that instant, Claudio felt that the distance between him and his two companions was fully compounded. In the time he had been away, their increasing familiarity had been taken to its logical conclusion. Now, they were a team; he would always be the outsider.

'They were probably more frightened than you were,' he said. 'But since you felt that you had to fire, I wish to God that you'd finished them *both* off. I've heard stories about these people. They've been known to go to great lengths for vengeance.'

Martin frowned. 'Worth going after the other one?' he inquired. 'He's got a bullet in him, it should slow him down some.'

Claudio shook his head. 'Not a good idea; not when he's on his home ground. Wounded or not, he'd cut our balls off and serve them to us on a plate.' He stared at the two of them again and the sanctimonious expression returned. 'You'd better finish getting dressed, both of you. Since fate has delivered a canoe into our hands, I vote that we use it straight away. I don't want to be here when those Xavantes come back to reclaim the body.' He got to his feet and strode back towards the campsite to collect their few possessions. Martin and Helen wandered back to their bathing place to pick up their discarded clothing.

'What's wrong with Claudio?' Martin muttered as he pulled on his boots. 'I get us the thing we need most in the world and is he grateful for it? No, he acts like some

257

Goddamned schoolmaster.'

'Well, I guess it must have put him in a difficult position. After all, he works for an Indian Agency. He's supposed to be looking after the Indians and you've just killed one and wounded another. How's he supposed to react to that?'

'But it was self-defence.'

'I know that. I suppose he does too, but still, he's bound to feel bad about the whole business.'

Martin shook his head. 'It's not so much *that* I'm talking about. You saw the way he was staring at us? Like maybe, I don't know . . . like he's jealous or something.'

'Claudio, jealous? No –'

'Sure, why not? He's got feelings, hasn't he?'

Helen reached out and squeezed Martin's arm. 'I dare say he has, but listen, just don't even talk about it, all right? I mean, life is complicated enough as it is.'

He nodded, laughed nervously. He was still riding on the rush of adrenalin that had resulted from the encounter with the Indians. Now everything felt faintly unreal, as though he was somehow outside the situation, observing it.

'Look,' he said, 'about *before*. I didn't have much of a chance to say anything but it was . . .' He shook his head, could not find the words to express what he wanted to say.

Helen smiled sympathetically. 'It was,' she agreed wholeheartedly. 'Very.'

Martin was not very adept at talking of such things but he was determined to make his point. 'I just wanted to say . . . well . . . I think you're one hell of a lady, that's all; and when we get out of this mess –'

But she had pressed the tips of her fingers against his lips. 'Don't talk about maybes,' she told him. 'We'll cross that bridge if and when we get to it.'

Claudio came bustling over laden with equipment,

anxious to be off. He dropped Martin's haversack at his feet and handed Helen the water jug.

'If you two are ready to go now,' he said, and there was more than a hint of sarcasm in his voice. Martin and Helen exchanged glances but said nothing. They got to their feet and trooped obediently in his wake as he gave them the inevitable pep-talk.

'Either of you been in an Indian canoe before? No? Well, I thought not. Don't worry, there's not that much to it. Here, take hold, let's get it down to the water. They're hard to balance at first and your legs will be cramped, but you'll soon get used to that. There now, Martin, you'll take the prow and use that paddle. Helen, you sit in the middle here. Try to avoid making any sudden movements. All right then. I think we're ready . . .'

The two men pushed the craft out into deeper waters while Helen sat amidships, gripping the sides of the hull. Then Martin scrambled aboard while Claudio steadied the canoe. With a last push, Claudio hauled himself over the side, making the canoe wobble precariously. For a moment, things looked very uncertain but then the two men took hold of their paddles and a few earnest strokes took them out into midstream, where they began to move along at a surprisingly brisk speed.

Crouched in the stern, Claudio threw a last apprehensive glance back over his shoulder at the dark impenetrable depths of *selva* that hugged the shoreline. Of course finding the canoe had been little short of a miracle; and yes, he was quite prepared to accept that the killing had been in self-defence. But letting the other man escape to tell tales, that was a mistake they might live to regret. He frowned, dipped the blade of his paddle deep into the river and pushed the canoe along on the already speedy current. He was anxious to get as far away from this place as possible.

The Indian watched from cover until the canoe had rounded the first bend of the river; then he emerged from his hiding place and walked slowly out across the *praia* to his fallen companion. He moved with difficulty because of the great ragged hole in his shoulder. Blood pumped copiously down his chest but he paid it no heed.

He dropped to his knees beside the corpse and prodded it a couple of times to ensure that the man really was dead. There was a dark bloody rent in the man's chest and after a few moments the Indian pushed his fingers deep into this, coating them with a layer of still-warm blood. He brought his hand back up and trailed the fingers across his own face, first one cheek and then the other, daubing them with the image of death. Then he turned and stared back downriver, spat venomously onto the sand. He remained in this position for a few moments, his eyes filled with hatred for the unseen occupants of the canoe.

Then abruptly he stood up, turned away. He paused only to collect the bow and arrow he had dropped on the *praia*. Gritting his teeth against the pain in his shoulder, he set off upriver at a steady run, veering left into the jungle at a point he knew would soon bring him to a trail that would take him back to his village.

In moments, he was lost to sight amongst the undergrowth. The *praia* stood deserted in the fierce light of the afternoon. A mantle of flies buzzed inquisitively around the still figure lying on the sand. High up in the vast blue emptiness of the sky, the first black vulture came riding the air currents in search of food.

PART THREE

Downriver

Chapter 12

They made good progress that day. After the interminable slog through the jungle, it seemed strange to have nothing to do; to laze in the canoe, paddling with the current as they slid effortlessly downriver between the silent over-hanging foliage of the jungle. The weather was clear and the sun, streaming down through the broad gap overhead, reflected up from the water into their faces, scorching their skin and dazzling their eyes. Claudio spoke of making a shaded canopy for the canoe when they had time to stop awhile; but Martin noticed that he was for ever casting apprehensive glances back upstream, as though expecting to see at any moment a whole armada of war canoes in hot pursuit.

Happily, such a vision did not materialize. The afternoon wore on uneventfully and, as the quick tropical twilight descended, they made camp on a convenient *praia* and cooked some supper of fresh fish and boiled turtle's eggs. Finding the river had naturally renewed their hope. Now, every mile they covered in the direction of home served to make them more confident. Helen and Martin felt reasonably sure now that the worst was behind them; Claudio, prudent as ever, simply announced that they would keep three-hour watches throughout the night.

In an uncharacteristic show of generosity, Martin offered to take first watch and, while the others snuggled under their wool blankets, he remained sitting by the fire cradling a rifle in his arms. It was silent save for the rhythmic chirruping of insects and the strange metallic hammering sounds that were made by tree-frogs. Beside him the river flowed silently past in the moonlight. For the very first time since he had been marooned, he was struck by the natural beauty of this wild, desolate place, a quality he would never have dreamed of attributing to it before. But then he was aware that something had changed in him and, though he was not exactly sure what it was, he knew that it had a lot to do with Helen Brody.

He turned his head to look at her. She was stretched out on her side, her head supported on one arm. Her face, illuminated by the waning embers of the fire, had a soft bewitching serenity to it that suggested she was at home, in the comfort and security of her own bed. A half-smile played upon her lips.

Martin was alternately intrigued and dismayed by the feelings she kindled in him. He was beginning to feel irresistibly drawn to her, he, Martin Taggart, the man who had never allowed a woman close enough to have any hold over him. Perhaps it was just the situation they were in. Sure, that was it. There was nothing like the fear of imminent destruction for making people reach out for things they'd never bothered with before. Still, for all that, it felt good. Like coming home after being a long time away; and it was also true that now he was thinking very seriously about survival.

He reached beneath his shirt and fingered the diamond in its worn leather pouch. Well, he still had that particular ace in the hole, and if he could hang onto it a while longer, it would give him a damn good start once he got back to the real world. Maybe Helen too, if she was interested. He hadn't quite made up his mind about that one. In a way, he wished she'd never found out about the diamond. No matter how much he cared for her, always at the back of his mind would be the fear that it had been the diamond and the kind of life that went with it that had initially drawn her to him. It had to be admitted, though, that it was beginning to look as if they had a

264

good chance of making it back to safety; but Martin reminded himself that 'safety' was a shaky term when applied to his own personal situation. News of the survivors' return was sure to precede their arrival in Belém; and there was surely not much news that eluded Charles Caine.

Martin jerked his head up suddenly as he sensed, rather than heard, something out in the black primeval night. He scanned the ranks of dark vegetation that flanked the muzzy periphery of his vision; nothing seemed amiss, and yet, abruptly, a strange sensation was with him, the powerful, insistent conviction that he was being observed.

This is crazy, he thought. *I'm just jumpy, that's all. Been listening to Claudio too much . . .*

But still, the feeling would not leave him. It nagged relentlessly at the back of his mind and, after a few minutes of doing his best to ignore it, he had to get up and pace slowly around the area of the campsite, his rifle ready for any eventuality. But it was a pointless task. He could see no more than a few yards into the tangled vegetation that lay on his right-hand side and to his left lay the cool silent run of the river. After a few moments, he came back to the fire. On impulse, he reached out and tossed a few more sticks onto the blaze. The fire crackled, belched smoke and then began to respond, eating greedily into the fresh supply of fuel. The level of light rose dramatically, casting a flurry of dancing shadows around the clearing. Glancing up, Martin thought he saw a long lean shadow detach itself from its surroundings and glide deeper into cover.

The effect was uncanny. It was as though the blood in his veins had abruptly turned to ice and he felt the hairs on the back of his neck stand up on end. He cursed beneath his breath, trained the gun on the area and waited. But now there was nothing. He tried to assure himself that all he had seen was a trick of the firelight, but somehow he could not convince himself. Nor could he calm his heart-rate, which seemed to be jolting along in his chest at a terrible pace. He glanced nervously back to the others and licked his dry lips. He wondered if he should wake them; but for what? To tell them that he'd been frightened by a shadow? They wouldn't be very impressed. He looked again at the place where the movement had been. Behind a screen of spiky ferns, there seemed to lie a hollow, a dark void, an emptiness.

Taking a deep breath, Martin reached down to the fire and snatched up the uncharred end of one of the bigger branches. He held the blazing end of it up above his head and watched as the emphasis of the light moved. Once again, didn't he discern the subtlest trace of movement there?

He shook his head. He had to be sure.

Holding the torch out in front of him and cradling the rifle in his right arm, he got slowly to his feet, his gaze fixed intently on that one spot. He took a hesitant first step forward, paused, stared until his eyes seemed to swim with coloured lights. Nothing. The blackness was still a blackness, an empty frame waiting to be filled. He took another step, another and each successive one changed the look of the area he was approaching. That dark hulking silhouette he had wondered about. Nothing but the stump of a fallen tree, rotten and pitted with decay. The thing that had vaguely resembled a coiled serpent waiting to strike. Nothing more startling than a hanging liana, dead and grey but hardly an object of fear. Light always explained the inexplicable. He had been acting like a child, afraid of the darkness in his bedroom.

He laughed at his own nervousness and turned to walk back to the fire. But the sound stopped him in his tracks. It was the faintest, the most imperceptible of sounds but it

266

brought fear back to Martin with a terrible jolt, set his skin crawling with apprehension.

It sounded, he thought, like somebody breathing.

Now this really is stupid, he told himself. *You're letting your imagination run riot.* But like a man in a trance, he turned back and continued to walk towards the darkness. He reached the edge of the jungle and was horribly aware that he was now some considerable distance from his companions. He pushed aside a low-lying tree limb and the dry wood crackled noisily in the silence; a silence so intense now that it was almost unbearable. What had happened to the insect sounds, for God's sake?

Maybe I'd better wake the others, he thought. A vision ran through his mind. Out in the darkness the Xavantes waited, armed and intent on vengeance. He would walk headlong into a trap and his companions would die in their sleep, never knowing what hit them. He was again on the point of returning when there was a rustle in the darkness that nearly made him turn tail and run like a frightened rabbit. He lifted the rifle and, filled with silent dread, took another step forward.

'Who's there?' he asked apprehensively. He felt vaguely ridiculous asking such a question; whoever was there would hardly respond. He became aware of a thick film of sweat moving down his forehead but, with both hands occupied, could not wipe it away. One more step carried him near enough to see that there *was* something crouched in the shadows . . . something moving from left to right across his vision.

Slowly, he raised the flaming torch a little higher so that the light flooded into the dark hollows beneath the undergrowth.

And then he was laughing with relief. The anteater was browsing happily at the base of a rotten tree stump, his long prehensile tongue scooping up mouthfuls of frantic termites who were spilling out from fissures in the ancient bark. He glanced up at Martin disdainfully, clearly relishing his dinner too much to allow this strange primate to scare him off.

'Well, feller, you surely put the fear of God into me!' chuckled Martin. He squatted down on his haunches, jabbed the torch into the soft ground and extended one hand towards the shaggy, striped creature in invitation; and then suddenly, with heart-stopping, sick-making abruptness, a face appeared from the darkness behind the anteater; a huge, feral, rage-filled face; yellow eyes that glittered fear and hatred, a gaping mouth that pumped the stench of raw meat past rows of ferocious pointed teeth. The anteater squealed and ran, while Martin could do no more than cower in terror as a long blasting roar seemed to shake the ground on which he squatted. He was literally rooted to the spot.

And then the jaguar was gone, melting back into jungle darkness like a great silent ghost. It had been lying up, readying itself to pounce on the anteater when Martin had come walking to within a few feet of its hiding place. Luckily it had been too frightened of the man and the blazing torch he carried to attack. Now, it was running fast along some hidden trail, seeking a less inhabited stretch of jungle.

For a long moment, Martin was unable to move. He stayed where he was and willed his heart to start beating again. At last it did, erratic but loud. He gasped, took a deep breath of night air. He still held the rifle in his right hand, a useless toy that he had never even thought to use, so lost in panic had he been. Now he felt drained, barely able to command his limbs. But with an effort he willed himself to get back to his feet and slowly made his way back to the camp. He had somehow expected to find the others awake, but nothing had changed. They both slept on, blissfully unaware that anything out of the ordinary had happened. He felt somehow betrayed. He could be nothing more than a heap of torn meat in the jungle by now and nobody would be any the wiser till morning.

With a sigh, he deposited his burning branch back onto the campfire and resumed the seat he had vacated a short while before. It would take something really significant to lure him away from there again. Glancing at Helen's watch, which lay across a log beside the fire, he saw that he still had another two hours to pass, but that was probably just as well. Any sleepiness he had felt earlier on had been effectively driven out of him by what was, after all, his second bad scare of the day.

He did not relish the dreams that would doubtless come to him later that night.

At first light they were on their way again, guiding the canoe out through the ethereal banks of mist that overhung the surface of the river. Claudio's plan was to get as much paddling done in the early hours as possible, before the cruel heat of the day began to take its toll. With this in mind, he had carved an extra paddle the previous night so that all three of them could put their backs into it at any given time. In the powerful tug of the current midstream, they once again made admirable progress, but the inactivity that had made such a pleasant change the day before had already outlived its welcome. The mechanical act of pushing the wooden oars through the water was boring and the journey soon became maddeningly uneventful. There was just the long silky stretch of the river and always the trees, crowding in on either side, dark and suffocating, pushing down greedy fingers to stroke the occupants of the canoe. Occasionally there were signs of animal life, the brief vivid flash of a macaw's plumage amongst the foliage or the elegant cautious gait of a *jabiru* – a white stork – wading through the shallows at the water's edge. But mostly it was just the silent desolation that they had come to know and hate.

They tried amusing themselves with spear-fishing for a while. The waters here teemed with fish, any number could be seen simply by staring down over the side of the boat into the clear water. There were huge whiskered catfish, electric eels and rays and a billion odd darting species that none of them could put a name to. Particularly numerous here were the black piranha, the broad, foot-long creatures whose ferocious habits had passed into legend. Claudio managed to spear one and he held it up so the others could examine it. Apart from the squat, tenacious jaws, it looked rather ordinary.

'You don't want to believe all the stories you hear about these things,' Claudio assured them. 'All that stuff about stripping a man to his bones in a few seconds ... that's nonsense.'

'Really?' Helen seemed remarkably unconvinced.

'Sure. It takes much longer than that. Ten, fifteen minutes maybe.'

'They are dangerous then?'

'Yes and no. I mean, for instance, you see those piranha down there?' He pointed out a thick shoal cruising alongside the canoe; and then, before anybody could stop him, had plunged his naked arm in amongst them. He held it there for quite some time, while the others watched him uneasily. The piranha investigated the arm curiously, approaching to within a short distance then shying nervously away from it. As soon as he felt he'd made his point, Claudio withdrew the limb.

'You see, they had every chance to bite me, but they didn't; because it's not just the presence of flesh in the water that sets them off. It's one of two things. First, fear. It's as if they can taste if an animal's afraid. I've seen an animal, say a capybara, fall in the water and get panicky, start struggling. Then the piranha are there, hitting into him. The other thing, of course, is blood. Watch this.'

He carefully removed the piranha from the point of the spear and, taking out his knife, slit the fish's belly wide open. Then he threw it overboard several feet ahead of the canoe.

The effect was startling. Almost as soon as the fish hit the water, it was surrounded by a flurry of dark bodies, attracted to the blood in the water like iron filings to a magnet. The area came suddenly alive with turbulence, a frantic flapping of silver tails and fins that seemed strangely to escalate in a wide area around the fish.

'In their haste,' said Claudio tonelessly, 'they sometimes bite at each other. Each stricken fish in turn becomes another victim.'

'Cannibals,' murmured Helen with distaste.

'Brazil is a country that specializes in them,' replied Claudio. 'The Xavantes, for instance, are known for some peculiar eating habits.' He saw that he had alarmed her and patted her shoulder reassuringly. They turned to look at the commotion in the water as it dropped away behind the stern of the canoe.

'Wherever you go in Brazil,' said Claudio, 'you're sure to meet someone who'll tell you a God's truth tale about some friend who went to wash his hands in a river and managed to leave his fingers behind.'

'The way I heard it, the guy was taking a pee; and it wasn't his fingers he left,' Martin said.

Claudio grinned. 'Yes, well I heard that one too. I was being polite.' He flushed slightly as he met Helen's inquiring gaze. 'The piranha, he's just a dumb creature like all the rest. Nothing so special about him really. And if this canoe overturned right now, we'd be perfectly safe.' Then he eyed Helen's raw ankles meaningfully and added. 'You might have something to worry about.'

'Thanks,' she replied. 'You know, Mr Ormeto, you have a way of making a girl feel really comfortable.'

Claudio smiled apologetically. He was on the point of

saying something else but seemed to think better of it.

The hours passed with slow mechanical precision. At one point, they spotted a huge fish, a *pirarucu*, cruising beneath the canoe. It was the length of a grown man and almost as wide. Martin grabbed a spear and managed to plunge it into the creature but was unable to hold it as it gave a great lurch to the side, almost pulling him headlong out of the boat. The fish took off upriver and they watched the haft of the spear jutting out of the water like a crazy periscope as it sped into the distance.

'It would have taken us a month to eat it anyway,' Claudio observed.

The mention of food reminded them that they were hungry, so a little after midday they pulled into a convenient *praia* and cooked themselves some of the fish that hadn't got away, together with more of the turtle's eggs which had a strong meaty flavour to them. Life was a good deal more agreeable than it had been back in the jungle and Martin remarked that a man could probably even grow to like it.

'Perhaps you should come and work for the Indian agency,' Claudio told him. 'This is very much the kind of life I lead. In fact, if it hadn't been for that damned crash, I suppose right now I'd have been coming up the *Araguaia* from the other direction. Now the trip will have to be cancelled, at least until after the rains.'

'How long before we meet up with someone?' Martin asked.

'By "someone" I suppose you mean white people; well, I would guess about a week. There's a mission station at a place called Bananal; the farthest upriver I've been before this. It's a small place run by some Dominican friars and, as far as I know, the first proper outpost we'll come to. They'll have a few creature comforts there. Whisky, newspapers, soap . . .' He glanced at Martin. 'Cigarettes.'

Martin was genuinely amazed to find that he had

272

virtually forgotten all about his former cravings.

As soon as lunch was finished, they went back to the canoe. Once again, Martin caught Claudio glancing apprehensively upstream.

What the hell does he expect to see? he wondered, knowing full well that Claudio was not the sort of man to worry without good reason.

They got the canoe pushed out onto the water and clambered awkwardly aboard. They were quickly getting accustomed to travelling in the canoe but there was inevitably a moment of uncertainty at the point of embarkation. The men dug their paddles into water and within minutes they were back in midstream. It was now the hottest part of the day and Helen and Martin began to wish that they had stayed long enough at the *praia* to build the sun-shade that Claudio had mentioned the day before.

'Tonight, when we make camp,' he assured them. 'We'll build it then.'

'I wish I knew how vital it is to hurry,' Martin complained. 'You really think those Indians would follow us all this way?'

'What do you mean, "all this way"? We've only been travelling a day and a half. Make no mistake about it, my friend, if the Xavantes took it into their heads to seek revenge, they'd follow us all the way back to Belém if they could. I tell you, I heard a story once about two garimpeiros who had killed a –'

Claudio broke off abruptly, noting the strange expression that had come over Martin's face. The American had turned his head suddenly and was staring back upriver, over the heads of his companions, his mouth open, his head tilted to one side. The others turned too, expecting the worst, but as far as they could see, the river was completely empty.

'What is it?' demanded Helen.

'Listen!' replied Martin urgently. 'Maybe I'm just going crazy out here but I do believe I heard something. I thought I heard . . .' He fell silent for a moment and then the low, insect-like drone that had existed only as a subliminal backwash in his eardrums began to rise steadily in volume. 'It *is* coming!' he muttered; and then his voice was louder, trembling with excitement. 'It's coming back! The sonofabitch is really coming back!'

Abruptly, it appeared around the bend of the river, flying low and following the long curve of the water: a small, red, single-engined biplane, its sleek belly seeming to skim dangerously close to the topmost limbs of the forest roof. The noise of its engine rose dramatically to a throaty roar, galvanizing the canoe's three occupants into action. They leapt to their feet, waving paddles, shouting joyfully and generally causing the canoe to pitch from side to side in a most alarming manner. The plane roared on overhead, so low that it seemed they might reach up their hands and stroke its gleaming flanks; and then, most wonderful, most gratifying of all, as it thundered on downriver, a flare shot out from the cockpit with a long, loud whistle and went whizzing luminously away to lose itself in green forest depths.

The pilot had seen them. He would mark their position. He would send help.

Yelling, they tumbled gratefully back into their seats, almost swamping the slender boat.

'It's the same one!' shouted Martin. 'The same as before! Don't ask me how I know, it just is! The beautiful sonofabitch must have seen our smoke after all. He came back for another look!'

'It *is* incredible,' admitted Claudio. 'But how else do you explain it?'

'If only it could just land and pick us up right now,' mused Helen. 'Why wasn't it a sea-plane? It could've just set down, right beside us . . .'

'That would be asking too much,' Claudio told her. 'We're well on our way home now. Most likely they'll send a boat upriver for us.' He patted her shoulder reassuringly. 'At least now somebody knows exactly where we are. That's a real breakthrough. Look, he's coming back again!'

The plane had turned around and was heading back towards them, waggling its wings slightly in a gesture of triumph; then, abruptly, it veered sideways and took off to the south-east.

'Doesn't it seem strange to think of Rio, still out there?' sighed Helen. 'Cafés, bars, electric lights . . . somehow you stop believing in things like that.'

Claudio nodded. 'You know, I can hardly believe our good fortune. The pilot finding us like that . . . that kind of thing just doesn't happen.'

'You're complaining?' asked Martin.

'Of course not. I'm very grateful; and when I get back to Rio, I want to shake the hand of the man who put that plane into the air.'

'The pilot? Maybe we'll meet him at Belém.'

'I don't mean the pilot. I mean the man who put out the money for the search. Whoever it was, he's a man with some real muscle behind him.'

Martin turned to stare at Claudio. The grin on his face faded. 'What do you mean?'

'Well, it's just that the authorities wouldn't have kept a pilot in the air for that long. Searching an area the size of the Mato Grosso, that's an expensive business; and, what's more, it must have taken some imagination to come looking for us so far from our proper route. The official searches are not known for their ingenuity or their persistence. Most of them give up after a day or so. That plane passing over our campsite the way it did . . . at first I put it down to a million-to-one chance accident. But I keep asking myself, what would a small plane have been

275

doing out there, in the middle of nowhere ... unless it was looking for us?'

Helen frowned. 'So how do you explain it?'

'It must be a *private* search. A rich man with a big interest in somebody who was on our flight, most likely Carlos Machado. You remember, Senhora Brody, the fat *fazendeiro* who was travelling with his daughter ...?'

Helen nodded. 'Yes, I remember.'

'Machado was worth a lot of money. I guess there would be plenty of people anxious to get him back alive.' He chuckled ironically. 'It looks as though his loss could be our gain, but I never thought I'd wind up being grateful to that evil bastard.' He glanced at Martin who had fallen silent in the prow of the canoe. 'Is something wrong, Senhor Taggart? You look worried.'

'Huh? Oh, no, I ... I was just wondering how long it might be before somebody comes out to meet us.'

'Impossible to say. As you know, until I sight something familiar, I'm just guessing about our position. We'll stick with our original plan and head on down to the mission station. Maybe they'll get to us before then; if not, we'll disembark and wait for them there. We may as well have what little comfort we can get. It will be interesting to see who reaches the mission first.'

He grinned and dug his paddle into the water. Martin nodded and followed suit. He said nothing, but he turned to stare at the treeline behind which the red plane had disappeared. The ghost of a suspicion had wormed its way into his mind and, though he tried hard to push it away, it kept returning, nagging at him repeatedly.

In his mind, he travelled back to his first meeting with Charles Caine, in that dingy foul-smelling office in Rio. Six long years ago and yet he remembered it as though it were yesterday: the dangerous gleam in the fat man's little eyes, the sickly smell of lavender water and, most especially, what Caine had said.

276

'Believe me, my friend, distance does not matter when a fellow has as long a reach as I have.'

But no, surely it wasn't possible! Even Caine's fat, greedy fingers weren't capable of worming their way into these remote backwaters. Martin had to believe that; to doubt it, even for a moment, was to fuel the conviction that every paddlestroke he made took him inexorably nearer to his own downfall.

'*Diabo!*'

Paolo coaxed the Beech up to its top speed and the 420-horsepower engine shook the frail craft from nose to tail. Suddenly all the comfort had gone out of Paolo's plans. How the hell had the survivors managed to get themselves a canoe? It was a move that he could not have predicted. He'd flown downriver confidently expecting to find his quarry working on a raft on the riverbank much farther upstream. Indeed, he'd been on the point of turning back, telling himself that they couldn't possibly be this far downstream when he'd spotted the canoe and its occupants ahead. At first he'd taken them for a trio of Indians on a fishing expedition, but as he got nearer he noticed that the middle 'Indian' had a shock of long, red and decidedly feminine hair spilling down from under her hat. Then they had all stood up in the boat and started waving excitedly. Paolo could see quite clearly that there were two bearded white men on either side of the woman. One of these matched completely Caine's description of Martin Taggart; the other was darker in colouring and more heavily built.

Now Paolo had to act quickly. He could not hope to reach base till late afternoon. Once there, he would ring Caine's office and, provided he could contact his employer, arrange for the 'rescue' party to leave for Conceiçao the following morning. With a refuelling stop at Goian, the trip would take something like nine or ten hours and they could not seriously expect to set out from Conceiçao until the following morning. Even with the obvious advantages of an outboard motor, it was debatable which boat would reach the mission station first. Paolo knew for a fact that there was radio communication equipment at the mission. If the survivors were allowed to make so much as one call, the whole of Brazil would know of their miraculous escape and that would make matters very difficult for Caine and his men.

It's not my fault, thought Paolo bitterly. *How could I know they would find a canoe?*

But in his mind's eye, he saw Charles Caine's fat face registering intense displeasure at Paolo's shortsightedness. There was nothing for it now but to try to make up for the error of judgment.

Despite himself, Paolo could not help but admire the survivors. What an ordeal to have come through! They had kept going despite all the odds and Paolo respected that. What a bitter irony to think that all their striving would (if Paolo's scheme succeeded) come to nothing. They were headed for retribution as grim and final as anything they could have encountered in the jungle, for it was hardly likely that Caine would allow any of them to escape with their lives. The world would never learn of their remarkable journey, would simply assume that they had perished in the crash, a futile and ignoble death.

Still, he could not allow himself to be sentimental. He was one of Caine's men now and to succeed at this he would have to make himself hard, cold, beyond the reach of any conscience. That was the way a man got to be somebody in this cruel world. Paolo had made his mind up a long time ago that, whatever the price, he was going to be somebody.

The rhythmic metallic croaking of tree-frogs rose and fell in an eerie cadence as the three travellers worked on their

278

canoe by firelight, plaiting a thick layer of broad palm leaves onto the framework of saplings they had already erected around the narrow vessel. Their skins were burned tender from another day's travel in the open sunlight; they were determined that tomorrow they would be better prepared. The resulting arrangement was bizarre and somewhat flimsy, a rickety hooped awning with wide openings at the sides through which the craft could be paddled. It looked as though a stiff breeze would lift the whole canopy clean away from its moorings but after the arid, airless day that had just passed the chance of any kind of wind seemed remote.

Since the arrival of the plane several hours back, the three had scarcely conversed apart from the odd monosyllabic phrase. It was as though, with the realization that they really were on their way back to safety, they had each retreated into a world of their own making, to brood silently on whatever was closest to their hearts.

Martin could not stop thinking about Charles Caine. Claudio's chance remark just after the plane's departure had set the American worrying, and through the long day the fear had grown within him. The mission station, he knew, would be the deciding point. Once there, Claudio had said, the plan was to hole up and wait for help to arrive. But Martin did not like the idea of sitting tight for too long. He might have to seek alternative means of escape. Perhaps he should take the canoe and head on downriver alone, evade any search party he encountered on the way and get Claudio to tell the rescuers that a man called Martin Taggart had died in an accident some time after the plane had spotted three survivors. But then there was Helen to consider. What was he to do about her? More importantly, what did he *want* to do about her? Part of him wanted to ask her to go along with him, another part realized that he would be inviting her to embark on a very uncertain future; and deep at the back of Martin's mind, there was a tiny nagging doubt that would not allow him to trust her. It all seemed hopeless and he did not see how he could expect to have arrived at a satisfactory conclusion by the time he reached the mission station. He glanced at Helen, who was working alongside him but she was too deep in her own thoughts to even notice his glance.

Helen was wondering how she might best pick up the pieces of her life. She had already decided, even before she took off on that fateful last flight, that she was going to get out of the airline business once and for all. It was expanding fast, the big companies were moving in to pick up the monopolies. The kind of shoestring operation that Mike Stone had run was already living on borrowed time. But, she wondered, what else was there for her? Go back to her rich family with her tail between her legs? Live out a boring, champagne-cocktail existence amongst the embassy fraternity, wrapped in cottonwool and shielded from the grubby touch of reality for the rest of her life? Hell no, she'd rather walk the streets than do that! Other option? Crazy Martin Taggart and his fabulous diamond. No, somehow she could not allow herself to treat that idea seriously. Despite what had happened between them, she distrusted him. Two people in a desperate situation were quite likely to fall into each other's arms without thinking too carefully about the consequences. It wasn't that she didn't care for him. She did, very much so. Perhaps she was even beginning to love him a little. But, she reminded herself, he was a man on the run and, if it ever came to a choice between her and his precious diamond, she was liable to lose hands down. Her guess was that as soon as they neared anything remotely resembling civilization, she would not see Martin Taggart for the dust of his passing. She sighed. She could turn her hand to most things, she decided and she would just have to adopt a 'Que sera, sera' attitude. Who could say, but maybe walking the streets wasn't such a bad idea after all.

She reached for a palm leaf at the same time that Claudio did and it tore in half. They gazed at each other for a moment and then, with a brief smile, he turned away and went on with his work.

Claudio was perplexed and vaguely surprised by the depth of feeling he had discovered within himself for Helen Brody. Strange. He had been quite unaware of it until a couple of days back, when he had returned to find a dead Indian and Helen and Martin half-dressed; it had shocked him to realize that it was the latter image that had caused him the most distress. There in his heart had been the bitter pangs of out-and-out jealousy. Of course, he had always admired the woman, had liked her style, her immense courage and determination. At which point that admiration had turned to love, he was unable to say, but the feelings existed within him and now all he could hope to do was to keep them in check. Besides, Helen had evidently made her choice. Claudio did not intend to become Martin's rival for her affections. He would continue as he always had, surviving as best he could. But of one thing he was certain. A woman like Helen Brody was worth a great deal more than any diamond.

His hands, working on the latticework of leaves, suddenly became still. He stood like a statue for a moment, listening, and then he glanced at his companions. They had ceased work also, and all three stared apprehensively away into the darkness.

The constant background noise of croaking frogs had stopped abruptly, as though somewhere an unseen hand had pressed the 'off' button of a tape-recorder. All around the *praia* on which they were camped was the intense, suffocating silence of death.

They spent a sleepless night on the *praia*, then pushed on at dawn, relieved to escape the awful atmosphere of that campsite. All through the night there had been a persistent feeling that they were *observed*, though they had seen or heard no evidence to support this notion. Nevertheless, the conviction remained with them and it was with intense relief that they steered the narrow canoe out through the banks of low-lying mist into the stronger currents of midstream. As they paddled onwards between the dark threatening flanks of thick vegetation, they waited nervously for an attack that never came.

The sun rose steadily in the east, creeping gradually up over the treeline and spreading a slow heat over the surface of the river. They passed into a long stretch where the water was rather shallow, plunging occasionally between huge granite rocks in a series of rapids. Here they were obliged to climb out of the canoe and guide it through the obstacles by hand, wading alongside in the thigh-deep water. They felt horribly vulnerable doing this; if an attack were launched now, they would be helpless. They would die, riddled with arrows, before they could reach the rifles which were lying in the boat. But no attack came; and once again the river widened, slowed to a more steady pace. They were able to clamber back aboard and resume paddling. But still they could not relax. Every little noise; every flap of a bird amongst the vegetation, every leap of a fish in the shallows, jangled their nerves. They were constantly searching the shadows amongst the trees for a glimpse of crouching figures waiting in ambush.

The long hours unfolded without incident, and gradually the fear subsided. They journied onwards and settled into the demanding rhythm of working the heavy paddles. A little after midday they noticed a thick pall of smoke drifting across the river up ahead of them. As they drew closer, they realized that the jungle on their left-hand side was ablaze, a not uncommon occurrence in these remote regions, Claudio said. Billows of thick acrid smoke curled around them, making their eyes stream and, as they moved on, they were assailed by waves of heat that forced them to drop back against the right bank. Peering to their left, they could see nothing but columns of fierce orange fire, gorging on the close-packed vegetation. There was a constant crackling thunder and the air was thick with sparks and blackened leaves. Occasionally, a piece of burning vegetation alighted on the awning of the canoe, where it began to smoulder dangerously. With the aid of the metal coffee jug, the area was doused liberally with river water. Like a trio of Charons sailing along the hellish waters of the Styx, they went onwards amidst the inferno and, after over an hour of this torture, emerged smoke-blackened and sticky with sweat on the far side of the blaze, which had finally veered away to the west.

'It's lucky we weren't still on foot in all that,' observed Martin grimly.

They all gazed up at a vast grey pall of smoke overhead which continued to block out the rays of the sun for another hour's travel.

They passed now into an area where a series of muddy *praias* edged the banks of the river and here for the first time, they saw *jacares*, the big heavy alligators of the das Mortes. They lay in twos and threes in the mud, torpid and indolent, seemingly uninterested in the little craft and its inhabitants. Once they surprised a big fellow who was drifting aimlessly across the river a few yards in front of their prow. Martin grabbed for his rifle but there was no need. Displaying all the signs of cowardice, the *jacare* turned away and submerged himself, leaving nothing but a thin stream of bubbles to mark his passing. Suspecting that at any minute the creature might resurface beneath the canoe, Martin remained on the alert but, happily, nothing untoward happened.

The shadows lengthened steadily into afternoon and

then, to everyone's surprise, the red biplane reappeared. Once again, it approached from upriver and went zooming past at low level, while Claudio and Helen, leaning dangerously out from under the awning, waved energetically. After a few moments, it came back and began to circle slowly overhead. Martin watched it silently with mounting suspicion.

'Strange,' muttered Claudio, peering up past the roof of leaves and twigs. 'I somehow didn't expect to see the plane again. Maybe he's just checking that we're all still safe.' He leaned forward and tapped Helen on the shoulder. 'Move back here, Senhora Brody, so the pilot can see you. Senhor Taggart, you lean out from the front. With this damned sun-shade, he's probably wondering if he's got the right boat.'

Martin frowned. He shifted forward, leaning his head out into the light. The plane continued to circle, buzzing slowly around like a great mechanized vulture, the sunlight flashing on its red wings. Again Martin was struck by a powerful sense of foreboding. He shielded his face with the flat of one hand, straining his eyes to try and see the occupants of the cockpit, but it was a useless endeavour. He moved back into the reassuring shade beneath the canopy and slipped one hand beneath his shirt to grip the leather pouch. Why did he feel so edgy? Why?

'It looks like they're moving on,' he heard Claudio say; and, glancing up again, he saw that the plane had indeed stopped its circling and was drifting rapidly away downriver.

'How come they're not going back the way they came?' he asked.

'Well, I suppose they're heading on down to organize some kind of reception committee!' Claudio chuckled. 'I dare say we do deserve the red carpet treatment after everything we've been through.' He was sitting beside

Helen in the stern of the boat and had draped an arm around her shoulder in a friendly, informal manner.

'It's a shame we can't radio ahead and tell them to have my bathwater ready,' said Helen brightly. She and Claudio fell into a lengthy, good-natured discourse on the various luxuries they would indulge themselves in once they reached a place that provided some. But Martin was not listening. Their voices seemed distant now, as though he were alone in the boat and they were left behind on the bank of the river.

Something bad was coming. He sensed it as surely as he felt the dark sway of the river as it slipped back beneath the hull of the canoe. Despite the heat of the afternoon a shiver ran through him and his shoulders sagged with the awful inevitability of it all. Somehow, he had always known that his run could never be as easy as he would have liked. That was simply not the way his life had been up till now. And nothing really changed when all was said and done. All he could hope for was that, when the test came, he would be ready for it.

He continued to paddle, his gaze fixed resolutely ahead. For the time being, he concluded, there was nothing else that he could do.

Charles Caine flung a last glance over his shoulder as the tiny boat far below him receded into the distance. The interior of the plane was cramped and incredibly hot and the unfamiliar khaki shirt he wore was sodden with sweat, despite the fierce wind that buffeted through the open windows of the cockpit. It had taken four uncomfortable hours to reach this point and there was still the grim prospect of another three before they reached Conceiçao. But for the moment that didn't matter. Caine's face was beaming with triumph.

'It *was* Taggart,' he announced grandly. 'I'm sure of that.'

Beside him in the pilot's seat, Paolo Estevez frowned. 'You said yourself, it's been over six years since you saw him. I don't see how you can be so sure.'

'Oh, it was him all right.'

'He was bearded, he was wearing a hat. You couldn't have seen his face properly.'

'I didn't need to see his face,' retorted Caine puzzlingly. 'He's our quarry right enough. I could tell by the very way he sat in the boat; the way he peered out from cover, while his friends waved their arms in invitation. The actions of a man who is very selective about who rescues him.' He smiled oddly, then turned and glanced back over his shoulder. 'How are you feeling, Otto?' he asked with exaggerated concern.

Schiller was slumped in one of the rear seats, a handkerchief clutched to his mouth. His usually pale face was now a startling shade of grey and for a reply he gave a formless groan of despair. Beside him sat Paco, Caine's big impassive chauffeur cum *pistoleiro*, who was rather insensitively crunching his way through a big bag of peanuts, his moustachioed face gazing blankly ahead.

'Paco, put those away,' Caine chided him. 'Can't you see you're making poor Otto feel even worse?' He giggled and slapped Schiller heartily on the shoulder. 'All I can say, Otto, is that it's a damned good job that they didn't have you in the Luftwaffe during the war. A fine lot of use you'd have been to them!'

Schiller groaned again, shook his head, and Caine turned back to address the pilot. In the confines of the cockpit it was necessary to talk loudly over the roar of the engine.

'Well, what do you think, Paolo? Can we beat them to the mission station?'

'Provided we get a good boat and start at first light, yes, I think so.' He jerked a thumb over his shoulder at a sizeable pile of loaded haversacks in the rear of the plane.

286

'I'm not so sure we'll need all that equipment, though.'

Caine spread his arms in an expansive gesture. 'Paolo, my dear boy, just because we're going into the back of beyond, it doesn't mean we have to forget our creature comforts.'

'It beats me how you got it all together so quickly.'

'That was remarkably easy! Why do you think I issue my *garimpeiros* with an address from which to buy their stores at a discount? It's very simple. I *own* the stores!'

'So . . . you lend them the money . . . and they go right out and spend it in one of your stores?' Paolo shook his head in admiration.

'It's a good system; and of course, having your own stores can come in handy sometimes. All I've done is borrow enough equipment to make our journey upriver a little more tolerable. Four days, you said?'

Paolo nodded. 'Maybe five, if the current's strong.'

'And you're sure there's no quicker way to get to them?'

'Not without a flying boat, I'm afraid; and like I already told you, there isn't one to be had at the moment, not at any price. But listen, Senhor Caine, if you don't much like the idea of the journey upriver, why not let the three of us go out while you stay at Conceiçao?'

'Very thoughtful of you, Paolo . . . very thoughtful indeed. But no. It strikes me that I could end up looking for you or Otto, instead of Taggart.'

Paolo smiled. 'Isn't there anybody you trust?'

Caine raised his eyebrows. 'Good heavens, no. What a curious suggestion.'

They travelled on for several moments in silence while Paolo thought something over. Below him, the river took a slow sinuous journey through the *selva*, an incongruous yellow worm that glittered occasionally beneath the rays of afternoon sun.

'It's a diamond, isn't it?' he ventured at last. 'It has to

287

be a diamond and a good one too, otherwise you wouldn't be going to these lengths. You're a patron and this man Taggart, he was one of your *garimpeiros*. He made a run with something he found.'

Caine looked at Paolo with something akin to respect in his piggy eyes. 'Remarkable, Paolo! Absolutely remarkable! And how, pray tell, did you arrive at that conclusion.'

Paolo shrugged. 'I just thought it out.'

'And has it ever occurred to you, Paolo, that you think too much for your own good?' Caine's voice, once again, had acquired a hard edge of menace. One minute Caine could be the absurd, ineffectual clown, all foppish good manners and undeniable charm; then abruptly, he could be something else, something infinitely more dangerous, a callous, cold dictator not to be crossed on any account. As Paolo watched, Caine changed tack again; his face relaxed, his little mouth changed from a curt snarl to an oily smile. His voice softened, became conspiratorial, patronizing.

'Well, Paolo, since we *are* on our way to Conceiçao, I see no reason why you shouldn't learn the rest of the story, such as it is. Yes, there is a diamond; at least, I believe there is, though I've never seen it, or heard any testimony confirming its existence.'

'Then how –'

'Because, Paolo, I understand human nature! Put it this way. The American, Taggart, was in my employ for something like six years. He never saw me in that time, but I took care to know everything that happened to him. In that time, he found several diamonds, some of them reasonably good ones; but he never saw fit to try and dupe me. Then suddenly, for no apparent reason, he made a run. Furthermore, he killed two men to protect whatever it was he found. The first was a fellow *garimpeiro*, whom I presume stumbled onto his secret. The second was Agnello,

288

my own right-hand man and, I might add, a ruthless and well-experienced *pistoleiro*. This suggests to me that he has got his hands on something of inestimable value.'

Paolo nodded, licked his lips nervously. 'Yeah *maybe* ... but, supposing he just went off his head or something? It happens to men out there, right? Maybe he was just getting the hell away from the place and those guys got in his way. It's possible that, after all this trouble, there *is* no diamond.'

Caine shrugged nonchalantly. 'Perhaps. In which case, as you say, all this ... *effort* will have been to no avail. But I'm a gambling man, Paolo and, I fancy, a shrewd judge of character. I'm prepared to bet that there *is* a diamond, a very exclusive one; and I believe that when we find Taggart, he will have it with him.'

'I hope so,' muttered Paolo between clenched teeth. 'I sure do.'

They fell silent now as they stared down at the endless meandering ribbon of yellow water that coiled and looped its way through the greenery below. There was an irony in thinking that the route they travelled now with comparative ease must be retraced slowly and laboriously over the following days. Later, they flew over the lonely outpost of the mission station where they intended to rendezvous with the survivors. It looked a very tranquil place. A couple of robed figures and a few Indians waved from a ramshackle jetty as the Beech zoomed overhead. Then the plane was moving onwards at top speed, eating up the miles as it raced downriver to Conceiçao.

Chapter 13

Paolo handed the haversacks out one by one to his **three** companions and then turned back to lock up the plane. It was late afternoon and a faint breeze stirred the short tufts of dry grass that covered the stretch of *campo* where he had landed. He noticed that Caine declined to take one of the haversacks himself. He stood some distance away from the others, looking vaguely ridiculous in an immaculate khaki bush-jacket and trousers and a flamboyant broad-brimmed hat. He carried a riding crop.

Paco, already heavily burdened, stepped forward to lift the extra haversack across his broad shoulders. He was obviously well used to doing the lion's share in Caine's outfit. Otto Schiller had made a remarkable recovery from his air-sickness the instant his feet had touched *terra firma*. Now he was his old self again, cold, impassive, humourless. Paolo wasn't sure he hadn't preferred him the other way. Schiller took one of the two remaining haversacks but left the other lying where it was, implying by this, Paolo supposed, that he didn't intend to allow himself to be loaded up like Paco. Paolo shrugged and, jumping down from the plane, hefted it onto his shoulder, noticing as he did so that it clinked as though it might be full of bottles. He led the way off the *campo*.

From here, a rough trail led down through patches of secondary jungle and scrub to the village of Conceiçao. They could see it through a gap in the trees a short distance below, a jumble of corrugated iron roofs disgorging columns of woodsmoke into the clear air. After ten minutes of energetic walking they were tramping along the muddy thoroughfare that was its main street.

Caine gazed about him with the expression of a man who had just had a piece of excrement thrust under his nose. There was no pity in his demeanour, just disgust. 'What a shit-hole,' he said at length.

For once, he had a point. Conceiçao was an unabashedly squalid little village, grey and sordid in its poverty. Not one of its four or five streets was paved, and the low, ramshackle buildings of painted plaster were of the very poorest quality. Here and there, the village's inhabitants sat out on their verandahs. Silent, indolent *caboclos* dressed in insanitary rags, they watched the arrival of the strangers with open suspicion in their dark eyes. They clearly had little to smile about and even less work to keep them occupied. Over the village hung a constant, all-pervading smell, an inexplicable mingling of poverty, disease and disenchantment. The inactivity of the older villagers was curiously contrasted by the liveliness of their children. Presumably too young to be affected by the grimness of their surroundings, the children were everywhere, naked, mud-splashed and voluble. They vied for prominence with the village livestock, which was plentiful and largely unconfined. Pigs rooted in the muddy streets looking for scraps of food, chickens trotted earnestly to and fro, scattering indignantly as the strangers walked carelessly amongst them. There were skinny goats and occasionally an even skinnier cow, while here and there, a captive macaw added a surreal splash of colour to the verandah of a house.

Several of the older children, noticing the superior clothing of these newcomers, began to trail along in their wake, holding out their hands and begging for coins. It was a futile and short-lived endeavour, cut short when the children got too close for their own good and Caine lashed out at them with his riding crop.

'Filthy little maggots,' he muttered sourly. 'Who knows what diseases they are carrying?' He glanced accusingly at Paolo. 'Where is this place we're headed?'

'Just a little farther, down by the jetty.'

Caine grunted. He glanced around again. Across the way, a couple of small children were having a ferocious tug of war with a live cat. One boy held its front paws, the other its tail, and they were apparently trying to find out which would break first. The wretched creature was

291

shrieking pitifully, unable to scramble free of their tenacious hold.

'Something should be done about places like this,' said Caine thoughtfully. Paolo was surprised. He had never thought of Caine as a philanthropic man.

'Well, it would take a lot of money, Senhor Caine; a lot of education. The soil here is good, it is really only a question of teaching the peasants more about farming and so forth.'

Caine stared at Paolo. 'Money?' he echoed. 'Education? My dear boy, I was thinking more along the lines of some well-placed sticks of *dynamite*.'

'Oh yes, of course . . .'

Caine giggled. 'You know, Paolo, you have, despite all your claims to the contrary, a decidedly soft nature. You should be careful. One day, such sentiments will get you into terrible trouble.'

Paolo shook his head. 'No, really, I just misunderstood. The people here, they are basically lazy and ignorant. They deserve everything they get.'

'Listen to him,' observed Schiller sarcastically. 'A real tough guy.'

Paolo glanced threateningly at the German. 'I don't recall asking for your opinion,' he snapped.

'Boys, boys!' Caine shook his head like a disapproving schoolmaster. 'Let's have a little civility between us. Remember, we've a long journey ahead.'

They had reached a place where the village outskirts plunged abruptly down to the edge of the river. A crumbling, lichen-covered wharf jutted out into the yellow water and around this a motley assortment of boats were moored. It was here at the water's edge that some of the most dilapidated houses were grouped, sullen and stained by earlier encroachments of water. Paolo indicated a long, low building that somehow managed to look even more insanitary than its neighbours. 'That's the place.'

'Delightful,' murmured Caine flatly; then he turned his head to stare at the cluster of canoes and launches by the jetty. 'And . . . the boat?'

'That's Hernandez's *batelão*,' said Paolo, pointing to a filthy old slop-bucket with a rusted outboard-motor fixed to its stern; then, noticing Caine's pained air of reproach, he spread his arms and added: 'You were expecting perhaps the *Queen Mary*?'

Immediately Caine was over-contrite. 'Paolo, you misjudge me! In the time, you've done a remarkable job. Quite remarkable. Please, lead on!'

Paolo led the way to Hernandez's shack. He knew the man only vaguely, had had dealings with him only once before and that a full year ago. But he knew that Hernandez owned the only motorized launch in these parts and that the man was considered knowledgeable on the Araguaia and the das Mortes. There was certainly nobody more qualified in Conceiçao to get the party to their destination. He knocked on a sun-blistered door and waited for what seemed an eternity before somebody opened it.

It was Hernandez all right, a stooped, grizzled little man of indeterminate age. His brown weatherbeaten face and wispy grey beard suggested advanced years and this was backed up by his almost bald head and rheumy eyes. But Paolo knew that living in these conditions could age a man prematurely. Hernandez stared uncertainly out at the newcomers, blinking as though he had just been roused from sleep; then he seemed to recognize Paolo and his lined face curved into a sheepish grin, displaying a few assorted stumps of rotten teeth. He was dressed in a ragged shirt and cotton trousers, both of which had once been white. Exposure to the elements had stained them to an unappealing shade of grey and they were blotched and torn at the knees and elbows.

293

'Yes, *senhors*?' he inquired cautiously. He evidently felt ill at ease with these strangers, disconcerted by their fine clothes and authoritative manner. He stood in the doorway squirming, like a man who had been surprised naked in broad daylight. Behind him, Paolo caught a glimpse of the interior of Hernandez's house – dingy, bare, cheerless. Over a rough stone fireplace, a greasy black cooking pot steamed, giving out the unmistakable aroma of a *feijoada*, meat and vegetable stew.

Paolo indicated his companions. 'These gentlemen have come all the way from Rio. They wish to charter your boat, Hernandez. They wish you to take them up the das Mortes.'

Hernandez stared at them for a moment with the open-mouthed, vacant stare of the habitually slow-witted. 'The das Mortes?' he mumbled. 'What . . . now?'

'Of course not right now! But tomorrow, at first light.'

'Oh, *senhor*, I am sorry but . . .' Hernandez was backing away from the door, shaking his head in apology. 'It is not possible tomorrow. My wife, *senhor*, she is very sick. She has the *maculo* and I cannot leave her right now. Perhaps in a week or so, when she has recovered her strength –'

'What do you mean, a week or so?' Paolo pushed his shoulder against the door as Hernandez tried to swing it shut. It had never for one moment occurred to the young pilot that Hernandez might refuse to undertake the work. 'Like I just said, these friends of mine, they've travelled a long way, it's taken them hours to get here. Now, they're prepared to pay good wages for the trip. I think you should reconsider.'

Again Hernandez shook his head. 'I tell you, *senhor*, I cannot leave her right now. Try Raoul Garcia, he has a *barco* for hire. He will take you, I'm sure.'

'Does he have an outboard motor?'

'No, but . . .'

294

'Then it's no use to us! We're in a hurry, we must get to our destination as quickly as possible. Now listen, what do you usually charge for a trip upriver? We'll give you a hundred cruzeiros on top of your regular fee.'

'Please, *senhor*, it's as I keep saying to you. It's not a question of money, though the God knows I could use some right now. You see, it's the *maculo*; and there's nobody to look after my wife, only my daughter, and I do not think that she is old enough to –'

'Excuse me, Paolo.' Charles Caine stepped forward, smiling warmly as he pushed Paolo gently but firmly aside. 'Perhaps if you would allow me to explain the situation to Mr Hernandez ...'

Hernandez bowed apologetically. 'Forgive me, *senhor*, but I can only tell you the same thing. I cannot –'

Abruptly, Caine brought his riding crop across Hernandez's face with a vicious swipe, making the man reel back into his house with a shriek of pain. Clutching at a red weal on his face, he lost his footing and sprawled backward onto the bare floorboards behind him. Paolo stood in the doorway, staring uncertainly into the house as his three companions sauntered past him. There was something dreadfully theatrical about the scene; Hernandez, cowering on the floor and staring up at the white men in horror while a thin trickle of crimson oozed from between his fingers; Caine, standing over the fallen man, legs astride, bending the pliable riding crop in his fat hands. Schiller and Paco moved past, seemingly indifferent to the villager's fate. Schiller strolled across to a battered wooden table which was littered with a few oddments of crockery, the remains of a recent meal. He swept them contemptuously aside with the flat of one arm, smashing the cheap items of pottery on the floor, and set his haversack down in their place. Paco moved over to the pot of *feijoada*, sniffed at it curiously and then, taking hold of a ladle that hung near the pot, he lifted some of the contents to his mouth. He gulped at it, then with an exclamation of revulsion, spat the food out, back into the pot.

Caine turned his head slightly and glanced at Paolo. 'Come in and close the door behind you,' he said quietly. Paolo nodded, did as he was told. As he entered, he noticed that Hernandez was staring at him entreatingly. He had to look away, could not meet the accusing stare in the *caboclo*'s eyes. 'Now then, Senhor Hernandez,' purred Caine, flexing the riding crop menacingly. 'Perhaps Paolo here didn't make the situation clear. You see, we're not *asking* you to take us to our destination, we are merely stating a fact. You will be our pilot. We have chosen you, you should be honoured. Now tell me, what is your first name?'

Hernandez was clearly confused by Caine's show of apparent friendliness. 'Francisco,' he whispered tremulously.

'Francisco!' Caine beamed patronizingly. 'Well, Francisco, firstly, I'm sorry that I hit you like that. But you see, you made it necessary. So long as you do the things I tell you to do, such actions will no longer be necessary. Do you understand?'

'Yes, *senhor* . . . but, my wife . . .?'

'Your wife, Francisco? Well, you do seem inordinately worried about her. Tell me, just exactly where is this wife of yours?'

Hernandez pointed across the room to an area where a grey woollen blanket had been hung across the doorway of an adjoining chamber. Paco went across to it and pulled the blanket aside. A woman was lying in a grubby bed, covered by several insanitary blankets. Her thin, almost cadaverous face was grey and beaded with sweat and she lay staring out at this room full of strangers, her dark eyes filled with an expression of terror. She was clearly too weak to move.

296

Caine took Hernandez's arm and helped him to his feet. Then he led him across the room to stand at the foot of the bed.

'Now look at her, Francisco,' murmured Caine. 'She looks very ill to me. She needs medicine, isn't that right?' Hernandez nodded slowly. 'And do you have any money to buy her medicine?'

'No, *senhor*, but . . .'

'Well, then, it makes perfect sense for you to take us upriver tomorrow. You'll be able to buy your wife the very best medicine and you may even have a few cruzeiros left to get her some clean sheets for that stinking bed.'

'*Senhor*, I understand this. But you see, I promised my wife when she began to be ill, I promised that I would not leave her. And you must understand, that I am a man of my word.'

Caine gazed at Hernandez for a moment and then he sighed. He shook his head. His smile faded abruptly and was replaced by an expression of anger. 'Francisco, you really are a most obstinate fellow.' He turned from the bed and strode back across to the table. He jerked a thumb over his shoulder at the curtained doorway. 'Cover the old bitch up,' he told Paco. 'The smell of her is making me sick. Otto, perhaps you can explain the situation to Mr Hernandez. He doesn't seem to respond to the friendly approach.'

Schiller shrugged indifferently. He got up from his seat at the table and walked across to Hernandez, gazing impassively at the man as though he were looking at nothing more than an object. Hernandez could see from the expression on the German's face that he had not an ounce of compassion in him. He began to back slowly away, his hands upraised.

'Please, *senhor*, don't cause trouble. I don't want to fight with you, I don't want –'

His voice dissolved into a gasp of pain as Schiller struck

297

him hard in the stomach, driving the breath out of his body. He doubled up and Schiller took a firm hold of his left arm, pulled him closer, twisting his own body sideways against Hernandez to hold him still.

'Mr Hernandez,' he said matter-of-factly. 'You have ten fingers. I'm going to break one of them, the little finger on your left hand. I want you to remember the pain this causes you; and I also want you to remember that whenever you question anything that Mr Caine tells you to do, I shall personally see to it that another finger is broken. Do you understand?' He took hold of the man's little finger and began to push it slowly back upon itself. 'I asked you a question, Mr Hernandez. Do you understand?'

Hernandez nodded frantically. 'Yes,' he gasped. 'Yes, yes, *senhor*, please, I'm sorry, I . . .' With an abrupt twist, Schiller wrenched the finger right back on itself, breaking the fragile bone like a dry twig. Hernandez's face froze in the expression of a silent scream, mouth open, eyes squeezed shut. He dropped to his knees sobbing. Schiller leaned forward and stroked his victim's head gently. 'Now then,' he whispered. 'You're going to take us upriver tomorrow, isn't that right?'

Hernandez nodded feebly, his bowed head dripping sweat onto the floor. He was barely conscious.

'Good fellow.' Schiller lifted him by the collar of his shirt and manhandled him across to the table, dropping him unceremoniously into an empty chair. 'Now, you just sit there and behave yourself.' Straightening, he caught Paolo's eye. The young pilot had been watching quietly from his position by the door. 'What's the matter, tough guy?' chuckled Schiller mockingly. 'You look a little pale.'

'I was just wondering if that was absolutely necessary.'

'Sure, it was necessary. He'll do as he's told now; and besides, broken fingers mend again. He's lucky I didn't break his neck.'

298

'All right you two, that's enough,' advised Caine wearily. 'I don't like this antagonism. Paco, there are some bottles of Scotch in one of the haversacks. Break them out will you. If we're going to spend the night in this piss-hole, we can at least have a drink or two.'

Paco grinned and set about locating the whisky. The others settled around the table. Paolo glanced at Hernandez. The man's head had sunk forward onto his chest and he was breathing raggedly. He was cradling his injured hand with his good one. The broken finger had swollen already, the skin blue and mottled. Paolo had not anticipated that it would be necessary to hurt the little river pilot; now he wondered vaguely how many others would be hurt before this mission was accomplished. Paco found the whisky and some little metal tumblers. He filled three and Caine raised his to propose a toast.

'To the successful hunting down of Martin Taggart.' The smooth Scotch was a rare pleasure and Caine called for the tumblers to be refilled. 'After this, Paco,' he said, 'you can see about getting us something to eat.'

The big man grinned. Since eating was his favourite pastime, he had no objection to this; and he knew that Caine had spared no expense in the purchase of stores for the trip. He began to empty out the contents of the food haversack, laying them on the table one by one.

'Give Hernandez some whisky,' Caine told Paolo. 'He looks as though he could use a stiff drink.' An extra tumbler was filled and Paolo held it to the man's lips. He coughed at first but then gulped at the liquid eagerly, spilling some down the front of his shirt.

Caine chuckled. 'It just goes to show. It doesn't matter how badly off a fellow is, he'll always drink good Scotch.'

At this moment, the door opened and a young *caboclo* girl stepped into the room, a smile on her face; a smile which faded when she saw the roomful of strangers. She stood hesitantly in the doorway, gazing inquiringly at her father. She was perhaps fifteen or sixteen years old, dark skinned and extremely pretty. She was dressed in a cheap cotton dress and was carrying a bucket of milk.

'Papa?' she said quietly; and then noticed his ashen complexion, the strange clumsy shape of his left hand. She set the bucket down carefully on the floor as though deliberating whether she should stay or run for her life.

Caine turned and smiled disarmingly at her. 'Ah, come along in, my dear, come along in. Your father and I are old friends. We were just having a little drink together.'

The girl shook her head apologetically. Clearly, she did not speak any English; but Caine's smile had reassured her. She took a step closer. Then Hernandez, rousing himself suddenly from his half-faint, became aware of her presence for the first time. He didn't speak but his agonized expression was enough to warn her that something was badly wrong. She spun round with the intention of making a dash for the door and, in the same instant, Schiller leapt up and made a grab for her, catching her around the waist and lifting her bodily from the floor. Twisting around, he kicked the door shut and then bore the girl, kicking and screaming, to the table.

'Well, well, what have we got here?' he chuckled gloatingly. 'A pretty little bird, wouldn't you say?'

'If you like that kind of thing,' replied Caine drily.

'Oh, but I do. I do like her. She's a pretty little thing.' Schiller set the girl on his knee and, grabbing his tumbler of whisky, he pushed it up against the girl's lips. 'Here, have a drink, little bird,' he coaxed. She resisted him so he put one arm around her, trapping her arms at her sides; then he pushed the tumbler to her mouth again, spilling the drink down the front of her dress. She spluttered, shook her head from side to side and Schiller laughed with obvious delight.

'Please, *senhor* . . .' groaned Hernandez. 'Please don't hurt her. She's only a child.'

Schiller gazed at the man calmly. 'You'd better watch out for your other fingers,' he warned.

'Hernandez has a point,' said Paolo bluntly. 'She is only a kid. Why don't you just leave her alone?'

'Oh, everybody listen! The tough guy just gave me a warning!' Schiller made a grimace of exaggerated terror. 'I'm frightened! I'm so frightened, I'm pissing in my pants.'

Paco guffawed and Schiller went right on with what he had been doing, while Paolo watched helplessly. He turned entreatingly to Caine, who was drinking his whisky, apparently unconcerned.

'Surely you are not going to let him carry on like that?'

Caine glanced perfunctorily at Schiller and the girl. 'Oh, I think Otto is old enough to determine his own destiny,' he replied. 'And besides, I don't see any great harm. A little whisky isn't going to poison the girl. Besides . . . it isn't every day that Otto takes a fancy to a young lady. I think we should let him have his fun.' He took the whisky bottle and refilled Paolo's tumbler.

'Let him have his fun?' Paolo was shocked by such a remark, even from a man like Caine. The American movies he loved so much had instilled in him the belief that there was an unwritten code of honour amongst criminals. 'That's just a child he's got there. A little girl.'

Caine glanced at Paolo thoughtfully for a moment. 'There you go again,' he said. 'That *soft* side to your character. I fear that you'll never make a good operator. Never.' He put his big hand on top of Paolo's and leaned forward slightly. 'Let me put your mind at rest. I know what you're thinking but you're really quite wrong. The girl's er . . . *honour* is quite safe. Otto has no interests in that direction . . . isn't that right, Otto?'

Schiller glanced up at Caine, his clear grey eyes open and unashamed. He did not admit or deny the allegation, but there was something about the horribly familiar way

301

he fondled the struggling girl that made Paolo shudder.

'Oh, we'll have some fine games together,' said Schiller quietly; and he stared at Paolo as he said this, smiling in a mocking way, knowing that he was provoking the young pilot. 'She's a pretty one. A real pretty. Have you seen her mouth, Paolo? Such a lovely mouth.' He slipped one hand beneath the girl's throat and tilted her head back so that he could pour more whisky into her mouth. Then he gave an abrupt yelp of pain as the girl lunged forward and buried her teeth in his right forearm. The tumbler fell from his hand and spread a slow dark puddle of whisky across the surface of the table. With an oath, Schiller stood up, tipping the girl forward off his lap. Then he brought the back of his left hand hard across her face. She tumbled sideways with a shriek and went sprawling onto the floor. Schiller was onto her in an instant. Grabbing her by the arms, he pulled her to her feet and administered a couple of hard slaps to her face, so that she slumped back into the crook of his arm, no longer resisting him. He examined his arm ruefully. Blood was welling up from the bite and the others could see, quite clearly, the distinct impression of two rows of teeth.

'Little bitch,' growled Schiller.

Paco laughed uproariously. 'Your pretty little bird has a sharp beak!'

'Shut up. Get me a bandage from the first aid kit.' He threw the girl contemptuously into his chair and she sat staring defiantly around at the others. 'You'll be sorry you did that,' Schiller told her coldly; but she gazed up at him uncomprehending.

'Well, you *did* say that she had a good mouth,' chuckled Caine. 'You'd better hope that she hasn't got rabies or something.' He waggled an empty whisky bottle. 'Paco, when you're through playing nursemaid to Otto, you can open another of these.'

Paco was helping Schiller to tie a dressing around his

arm. 'You had better be careful, Senhor Schiller,' he said. 'In the heat of the jungle, a bite can soon be infected.' He turned away to search out another whisky bottle. Schiller finished tying the knot himself with some difficulty. Then he stood looking at the girl, his eyes fierce and terrible, but for the moment at least he did not attempt to touch her again. Instead he slipped his left hand into the pocket of his bush-jacket and there was the familiar clicking sound. It was suddenly very quiet in the room and, Paolo thought, rather cold. He was only dimly aware of Caine filling his empty tumbler back to the brim.

'Why so wistful, Paolo?' Caine slapped the young pilot's shoulder. 'Thinking of all the money you're going to own?'

'Sure ... that's it, Senhor Caine. The money.' And impulsively he raised the tumbler, falling back as he generally did in times of uncertainty on the easy escape of alcohol. Drinking made ugliness easier to accept. And right now he had a powerful thirst deep in his guts.

'That's right,' purred Caine. 'Liquid fire. Once you get the taste for Scotch, you'll want nothing else. Better than *cachaça*. Better than anything.' He made a great show of gulping his own drink, but in reality, only sipped at it. He watched with quiet satisfaction as Paolo tilted the liquid back in one long swallow; then, with a smile, leaned forward and filled the tumbler again.

Another fire, another sandbank, thought Martin. *And they all look exactly the same.*

Sometimes it was hard to believe that the canoe was making any kind of progress. And yet, every evening when they camped, Claudio would reel off his estimate for the distance they had covered. It always sounded impressive. But what if there were no end to this lousy river? What if those slow yellow waters just slid silently onwards for all eternity, until you died or went mad, between those oppressive waiting lines of jungle? A man could believe that kind of thing out here all too easily.

He cradled the comforting wooden stock of the rifle and stared thoughtfully into the flickering light of the fire. It was late and it was his watch. It was *always* his damned watch, or so it seemed to him.

Since the last appearance of the plane, he had thought long and hard about Caine and had almost managed to persuade himself that the fat patron could not possibly have discovered his whereabouts. The country was just too big, too remote for that.

He turned at the sound of a light footstep behind him. It was Helen.

'I couldn't sleep,' she said. She sat down beside him, resting her head on his shoulder.

'All this soft living you've been doing,' he told her.

She laughed. 'Just one long holiday really.' She sighed. 'A holiday you can't get away from. Sometimes you feel like you'll be travelling like this for the rest of your life.'

'I was just thinking the same thing.' He poked at the fire with a length of stick, watching the flurries of sparks that danced skywards from his attack. 'You know, Helen, I've been thinking . . . my diamond and all. Once we reach the mission station, I'm going to have to move on pretty damned quick. I don't want to get caught out here in the open. So, there may not be time to say much.'

She looked at him with a trace of mockery in her eyes. 'What would you want to say?'

He shrugged, looked away a moment. He felt suddenly rather uncomfortable. 'Hell, you know . . .'

She stilled him with the touch of a hand on his bearded face. 'Listen,' she said. 'Martin, I'm not a little girl. I don't depend on things, you know? I know how it can happen between two people. All right, so the two of us have got something for each other, but it may not mean very much back in the city. You don't *owe* me Martin, I accept that.'

304

'Supposing I *want* to owe you?' he asked her.

She gazed at him blankly for a moment. 'Come again?'

'I said, supposing I want to owe you? To tell you the truth, I've been thinking of ... of asking you to come along with me. What would you say if I did ask you?'

She pondered this for a few moments. 'Well, naturally, it would depend on where you were planning on going.'

He shrugged. 'Haven't thought it out too carefully yet. Europe, most likely. Switzerland, Sweden, somewhere like that. From there, back to the USA. One thing's for sure, I wouldn't want to cool my heels in Brazil for too long. It might be rough getting out but we'd have the tarantula and ...'

'The what?'

'The tarantula. That's what I call the diamond.' He patted the leather pouch beneath his shirt and then he grinned. 'Hell, I've just realized. You haven't even seen the diamond, have you? Neither has Claudio. It seems strange to think I've been carrying it all this time and never shown it to you.' He pulled the pouch out from under his shirt.

'Well, you know what they say,' replied Helen. 'When you've seen one diamond ...'

'Not true,' he assured her and tipped the tarantula out onto the palm of his hand. 'There, take a look.'

She took it from him gingerly, handling it with care as though she thought it might shatter like a fragile eggshell.

'Lord, it's big,' she whispered. 'Are you sure it's real?'

'I hope to God it is! Otherwise, I've gone through hell for no reason at all. No, it's real all right. Here, look, hold it up to the firelight and look through. You see the tarantula?'

'No.'

'Sure you do. Right in the middle there.'

'No, I ...' She broke off in mid-sentence and then gave a brief gasp of surprise. 'Yes. Yes, I see it now. God, isn't

305

that strange.' She shuddered abruptly and then handed the diamond back. 'I don't like it,' she concluded. 'It gives me the creeps.'

He stared at her. 'What do you mean?'

'I don't know. There's something unnatural about it. It looks so perfect, that design. Like it's been *drawn* in there somehow. Don't you ever wonder how it came to be that way?'

He shook his head in disbelief. 'Well, isn't that just like a dame. I show you the most valuable piece of rock in all South America and you worry about the way it looks! You'll be telling me next it's got a curse on it.'

It was meant as a joke but she didn't smile.

'Things don't happen by accident,' she insisted. 'That design. It must mean something.'

'It's an accident of nature, that's all. Just think of it in terms of what it could buy. That's a whole mountain of fur coats I'm holding, right there in the palm of my hand.'

She shrugged. 'A fur coat wouldn't be much use to me here.'

'No; but it would in Europe. They get cold winters out there. Snow.'

'Then . . . you *are* asking me?'

'I might be.'

'God, Martin, this is impossible! You're not sure if you're asking and I'm not sure if I want to accept. Let's just think about it a while longer, all right?'

He frowned. 'Yeah, well I guess that makes sense.' Martin slipped the tarantula back into its pouch and he and Helen fell silent for a while. Across the gently lapping river the long strip of black velvet sky that overhung it shimmered with countless stars, flung like a handful of tiny rhinestones into emptiness.

'Beautiful,' whispered Martin impulsively. 'Absolutely beautiful.'

Helen turned to look at him. 'What is?' she asked.

306

'You are,' he told her; and, leaning forward, he kissed her gently, cradling her face in his hands and stroking her hair. She pulled away from him, laughing.

'That's not what you meant at all,' she protested. 'You were talking about the –'

She broke off abruptly and stared at Martin in alarm, as though doubting that the sounds that had interrupted her really existed. But the grim look on Martin's face confirmed her fears. He rose cautiously to his feet and gazed around. The sounds rose, throbbing and pulsing on the night air. Impossible to say whether the drums that pounded out that urgent constant rhythm were close or far away, but they were loud and there were many of them. The individual beats echoed hollowly in the darkness and then fragmented, so that it seemed there were literally hundreds of pairs of hands beating in time, somewhere out in the vast unseen depths of the jungle. It was frightening, threatening.

Claudio came running over, his blanket draped around his shoulders like a poncho, his rifle held ready for action. He glanced nervously at the others, then stared slowly around the pool of light from the campfire.

'Has this just started?' he inquired, blinking the sleep from his eyes.

Martin nodded. 'A moment ago. What does it mean?'

There was a brief silence. 'I don't know,' replied Claudio. But there was something evasive in his manner.

'You must have an idea,' reasoned Helen.

Claudio shrugged. 'Whatever it is, it isn't good news. I think we should forget about the camp for tonight and push on in the dark. What do you say?'

'I don't think either of us will argue that point,' said Martin. 'What are we waiting for? Let's go.'

They scrambled for their equipment, stumbling and bumping into one another in the darkness, their nerves jangling in grim accompaniment to the drums, which seemed to grow louder and louder by the minute. At last, sweating, cursing, they threw their last few belongings into the canoe and pushed out into the blackness of the water. Luckily, there was moonlight. It filtered through the gap in the trees, gilding the middle of the river with a ghastly glow. The ranks of jungle on either side were black voids, eerie and unfathomable.

On the *praia* they had just vacated, the campfire burned, a lonely twinkling beacon, dwindling rapidly as the canoe journeyed onwards. Martin was amazed to realize that he could hear the beating of his own heart. It seemed to him even louder than those terrible unseen drums, which continued their thunderous rhythm all the rest of that night as the three of them paddled downriver beneath the stars.

Paolo woke abruptly from sleep and lay where he was for a moment, allowing his confused senses to pull together into some kind of order. He was lying slumped forward across the table, beside the empty whisky bottle. A dull redness pounded in his head as he eased himself slowly upright. His mouth was arid, his tongue and lips sticking together so that he could barely swallow. Instinctively, he reached out for his tumbler, which still had a few drops of whisky at the bottom of it. The sour smell made his stomach recoil momentarily but he swilled the contents down anyway, grimaced fiercely and then sat peering blearily about in the darkness.

After a few moments, he was able to make out the large hunched shape of Charles Caine, stretched out on the floor beneath an elaborate arrangement of blankets. Paco was slumped in a chair at the other end of the table, snoring prodigiously, his face buried in his arms. Beside him on the table top lay the haversack that contained the bottles of whisky. Paolo licked his dry lips. Steadying himself with one arm, he got uncertainly to his cramped feet and began to move around the table, intent on securing another bottle to get him through the night; but he had only gone a short distance when he stumbled and almost fell across something that lay stretched out on the floor against the back wall.

Gazing down, Paolo saw that it was Hernandez. The man had been tightly bound and gagged with a length of rag. In the gloom, Hernandez's eyes stared pleadingly up at Paolo, as though asking his help. Paolo stood looking down at the little *caboclo*, wondering who had trussed him up in such an elaborate fashion. Restraining him was one thing, but a gag ... and then, for the first time, it occurred to him that Schiller was not in the room.

A sharp stab of suspicion hit Paolo. The girl was gone too. What the hell was going on?

Glancing nervously around, Paolo noticed that there was a faint strip of light showing from beneath the grubby curtain that masked the house's bathroom, a tiny, insanitary affair that Paolo had been obliged to visit earlier that night. As he watched, he became aware of movement in there, as somebody's feet passed in front of the light source, and he could just make out the faint sounds of somebody talking in a low hushed tone. It was Schiller's voice all right. For some reason, a brief chilling shudder of apprehension rivered through Paolo's body, driving the last traces of drunkenness away.

Puzzled, he moved carefully away from Hernandez and crept slowly across the room, taking care not to blunder into anything in the darkness. He approached the curtained doorway and, easing the material aside with one hand, peered into the bathroom. A hurricane lamp had been set up on a small table and Schiller was arranging some items on it while he talked in a calm, assured voice to the girl. She was seated in a large cane chair and, like her father, had been gagged; furthermore, Paolo could see that the girl's slim wrists and ankles were

309

lashed tightly to the framework of the chair. Her large dark eyes, watching Schiller as he worked, were absolutely terrified.

Paolo took a breath. What the hell was the German up to now? He tried to catch what the man was saying.

'Now, let us see what we have here. Only the very finest equipment, you can be sure of that, little bird. And sharp. I always keep them sharp. Yes, let me see now . . .'

Schiller had moved slightly to one side and now Paolo could see what he was arranging on the table. His blood seemed to freeze in his veins. He was looking at a glittering array of dental implements, tiny knives, hooks, hypodermics. He was setting them out in a particular order, taking great care over this as though it was of the greatest importance.

'You must be taught not to bite people,' Schiller was saying matter-of-factly as he filled a hypodermic from a glass phial. The girl's eyes bulged in terror and she tried to scream against the gag which held her tongue. 'Firstly, a little shot of something to calm you down a bit; then we'll see about those sharp little teeth of yours . . .'

Paolo felt an abrupt dull sickness lurch in his belly. He had seen enough. As Schiller turned to lean over the girl, Paolo stepped quickly into the bathroom. He grabbed Schiller by the shoulder, spun him quickly around and punched him hard in the face, sending his thin body reeling across the small room. The hypodermic dropped from the German's hand as he tripped backwards over the low jut of the verminous-looking bathtub and half fell into it. As he did so, something spilled from the pocket of his jacket: hundreds of tiny white objects that went skittering noisily across the enamel surface of the bath. Paolo gave a soft curse and he took a step closer, staring down into the bath in uncomprehending revulsion.

Not pebbles as he had previously supposed. No. They were teeth. Human teeth. Schiller must have been

310

collecting them for a very long time.

'What kind of sick animal are you?' gasped Paolo, in disgust. 'What kind of a filthy pig that you would do such a thing to a little girl? Tell me, goddammit! Make me understand.'

Schiller said nothing. He lay on his back in the bathtub, leaning on one elbow and staring up at Paolo, a curious smile on his bloody lips. Paolo was vividly reminded of a Hollywood vampire emerging from a coffin, an image from a film he must have seen years ago. He watched in silence as Schiller raised one arm to wipe the crimson trickle that was coursing down his chin. Then, slowly, he got back to his feet and glanced down at the white specks that littered the inside of the bath. As he climbed out, a tooth crunched to powder beneath his foot.

'You shouldn't have done that,' he said tonelessly. 'That was a very stupid thing to do.' He slipped one hand into his pocket and it emerged holding the pearl handle of his stiletto flick-knife. A touch of his thumb and the long blade shot out, glittering dangerously in the harsh light of the lantern. 'All right then, tough guy. Let's see how good you really are . . .'

Schiller took a step forward and instantly Caine's voice intervened. He was standing in the doorway, his hair rumpled, his face bearing the indignant look of a man rudely awakened from sleep. Behind him, Paco too peered in at the commotion.

'Otto, put the knife away! We'll have no fighting under this roof.'

Schiller shook his head vehemently. 'Oh no, Caine, the punk attacked me. Nobody does that without being brought to task for it.'

'All right, Schiller,' said Paolo. 'Put down the knife and we'll go outside and settle this.'

Schiller's mouth curved into a mocking grin. 'Don't be stupid. What do you think this is, some kind of chivalrous

311

game? I'm going to cut you to pieces, boy. The fact that you are unarmed only makes it twice as enjoyable for me.' He raised the knife and took another step forward.

'Otto, I'm warning you!' snapped Caine. 'Paolo is a valuable member of this expedition. Any personal grievances you may have can wait until after the job is finished. Put the knife away and come out of there.'

Schiller hesitated. He glanced at Caine and then back at Paolo. He seemed to make a conscious effort to control his temper.

'Very well,' he conceded at last. 'But it's not over.' He jabbed a finger in Paolo's direction. 'You remember that, tough guy. When this trip is finished you'll still have to answer to me.'

Paolo nodded grimly. 'I'll remember. And I'll also remember what you were about to do to that little girl. You sick bastard, you don't deserve to live. Somebody should put you out of your misery like a mad dog.'

For an instant, Schiller's eyes bulged with anger. Then his features lapsed into a contemptuous sneer. 'Go ahead, say whatever you like. Every remark from now on is just another cut with the knife before you die.'

From anyone else, the line would have sounded ridiculously theatrical. From Otto Schiller it sounded like nothing less than a firm promise. He carefully folded the stiletto and slipped it back into his pocket; then, kneeling down, he set about picking the teeth out of the bathtub, searching them out as carefully as if they were precious jewels.

'Come along, Otto, you don't have to do that now,' complained Caine tetchily. 'Leave them till morning.'

'They are my good luck,' muttered the German tonelessly. He crammed a few more into his pocket and then, with a sigh of resignation, pushed roughly past Paolo and went out into the main room, barely glancing at Caine as he went by. After a few moments, Paolo heard the outside door open and close.

Caine smiled ruefully and stepped into the bathroom. 'Gone to work out his frustrations in the village, no doubt,' he observed. 'Some poor fellow is liable to have his throat cut if he gets in Otto's way.' He walked over to the collection of dental implements and fingered them. 'A curious hobby this. I believe he picked up the taste for it at Auschwitz.'

Paolo ignored Caine. He untied the girl and gently removed the gag from her mouth. She began to sob hysterically in a mixture of terror and relief, and she clung to Paolo shaking while he stroked her hair.

'It's all right now,' he told her. 'Nobody's going to harm you.'

Caine chuckled. 'There you go again, Paolo,' he observed. 'That soft nature of yours. It will get you into trouble one of these days.'

Paolo gazed at Caine contemptuously. 'Maybe you think I'm old-fashioned. But torturing children has never been my style.' He led the girl back out to the main room and watched as she ran over to the slumped figure of her father. Paco took a step towards her as if to intervene but Paolo held him back.

'Let her go to him,' he said. 'I'll watch them.' He went over to the haversack and took out another bottle of whisky, uncorking it with his teeth. Paco threw an inquiring glance at Caine but the fat man dismissed the matter with a wave of his hand. He watched thoughtfully as Paolo took a long swig.

'You look as though you have a powerful thirst.'

'It gets stronger by the minute,' admitted Paolo.

'Well, if I were you, I'd take great care from now on. Making an enemy of Otto Schiller is very unwise. And I may not always be around to call him off.'

Paolo shrugged. 'I'll keep an eye open for him,' he said. He watched the girl as she untied her father and eased the gag from his mouth. She was still sobbing, her pretty face streaked with tears. 'One more thing, Caine. If anything happens to that girl before we leave, I'll blow this whole operation wide open. You'll have to find another pilot to fly you out of here.'

Caine gazed at Paolo for a moment, a smile of amusement on his fat face. 'Yes, Paolo. I think I get the general idea.' He yawned, stretched himself in an exaggerated display of sleepiness. 'Now, if you'll excuse me . . . I think I'll try and get some sleep. I trust that you will keep an eye on Hernandez and his daughter.'

Paolo nodded. Somehow, he didn't feel sleepy at all. He watched as the fat patron returned to his bedroll. Paco had already settled back into his chair and within a matter of moments was asleep again, his heavy snores punctuating the silence at regular intervals. After checking on the girl's mother behind the curtain, Hernandez and his daughter curled up on the floor together and at length her sobbing subsided as exhaustion claimed her.

Paolo was left alone with the bottle of whisky, drinking steadily as he waited for Schiller to return.

Chapter 14

At first light, Hernandez and Paco went out to the *batelão* and loaded it with provisions for the journey. Some spare petrol cans were filled from Hernandez's precious store. It was a grey, chilly morning and Paolo, suffering from a debilitating hangover, could do little but hang about on the wharf, waiting to depart.

Schiller had not returned until an hour or so before dawn and then he had barely acknowledged Paolo's presence. It was as though he had dismissed the previous night's skirmish from his mind, at least for the time being.

He said nothing about where he had been all night.

At last the *batelão* was deemed ready for departure. Paco climbed down to it first and sat himself in the stern alongside Hernandez, so that he could keep the little *caboclo* covered with his pistol. Schiller, aloof and silent, took a seat in the prow and kept his gaze fixed on the broad muddy sweep of river up ahead. Caine clambered awkwardly down the rickety ladder of the wharf and took a seat amidships, then beckoned Paolo to follow him.

'You sit here with me,' he suggested. 'I want to keep you and Otto well away from each other.' He glanced back at Hernandez's house, where the face of the little girl watched apprehensively from a dusty window. 'I hope, Francisco, that you have schooled your daughter on the subject of your sudden departure,' he said.

Hernandez nodded wearily. 'She is to tell anyone that asks only that I have gone on a trip upriver, *senhor*. She does not know where I am or when I will be back. She has promised not to say anything more than this.'

'Good. All right, let's go.' Paco grinned and jabbed the barrel of the gun into Hernandez's ribs. The *caboclo* jerked the starter cord but the engine was cold and it merely spluttered dismally. It took perhaps half a dozen attempts to kick it into life before, at last, the boat chugged steadily away from the wharf and began to pick up momentum as it slid upstream. Paolo stared vengefully at Schiller's back. 'I don't understand,' he murmured. 'What kind of a man could fall so low as to do what he tried to do, last night.'

Caine chuckled. 'I'll admit,' he said, 'Otto is a strange one. There are very few like him and that's probably just as well for the world. But men like that have their uses. They have a seemingly insatiable appetite for the dirty jobs in life and, whether we admit it or not, those jobs have to be done by somebody. In the human jungle, Otto is a predator. He feeds on the weak and the sick and the indecisive. He has some unsavoury habits, but it was the war that did that to him. He doesn't choose to talk about his career back then, but I've managed to find out a lot about it. No man can come through the experiences he's had without acquiring a few ... deviations.'

'That doesn't excuse what he tried to do,' snapped Paolo fiercely. 'The girl would have been marked for life ...'

Caine spread his hands. 'And what kind of a life does she have in store, Paolo? A life of poverty, disease and squalor.' He gestured at the last few buildings perched on the very edge of the jungle. 'You must stop thinking of them as people such as you or I. They're little short of animals, lazy, dirty, ignorant. You think that they deserve the same consideration as *decent* people?' Caine shook his head emphatically. 'Let me tell you, they will always be like this, because basically, they aspire to nothing more than this degradation in which they exist. There's not one of them who has the *stuff* to stick his head up out of the slime and say that I'm wrong. Animals, Paolo. Nothing more than that.'

'And that gives us the right to torture and kill them, whenever we see fit?'

Caine considered the point for a few moments. 'Yes,' he replied at last. 'I think so. Do not gods play with mankind for their amusement? So, in turn, the more elevated men tinker with the destiny of such people as these. Look at Hernandez here.' He turned and indicated the grizzled little pilot in the stern. 'We have beaten him, we have inflicted pain upon him. We have almost certainly left his wife to die back there. Events that you might suppose would drive him mad with rage. Does he attack us? Does he refuse to comply with our orders? No. He sits in the boat and pilots it upriver, the only thing he has ever learned to do. He hates us and what we have done to him and his family, yet in the end, he accepts it all with the age-old fatality of the peasant. He's contemptible. A poor joke that the gods have played on mankind.'

He turned again and put an arm around Paolo's shoulders. 'People like *us*, Paolo, we put ourselves above such silly twinges of conscience. Brazil belongs to men like us because we have taken it by right of conquest. Never weaken, Paolo. Be firm in your resolve and the world will be yours.'

He stooped and reached into one of the haversacks by his feet, pulled out a nearly full bottle of whisky. He opened it and savoured its aroma for an instant, then took an ostentatious swig, aware that Paolo was watching him. He lowered the bottle and wiped his mouth on his sleeve.

'And this is the drink for men like us,' he continued. 'In those amber depths a man can find an explanation for most anything that troubles him. Learn to love whisky, Paolo. She's a good mistress and she'll never disappoint you.'

He watched with quiet satisfaction as Paolo took the bottle in his unsteady hands and tilted it to his lips, trying as he gulped down the bitter liquid to forget the frightened, sobbing face of the young girl he had saved in the gloomy evil-smelling bathroom of Hernandez's shack. As the whisky burned like fire in his stomach, it felt as though he would never satisfy the terrible thirst that raged at the back of his parched throat.

'That's the way,' observed Caine approvingly. 'Drink hearty, my boy. You'll travel easier with that inside you.'

Martin peered wearily ahead as the last traces of morning mist began to disperse. It had been a nightmarish journey through the darkness, and even now, with the reassuring touch of sunlight filtering down through the trees, the ordeal was not yet over. The sound of the drums had faded, it was true, to a low ominous undercurrent

317

booming in the distance, yet still all three occupants of the canoe felt the closeness of danger, the awful sweat-inducing fear of an imminent attack.

As always, it was Claudio who drove them on. Like the cox at a university boat race, he was constantly urging them to keep up the pace, as though he sensed a second, wilder crew breathing down his neck. But though time and again he cast anxious glances back upriver, there was no sign of any pursuit; only the feeling remained, strange, intangible, that the Indians were not very far away.

By midday, the sound of the drums had faded altogether and the full heat of the sun beat down upon them, seeming to cut like a knife through the insubstantial awning of leaves and twigs. Martin's sleep-deprived eyelids were as heavy as lead and he began to experience the strange lapses of time that come as a man falls victim to short bouts of sleep. He would close his eyes for an instant, just to rest them. When he opened them again, the canoe would have travelled several hundred yards downriver. The current here was fast and he decided to ship his paddle and take a short rest. Helen was already asleep, hunched silently forward, her paddle resting across her knees. Behind her even Claudio was struggling to keep going, his face bearing the tortured expression of a long-distance runner fast reaching the limits of his endurance.

Martin turned back to gaze downriver. The prow of the boat was pointed unerringly into the flow of the main current. He would close his eyes for just a few minutes. Claudio would soon shout a warning if the canoe began to nose towards either shore. Yes. A few minutes wouldn't do any harm ...

It was no longer the river down which he travelled but a gloomy underground tunnel, its walls and low ceiling worn smooth by the passage of ancient waters long since vanished. It seemed endless, and he carried a flaming torch to light his way. His footsteps echoed a hollow drum-like rhythm in the eerie subterranean silence and his eyes searched the way ahead hopefully, anxious to spot some sign of what he was seeking here. He seemed to walk for an eternity, discovering nothing more substantial than darkness and yet more darkness, waiting for him in the constantly unfolding distance; but then, at last, he glimpsed a flicker of light up ahead, a dancing beacon that seemed to sway from side to side as he approached. He realized then that this was simply the reflection of his own torch, mirrored in something large and round that he could not, as yet, make out.

He emerged into a square rock-hewn chamber and saw to his surprise that the tarantula stone stood in the very centre, supported by a pedestal of black granite, but it appeared to have grown to twice its usual size. It was this that had reflected his torch. Around the pedestal, as though in the act of worship, kneeled several Indians of a tribe he did not recognize. They were dressed in elaborate feather head-dresses and wore heavy cloaks woven with gorgeous colours and intricate designs. Martin hesitated at the entrance of the chamber, unsure whether his presence there would be tolerated; but then, the Indians turned and smiled welcomingly. Their dark faces were handsome and placid. They beckoned him to approach.

He did so cautiously. From somewhere, a slow drum-rhythm had started up, booming strangely around the confines of this underground labyrinth. The Indians, whom Martin somehow sensed were priests, had turned to gaze lovingly at the tarantula stone. Now one of them pointed and gave a shrill cry of exaltation. Martin looked at the diamond and saw with an abrupt thrill of terror that it was growing bigger. Impossibly, inexplicably, it was bulging outwards in every direction, yet retaining its perfect symmetry. Within its icy heart, Martin could see the perfect shape of the tarantula itself. There was, he thought, a fullness to it, a three-dimensional quality that

319

he had never noticed before. It seemed to him that its body was pulsing with a slow, regular rhythm just like that of the unseen drum. It was as though it was actually possessed of life and the centre of the diamond a hollow in which the spider slept.

The diamond continued to grow. Now it was the size of a grapefruit; now, a melon; now, a great round glistening sphere with which nothing could compare. The kneeling Indians were obliged to shuffle back from its crystalline flanks as it pushed at them, swelling upwards and outwards until it seemed to fill the very cavern in which they stood.

Martin could see the massive tarantula in every detail. He could see the rippling of the fine hairs on its powerful legs, the ugly brown carapace onto which those legs were jointed; and he could see the creature's huge jaws, opening and closing on emptiness. It was a creature born of man's most ancient fears, a study in terror; and it seemed to be growing restless in its crystal prison ...

Suddenly, it gave a great spasmodic lurch with all eight legs and the unthinkable happened. The diamond crumbled and shattered like an insubstantial shard of ice, crashing open with a thunderous roar to rain fragments of itself down into the interior of the cavern, fragments that glittered magically. Martin caught a handful of them as they scattered all about him. Each of them was a perfect, multi-faceted diamond that would grace the hand of any fine lady. But Martin did not look at his treasures for long, for a loud bellowing roar made him snap his head back up in wide-eyed terror.

The tarantula crouched like a great black hand on the pedestal. Its long legs twitching experimentally, it stared down at the tiny primates who shared its domain.

The Indians seemed to have fallen into some kind of trance. Yelling in exaltation, they ran towards the spider, waving their arms in worship. The tarantula reached out

320

his forelimbs to the leading figure and grasped him in a quick but horribly gentle motion, lifting him from the ground and raising him smoothly to its waiting jaws. The expression on the Indian's face was one of rapture; an instant later, his head was crushed like a walnut between the tarantula's massive jaws.

The sight of this galvanized Martin into action. With an oath, he turned and ran back along the tunnel, holding the torch out in front of him to light his way. From behind he heard the brief death-screams of the other Indians and then there was a terrible silence in which he imagined the spider's jaws munching obscenely.

Perhaps, Martin reasoned, the tunnel would be too narrow for the tarantula; but glancing back he saw to his horror that the creature was already entering it, lured by the distant bobbing of Martin's torch. The spider's many sets of eyes seemed to glow with a feral malignance and worst, worst of all, was the sound it made as it came scuttling down the tunnel on silent legs. It roared. It gave out a long, thunderous roar, a fluid, hissing, bubbling sound that grew steadily in volume as it began to gain on the fleeing man.

He responded by running at full tilt, oblivious to anything but this wild flight along the twisting, turning tunnel. He dared not look back again, but he could imagine the tarantula's jerky, clockwork scramble close on his heels and meanwhile there was the sound of it, that awful, ear-shattering roar to remind him of its proximity. His skin crawled at the imagined impact of those powerful legs and jaws and he could no longer control his breathing. The tunnel was endless and his legs were rapidly giving out on him. The roaring!

With a last desperate lunge, he flung himself around the next bend and ran headlong into a gigantic web. The torch slipped from his hands and he struggled helplessly in the darkness, aware of a huge shadow closing over him . . .

'Jesus!'

Martin had never been so relieved to be awake. He was slumped forward in the canoe, the paddle gripped in his sweaty hands. The boat seemed to be moving forward at a terrific rate and for some reason . . . the roaring of the spider still filled his head. He sat up blinking, wiping his eyes on the backs of his hands. He fought off a yawn and shook his head to clear it of the last traces of sleep.

That noise . . . what the hell was it?

He stared downriver, wondering for the moment if he weren't still dreaming. Then abruptly, he knew only too well that he was not.

'Sweet Jesus,' he said quietly.

The roar he could hear was the sound of massive amounts of water less than fifty yards ahead, where the river plunged dramatically down through a series of terrifying rapids, smashing into foaming clouds of vapour on the jagged granite rocks that jutted up from its stony bed. Through its centre ran the narrowest of channels and the rocks looked hungry for the keels of flimsy boats like this one.

Glancing back, Martin saw that both his companions were asleep. He screamed something incoherent at them and then, digging his paddle into the water, attempted to edge the canoe out of the current. But the powerful grip of the water could not be denied, even when Claudio and Helen lent their efforts to the task. Though they paddled till their muscles ached, the water held them in a deadly embrace.

'It's no good!' yelled Claudio, above the roar of the water. 'We'll have to go through as best we can!'

'Go through?' Martin shook his head. 'We'll smash to pieces in there! Let's swim for it!'

'Too late for that!' cried Helen. 'We'd have even less of a chance that way! Claudio's right!'

'Jesus, we can't just –' But he never finished the conversation. The canoe lifted on a sudden rush of water and went catapulting headlong down the torrent towards the first hunk of granite. There was no time to do anything but brace himself and stand ready to fend the canoe away from the rock with the short length of his paddle. It seemed a hopelessly ineffective course of action. Most likely he would have to pay a terrible price for that half hour's sleep.

Paolo lay slumped in the *batelão*, cradling the bottle of whisky and staring up at the strip of blue sky above his head. The steady chugging of the outboard motor seemed to reverberate through the heavy hull of the boat and deep into his drunken mind, turning over and over its jumble of confused thoughts.

He was dimly aware of the oppressive heat and the attendant ranks of thick jungle that reared up on either side. From time to time, a face would loom into his field of vision; usually that of Charles Caine, fat, contented, staring down with a smug smile. Other times, when he shifted his head slightly, he saw Paco, big, impassive and invariably eating something. Beside him crouched Hernandez, resembling a small squashed bug, his shoulders stooped and weary, his grizzled face lined with misery. Occasionally, a snatch of disembodied conversation would reach Paolo, though the words rarely registered as anything but a meaningless babble. He lay there trying to figure them out.

'. . . dangerous, I tell you. I just think it was a mistake bringing him along . . .'

'. . . told you, Otto. Right now, he's necessary. He won't *always* be. Besides, look at him, he's harmless. Poor stupid . . .'

'Goddamned *amateur* . . . one debt I shall look forward to collecting.'

323

Paolo groaned, attempted to heave himself up and over onto his stomach. The world appeared to be spinning in a tight halo around his head and he could barely control the actions of his limbs. How had he got into this condition? His dry throat craved another drink and he reached for the bottle with clumsy fingers. But an image of the tortured girl's face rose from the dark pool of liquid in his head, like a carnival ghost in a fright mask. He groaned, tried to wish the vision away, but it persisted. There were some things, he realized, that a man could never drink away.

With an effort, he craned himself up over the side of the boat, making it rock dangerously in the water and provoking a string of curses from his companions. He ignored their oaths and gazed across the placid surface of the river, marvelling at the golden patterns the sunlight doodled upon it. He hummed to himself, some strange half-remembered theme from a movie he'd seen.

Abruptly, a strange shape slid up out of the water a short distance away; a mischievous bear-like face, whiskered and covered with fine brown fur, stared up at him with large intelligent eyes as black as tar. It hung suspended on empty air for a moment and then flipped over backwards, submerging with a slap of a furry tail, vanishing as suddenly and silently as a ghost.

Within moments, it reappeared, swimming alongside the boat and regarding the passengers with a placid, friendly gaze. A second head appeared beside the first and took a playful nip at his companion's neck. She reciprocated and instantly the two creatures crashed together in a playful fight, splashing around in an agile display of skill and high spirits.

They were river otters, large, handsome beasts and, Paolo knew, already very rare on this part of the river, for they had been hunted near to extinction for their fine pelts, the hunters taking full advantage of the otter's friendly disposition. Paolo had never seen such trusting eyes. The otters came swimming right up to the boat, raising themselves half up out of the water to peer inside; then they would tumble backwards, head over heels, and dive into the silent depths only to come rushing back to the surface in a flurry of foam.

Delightedly, Paolo grabbed one of the fish that had been hauled in from the *batelão*'s fishing lines earlier that day and, holding it over the side, gestured for the otters to come closer.

'H'lo otters,' he slurred. 'I'm Paolo. Pleased t'meetchu. C'mere. Come and get the fish . . .'

The nearest otter, the female, did edge nearer to the boat, gazing curiously at the fish in Paolo's hand, yet holding herself ready to dash to safety if necessary. Her tiny nose crinkled as she caught the scent of the fish and she came even closer, so near that Paolo could almost reach out and touch her . . .

And then suddenly, horribly, the boom of a pistol shot crashed out a few feet from Paolo's ear, half deafening him. The otter was slammed backwards into the water as the bullet struck her full in the face and she began to kick and shudder spasmodically, trailing a thick cloud of crimson. Her mate came swimming frantically towards her, calling out in a frightened snuffling tone. He cradled her in his paws, prodding her shuddering body with his nose, mystified by her lack of movement.

'Get away!' cried Paolo desperately. 'Get away or they'll kill you too . . .'

But then a second shot rang out, smashing the male otter down beside his mate. The two beautiful corpses were left floating in a pool of blood as the piranhas began to gather.

Paolo turned away, his eyes filling with moisture. He saw that it was Paco who had fired the shots. He was grinning proudly at his companions, twirling the pistol on his finger like a Hollywood cowboy.

'Why?' croaked Paolo, unable to comprehend such a thing. 'Why, Paco? Why did you shoot them?'

'Target practice,' replied Paco. 'Why, something is wrong?'

Paolo shook his head wearily. 'No,' he muttered. 'No. Nothing wrong. Nothing . . .' He slumped back down into the boat and suddenly, he was no longer drunk. He knew with a clear-cut, rational clarity exactly what was happening to him. He knew that the *batelāo* was a boatload of death, on a river of death; and that anything his ruthless companions touched became itself infected with death. Also in that instant Paolo knew that there could be no partnership with men like that. He had been stupid to envisage it. They had use for him now, but when that usefulness was over, they would get rid of him, as coldly and methodically as Paco had despatched the otters.

The toe of a boot prodded him and a voice said his name but he ignored this. He lay very still, feigning sleep while he listened to the others talking.

'It's all right, he's out cold again.'

'I tell you, I'm getting tired of his carrying on! If he makes such a fuss over the death of a piece of river-vermin, what will he do when we reach the mission?'

'Otto, you should relax. Personally, I find him rather amusing. And as long as the whisky supply lasts, there's no reason why he should cause any real problems. As I have already told you, we need that plane of his and we need him to fly it. By the time we reach the mission, it's all he'll be able to do to stand up! Now, let me hear no more about it.'

Paolo gritted his teeth, his face hidden in the crook of his arm. So that was how Caine saw him, was it? A clownish lush who couldn't refuse a drink to save his life. Well, perhaps there was some truth in it when all was said and done; and if that was what Caine wanted, let him go on believing that. Paolo could play the helpless drunk easily enough, even if it meant surreptitiously dumping most of the whisky in the river. From now on, he'd be a quiet, well-behaved boy. He'd get the others to feel that he could be left absolutely unattended. They still did not know about his gun and he would take steps to ensure that they didn't discover it. Then, when the time was right, he'd make his move. He'd do it just like Gable, cool, assured, brilliant. After all, he'd rehearsed the part often enough in his mind. This time it would be for real.

Meanwhile, he told himself, no more drink, no matter how thirsty he felt. He had to get himself thoroughly sobered up by the time he reached the mission. And he knew the best way to go about that. Gratefully, he allowed his senses to shut down one by one so that he could drift off in sleep.

The canoe bellied into the great slab of granite with a force that shook Martin from head to foot. He pushed at the rock with his paddle, putting all his strength into the task, but for a long, terrible moment, the canoe clung to the rock like a tenacious leech, its fragile hull groaning under the strain. Then, in an explosion of shattered water, it lurched upwards and swung giddily away to the right, then hurtled headlong down a steep valley of rock-haunted water, moving at a terrifying speed. The occupants could do nothing but cling grimly on as it vaulted into the raging waters beyond. The prow nosed heavily beneath the surface and an alarming rush of water came swarming into the hull; then the canoe see-sawed upwards again until it stood almost on end, flinging the three passengers backwards towards the stern and dousing them liberally with water. Items of light equipment went spinning away into the river and Helen just managed to grab hold of the precious coffee jug, before the canoe found itself a new goal and lit out for it at top speed, bobbing like a gigantic cork on the rushing water.

Martin clawed himself upright just in time to see a second rock lungeing out to meet them. Before he could reach out with his paddle, the prow had smacked into it with a terrifying thud and then the stern was snatched around, making the canoe spin a perilous half circle in mid-stream. Everybody dug their paddles frantically into the water in a desperate bid to straighten the craft as it was sucked onwards to the next obstacle, a series of descending ridges that resembled nothing so much as a liquid staircase.

The canoe shot forward like an arrow from a bow, seemingly eager to be smashed to pieces. It rushed out over the first descent and seemed to hang motionless upon the air, a long terrible eternity before dropping with a heart-stopping suddenness to hit the rock-studded shallows below. The impact shook everybody to the bone and more water rushed into the already swamped hull.

'Bail!' screamed Claudio above the thunder of the rapids, as the canoe plunged rattling and shuddering down the staircase, bumping and scraping its shallow hull against half-submerged moss-covered boulders. Hands flew to the task with a will born of desperation and once again, the coffee jug proved to be worth its weight in gold. Helen scooped out water with that while Martin and Claudio employed their cupped hands. They worked in frantic desperation, aware that deeper water lay only a short distance ahead and that, weighted as it was, the canoe would sink like a stone. Somehow, they got the level down sufficiently. The vessel was low in the water but it floated, its pace unchecked as it raced towards the next hurdle.

Martin stared at it transfixed. It was a long claustrophobic passage where the river ran frighteningly narrow between vast overhanging walls of granite. He was briefly

328

reminded of childhood tales of Jason and the Clashing Rocks, but these granite slopes were far too solid to be dismissed as fantasy. He dipped his paddle into the water, straining his muscles to keep the canoe on an even keel, knowing that above all costs the nose must be kept pointed directly into the very centre of the corridor of water. In the wet season, he knew, the level of the river would rise enough at this point to make the passage an easy one. But now the water was frighteningly low. A slight veering to left or right would smash the canoe to matchwood on those waiting rocks.

'Keep your arms in!' he yelled back over his shoulder as the canoe raced unchecked into the narrow opening. The sun was abruptly extinguished and the sheer walls of granite seemed to blur into insubstantial mist as the canoe sped by; but occasionally the craft drifted slightly to one side and the ominous tearing sound that issued from the friction of contact told the travellers that the rocks were indeed depressingly solid. The wet wood of the hull began to smoke ominously, and at one point the flimsy structure of the canoe's awning collided with an overhanging rock and came tumbling down onto their heads. They struggled to push it away, terrified that it might snag and send the canoe tumbling end over end.

For a moment, it seemed as though the tunnel had no end; but then, abruptly, the canoe shot out into open water, like a cork from a champagne bottle. Ahead lay a nightmarish obstacle course of rocks, falls, twists and turns. They snatched up their paddles again as the canoe, an idiot leaf borne by a storm, raced headlong to its next confrontation with destiny.

For the three occupants time seemed no longer to exist as they bounced and lurched downriver, their hearts thumping, their arm muscles aching with the effort of working their paddles. The canoe seemed to possess a charmed life. It bounced off rocks, skidded over boulders

329

and described intricate patterns in the raging water, while its desperate sailors were thrown left and right, backwards and forwards; yet somehow, it survived. A full mile downstream, the rapids emerged at last into a wide, slow-moving curve of untroubled water whose very tranquillity belied the horrors such a short distance upriver. Into this oasis, the canoe finally limped, scarred, battered, half swamped but otherwise intact. With their last shreds of energy Martin, Helen and Claudio paddled wearily to shore. They staggered out onto the *praia*, dragged the canoe safely onto dry land, and then collapsed onto the hot sand where, oblivious to the depredations of flies and ants, they slept. For the time being, they had forgotten about the drums, the unseen Indians, the constant fear of attack. Now, in the grip of total exhaustion, they lay like the dead, dreaming of nothing.

Charles Caine cursed softly and slapped with the palm of one hand at the rolls of fat behind his neck, mashing yet another biting-fly to sticky redness. He trudged slowly across the *praia* until he reached a large flat rock, lowered his bulk onto it with a sigh of relief and sat watching his companions as they unloaded the *batelāo*.

Four days of travel had worn his patience thin. Four nights of mosquitoes and tinned food and excessive heat had worn it even thinner. In the years of comfortable existence that his money had brought him, he had forgotten that journeys could be like this. But then, he reminded himself, this one was very nearly over. Some time tomorrow morning, Hernandez had said, they would reach the mission station; and if Caine's beliefs proved to be well-founded, the return journey should prove much easier to bear.

Paco came plodding over with a large canvas bag slung across his shoulders. 'Where shall I pitch your tent, Senhor Caine?' he inquired.

330

'Oh, over there will do, away from those trees. And make sure the mosquito net is properly secured. I was damned near eaten alive last night.'

Paco nodded wordlessly and moved away. He did not question the fact that Caine slept in a tent while the others had to make do with simple bedrolls on the sand.

By the beached boat Hernandez was wiping down the outboard motor with an oily rag. He kept throwing surreptitious glances in Paco's direction, for he had noticed that the big man carried a machete in his belt and that the handle of the weapon stuck out at a careless angle.

Schiller meanwhile was helping Paolo out of the *batelão*. Gripping him unceremoniously by the collar, he dragged the young pilot across the sand. Paolo was singing tunelessly to himself, clutching a nearly empty bottle of whisky to his chest.

'Thanksh, Otto,' he slurred happily. 'Do the shame for you shumtime. It'sh really *decent* of you.' He was mimicking the refined tones of Charles Caine and the fat man laughed appreciatively.

'I think Paolo here missed his vocation,' he chuckled. 'He should have been on the stage.'

Schiller grunted disdainfully and flung Paolo headlong onto the sand. 'He should be in a *home*,' he said flatly. 'A home for stinking alcoholics. He's contemptible.'

'Thanksh old boy. Delightful.' Paolo waved regally from his place on the sand and Schiller had to restrain himself from aiming a kick at the young pilot. Instead, he contented himself with kicking a large chunk of *praia* into Paolo's face.

'Oh, I say! Dinner already! Thanksh awfully old chap!' Paolo made an exaggerated display of chewing a mouthful of sand and Schiller turned away with a sneer. He unslung his haversack and dropped it at Caine's feet, then stood regarding the fat man sullenly.

'I can't stand much more of this,' he said.

'Relax, Otto. You heard what Hernandez said. Tomorrow, we'll reach the mission station. Then we'll be able to settle down in relative comfort and wait for Taggart to arrive. You know, Otto, the trouble with you Germans is you're too dour. There's a lot of humour in our current predicament, if you only choose to look for it.' Caine leaned forward and began to rummage in the haversack that Schiller had laid at his feet. He found a tin of crabmeat and a can opener and set about removing the lid.

'I'll organize some food,' muttered Schiller. He turned and strolled back to the *batelão*. 'Hernandez, you can start getting some firewood gathered.' He shot a glance at the little *caboclo* who was gazing thoughtfully at him. 'What are you looking at?' he snapped sourly. 'I said firewood. Now!'

Hernandez bowed his head and shuffled quickly across the *praia* to the edge of the jungle, where he set about collecting a pile of sticks; but he still continued to dart glances across at Paco, who seemed engrossed with the problems of erecting the tent . . .

Schiller returned to the canoe and lifted out the large collection of fish that had been hooked earlier that day. Caine's tinned food was intended only as an appetite whetter and, furthermore, the Englishman would not offer anybody else a taste. He knew, too, that when the fish were cooked, it would be Caine who would devour the lion's share. He turned to glance back at Caine, noticing how the fat man reached daintily into the open can with a thumb and forefinger, how he savoured each morsel of crab before putting it into his mouth. What a ridiculous, foppish creature Caine was; and how easily he could be removed if it weren't for those damned letters! Indeed, the letters might not even exist but he dared not assume such a thing. He was helpless, obliged to serve a

332

man he despised simply because Caine had outwitted him. South America, the one continent in which he had thought himself safe, was now a deadly trap from which he could not extricate himself. There was simply nowhere else to run to.

Now, here he was, nurse-maiding a fat pig of a patron, an alcoholic pretty boy, a big stupid lout and a stinking peasant. With a grunt of disgust, Schiller laid the fish down on the ground and turned to shout to Paco.

'You can gut these,' he shouted to Paco, 'when you've finished with the tent. For God's sake get a move on.'

'OK, Senhor Schiller. I'll be just a few minutes.'

'Why don't you gut them, Otto?' suggested Paolo brightly. 'I thought you were the one who couldn't wait to get the knife out?'

Schiller turned and eyed Paolo coldly. 'Oh, I'm saving that for *you*, pretty boy. I'm going to carve you up slowly and pull out those film star teeth of yours. I don't want to go blunting my blade on those fish, now do I?'

He began to stroll back towards Paolo and did not notice that Hernandez was edging slowly towards Paco, his eyes fixed resolutely on the handle of the machete.

'Aww, you're just being *sore* at me!' persisted Paolo. 'What shay we have a little drink together and be pals, huh?'

'Don't flatter yourself, Estevez. Go back to sleep . . . and stop bothering me.'

Hernandez was now very close to Paco. The big man was kneeling, helplessly trying to slot together two sections of pole. Hernandez took a deep breath and then leapt forward, snatching the handle of the machete and whipping it out of its sheath. He did not waste any time on Paco, but instead raced straight at Schiller, the machete raised to strike at the German's unprotected head.

At the last instant, Schiller sensed somebody behind

him and he ducked, the blade missing his head by scant inches. In one fluid motion, he whipped around, administering a savage kick to the *caboclo*'s ribs as he lurched unsteadily by. Hernandez staggered a few steps but whirled quickly around, intent on vengeance, to find that, as if by magic, a long steel blade had blossomed from the German's right hand. Hernandez hesitated, licking his lips nervously. He began to circle the German slowly, the machete swinging left and right as he sought an opening.

Schiller grinned wolfishly. 'So, the little maggot has some guts after all,' he murmured. He crooked a finger in slow invitation. 'Come on then, maggot. I'll *gut* you. Let's see what you can do.' He snapped his head sideways at the sound of a gun cocking and suddenly his voice was angry, possessive. 'Keep the hell out of this, Paco! He's *mine*.'

Hernandez used the distraction to make a lunge, stabbing forward with the broad blade of the knife into Schiller's stomach; but the German weaved nimbly aside and brought his own arm up in a seemingly casual flick. The tip of the blade carved a straight red furrow in the *caboclo*'s right cheek and he reeled backwards with a yelp of pain.

Paolo, supposedly drunk, could only sit watching the scene in silent dread. He glanced at Caine and noticed, with a sense of shock, that the fat man had not even bothered to stop eating. He was observing the fight with the jaded air of a man watching an already familiar newsreel.

Hernandez wiped his bloody cheek with the back of one hand and then began to circle again. He looked frightened now, reluctant to strike again.

'What's the matter, maggot?' whispered Schiller. 'Don't you like the feel of the knife? There are some who do, you know. Take that daughter of yours, for instance . . .'

Hernandez's eyes widened with rage. He leapt forward,

hacking wildly at Schiller, but the German simply retreated confidently from the blows, evading the heavy blade by scant inches while he continued to taunt.

'When I get back to Conceiçao, maggot, I will go looking for that precious daughter of yours . . .' Again Hernandez lunged, again Schiller evaded the machete. He laughed mockingly. 'Now the maggot's angry! Don't you know, maggot, that's the worst mistake you can make? Once you lose your temper, you're as good as finished.'

Hernandez threw himself at Schiller with a yell of hatred and, like a toreador, Schiller sidestepped and brought the stiletto up in a tight, scything arc. Hernandez screamed and clutched at his ear, the lobe of which had been neatly sliced away. He stumbled onwards a few steps and then turned to face his adversary. The little man was nearly blind with pain and hatred.

'Now then . . .' Schiller readied himself for the death-stroke, holding his knife out in front of him like an artist contemplating the creation of a canvas of butchery. 'Just where to put the blade, I wonder? The belly? The heart? The liver?'

Schiller's face was a picture of perverted joy. He ran his tongue across his lips, savouring the moment. Sobbing, Hernandez lifted the machete and steeled himself for a last desperate lunge. He was sweating and his grizzled face was a mask of blood. He took a deep breath and, with an abrupt scream, he ran at Schiller, the machete poised; but the German ducked coolly under the blade and stepped in close, pushing the very tip of the knife into the *caboclo*'s stomach while, with his left hand, he gripped the wrist that held the machete. He held Hernandez there on the point of the knife, raising it slightly so that the man had to stand on tip-toe. He looked deep into Hernandez's eyes and smiled, a sweet smile of contentment. Hernandez's eyes closed and his lips moved in a swift, silent rhythm. He was praying. Then,

Schiller half turned and looked at Caine.

The fat man shook his head. 'We need him, Otto. He knows the route back to Conceiçao and he can repair the engine if it breaks down.'

Schiller nodded wearily. 'Somehow, I had a feeling you'd say that.'

'I think you've taught him a lesson he'll remember.' Caine mopped up the last few remnants of crabmeat with his fingertips, then sucked the fingers clean.

Schiller sighed. 'You've been very lucky,' he told Hernandez. 'There are few men who try a trick like that on me and live to tell about it.' He removed the blade of the knife from the *caboclo*'s stomach and wrenched the machete from his hand. Hernandez dropped to his knees sobbing helplessly. Paolo let out a secret sigh of relief. Afraid of blowing his cover, he had resigned himself to watching an innocent man die. Nothing, he had told himself, must be allowed to get in the way of his own plans. It had been hard to sit by and do nothing and, he suspected, it would be doubly so when the party arrived at the mission station. The missionaries were doomed to die, he knew that now. Yet, he would continue to play his part. That way, he himself had a good chance of emerging from this venture, rich. He would tackle the matter of his own conscience some time in the future. He watched dumbly as Schiller stalked back to Paco and thrust the machete into his hands.

'Just be more careful in future,' he snarled; then he turned and strode away along the *praia*, looking for all the world like a small boy denied a favourite toy.

Caine chuckled, shook his head. 'Poor Otto,' he said. 'It seems I'm always spoiling his fun. Still, he'll get plenty of that kind of thing when we reach the mission station.' He gazed impassively at Hernandez for a moment and then threw the empty crabmeat can at him. 'Don't sit there snivelling, man, get on with what you were doing. The

336

firewood.'

Hernandez glanced up. His eyes had the eerie stare of a man who has wandered too close to the brink of insanity. Staring out from a blood-soaked face, the eyes were very unsettling. He got obediently to his feet and limped slowly back to the pile of wood he had been collecting.

Caine reached out and tousled Paolo's hair. 'Well, what do you say, drunkard? Tomorrow we'll have a little more comfort on our side. Then we'll see if this whole business has been worth the effort. Tomorrow.' He nudged the bottle in Paolo's hands. 'I'd say that's worth drinking to, wouldn't you?'

'Yesh,' gurgled Paolo, nodding like an idiot. 'Heres'h to tomorrow.' He raised the bottle to his lips, draining its meagre contents.

Yes, tomorrow, he thought. Then we'll see who holds the best hand in this game of poker.

And with a wild laugh, he flung the empty bottle out into the blackness of the river. It floated for quite some distance downstream, but then the moving water found its open neck and began to spill in. The bottle slowed, foundered, wallowed and then sank slowly into the cold heart of the river, leaving only the briefest of ripples to mark its passing.

Chapter 15

It had been four days since they had escaped the rapids; four uneventful, heat-racked days through which they had paddled gamely downriver, their back muscles aching with the constant strain. The threat of attack seemed to have lifted now. Perhaps the Indians had not cared to follow down the twisting crashing madness of the rapids. The constant fear and uncertainty had given way to a curious calm and contentment. They had survived against all the odds. The plane crash had not killed them, nor the rebel attack, nor the jungle. They had escaped the Indians and they had cheated the rapids; truly, their lives were charmed. They travelled these last paltry miles in a state of exaltation, the winners of a gruelling marathon performing a lap of honour.

And then, early on the fifth day, Claudio stood up suddenly in the canoe and pointed excitedly to the wide mouth of a river branching off into the jungle to their left.

'The Tapirape!' he yelled. 'Now I know exactly where we are! The mission station is only a few hours away.'

Eventually, the right bank of the river reared upwards into a series of lushly forested hills; and amongst the trees they spotted a derelict stone tower. Remote and partially encroached by jungle, it was nevertheless a sign that white men had put their stamp on this part of the jungle.

'That's the *old* mission,' Claudio assured them. 'The new buildings are just a short distance ahead.'

A terrible suspense took hold of them as they crept around each successive curve. Supposing the mission was no longer there? Suppose all this way they had been pinning their hopes on something as insubstantial as a memory? A silence settled over the river, total and oddly unsettling. It was as though even the very birds were holding their collective breaths.

'There!' cried Claudio at last. And the others saw a stubby little wharf jutting out from the right bank. It seemed to be completely deserted. They let the canoe glide in beside it, tied up with an old length of rope that trailed from the mooring and then clambered ashore. Claudio gazed thoughtfully about.

'Odd,' he murmured. 'I should have thought that there would be a few Indians about. Still, there's a second landing stage further downstream. Most likely everybody is working down there.' He glanced at the others, smiled

338

reassuringly. He indicated a well-beaten track that led upwards through secondary jungle and quickly lost itself amongst the trees. 'The mission is this way.' Shouldering his rifle, he led the way.

They walked in single file, toiling slowly up the hillside through the late morning heat. Amongst the trees, the birds had begun to sing again. Claudio walked a short distance ahead of the others, staring this way and that. He seemed vaguely perturbed by the absence of any life. Martin, however, was hardly aware of this, because he was deep in his own thoughts. He glanced at Helen but she seemed to have forgotten that she had promised to make a decision when she reached this place.

They emerged into a clearing at the top of the hill. There were more obvious signs of habitation here. A stone well had been built beside a carefully tended vegetable garden; and set some distance back from this was a low, single-storey white building with a thatched roof and a stone chimney, from which a reassuring column of smoke rose. Another hundred yards back and there was the church, a simple structure of grey brick, looking oddly civilized in this wild location.

'Well, here we are,' announced Claudio. 'And if either of you are longing for a clear, sweet drink, that well has the best tasting water in all of Brazil.'

'I'll draw us some,' offered Martin.

'All right. And I'll go up to the mission and introduce ourselves . . .' Claudio glanced at Helen expectantly, but Martin had taken her arm and was leading her across to the well.

'We've got something to discuss,' he told her.

Claudio shrugged. Turning, he continued on up the hill. Martin and Helen walked slowly together to the well. The wooden bucket was empty and Martin nudged it over the side so that it went rattling downwards into darkness to splash into the water far below. He gazed thoughtfully at

Helen.

'So?' he asked her.

'So what?' She looked back at him defensively.

'You were going to think it over and give me a decision when we reached the mission. We're here. My plan is to stick around for just a day or so, then push on downriver with the canoe. So . . . what do you say? Yes or no?'

Helen pursed her lips and shook her head angrily. 'Goddammit, Taggart, I'm still waiting for you to *ask* me!' she cried.

'Uh . . . I . . . I thought I had.'

'Not in so many words, no. All I've heard is that you *may* ask me, or you're *thinking* of asking me. Martin, it's all so vague. Now, I understand that you're not much of a talker and I understand that maybe you're afraid to commit yourself, but at the end of the day, a question is a question, right?'

He nodded awkwardly. 'All right then. I'm asking you now. Er . . . Helen, will you . . . that is would you *like* to . . . umm, come along with me. In the canoe. Huh?'

She smiled at his obvious discomfort. 'That's it?'

'I guess so.' He stared at her uncomprehendingly for a moment and then realized that she was waiting to be kissed. He moved clumsily towards her and gave her a quick, perfunctory peck on the cheek. He stepped back and noticed that she was still looking at him in mild disbelief. He became irritable. 'Well, hell, that's my offer!' he said gruffly. 'Take it or leave it.'

She stood for a moment with her hands on her hips and then she shrugged, sighed. 'Martin Taggart, damn you for being a silver-tongued, sweet-talking son of a bitch but I do believe you've done talked me into it.' She stepped closer and prodded his chest with her forefinger. 'But listen to me, Mr Taggart, before you go congratulating yourself. Don't you *ever* let me down, or so help me, I'll break every Goddamned bone in your body.'

Martin laughed. 'All right, princess, you've got a deal.' He moved back to the well and began to wind the bucket back up. 'Let's drink to it.'

'Hold on a moment. I'd better chase after Claudio and explain the situation. He's liable to sit right down at a radio set and give the game away . . .' She stared at him thoughtfully for a few moments. 'You're sure this is what you want?'

He nodded. 'Yes, I'm sure.'

'All right, I'll see you in a little while. Save me a drink.'

She turned and hurried up the track after Claudio, who had just stepped through the doorway of the white-painted building. Martin gazed after Helen for a few moments and felt a terrific sense of calm settle within him, now that he had accepted his true feelings. As he watched, he continued to wind up the full bucket. It was very heavy and it took some time to raise it to the surface. He gazed at the surrounding landscape. There was a serene tranquillity to this place that was reassuring after the arduous journey. Perhaps he and Helen could rest up here for several days before pushing on again. It all depended on the rescue party, of course. If the missionaries would go along with it, there was nothing to stop him from hiding somewhere nearby until the party had set off for Conceiçao with Claudio. Then all Martin would have to do was trail the party back downriver and make his own way from there, passing Helen off as his wife. Claudio had said that the village was no more than four days' travel away.

The full bucket rose into sunlight and Martin swung it across onto the edge of the well. Somewhere, a bird sang, a shrill tone of warning. He turned his head and gazed slowly around, but the glades seemed empty. From the track ahead, Helen waved. He waved back, unslung his rifle and leaned it up against the base of the well. Then he took the ladle that hung from the spindle above his head

341

and dipped it into the bucket. He raised the ladle to his lips. Then he froze, staring into it, his eyes wide with shock.

The water was bright red.

He swore softly, let the ladle fall back into the bucket. Crimson droplets splashed upwards from the contact. Slowly, Martin leaned forward and peered down into the darkness of the deep hollow. At first, he could see nothing; but then, as his eyes grew accustomed to the gloom, he began to make out things. Things floating in the water. An abrupt numbing chill ran through him. They were bodies, impossible to say how many of them, piled one on top of the other. Some wore the distinctive black and white habits of friars. And instantly Martin knew, with a terrible conviction, the name of the man responsible for this killing.

'Caine . . . oh God, no . . . Helen!' He whipped around to shout a warning to her, just in time to see her step in through the open doorway of the mission house. The door swung shut behind her.

In a frenzy of fear and panic, Martin snatched up his rifle. He stood staring at the station for a moment and then gazed aside, to the trail leading back down to the river, the canoe and escape. No choice at all really. Without a moment's hesitation, he began to run back down the trail. Fuck the heroism. He still had a good chance of getting out with his skin intact . . .

He ran for maybe ten yards. Then he slowed to a halt and stood very still, his shoulders heaving, his head bowed, knowing in his heart that he could not run and leave Helen and Claudio in the hands of such a man. For the first time in his life, love had him trapped. He gave an involuntary groan of despair. It was pointless to go up to that white-painted building, he was as good as dead the moment he stepped through the door. It was a shallow, futile stupid gesture; but nevertheless, he was

342

going to do it.

He turned and began to climb the hill, holding his rifle in front of him.

Idiot, he told himself. *Think this proves something? You had your chance to get out and you loused it up. Goddamned tin-pot hero!*

He walked slowly because he was in no great hurry to die. The irony of it struck him like a lead bullet. To have come all this way only to find his oldest, most powerful adversary waiting for him. What a waste of time and effort. He might just as well have died back there in the plane.

He reached the paint-blistered doorway and stood in front of it for a moment, readying himself. Then he prodded the door with the toe of his boot. It creaked slowly open.

There were several people in the room. Martin stood regarding them silently. Helen and Claudio were crouched against the wall to his left. A big moustachioed man whom Martin had met just once before was standing over them, holding a pistol to Helen's head. Against the right wall, a grizzled little *caboclo* with a scarred face sat, head in hands; next to him, a young man in a leather jacket leaned back on one elbow, nursing a bottle of whisky. He appeared to be drunk. But it was the figure that sat behind a wooden table in the centre of the room that captured Martin's attention. He sat leaning on his elbows, his fat hands clasped in an attitude of prayer, the tips of the fingers touching against his moist pink lips. He smiled welcomingly at Martin and spoke in a warm, cultured voice.

'Ah, Mr Taggart, we meet again at last. You wouldn't *believe* the lengths I've had to go to, in order to find you. Come in, please.'

Martin edged slowly into the room, keeping the rifle pointed straight at Caine's chest.

'I'm afraid I shall have to ask you to put down the gun, Mr Taggart. Otherwise, Paco here will be obliged to blow a large hole through this young lady's pretty head. I'm sure you wouldn't want that.'

Martin opened his mouth to reply and almost instantly there was the cold pressure of a knife-blade against his throat as somebody stepped out from behind the open door. It was so inevitable that Martin could only shake his head and laugh bitterly. He allowed the knife-man to take away his rifle and then the door closed behind him and he was backed up against it.

'I'm glad you can see the humour of the situation,' chuckled Caine. 'I like a fellow with a sense of humour. Allow me to introduce Otto Schiller, Mr Taggart, a man with no sense of humour whatsoever. He inherited Agnello's old job and, I might add, he's very good at it. Very good indeed.'

Martin turned his head slightly sideways and looked into a face that had forgotten the meaning of pity.

'Congratulations, Caine,' said Martin. 'I didn't think it was possible but you found somebody *twice* as ugly –'

He broke off with a curse as Schiller's knee jerked upwards into his groin, doubling him over with a jolt of pain. Then he was thrown back hard against the door and the knife was pressing even harder into his throat.

'Don't make Otto angry,' advised Caine calmly. 'He'd enjoy nothing better than slitting your throat.'

'Like he did to the missionaries, you mean?'

Claudio sat up when he heard this. 'They've killed the missionaries?'

Martin nodded. 'Every Goddamned one of them. I found them in the well. You can cross a drink of water off your list of priorities, that's for sure.'

Claudio stared at Caine accusingly. 'In God's name, why?' he whispered. 'They had nothing to do with this . . .'

'They were in the way, my dear fellow. A necessity. Nothing personal, you understand, just as I have nothing against you and this charming young lady. But as associates of Mr Taggart, I hope you will understand when I say that I cannot allow either of you to walk out of here. Unfortunate, I grant you; but that's the price of knowing a man like that. You should have chosen your friends more carefully.'

'So, it *was* you in that plane,' said Martin. 'But how in the hell did you . . .?'

'Find you? That, Mr Taggart, is a long and complicated story, which I don't intend to bore you with. Suffice it to say that my good friend Mr Estevez here was instrumental in locating you. He's the pilot of the plane you saw.'

'A pilot? Him? It's a wonder you got here in one piece.'

Caine smiled. 'He's not at his best right now. However . . .' He stared intently at Martin. 'Much as I would love to chatter the day away with you, I think we should get down to some business. I think you know why I'm here. The diamond, Mr Taggart.'

'Diamond? What diamond?' Again Schiller's knee crashed up into Martin's groin, doubling him over with a groan. 'All right,' he gasped, straightening himself up with an effort. 'I . . . get the general . . . idea.' He fought to regain his breath. 'What say . . . we make a deal on this . . .?'

'A deal, Mr Taggart?' Caine laughed sardonically. 'Excuse me, but I'd say you're in no position to make a deal right now. A *deal* was what you originally had with me. Fifty per cent. Instead, you saw fit to try and cheat me and it's taken a lot of time, trouble and expense to locate you. A deal, Mr Taggart? I hardly think so.'

'No, listen. I'm not talking about money! The woman . . .' He indicated Helen. 'At least let her go, huh? She doesn't know anything about any of this, she isn't going to talk against you. What say you take her back with

345

you?'

Helen had turned to stare imploringly at Martin. Caine noticed the look that passed between them and he nodded understandingly. 'How very romantic,' he observed. 'It would seem that love has bloomed in no-man's land. Touching. Quite touching.' He sighed. 'But unfortunately, womankind is not noted for its ability to keep its mouth shut.' He considered for a moment. 'I tell you what we might do. My man Paco here has an appreciative eye for the ladies. We might pass her over to his keeping. Then, if she can *persuade* him that she is worth taking along with us —'

'Go fuck yourself, fat boy!' snapped Helen, staring at him defiantly. 'I wouldn't climb into a boat with you if you paid me!'

Caine gazed at her placidly for a moment. 'So much for deals,' he concluded. 'Paco, you can have the ill-mannered bitch anyway and you can do what you like with her before we leave. After that, you can turn her over to Otto. She won't be coming with us.' He turned back to Martin and smiled sweetly at him.

'Caine,' said Martin quietly. 'You really are a prime hunk of dog-shit.'

An instant later, he slumped down against the wall as Schiller smashed a fist hard into his face.

'Shall I kill him now?' asked Schiller tonelessly.

'No, not yet, Otto. First let's ensure that he has the diamond on him.'

Schiller leaned over Martin, keeping the stiletto tight against his throat. He began to paw the American's body with his free hand, thrusting it into pockets and beneath his clothing.

'Does this mean we have to get married?' muttered Martin between clenched teeth. The German's last blow had split his dry lips open and blood trickled copiously down his chin.

346

'You don't learn quickly, do you?' snapped Schiller. It only took him a few moments to locate the leather pouch. He pulled it out from beneath Martin's shirt and slit the rawhide thong with the blade of the knife.

'This looks like something,' he announced. He tossed it across to the table and Caine caught it, examined it doubtfully.

'This *can't* be it, Otto,' he protested. 'No diamond could be this size ...' But he opened the pouch and extracted the tarantula stone with clumsy fat fingers. His intake of breath was audible to everybody in the room. It was suddenly very quiet as he stared at the diamond for a very long time as though he disbelieved his own eyes. He turned it over and over in his hands, weighing it, trying in vain to evaluate it. When he spoke, his voice had the strange calm tone of a man speaking in a hypnotic trance.

'Yes, Mr Taggart. Now I understand why you killed Agnello. Who wouldn't risk everything to possess such a stone as this? To tell you the honest truth, I would never have honoured our arrangement for something so valuable. It's incomparable. It must be worth a king's ransom.' He raised the diamond slightly, peering into it with his tiny, piggy eyes. He had noticed the strange shape etched into the diamond's crystal heart.

'Why, good Lord, it looks like a t–'

He broke off abruptly, his trance rudely interrupted by the prod of a cold gun-barrel against the back of his neck. His eyes bulged grotesquely as he tried to peer backwards without turning his head.

'P ... Paolo?' he inquired weakly.

'That's right, Senhor Caine.' Paolo's voice was unexpectedly sure of itself, unslurred by alcohol.

'But ... but what are you doing?'

'I'm double crossing you, of course.' Paolo glanced quickly around the room. 'All right, don't anybody make a move or I'll blow Caine's head away.' He cocked the trigger of the ancient .45 pistol and Caine's face lapsed into an expression of blind panic.

'Do as he says! He means it!'

'He's bluffing!' Schiller sneered. 'He hasn't got the guts to kill anybody.'

'Let me be the judge of that!' Caine's voice was shrill with terror. He took a deep breath, tried to control his erratic breathing. His already moist face was now dripping with sweat.

'All right, Paolo, what's this all about?' he demanded. 'Where did you get the gun?'

'It's *my* gun. I've had it all along. Just one little detail that you forgot to check.'

'Check? But my dear boy, there was never any thought of checking on you; after all, we're partners, aren't we?'

'Partners!' Paolo laughed. 'Oh sure, sure, partners. And you never had it in mind to double cross *me*?'

'Of course not. Why, that's a ridiculous notion. Now listen, Paolo, put the gun down and we'll talk this over together, just the two of us.'

'Shut up, Caine, you talk too much!' Paolo gazed slowly around at Schiller and Paco, then back down at Caine. 'Animals,' he murmured. 'A pack of animals. And I'm ashamed to admit that I'm nearly as bad. Oh yes, I was greedy for the diamond, just the way you were. But I've watched you kill and maim and stink your way upriver. There should be a new name invented for animals like you. You have sunk so low, you don't even have a code of honour amongst yourselves. You were even going to kill me.'

'That's not true, Paolo,' protested Caine.

'Shut up!' Paolo prodded his fat neck with the gun. Then he noticed that Schiller's knife hand was moving slightly away from Martin Taggart's throat. 'I told you, Schiller, don't move unless I say so!' He indicated a small open window in the left-hand wall of the room. 'I want all your weapons out of that window,' he announced. 'I'm going to count to twenty. If it isn't done by then, I'll blow Caine's head through the roof. Now get moving.'

Caine's face was unnaturally pale beneath its layer of sweat. 'Do as he says,' he croaked. 'Quickly.'

There was a long silent pause. Then Paco clumped reluctantly across to the window and threw his pistol out onto the ground beyond.

'The machete too,' Paolo prompted him. 'All right, that's good. Now, those two rifles. Hurry it up, I'm still counting. Good! Now, Senhor Schiller, that just leaves your knife.'

Schiller was gazing accusingly at Caine, an expression of contempt on his face. 'So, the boy is drunk, is he? He's under control is he? He amuses you, does he? You fool, I warned you about this. Now look where your selfish stupidity has got us!'

'Shut up,' whispered Caine, aware of the seconds ticking away. 'Just do as he says. Remember, if I die, you're dead too.'

Schiller sighed. He hesitated a few moments more and then, with a shrug of resignation, threw his knife out. Paolo spent a short while assuring himself that his was now the only weapon in the room. He checked Caine, expecting to find a gun tucked away somewhere in one of his pockets but surprisingly there was nothing. Satisfied, he glanced up at the ragged circle of faces that peered at him from all points of the room.

'Good,' he said. 'Now then, Senhor Taggart. I have a deal for *you*.'

Despite himself, Martin had to laugh. 'Hell, do I get any choice?'

'Maybe not. But it's a fair deal and I think, under the circumstances, you'll accept it.' He reached out and took hold of the tarantula stone, wresting it with some difficulty out of Caine's grasp. '*Your* diamond, Senhor

349

Taggart,' he said, holding it up. 'I don't dispute that. All I want is a twenty per cent cut of what you get for it. Down the track out there, there's a *batelão* with an outboard motor. I'll take you and your friends back to Conceiçao.'

'All right,' Martin shrugged, 'sounds reasonable. But what assurance do you have that I'll keep my part of the bargain.'

'For one thing, *I'll* keep hold of the diamond. From here on, I'm going to stick like glue to you until some kind of transaction is made. Meanwhile, you have my word of honour that twenty per cent is all I want.'

'Hell, this is the funniest thing I've come across in months.'

'It would be very easy for me to just take the diamond and run.'

'Yes, so why –'

'Oh, don't get me wrong, Senhor Taggart, I'm no plaster saint. But I ain't no murderer, neither. I came on this trip for greed but I wasn't willing to kill innocent people on account of it.'

'Standing back and letting it happen is just as bad,' Claudio observed. 'It's too bad your change of heart didn't come in time to save the missionaries.'

'I wanted to help them, but the chance just didn't arise. I had to have everybody in one place, where I could handle them easily. They would have killed me just as readily as those monks if I'd botched it. Besides, I wanted to be sure of getting the diamond, too.'

'Admirable priorities.'

'Perhaps, *senhor*; that's something for my own conscience to handle. Meanwhile, I still want a stake in that diamond. So I'm taking a risk. I'm offering you part of the deal I made with Taggart. I'm offering the three of you your lives as part of the exchange. I think you'll agree, twenty per cent is a cheap price to pay.'

Martin frowned, scratched his head. 'When you put it

that way, I have to agree with you. All right. It's the craziest damned deal I ever heard of, but I'll go along with it.'

Paolo glanced at Claudio and Helen. 'I want you two to be witnesses to this,' he told them gravely. They both nodded.

'What happens to these sons of bitches?' Martin inquired, indicating Caine, Schiller and Paco.

'We'll tie them up here and send the authorities back for them.' Paolo turned and waved Hernandez to his feet. 'I want you to go to the *batelão*,' he said. 'Bring back the ropes we left by the wharf. I promise you these men will be made to pay for what they did to your daughter.' Hernandez nodded. He shot a meaningful look at Schiller and then went out of the room, letting the door swing shut behind him. They heard the sound of his naked feet slapping against the hard earth of the trail that led downwards to the second wharf farther downstream.

'Can he be trusted?' inquired Claudio anxiously. 'All the guns are out there; and there's nothing to stop him from just taking off.'

Paolo shook his head. 'Don't worry. He's the one man here I *do* feel sure of.'

'I don't mean to be critical,' said Martin, 'but I think you'll be making a mistake if you let these men live. You said yourself that they were planning to kill you. I think you should finish them off and have done with it.'

'There's been enough killing,' Paolo said quietly. 'Oh, I'll pull this trigger if they force my hand, but I won't appoint myself executioner. They're murderers, the law will take care of them.'

'I wouldn't be so sure about that.' Martin indicated Caine. 'That's not a man sitting there, it's a dog turd greased with vaseline. He could wriggle out of any tight spot; he's got the money and he's got the connections. Pass them over now and we could all live to regret it.'

Again Paolo shook his head. 'No, I won't sink to their level! We'll radio in an anonymous call before we leave. By the time the authorities get onto it, we'll be well away from here. The missionaries are dead, Caine will never be able to explain his way out.'

'I don't like it. Too many loose ends. Listen, give me the gun . . .'

'I told you, Senhor Taggart, I'm calling all the shots here. We'll do it my way or not at all.'

Schiller laughed derisively. 'Why don't you just admit that you haven't the guts to do it?' he said.

'Don't push so hard,' Paolo warned him. 'I only need the excuse.'

Caine found his voice at last. 'You can't just leave us tied up here, Paolo. It will be days before anybody finds us. We could starve to death.'

'You won't starve, Senhor Caine. You'll just get very, very hungry.'

'Paolo, it's not too late to work something out between us! Just think about what you're doing for a moment. You really think you can trust a man like Taggart to keep his word? Why, he'll most likely kill you the moment that your back is turned. Now, I've no idea where you got this ridiculous notion that I was planning to double cross you . . .'

'Maybe because I heard you and Schiller discussing it when I was supposed to be asleep.'

'No, you've got it all wrong, Paolo! It was *Schiller* who wanted you out of the way. Schiller. I was arguing on your behalf. Believe me, I never had any intention of –'

'Shut up, Caine, you fat oaf!' It was Schiller who had spoken. Caine stared at him, his mouth open in outrage. 'Can't you see that you've ruined everything? At least try to accept your fate with a little dignity.'

A silence fell over the assembly. It was very hot in the room and everybody waited, watching Paolo who still

352

held the pistol against Caine's head. Outside the hut a bird shrieked somewhere in the near distance, a brief shrill cry.

'Look,' said Martin after a lengthy interval. 'Why don't you let Claudio and me get the other guns now? We could take some of the pressure off you.'

'No, you stay put. I told you, I want mine to be the only gun from here on. As soon as these pigs are secured, the rest of the weapons go straight into the river.' He smiled apologetically. 'No offence, but I'll feel a lot more comfortable that way.'

'But I thought we had a deal.'

'I had a deal with Caine and look how that turned out.'

'That fellow is taking an awful long time with the ropes,' observed Claudio.

'Think so?' Paolo stared thoughtfully out of the open window but could see very little. 'We'll just wait awhile longer,' he announced.

Time passed, the seconds ticking away, but still Hernandez did not return. The heat in the room was becoming stifling. Again they heard the bird call, and this time there was an answer, somewhere off towards the river. Paolo mopped at his brow with the sleeve of his jacket and swore softly to himself. It was only a short run down to the wharf, what the hell was keeping Hernandez? His gaze wandered quickly over his various captives, searching for any subtle movements but everything seemed to check out. He bit his lip nervously, straining his ears for the sound of the *caboclo*'s naked feet slapping on the hard earth. But there was only silence, interminable, suffocating silence.

'All right then, Schiller, Paco.' He had decided on a new ploy. 'I want you to move over to the right side of the room. Let's have your hands up where I can see them. Come on, hurry it along! You others, I want you in one bunch, here on the left.' He watched anxiously as the figures shuffled to their designated positions. Schiller was smiling mockingly at him.

'What's the matter, tough guy? Beginning to panic?'

'Shut up. Just stay right where you are . . .' He backed a few steps away from Caine and then circled around him and began to edge towards the door, keeping the pistol trained on the fat man and holding the diamond in his left hand. His mouth felt so dry he could scarcely talk. 'All right now, don't anybody get excited. I'm just going to step out of the door for a look around. The first person to try anything – and that goes for all of you – gets a bullet.' He moved backwards slowly, placing each step with great care, aware that a stumble now would be disastrous.

'Give *me* the gun,' pleaded Martin. 'I'll cover them for you while you look.'

But Paolo, mindful of his earlier double cross, shook his head. Now he had reached the wall beside the door. He edged it carefully open with his left elbow and backed a few feet into the open, holding the door ajar with his foot and pointing the gun into the room, straight at Caine.

'Hernandez?' he yelled. His voice echoed strangely through the trees. At the back of his mind was the fear that the little man might have decided to just get the hell away from there; and yet surely he hadn't taken the *batelão*, because there had been no sound of an engine starting. Unless . . . unless he'd simply unhitched the line and let the current take him on downriver. Suddenly, the conviction came to Paolo that this was what had happened. He had been a rash fool to trust the little man like that. Now he was almost certainly stranded here, with just Taggart's slow-moving canoe in which to effect an escape. But then, just as he was accepting defeat, his ears caught a faint rustle of movement in the trees to his rear as somebody came running up the trail. Relieved, he opened his mouth to shout again.

'H–' The word died in his throat in an abrupt

exhalation of air as something struck him a terrible impact full in his back, knocking him several paces forward. He was aware of pain; intense tearing pain rivering down his spine, and he could see the shocked expressions on the faces of everyone in the room as he came lurching forward, his eyes bulging with shock, his mouth open to form a long scream of agony. He tried to turn around but his legs were like columns of jelly and a powerful rushing blackness swarmed up from behind his eyes and into his brain.

Paolo gave a last convulsive shudder and then fell forward onto the tabletop. The gun and the tarantula stone slid away from his twitching fingers. For the first time, the occupants of the room could see the yard-long arrow between his shoulder-blades.

Chapter 16

There was a long awful moment when nothing happened. Everything seemed frozen, numbed into immobility. Paolo's corpse was stretched out face-down and unmoving on the tabletop and the others simply stared at it in shocked silence. Then, abruptly, the spell was broken. There was a brief scramble for the pistol on the table. Both Martin and Schiller made a grab for it, but it was the German who snatched it up with an exclamation of triumph. He jabbed it into Martin's chest and cocked the trigger.

'Get back,' he growled; and Martin was obliged to move slowly back to his seat by the wall, watching in disgust as Caine's fat hands closed for a second time around the tarantula stone.

Another arrow whizzed in through the open doorway, missing Caine by a few inches. It embedded itself in the

355

soft plaster of the far wall with a loud juddering sound. Caine stared at it blankly for a moment and then dropped, in an ungainly heap, onto the floor. Everybody scattered, pressing themselves flat against the wall.

Martin heard Claudio chuckle grimly. 'The Xavantes. They followed us after all.'

'Looks like it,' admitted Martin.

'What are you two talking about?' demanded Schiller.

'These Indians are old friends of ours,' Martin told him. 'Seems they've been trailing us downriver for more than a week. We thought we'd shaken them off.'

Paco had edged himself upwards to peer cautiously out of one of the windows. 'I don't see anything.'

'You won't,' Claudio told him with morbid glee. 'Not until an arrow hits you.'

Caine had crawled underneath the table. He peered out at the others, the tarantula stone clutched covetously to his chest. 'We ... we surely aren't going to let a few ignorant savages get the better of us?'

'What do you suggest?' sneered Schiller. 'Thanks to that idiot Estevez, we've only the one gun in here.'

'There are others outside.'

'Admittedly. Would you care to go and fetch them?'

As if in answer to the question, an arrow shot in through an open window and thudded into the tabletop a few feet from Paolo's corpse. Caine glanced apprehensively up at the quivering shaft just above his head and his face turned white with fear.

'P ... perhaps we can wait them out,' he croaked, his voice barely more than a whisper.

'Very unlikely,' said Claudio. 'They want revenge. We killed one of their warriors upriver.'

Caine pointed a shaking finger. 'Then ... then it's just *you* that they want!'

'The Xavantes are not known for their discrimination,' Claudio laughed. 'When they're in this kind of mood,

356

they'll kill anything that moves.' He slipped his arm protectively around Helen. 'If any of you know some good prayers, this would seem a good time to say them.'

Schiller had opened his mouth to reply but was interrupted by a sudden cry from outside; a long, drawn-out wail of fear.

'Jesus!' Paco called out from his place at the window, 'They've got Hernandez!'

The four Indians had just emerged from the trees into a clearing some distance down the trail. They were carrying the skinny, naked figure of the little *caboclo*, who was twisting and writhing helplessly in their grasp as the Indians laughed outright at his pathetic attempts to escape.

'Maybe you could pick them off from here,' suggested Caine, glancing hopefully at Schiller. The German shook his head.

'They're well out of range,' he said. 'I'd just be wasting my bullets.'

'Well, we've got to do something!' Caine lifted his head. 'What are they up to now . . .?'

Two more Indians had emerged from cover. They walked slowly, openly, as though they were quite aware that they were in no danger. One of the men was carrying a long, stout wooden stake one end of which had been sharpened to a point.

'What are they going to do?' whispered Helen fearfully.

Claudio tried to ease her away from the window. 'Don't watch,' he advised her. 'This isn't going to be pleasant.' But she shrugged him away.

Now the four warriors were pulling on Hernandez's arms and legs, lifting him clear of the ground. He was sobbing, calling out to the others to come and help him. He looked impossibly small and frail beside the powerful naked figures of the Indians. Now the other two warriors stepped forward, both of them holding the stake.

357

Hernandez's legs were forced apart and the point of the stake inserted between them. The two Indians began to push with all their strength.

'Oh God,' whispered Helen. She turned away from the window and hunched down on the floor as Hernandez's screams began to echo through the trees. Long, shrill, they seemed not of human origin at all, but the sounds made by a wild beast in its death throes. Hernandez went on screaming for a very long time and one by one the others moved away. Only Schiller remained, watching till the bitter end, when the point of the stake emerged from Hernandez's open mouth, preventing him from screaming any more.

After that, a terrible silence settled in the room. Everybody sat gazing at the floor as the full realization of their predicament sank home.

It was Caine who broke the silence. 'Send Taggart and his friends out there,' he demanded. 'Perhaps they'll spare the rest of us.'

Schiller shook his head. 'You think you can reason with creatures like that?'

'We've got to try something. We can't just sit here and . . .'

'Shut up a moment! I'm trying to think.' Schiller scrambled across the floor to the other side of the room. He peered out of the small window through which the guns had been thrown. 'It looks very quiet out here,' he murmured. 'Perhaps they haven't covered this side of the building. It's only a short distance to the *batelão*. Perhaps if we make a run for it . . .'

He broke off in mid sentence at a sudden noise above his head, a loud crackling sound. Almost instantly, clouds of thick smoke began to coil down between the roof beams.

'The roof!' wailed Caine in terror. 'They've set it alight!'

Within moments, the dry thatch of the roof was an inferno, raining sparks and burning thatch down into the room. The smoke thickened, came billowing down in blinding grey clouds, wrenching moisture from their eyes. The heat was intense.

Schiller somehow managed to stay in control. 'We're going out through this window,' he shouted. 'Paco, you go first and collect up the guns.'

Paco looked apprehensive about his election, but there was no choice. He grabbed a chair, put it beside the window and clambered up. He levered himself fearfully onto the window ledge, dropped to the ground and crouched beside the wall, glancing fearfully this way and that. Nothing happened, so he began to gather up the various weapons. Shoving his own pistol into his belt, he found the two rifles and also Schiller's knife. Then he located the machete and pushed that back into its sheath.

'All right,' he shouted back. 'That's everything.'

Schiller nodded. The heat in the room was now almost unbearable. He waved his pistol at his three captives. 'Now you three,' he snapped. 'Out you go!'

Caine scrambled over to Schiller and tugged at his sleeve. 'Why them?' he shrieked. 'Leave them and let's get the hell away!'

Schiller shook his head. He was obliged to shout over the roaring of the flames. 'We'll send them ahead of us when we make *our* run,' he yelled. 'They will take the first arrows. The more targets, the better our chance of getting out of this.' He watched as the three of them launched themselves headlong out of the window and then slapped Caine hard on the shoulder. 'Now you!' he instructed. 'Hurry man!'

The first beams were beginning to crack overhead; and occasionally, a questing arrow would rush into the room through the open doorway. Schiller swore and, pulling a handkerchief from his pocket, held it across his mouth

359

and nose. Caine was struggling pathetically to lever his body through the small window, which only just admitted his massive torso. Schiller pushed unceremoniously at the man's rear and at last Caine tumbled through to land in an ungainly sprawl on the far side.

There was a great rush of air as the centre beam of the roof collapsed inward, but in the same instant, Schiller had vaulted headlong through the window. He struck ground, rolled awkwardly and found his feet, joining the others pressed up against the wall. For the moment, they seemed to be shielded from the Indians. But the fire was encroaching fast and they could not hope to stay put for very long. Schiller crawled over to Paco and took one of the rifles from him. He slipped his knife back into his pocket and slid Paolo's pistol into the belt of his trousers. Then he turned to look at the others and indicated a dirt track that led downwards through the trees.

'The *batelão* is at the end of that track,' he said. 'Start running.' He pointed the rifle at them. 'If you won't run, I'll shoot you here and now. It's up to you.' He watched for a moment as the three captives exchanged glances. Then Martin took a deep breath and took hold of Helen's arm.

'Come on, princess,' he murmured. 'With any luck, we'll get through and those bastards will get all the arrows.' He nodded to Claudio. 'Good luck.'

'Thanks. The same to you.'

'Go!' screamed Schiller.

The three set off in the direction of the track, running with all the speed they had left in them, their heads low, their bodies cringing from the imagined impact of one of those massive arrows. Instantly, the air seemed thick with flying projectiles. Too fast to be really visible, they registered on the vision as a brief streak of light passing before the eyes. Martin felt the hard edge of one arrow tear a bloody furrow across the top of his shoulder, but he did not pause to consider the closeness of it. Gripping Helen's arm tightly, he lunged onwards as more arrows ripped noisily through the vegetation on every side.

As soon as the first volley was released, Schiller, Caine and Paco ran too, hard on the heels of their enemies. Schiller's plan seemed to have worked, for they crossed the open stretch of ground largely unopposed. As Caine went lumbering after the others, Schiller and Paco turned at the top of the trail and fired a fusilade of rifle shots into the thick vegetation behind them. Not pausing to see if their aim had been good, they turned and ran on, their heavy boots pounding on the hard earth.

Farther ahead, Martin, Helen and Claudio were racing down through the gloom of the surrounding trees, horribly aware of movement in the undergrowth on either side. More arrows skittered across the track, flashes of insubstantial light against the relative darkness. They could hear voices yelling excitedly in the *selva*. Behind them, more gunshots indicated that Schiller and Paco were firing at anything that moved out there. Glancing back, Martin saw Caine a short distance behind him, running for all he was worth. There was a look of exhaustion on his face and he was puffing and blowing like an old steam engine. He still held the tarantula stone, clutching it to his chest as though it was a rugby football.

Suddenly, Helen cried out as a naked figure came leaping out of the bushes to Martin's left brandishing a spear. The Indian lunged at Martin, who managed to twist sideways, avoiding the full impact of the blow. The point of the spear grazed his ribs and, with a wild yell, he dashed his elbow up into the Indian's face, smashing his nose. As the Indian reeled back, Martin wrenched the spear from his hands and struck him hard across the throat with the handle of it. He did not hesitate to watch the man fall but dropped the spear and continued to run. He almost collided with Helen who, he realized with a

361

sense of shock, had stopped to wait for him. He pushed her on ahead of him.

'You all right?' she yelled.

He nodded and pressed a hand to the rapidly spreading crimson stain on his shirt.

They seemed to be clear of the arrows now, but the thunder of gunfire only twenty yards behind them suggested that Schiller and Paco were not so fortunate. A crowd of Indians had started after the party in hot pursuit and they seemed oblivious to the rifles' bloody retribution.

'The bastards keep on coming,' observed Schiller coolly as he pumped another cartridge into the breech. 'Come on, let's move out.'

Paco was gasping for breath, his face shiny with sweat. 'I don't know if I can go on.'

'Of course you can! If that fat bastard Caine can run, so can you!'

'Just let me get my breath. I can't –' His voice dissolved into a shriek of pain as an arrow thudded into his side. His legs buckled and he crumpled to the ground, where he lay looking up at Schiller with wide, frightened eyes. 'I can't get up!' he gasped in terror. 'Senhor Schiller, I can't move my legs!'

Schiller stooped and squeezed his shoulder reassuringly. He pushed Paco's rifle back into his hands. 'Hold them off for a moment. I'll get someone to help carry you.' He scrambled to his feet but Paco clung to him, his eyes filling with tears.

'Senhor Schiller, I beg you, don't leave me!'

'Let go of me! I'll be back for you, I promise!' Schiller pushed the big man away and raced onwards down the trail.

'Please! Oh Mother of God, don't leave me! Don't leave me!'

Paco's voice came wailing pathetically down the trail

362

for several moments and then, after a brief pause, there was the sound of his gun firing, once, twice, three times. Schiller caught up with Caine.

'Paco?' gasped the fat man inquiringly.

Schiller shook his head.

'He'll buy us a little time,' he said. They had passed now into an area of dry *campo* and a faint breeze was blowing in from the river. Schiller abruptly ordered everybody to halt. He asked Caine for his cigarette lighter.

'My lighter?' wheezed Caine. 'But . . . why . . .?'

'Never mind why, just give it to me!' He watched with terrible impatience as Caine fumbled in his pockets. But at last, the gold lighter was found.

'Good,' whispered Schiller. 'Now we'll give the bastards a taste of their own medicine.' Kneeling down, he set fire to the dry grass at his feet. The effect was magical. A thick plume of flame danced upwards and began to fan rapidly outwards, spreading in a wide band across the trail. A thick cloud of smoke drifted back on the wind. In the near-distance, they could still hear Paco's rifle firing at regular intervals.

'Paco,' murmured Caine, staring apprehensively at the flames.

'He'll be dead by the time that reaches him,' replied Schiller bluntly. He turned back to the others who were waiting a short distance away, regaining the breath that they had lost on the run down. 'All right, let's go on,' he said. 'Come on, move!' They stared sullenly back at him for a moment and he fired a shot into the ground by their feet, flinging up clods of stinging dirt into their faces. Reluctantly, they turned and went on, at a slower pace this time. Behind them, the jungle was rapidly becoming an inferno, a great searing wall of flame eating its way backwards into the heart of the *selva*. It would surely be some time before the Xavantes could push through it. As they ran, they counted the shots from Paco's rifle; another four shots before his gun fell abruptly silent.

Turning a last bend in the trail, the runners saw the river a short distance ahead of them and jutting out from the near bank was the short stubby stretch of the wharf. Schiller grinned triumphantly but his pleasure was short-lived. As everybody clumped onto the wooden board-walk, he noticed that the *batelão* was no longer moored alongside it. It had drifted away, some considerable distance downstream. About thirty yards from the shore, it had snagged on a half-submerged tree-limb and there it sat, the one means of salvation in a desperate situation.

'We'll have to swim for it,' gasped Caine. 'That stupid *caboclo* couldn't have moored it properly. Kill Taggart and the others and we'll go.'

But Schiller was shaking his head. 'I can't swim,' he murmured, a look of dread on his face.

'What do you mean?' Caine stared at him in disbelief. 'You ... you must be able to.'

'I can't, I tell you! I've just never learned. I ... I have a fear of the water. I can't go in.'

'Well, for God's sake, we can't just *sit* here. That fire isn't going to hold them for ever. We'll have to –'

He broke off in alarm as an arrow came hurtling downwards, apparently out of the open sky, to embed itself in the boardwalk a few inches from his left hand. 'My God,' he whispered, 'where the hell did that come from?'

'There!' Schiller pointed upriver. Unable to get through the wall of fire, a few warriors had worked their way to a broad *praia* fifty yards away and from there were casually lobbing high shots onto the unprotected wharf. Even as Schiller spoke another two arrows came scything down from blue emptiness to smash headlong into the wood with a couple of ominous thuds.

'Shit,' said Caine very quietly. Suddenly, everybody was

364

clambering over the side of the wharf to take refuge on the Indians' blind side, amongst the various beams and spars that supported the construction. Schiller slipped on a mossy foothold and his rifle dropped into the river by his feet. Ever watchful, Martin steeled himself to leap but in an instant, Schiller had pulled Paolo's .45 from his waistband and was pointing it menacingly at his captive.

'One of *you* will swim out and bring the boat back,' he informed them.

'Fuck you,' snapped Martin. 'Why should we? You're going to kill us anyway. I'd rather die here than in the water.'

'I had a deal in mind.'

Martin laughed in his face. 'Another deal?' he sneered. 'You people make deals like others have dinner.'

An arrow rushed past them and immersed itself in the water a few inches below their feet, Everybody looked at it in silence for a moment.

'You want to hear the deal or not? If one of you men will fetch the boat, I'll take the woman back with us. I promise she'll be unharmed.'

'Take a hike, Fritz,' snapped Helen bitterly. 'I don't *want* to go with you. I'd rather stay here and take my chances with the others.'

'Keep out of this,' said Schiller quietly. 'I was asking *them*.'

'What do you mean, keep out of it? It's *my* Goddamned neck we're talking about. If you're going to kill us, I just wish you'd get it over with.'

'Very well.' Schiller cocked the hammer of the .45. 'You first, my dear.' He put the barrel of the gun against Helen's head.

'No, don't do that,' said Claudio suddenly. 'I'll go.' He sat down on the spar and began to remove his boots. An arrow glanced off the edge of the wharf and went spinning crazily down to the water.

365

Martin stared at Claudio helplessly. 'Are you crazy?' he demanded. 'You really believe he'll keep that promise? You've seen the kind of shit he is. Don't do it, Claudio!'

Claudio gazed up at Martin calmly. 'What other option do we have?'

'Martin's right,' agreed Helen. 'They don't intend to let me get into that boat. I say let them get themselves out of this mess. Please don't . . .'

Claudio stilled her with a touch of his hand. He grinned oddly. 'My one chance to be the big hero and you want me to pass it up? Helen, I . . .'

'Get on with it!' snapped Schiller. 'My patience is wearing thin.'

Claudio nodded. He turned back to face Schiller. 'You promise, on your word of honour? She won't be hurt?'

'Yes, yes. Now get going.'

Claudio stripped off his shirt and then lowered himself slowly into the water. He inched himself out along the length of the wharf until he was peeping out from the end of it, took a quick bearing on the *batelão*, gulped down a deep breath and then launched himself for his objective, keeping his body under water for as long as possible.

Martin watched him in silent dread. It was all so pointless. Schiller had not the slightest intention of keeping his word. He slipped his arm protectively around Helen's waist, wishing helplessly that he could have the opportunity to say all the things he wanted to say.

'I'm sorry, princess,' he murmured. 'We gave it our best shot but I guess the dice were loaded.'

'We're not finished yet,' she told him fiercely and he was genuinely surprised by the look of defiance on her face.

Now Claudo surfaced, still some distance from the boat. He struck out in a fast crawl and a series of yells from the Indians upriver informed him that he had been spotted. The intervening screen of fire and smoke might hold back the Xavantes, but it could not stop their arrows.

'Come on, you fool,' whispered Schiller. 'They're onto you.'

Arrows began to rain down around Claudio and, gulping more air, he dived again, still pushing towards the boat. But the arrows' own impetus drove each one of them deep into the water and inevitably Claudio rose abruptly to the surface with one sticking out of his back. The others could see him thrashing about in the water, an agonized expression on his face as he attempted to pull it free. Clearly, it had not pierced him very deeply, because he had it out in a few moments; but a thick cloud of blood swirled into the water. Gritting his teeth, he kicked himself onwards and somehow reached the *batelão*. Circling round to the blind side of the boat, he began to laboriously push it back.

'It's going to be all right, Otto,' shrieked Caine excitedly. 'He's still going strong!'

But Martin, staring out from his vantage point on the wharf supports, noticed a brief flash of silver in the water some distance behind Claudio's kicking legs; then another and another.

'Oh God,' he whispered. 'Piranha . . .'

There was an abrupt turbulence in the water around Claudio, a dark moving mass that seemed to be closing rapidly around him. Claudio's head was up, he was swimming hard for the wharf. He did not see the danger that hung close on his heels.

'Claudio, leave the boat!' screamed Martin. 'Swim for it, the –'

He reeled backwards with a groan as Schiller brought the heavy gun barrel down against his face, almost knocking him from his perch into the water. Helen grabbed Martin's arm and steadied him. The *batelão* was close now but suddenly Claudio's face contorted into an expression of pain and surprise. He was the centre of a wriggling, churning attack that began to smash the calm water into foam. Clouds of blood began to seep into the water and from his open mouth, there issued a shrill, unearthly scream of agony. Yet he kept swimming onwards, pushing the boat inexorably nearer, his gaze fixed on Helen as though the boat was his personal offering to her. She crammed a hand into her mouth to prevent her own cries from escaping and then could not look any more at the screaming, swimming man, his body festooned with thick clusters of wriggling fish that clung tenaciously to every square inch of unprotected flesh. He went down beneath the surface but rose again, struggling to push the boat the last few yards to the wharf. The water around him seemed to boil with a crimson ferocity.

'Get into the boat,' Schiller told Caine, who seemed mesmerized by the vision. 'Did you hear me? I said, get in!'

Caine nodded dumbly, clambered aboard. He took a seat in the prow, gazing nervously over the side at Claudio's death struggles. He held the tarantula stone now as though it were some fabulous talisman that would ward off any danger. Schiller too climbed in and stood looking down at Claudio for a moment, and he, in a last desperate bid for rescue, extended his hand to the German. Schiller grinned, shook his head. He leaned forward and struck Claudio very hard across the forehead with the barrel of the gun, stopping the man's struggles once and for all.

Martin's eyes filled with involuntary tears. Leaning on Helen's shoulder, the blood trickling from the recent wound on his face, he croaked his last heartfelt curse at Schiller and Caine.

'You motherfucking bastards,' he hissed. 'May your black souls rot in hell.'

Schiller smiled sweetly. 'You're a bad loser Mr

368

Taggart,' he observed. 'But as they say, you can't win them all.' He raised the .45, clasping it in both hands, and pointed it at Martin's head. 'Goodbye, Mr Taggart,' he said; and he squeezed the trigger.

The blast of the gun was somehow too loud. Martin had flinched from the imagined impact of the bullet as it smashed through his skull, but he remained upright, totally unharmed; instead, the gun had exploded in Schiller's hands, blasting backwards in a tangle of hot metal to claw deep into the German's thin face. Schiller made a kind of gurgling scream as he lurched over backwards, his shattered hands gesticulating like an out-of-control marionette. He crashed into the piranha-infested water with a scream of terror and the greedy fish were onto him in an instant, their instincts already sharpened by the taste of blood. It was over in a matter of moments. There was a brief frenzy just below the surface and Schiller's lean body jerked and twisted in a foul parody of life. Then, heavy with fish, his corpse sank to join Claudio's, deep in the blood-embroiled waters.

Caine was left alone in the boat. Unarmed, unsupported, he looked suddenly very small and vulnerable. He watched apprehensively as Martin and Helen climbed in.

'Start the engine,' Martin told Helen. 'You know how to do it?'

Helen nodded. She was aware that arrows were still falling periodically into the water to their right; and glancing between the dark skeletal supports of the wharf she could see that the fire had almost died away and that the Xavantes were working their way hurriedly along the river bank. She knelt beside the engine, took hold of the starter cord and gave it a tug. The engine gave a brief apologetic splutter and promptly died.

'Try again,' said Martin quietly. He turned his gaze towards Caine. 'Now, you sonofabitch,' he said. 'Give me my diamond.'

Caine shook his head slowly. 'It's not *your* diamond,' he hissed. 'It's mine.'

Martin shook his head and began to walk slowly towards Caine. An arrow whizzed past his head a short distance away but he scarcely noticed it.

'The diamond,' he said.

Behind him, the engine spluttered, died.

'Goddamn you, no!' Caine's face was wild. He was close to breaking point. His black curls were in oily disarray, his fat face was streaked with grime and sweat. A trickle of saliva dribbled from his mouth and he began to back away towards the prow, the tarantula stone clutched tight in his clammy hands.

'A deal?' he whined. 'Some kind of deal?'

'No more deals,' said Martin blankly.

The engine sputtered, burst into a short sporadic rhythm and then died. Helen became horribly aware of shouting figures emerging from the smouldering bushes on the riverbank behind her. She swore, opened the choke a little, pulled the cord hard.

The engine made a hoarse, coughing noise and fell silent again.

'Martin, it's not working!' she sobbed.

'Try again,' he told her. His voice had the calm distant tranquillity of a man talking in his sleep. He was very close to Caine now. The fat man was scrambling steadily backwards, shaking his head from side to side, sobbing with terror. He tried to step back onto something that wasn't there and, with a shriek, fell out of the boat. He came up spluttering, frightened, holding the tarantula stone up in one hand as though he feared that it might dissolve, like a pearl in wine. His fat legs kicked the water into motion.

Helen took a deep breath, opened the choke a little wider. Whatever happened she mustn't flood the engine. She pulled the cord hard. This time it almost caught,

370

almost, but not quite. As it died, she became aware of the first warriors running out onto the wharf. Arrows lanced the water on her right side.

Caine was floundering in the river. Martin flung himself down in the prow of the boat and stretched out his hand for the diamond. He could not quite reach. A dark moving mass came twisting up in the water below Caine, lured by his flailing limbs and the heady taste of fear.

Naked feet thundered the boardwalk.

Martin strained his fingers to reach the diamond. It was scant inches away.

Caine screamed suddenly, his eyes widening in the awful realization that he was about to be eaten alive. His body arched, twisted. He began to sink slowly beneath the surface.

'No,' whispered Martin. 'No!'

Arrows thudded into the stern of the boat. Sobbing, hardly able to breathe, Helen pulled the cord one last time. The engine fluttered, caught, rose to a steady vibrant rhythm.

Caine lunged back to the surface screaming. His bulging eyes peered out through a mantle of fish, his flailing arms heavy with their silver bodies. The tarantula stone rose one last time, catching the rays of clear sunlight. Martin lunged, almost overturning the boat. But it was too late. Caine sank for the last time. For an instant there was just his outstretched arm and the diamond glinting slow, slow, as it slid into the chilly water's embrace.

The *batelão* lurched forward and raced for the open river braving a fusilade of arrows. Martin, sprawled in the prow, screamed in agony as an arrow bit into his thigh. He slumped down onto his face, teeth gritted against the pain, and barely knew that the boat was away from the wharf and racing at full speed downriver. With a groan of despair and exhaustion, he closed his eyes and, gratefully, let the blackness fill his head with sleep.

When he opened his eyes again, they had travelled several miles. He sat up and the arrow in his leg set fresh spasms of pain jangling through his thigh. He examined it ruefully. It had gone clean through to the other side. Gritting his teeth, he managed to snap the head off the shaft and draw the wood out, though the effort of doing this nearly sent him back into unconsciousness. He steadied himself, took a few deep breaths and then looked up at Helen. She was leaning back against the stern of the boat, handling the rudder. She gazed at him for a moment and smiled sadly. Martin's eyes welled with tears.

'I lost it,' he sobbed. 'I was so close . . . so Goddamned close. But Caine got it after all.'

Helen nodded. 'I saw,' she said.

He began to crawl towards her, pulling himself over the various obstacles in the bottom of the boat, dragging his useless leg behind him.

'All that way,' he whispered bitterly. 'Carrying it with me every damned day. Planning. Scheming. And now it's gone. I've got nothing.'

'You're alive,' she told him.

'Alive.' He laughed bitterly. 'What's that worth without the diamond? What's it worth?'

'A lot,' she said. 'A whole lot, Martin. I only realize that now. Besides, the diamond isn't going anywhere. You can come back for it, another time.'

The idea excited him. He had not even considered it. He clambered the last few feet and slumped down beside her.

'Yeah, that's it . . . that's it! Crazy, I wasn't thinking straight. The Xavantes won't always be around and nobody else knows where it is. If we get to it soon enough, it won't have drifted far. All we'll need is a boat and a diving suit.' He warmed to the theme. 'Sure. With Caine gone, there'll be nobody to get in our way. We'll have all the time we need. All the time in the world, princess. We can do it, you and me.'

She shook her head wearily. 'You Martin. *You*. Think about that. It will keep you alive –' She gritted her teeth suddenly and her body shuddered. For the first time he noticed the paleness of her face, the strange vacant gaze in her eyes. Then he saw the red stain seeping slowly across the side of her shirt.

'Princess?' he whispered fearfully. 'Oh princess, no . . . no!' He raised his head to peer apprehensively over the stern of the boat. The arrow had gone clean through the thick wood of the hull and deep into her side. There was no way of pulling it out without tearing her even more. He shook his head slowly, knowing she was doomed but not wanting to accept it. It came to him then, how selfless she'd been. She'd piloted the boat out of danger while he'd been on his face, scrabbling for the diamond. He had never felt more ashamed. He reached out and stroked her face. 'It's not the diamond,' he told her, his voice tremulous with grief. 'It's you, princess, you. It's always been you. Don't you see?'

She was shivering now and when she spoke again, her voice was faint.

'It's better this way, Martin. Best. You never really did trust me, you know. You tried. I know you . . . tried.' She pulled him closer suddenly, her eyes wide, her voice urgent. 'Come back for your diamond, Martin! Be sure of that. You'll never be happy if you don't. Promise me . . . promise . . .' Her eyes seemed to focus on something just in front of her and a strange glint of recognition dawned in her eyes. 'Hold me,' she said; and as he pressed himself against her, he heard the last slow exhalation of her breath. Her body went limp in his arms.

The grief came swelling up within him until it burst like a bitter explosion in his chest. He cried then like a lost child while he held Helen tight in his arms. When the tears had subsided a little, he began to talk to her; he tried to assure her that she would be all right, that he would get her home safely if only she could hang on a little while longer. They were going home now. They would soon be home.

It was a passing launch that found them drifting a couple of days later. The *batelão*'s outboard motor had run out of petrol and had not been refilled, even though there were spare cans of gasoline on board. The man was half mad, burned red raw by exposure to the sun and weak from loss of blood. He kept babbling some nonsense about tarantulas and diamonds and he kept repeating the name of the dead woman he cradled in his arms. The Xavante arrows that riddled the hull of the boat told their own grim story but it was unclear what the two travellers had been doing out in the remote backwaters of the Rio das Mortes. He was taken on board the launch and carried to the nearest place of habitation.

At Conceiçao they patched up his wounds and got him on his feet again. When they found that he was the sole survivor of the recent aircrash, the villagers talked excitedly of a hero's welcome for him back in Rio; but he did not want that. He had a little money with him and he used that to slip quietly away on the last launch up to Belém before the rains began.

The rains were very bad that year. Even as his launch began to move away downstream, it began to fall, an angry grey torrent that soaked everything beneath its wrath. The villagers who had tended the American noticed how he stood on the open deck, staring vacantly into the dark depths of the river while his fellow passengers sheltered from the downpour. He did not even wear a hat.

The crazy American was the talk of Conceiçao for a day and a half but then the villagers, troubled by the

374

problems of everyday existence, forgot all about him. The grey rain continued to fall, day after day, and it was a long, lonely eternity before it stopped again.

Epilogue

Austin was momentarily surprised by the darkness in the bar. The hours had lengthened out into late afternoon and it would soon be time to turn on the lights. He glanced thoughtfully at Taggart. The old man was hunched over the bar gazing sadly into his drink.

'And you never did go back?' Austin asked softly at last.

Taggart shook his head. 'Meant to. Always meant to. Somehow, I just couldn't bring myself to get started.' He tapped the crumpled piece of paper with the tip of one finger. 'I even made this damned chart up. Studied the currents in the area, worked out just exactly the one place where Charlie Caine's skeleton must've finished up. He was gripping that tarantula stone real tight. Guess he still is.'

Austin took out his cigarettes, went to offer them to Taggart and then remembered.

'Oh sorry,' he muttered. 'I forgot. Mind if I . . .?'

'Hell no, you go ahead.'

Austin lit his cigarette and inhaled. 'One heck of a story,' he murmured. He glanced at the chart in Taggart's hand. 'You er . . . ever consider *selling* that.'

'Selling it?' Martin Taggart stared at the paper as though aware for the first time of its existence. 'Hell no. Never even *told* anyone about it till now. And who the hell would want to buy a piece of paper from a broken down old feller like me?'

'I would,' replied Austin without hesitation. 'Now look,

375

I've got my cheque book right here. I can give you a personal cheque for ... shall we say five thousand dollars?'

'Hey whoah, steady on now!' Taggart stared at Austin in alarm. 'A feller needs to think very carefully about a thing like this. That all happened a long time ago; there's no guarantee of you finding anything.'

'I know that,' said Austin calmly. 'But then, I won't just be buying the map. I'll be buying the story too. That way, nobody can say I've stolen it.' He had taken out his cheque book and was writing out the figures in a quick, well-practised scrawl. 'Now,' he said. 'You just take this up to the Chase Manhattan Bank uptown. You have my word that they'll honour it. There's my number on the back, see?'

Taggart scratched his head. 'Oh my Lord,' he muttered. 'I don't know about this. I mean, you're surely not thinking about using any of that stuff are you? I'll tell you, boy, all that was a long time ago. The world isn't interested in that kind of stuff any more. Old men telling the story of their life; that's strictly for the bar-room.'

'Maybe,' Austin smiled, 'maybe not.' He handed Taggart his cheque and pressed the old chart into the pocket of his shirt. 'I have to go,' he said apologetically. 'I'm meeting some officials for dinner and I'm already half an hour late. But listen, will you be around tomorrow? I'd like to come back with a recorder and get a few facts down on tape.'

Taggart shrugged. 'Tomorrow afternoon? Hell, I'm here every afternoon as a matter of fact. But listen, didn't you say you were going up-jungle tomorrow? Lookin' for adventure, that's what you said.'

'That's right,' agreed Austin. 'And now it seems that there's no need to go up-jungle. I've been there all afternoon. I'll see you tomorrow.' He shook Taggart's hand and hurried towards the door; but he paused for a moment and said, grandly; 'We can call it *The Tarantula Stone*. I like the sound of that.' And then he was gone, pushing through the swing door into the last rays of afternoon sunshine.

It was very quiet in the bar after that. Taggart sat regarding the cheque in his hands, an expression of bewilderment on his grizzled face; then he folded it neatly and slipped it carelessly into his pocket. He topped up his glass with the last of the *cachaça* and, holding it in front of him, gazed long and hard at his reflection in the mottled, fly-blown mirror that hung behind the bar. After a few moments, a second face seemed to appear in the glass beside his own, a youthful, pretty face, staring helplessly back at him across the terrible void of time. Taggart's eyes filled and the woman's face blurred, dissolved like soft wax melting.

'Here's to you, princess,' he said quietly; and tilting the glass he drank to her memory, just as he did every day of his life.